MORTAL TRINITY

KELLY ST. CLARE

Mortal Trinity
by Kelly St. Clare

Edited by Melissa Scott and Robin Schroffel
Cover illustration and design by Amalia Chitulescu Digital Art
Map Art © 2018 by Laura Diehl, www.LDiehl.com

MORTAL TRINITY

Exosia
Kentro
Maltu
Pleo
Selkie's Cove
Syraness
Portum
Febribus
Charybdis
Neos
Zol
Caspian Sea

Dynami Sea

Davy Jone's

Medusa's
Lair

N
W
E
S

Exosian Realm

"Everybody is a genius. But if you judge a fish by its ability to climb a tree, it will live its whole life believing that it is stupid."

- ***Albert Einstein***

ONE

Ebba knew the black-and-crimson stone of Davy Jones' Locker better than she knew herself.

The fiery stone island that formed the outer cliffs of hell was plain at first glance, aside from the crimson hue contained deep within. But after a few days of staring at the same rock, the slight fissures and pockmarked erosion from the sea salt became apparent.

Tiny crabs and leaping sea lice had stayed away when she was deposited here, but now they moved across the rocks without fear. Or maybe she'd become the stone. Except her fissures were soul-deep, gaping wide open.

Her erosion was bared to all.

Most of the time, Ebba wasn't sure she existed anymore. Her thoughts belonged to some distant space, and she was grateful for that one mercy; remembering his name and face would surely be the end of her. Admitting what had happened would cease her existence.

Ebba had to get the missing part of herself back. Without him, she was void.

She just wasn't.

An empty shell.

An eerie whisper on the salty breeze.

There were other times, too few to count, when something disturbed her mindless pain. An annoying reminder that wouldn't let her be. That pestering thought hovered at the jagged edges of her mind. It couldn't get in. She didn't want it to get in. But the thought continued to pester and hover, regardless.

"Ebba-Viva, lass. Ye need to eat and drink. Please, lass, just a couple o' mouthfuls."

Peg-leg was upset. She didn't want him to be upset, but she wasn't in control of her body and mind any longer—not without the missing part. Ebba would stay here and become part of this stone island. Her shell would die and shrivel and rot like her being. That was how it should be now.

"Soon, ye won't give us any choice but to force it down yer gullet," he said roughly.

He left.

The words felt familiar. As though he or her other fathers had done the same a few times already.

Other fathers.

Ebba sucked in a sharp breath, feeling a crack on her lip split open. Hot blood dribbled down her chin. She was relieved to see her body—her shell—wasn't faring too well. They were outside of hell now, situated atop the twenty-foot cliffs that bordered the entrance to Davy Jones' Locker. Her fathers had placed her between two boulders about knee height right by the edge of the towering cliffs. Ebba rested against the one at her back, but she could see over the one in front of her—if she chose. Here, on this small, barren island, they were exposed to the elements. The strong wind of the Dynami Sea and the chilly temperature had taken their toll.

Angry voices floated up to her.

"—It ain't natural-like, her reaction. It's like she ain't even there—"

"—We need to get water into her. She hasn't slept. I don't know how she's still upright—"

"—Maybe you need to talk to her about Plank's death—"

No.

Ebba hunched as molten-red agony ripped through her aching soul, tearing the weary pieces left of her to shreds, and leaving her in a cowering, ruined mess.

The last comment belonged to Caspian. He'd been her friend back when she'd felt like a human. That was a different life.

"—We don't know what that'll do to her—"

"—First things first, she has to survive." Locks' voice held grim determination. "We need to get water in her."

Water wasn't what she wanted. Water would sustain her shell.

Ebba dragged open her gritty, stinging eyes as footsteps approached. Swallowing and licking her lips, she worked her throat, forcing words out. "Don't touch me."

That stopped them.

Would that it was so easy to leave this realm forever. She swayed on the spot. *So close to death.* Only a couple more days, if that.

Her fathers and Caspian threatened that future.

For the first time since waking up here, Ebba looked up from the boulder in front of her. She blinked down at the churning waves of the Dynami Sea where they struck the base of the twenty-foot cliffs below. The tide was currently low and, far beneath her, the rocky pathway to Satyr Island was exposed and narrow, extending in a straight line into the distance.

She traced the jetty back toward the entrance to hell—but the sea-level gateway to the Locker was out of view around the cliffs to her left. The island housing the entrance to hell just seemed like a choppy gathering of cliffs. As though the land beneath had clashed and sent spears of the fiery stone stabbing up through the sea in a cluster. Inhospitable. *Barren.*

Ebba couldn't see the entrance, but directly below where she sat between the two low boulders, a kraken bobbed in the water. Its great octopus head stuck out above the dark, choppy swell, the immortal's beak just visible.

As she stared, the kraken lifted a tentacle and waved.

"Hey," the immortal called up, its beak chopping up the word.

Ebba turned away from the sea and the kraken, swallowing again. Instead, she looked at the men who'd gathered to force water down her throat.

Grubby, Peg-leg, Locks, Stubby, and Barrels.

Her fathers looked almost as bad as she felt. Rips decorated their clothing, which now was dirty and stained. Dark patches marred the area beneath their eyes. Their lips were cracked, eyes red-rimmed, and blood caked over various wounds on their faces, arms, and legs.

Escaping Davy Jones' had truly been a battle for their lives. And all for what? Mutinous had gotten away with the parts of the root of magic. And really, they were just sitting right by the entrance to hell anyway.

Yet, that problem was so tiny and insignificant it almost amused her. The end of the realm, the taint of all, and the ruination of mortal and immortal alike was so . . . unimportant. Because Mutinous took something else from her. Not the person who'd disappeared with the missing piece of her.

Another person.

She blinked, realizing the pestering thought she wasn't allowing herself to recognize kept her from fading from this realm peacefully. It wasn't a thought at all. It was a pestering *person*.

That person wouldn't let her be, but Ebba couldn't let herself remember. It was too painful. She had to leave this place.

"Ebba," Barrels spoke.

"Don't touch me," she croaked. The words ripped through her parched throat.

Grubby was crying. Peg-leg didn't appear far behind. Ebba noted their emotions dispassionately.

"I'm afraid ye've given us no choice," Locks said. He stepped forward, an unstoppered flagon in hand.

Anger swirled through her arms and legs, and the inkling to defend her right to die stirred within.

Ebba wavered where she stood. If they attempted to force her to drink, she'd resist with all her strength—which probably wasn't much right now. But they were ten feet away, and she did have enough time to. . . .

"I'll throw myself off the cliff," she told them, eyes vacant, hair limp.

Their shocked gasps didn't touch her. She might have cared that her actions would hurt them once. But she didn't anymore. Nothing mattered.

"Ebba, please don't speak that way," Stubby whispered. "We'll figure it out; ye know we will. Plank—"

"*Don't speak that name*," she said harshly. Ebba held up a hand, her limb heavy and sluggish to her command. "Never again."

They fell into a silence only broken by the howling wind.

Barrels spoke again, softer this time. "Our job is still the same, Ebba-Viva. We need to get the parts off Mutinous and assemble the root of magic to defeat the pillars."

Insignificant. Did he think that would stir her?

"If ye don't live, ye're doin' a disservice to his memory," Peg-leg said.

She recognized the heated bitterness in him, except hers wasn't hot but deathly, deathly cold. So what if dying was a disservice to him? He'd done a disservice to her. He'd chosen his fate. He'd knowingly put himself in a position to . . . leave her.

"I mean it," Ebba said, turning back to the sea.

Why hadn't she thought of jumping earlier? The rocks below were perfect.

She knew why.

That damned pestering person she didn't wish to think about. That annoying reminder that there was something unfinished. Some other reason to live lingered on the tip of her tongue like a fact she couldn't recall.

Someone did approach her then. Not her fathers, though she could see them edging around behind her. Their ploy didn't matter. She wouldn't even need to stand to heave herself over the small boulder between her and thin air. She'd fall onto the jagged outcrop below.

She didn't, yet, because Caspian approached. Not a threat.

He crouched close by, and Ebba kept track of his movement from the corner of her eye. Weary muscles coiled to embrace her chosen fate just as her father had. Why should he be the only person allowed to choose an easier existence?

Caspian studied her, weighing his thoughts before speaking as he tended to do.

"We need to save our friends on Zol," he said quietly. "Remember? Verity, Marigold, and my sisters. All the children there. And Sally, remember her, Mistress Fairisles?"

Sally. Ebba let out a breath. She did recall the sprite.

For a moment.

Then the thought flittered away.

Caspian spoke again. "The taint is spreading. Grubby's octopi reported that sea creatures are fleeing here. The waters back home are oily with the pillars' power. Their taint has crept over all the land closest to Exosia for certain. The octopi say the taint wasn't quite at Zol when they left, but our friends don't have long. We—"

"I don't care," Ebba said, a hollow echo to her voice.

She didn't care. Or perhaps just couldn't access the emotion. Something wouldn't let her care. Something intrinsic and beyond her control or understanding. Something had broken. Whatever had made her Ebba was no longer there. Feeling stood on one side of the river and she stood on the other.

"Thousands will die."

He was getting angry.

Ebba listened to the *tap-tap-tap* of her father's peg as the crew surrounded her. She still had time to throw herself over. If only she could remember who that pestering person was, she'd happily surrender to the rocks.

Frustration briefly reared its head through the dark, cloying pain —the first emotion she could recall feeling since exiting hell.

Caspian inched closer. Just shy of too close. "Mutinous has him."

Ebba blinked and turned to him.

The exiled king shuffled closer still. So did her fathers. "We need to get him back," Caspian said.

Aye, they did. She knew that. And yet, who was the person he referred to? The pestering thought just beyond her reach grew stronger in her mind.

"We need your help to do it. Without you, he'll die."

Death.

Finality.

That couldn't happen to the person Mutinous had taken. The notion pierced through the cloud and hovered just within her awareness.

Shakes wracked her body, energized fearful shivers that jolted her weary frame.

Ebba fixed her eyes on Caspian, noting the dark flicker in his amber eyes.

"Mutinous has Jagger, Mistress Fairisles," he said, holding out a trembling hand to her. "Will you help me get him back?"

Jagger.

A choking sound forced its way from her lips. Ebba jerked her prickling fingertips to her bloodied lips. *The pestering person.*

"J-Jagger?" she repeated.

"Jagger," Caspian repeated in a stronger voice. "Jagger needs you."

Jagger needed her.

The reminder finally crept inside her. Feeling stood on one bank and Ebba on the other, but Jagger was the river raging between them. The haze around her mind dissipated, in part, and Ebba felt something deep within, a tiny ember in the deathly cold void.

The ember didn't grow, but neither did it flicker and die.

"We need your help," Caspian repeated.

She took a breath and nodded, still shaking from head to toe like a trapped leaf in the wind.

Ebba would help Jagger.

TWO

Since yesterday, Ebba had eaten and gulped back a few sips of water. She'd also moved to a different rock, lower on the cliffs, only twelve feet above the water. The ember within her hadn't grown to a flame, but it still smoldered. So instead of staring at the black stone, she now stared at Satyr Island—the island housing Cannon's tainted damned and the Satyr themselves—half-goat, half-human immortals who worked for the pillars and had imprisoned the female Capricorn for nearly fifty years.

Cannon had the pieces of the root . . . and Jagger.

Her crew needed the root parts back. She needed Jagger.

"I guess we'll be bringin' ye up to speed then," Stubby said. "We've kept ye in the loop, but I ain't sure ye heard much."

They'd told her stuff?

"Tell me again." Her voice was still raspy from disuse.

Stubby sighed, his blue eyes dull. "Ye were nearly lifeless yerself when Plank—"

Ebba inhaled sharply, and he cut off before hurrying on.

"Tainted damned were explodin' out o' Davy Jones'," he blurted.

"We would've all been goners, but for Matey, who was still waitin' for us outside the entrance."

A tentacle inched above the cliff edge and patted Ebba's ankle, leaving a slimy streak in its wake. She leaned over the edge to peer twelve feet down, tracing the sucker-dotted length of the huge tentacle to its owner.

Matey was sprawled out across the surface of the water like a jellyfish, the expansive reach of his tentacles and his sheer size never clearer than from her bird's eye angle.

"Are we deciding stuff?" he called eagerly. "Hey, Ebba."

She shifted her gaze to the kraken's eyes, not answering. He slowly lowered his tentacle back down to the water below, drooping.

"Aye, I was just tellin' her that ye saved us," Stubby said.

Matey drew himself up tall. "It wasn't easy. The entrance of Davy Jones' split in two, and the damned poured out. I thought they'd never stop coming—all of them running across the path to reach Satyr Island. Then I saw your fathers dragging you out, so I collected you all up and placed you up here on the cliffs. There was a fierce storm that day, so trying to save you while fighting the current was really hard. I had all those barrels of your crew's stuff too. A lucky thing I have eight arms, let me tell you that."

Barrels? Ebba glanced at Stubby.

"The stuff we saved from the ship," he said. "Yer scrapbook and the bangle from Marigold, savvy?"

She closed her eyes. The scrapbook filled with her fathers' memories of her childhood. "Where are they?"

Hopefully the book was at the bottom of the Dynami.

"Matey put the barrels up here with us. They're just down the cliff a way," Stubby said. "Safe."

Great.

Locks hunkered down beside her. "When enough evil left the Locker, the balance o' light and dark was restored. Soon after we got out, the entrance sealed again. Not all o' the damned got out afore the door shut on them. And we're guessin' that some were killed in the stampede to get out. Not all o' the tainted pirates who got on the path made it across afore the sea came in and swept them away. They'll have regenerated back inside Davy's with the ones who were killed in the stampede. So that be sumpin'."

In hell, she'd killed Riot, only for him to regenerate six hours later at the entrance of Davy Jones'. Once dead, a person couldn't be killed again. They just came back over and over. However. . . .

"We can use that to put Mutinous and the others back inside," she said.

Ebba wanted a plan. She needed to know how long she needed to fight. How long before she could return to thoughts of fading into death.

"There be a lot o' tainted damned that got out, lass." Locks shook his head. "And a lot of plain ol' damned that are probably tainted by now, too."

Caspian perched on a rock behind her. "We need to leave the tainted damned leaderless. Then they're no different to any of the other tainted in the realm. Kill Mutinous and Pockmark, maybe Riot and Swindles. Get Jagger and the weapon parts, then get out and continue our quest."

That would be great . . . if it worked. Who knew how many were guarding Jagger? And the parts wouldn't be left unguarded by the pillars, whom Cannon and Pockmark had no choice but to obey.

Locks narrowed his eye, adjusting the patch covering his empty socket. "Matey, ye're on land. Have ye always been able to do that?"

"Yes, but land makes me feel fat and heavy," the kraken replied, stiffening. "So let's hurry this up."

Barrels picked his way through the loose stone toward Ebba and held out a flagon of water. She obediently took a few sips and passed it back. Matey had to be bringing supplies—she doubted any food or water existed up on this barren outcrop.

"Matey wasn't the only one waiting out here for us," Barrels said, corking the flagon again. Her eldest father was bereft of a cravat, a doublet, and his buckled shoes. He appeared more like a pirate than she'd ever seen him, and far less like a quartermaster who'd accidentally found himself on a pirate ship.

He continued, "Two of Sally's subjects were here, too. It seems the queen of the wind sprites heard your shouted plea for help when we were walking across to Davy Jones'."

Ebba lifted her head. She could barely recall doing that. She could barely recall a lot of things. There was only the distant, irretrievable memory of how everything was before she broke apart. A white glow edged the memory of them crossing the jetty from Satyr Island; even as they'd marched to hell, the moment was perfection because they were all together. All nine of them.

Locks grunted. "We sent one sprite back to Sal, alertin' her to what had happened in the Locker, and the second to find the Daedalion. It be time to call in our favor with them."

Right. They had no ship. But— "How is Mutinous gettin' to the pillars with the parts?" she asked.

A grim silence met her words.

"Seems the Satyr were workin' on a project for Cannon," Peg-leg said, taking a seat on her left. "They have a ship, lass. Must've been at it for years. And from Grubby's reports, the Satyr and tainted damned started loadin' her up yesterday."

Which meant they'd soon set sail.

"Ye've been scoutin', Grubs?" she croaked.

The face of her youngest father was pinched, and Ebba guessed she was to blame for that. He'd somehow kept ahold of his Monmouth cap through everything. Except the hat had been twisted so much with his anxious hands that it was a frayed wreck.

"Aye, I've been swimmin' over every day. Ain't seen much o' Mutinous and nothin' of Jagger. I'm thinkin' they must keep him below deck," Grubby replied, smiling his toothy grin.

Below deck.

Jagger might only truly fear the loss of his loved ones but being below deck came a close second. Surrounded by such strong taint and devoid of sunshine and fresh air, there was no telling what state he'd be in when they got him back.

If they got him back.

"I've seen a whole heap o' Pockmark and his two cronies around," Grubby said, hovering before her, his eyes fixed on her face.

Her attempt to smile reassuringly at him resulted in a twitch of the lips. But her thoughts quickly turned to Mercer Pockmark, grandson of Mutinous Cannon. He wasn't the real danger, perhaps, but he'd taken too much from her to be forgiven.

"I want him dead," she whispered. Ebba had only felt murderous a few times in her life. Really only toward the pillars and Mutinous. At times she'd felt pity for Pockmark, but that was cold and dead now, along with the rest of her. Now he stood between her and Jagger.

Ebba wouldn't hesitate to end him.

"I'm goin' scoutin' again," Grubby declared, standing suddenly.

"I'll come with ye," Ebba said.

Peg-leg rested a hand on her shoulder, pushing down. "Nay, lass. Mayhaps when yer strength be up. Ye're a liab'lity out there right now, bein' so weak."

Considering her legs shook at the mere thought of standing, he was probably correct.

"Aye, tomorrow then." She'd eat more today if food was available.

Peg-leg blinked, eyeing her, a wrinkle between his brows. He'd expected her to fight the issue?

Ebba had only enough fight left for Jagger, nothing more, nothing less. Peg-leg's reasoning was sound.

"Wait, Grubby. Before you go," Caspian called after him, "what news from the octopi?"

Her father spun back, smiling wide again. "The octopi ain't headin' back to Zol again. Said the water be dark now and unsafe. I sent a message with a jellyfish and a turtle who were goin' to try their luck that way, but the turtles be matin' at the minute. So might be a bit. And jellyfish ain't really got control o' where they go, so there be that."

Caspian's mouth formed an 'O' before he shook himself. "Could you tell a fish, perhaps? Or a stingray?"

"Fish don't like to uproot their families too much. And stingrays be fierce bad luck. Thought ye'd know that by now," her father gently chided.

The exiled king opened his mouth and then closed it with an audible click. "Right. I'll just leave things to you."

Grubby left with a distant splash, and not long after, Ebba glimpsed her part-selkie father cutting through the churning waves on the way to Satyr Island.

"Matey," Stubby said. "Anythin' new from the male Capricorn?"

The male Capricorn? Ebba twisted to look at the kraken. As far as she remembered, the male Capricorn were on the pillars' side. Not because they wanted to be but because the Satyr had held the female Capricorn captive for nearly fifty years.

Matey caught her look. "The male Capricorn have had enough. They're helping us in secret, bringing food and water and whatever news they can. Nothing to report," he answered Stubby. "They're still saying the Satyr plan to sail with Cannon and the tainted damned to Exosia to join up with the pillars. They're taking the six parts of the weapon, of course. But they've heard no mention of where the pieces are kept—or Jagger."

He'd tagged Jagger on like an afterthought. And Ebba supposed that to the rest of her crew and friends, the six parts of the root of magic were more important than one person. Without the weapon, the six pillars were nearly invincible. *With* the weapon, the pillars were powerful beyond measure. Ebba and the others needed to assemble the root to take the pillars down and save the realm.

She just couldn't bring herself to care about that.

Though Ebba really couldn't understand why the six immortals—who'd melded their minds into one consciousness—weren't coming to retrieve the parts themselves. The pillars controlled the will of others through their taint, feeding on mortal and immortal souls alike. Through the eyes of their tainted, the pillars could monitor the realm. And the six evil immortals knew Ebba, Caspian, and Jagger were the three watchers who could assemble and disassemble the root of magic.

But maybe there was her answer—Mutinous *had* Jagger, one-third of the three watchers. Perhaps the pillars were simply content to possess the pieces, which provided individual powers to those who held them, to ensure the root was never assembled and used against them.

"I know we need to get Jagger back, but I'm wonderin' if we have the best chance of savin' him if we have the parts. If we go for those first, Ebba can assemble the weapon quick-like, and then we can use it against Cannon and the tainted damned."

Ebba frowned. "What?"

She'd missed something. Not unlikely considering her rock-staring vigil of late. The three watchers had to assemble the weapon, not just her . . . right?

Everyone stopped talking to look at her. Understanding dawned on Caspian's face first.

"Matey retrieved his grandfather's journal. We know a lot more about the three watchers than we did," he explained.

They did?

Caspian walked toward her, and Ebba found herself observing him.

Something was different.

His expression was grim and determined, not so unusual. But his eyes blazed like they did when he forgot his troubles. Since losing his arm, his eyes had only blazed intermittently, but the burning intensity of them wasn't quite the same. Normally, the orbs fixed on the object of attention with single-minded intensity. Now, his focus seemed expansive and wide. Instead of tunnel vision, he appeared keenly aware of his surroundings and the people in them. His gaze was sweeping but calm.

Caspian always tried to hide his empty sleeve from sight. Because of that trait, she'd always found herself looking at his missing limb first—drawn to see what he was ashamed of. This time, Ebba hadn't looked there first.

His shoulders were straight, his chin raised; the exiled king appeared as regal as at their first meeting though a darker knowing to his eyes. Dark like she felt. Dark as they probably all felt. In the Locker, in the wake of the intense regard between her and Jagger, Caspian had distanced himself. She'd watched as he tried to shake off the demons that had plagued him since his father's death and maybe since losing his arm.

Somewhere between exiting Davy Jones' and this moment, he'd gone from showing a pretense of strength to the real thing. What had happened to drag such confidence and surety from him? This Caspian was almost unrecognizable.

Or maybe it was she who had changed. There was that.

He sat on her right. "We pretty much knew what Jagger's role in the three watchers was. He's immune to all magic, so he can make unbiased decisions concerning the assembling and disassembling of the weapon without being influenced by immortals."

"Do ye know what shape the root o' magic is then?" she asked.

He shrugged his shoulder. "Matey's grandfather only mentioned that the six parts fit together. I'm afraid we haven't been able to come up with an answer as to what the parts form or just how that's meant to happen."

Most of the parts they'd collected had a cylinder-like appearance. Some had rounded ends, some pointy, and some flat. Then there was the question of how *veritas*—the sword part—was meant to fit. She had no idea either.

"And what about ye? The bearer," Ebba asked.

"Really, it's in the name. What we understand from the journal is that I carry the parts to you one at a time, but as the assembler, *you* must put the six parts together—"

Sink her. Did that mean she had to figure out how to put them together in order to save Jagger?

Ebba licked her lips and saw Caspian's eyes drop to watch her response before he met her gaze again.

"Why would ye need to carry them to me?" she said. "I can hold a few at a time."

He leaned back. "Another thing we couldn't uncover an explanation for in the journals. However, Matey's grandfather *did* make mention of the six people accompanying the assembler."

"Six. . . ." Ebba had learned not to dismiss coincidences by now. There were six pillars, six parts, and she'd had six fathers. "Did he mention what that meant?"

Stubby grumbled, "Not a damned word."

Matey's beak dropped open, and his eye blazed. "You know, less attitude would go a long way. I didn't *have* to share his journals with you." He pressed the back of a tentacle to his forehead, eyes squeezed shut as though pained. "I *certainly* didn't need to save you all from H-E-L-L."

Caspian stood slowly. "Your deeds are much appreciated by the realm, Sir Matey."

The tentacle lowered, and Matey peeked over the top, the angry glow of his eyes dimming slightly. "*Sir* Matey?"

"*Sir* Matey," Caspian repeated.

"Can you knight someone, being exiled and all?"

"Uh." Red crept over Caspian's jaw. "I guess that would just make you an exiled sir. Are you okay with that?"

The remaining fearsome glow in the kraken's eyes died.

If Ebba had to venture a guess, she'd say the wild notion of being exiled was preferable to the kraken. *Greatly* preferable.

"Anyway. . . ." Barrels glanced between the kraken and Caspian. "I agree with Stubby. We stand a better chance of saving Jagger if we retrieve the parts first. Ebba can put the weapon together, and we won't have to battle an entire army of tainted damned with mortal powers."

They really had no idea what the weapon could do, so Ebba wasn't going in without a plan B. If they took the parts, she'd have a bartering chip to use with Cannon for Jagger's life. Barring that, plan C was shoving the parts down Cannon's gullet one at a time.

Ebba glanced out across the sea to the island where Jagger was trapped. Hunted and hurting because his immunity painted him as a valuable asset to the pillars. It took everything within her to not march across the exposed path this very second. Well, that, and there wouldn't be enough time to cross. She wasn't screwing this up. Ebba wouldn't go in without exploring every possibility first. She couldn't afford to let things go south this time.

Jagger would live. No matter the cost. She'd free him or die trying.

The whistling wind swirled around her, cold company for her cold thoughts.

Peg-leg stilled. "Did ye hear that?"

With the others, she turned to look at him.

Ebba strained to listen. There was only the hiss and slap of the waves against the rocks and the path below. The howling of wind. The occasional caw of a bird from high above.

"That's what a diet o' seaweed will do to a well-eaten bloke," Locks joked.

But the smile on his lips died as a booming *crack* rent the air.

The ground beneath them shook. The wind lifted, howling like wolves closing in on prey. And beneath all of that were distant shouts and screams —an increasing rumble and roar.

"What is it?" Barrels called over the wind, his peppered hair whipping about his face.

The sounds were growing louder. And coming from directly underfoot. In this corner of the Dynami Sea, there was only one thing it *could* be.

"Davy Jones'," she and Caspian chorused.

The small stones on the clifftop began to leap and jump, and everyone shot to their feet. In the midst of the crew, she crept to the edge and peered down to the entrance of the locker.

The cracked entrance.

"Shite," Locks hissed. "It's open again."

Which accounted for the rumbling roar that was near-deafening by this point. The damned within were stampeding once more for the exit.

But then, as though snuffed out, the shouts and screams and pounding footsteps of hundreds died, leaving a throbbing and hushed quiet that was somehow louder than the stampede of a few moments prior.

"I ain't likin' that silence one bit," Stubby whispered.

"The path'll disa'pear soon, though," Ebba added, looking to where the water was beginning to flood over the top of the narrow rocky protrusion. "Not all o' them will get onto it, and none will make it across."

She blanched at her next realization. "When that happens, they'll come up here. They won't go back inside. Not for anythin'."

Caspian threw her a curious glance.

Barrels spoke. "None of the damned have managed to get out since we left. As soon as we—the light souls—left, balance was restored, and the entrance shut. Why has it opened again?"

In her pirate opinion, now wasn't the time to solve puzzles. It was the time to live so that she could save Jagger.

"If it's open now, then the balance has been upset again," Caspian replied. "No one has entered the Locker, so something must've happened out in the realm. The pillars' power must have grown. A lot."

"Matey," Locks said as he turned. "We'll be needin' to relocate. Can ye. . . ?"

When he trailed off without finishing the sentence, Ebba peered back over her shoulder. Her eyes widened at the person standing there.

She slowly reached down to shake Caspian's shoulder. "Ye'll be wantin' to see this," she told him.

"See what?" he asked her, glancing back.

Caspian went utterly still.

The kraken was nowhere in sight, but someone else was.

One by one, her remaining fathers turned. . . .

. . . To stare at Caspian's father, King Forge Montcroix.

THREE

"Sink me," Stubby said grumpily. "Don't he ever die?"

Ebba wondered the same thing; the monarch had more lives than Pillage.

King Montcroix ignored Stubby.

"Son," he said, rusted amber eyes set on Caspian.

The royal father and son had spoken multiple times in recent weeks, but a boiling river had stood between them. When they last saw the king, Cannon had killed him. With the damned only regenerating at set times, and with the entrance closing, Ebba doubted any of them had expected to see the king again.

The current meeting felt tense, but it had to be nearly unbearable for Caspian.

Caspian's strong voice surprised her. "Father," he said in greeting. "You're alive."

Father. You're alive.

The words were like a knife to her innards. How casually the prince said them upon seeing his father was alive. He only had one parent, and that father was dead and damned. How could he be so casual about seeing him again? Or was he just better at hiding things now? Even if he didn't love the king, and truly didn't care whether he was alive or not, how was it that *she* had ceased to be when her father left and he was . . . coping?

If Plank had regenerated, she—

Gasping, Ebba lurched forward. "Plank," she said to the king, reaching for his hand.

The monarch reeled back. "Don't touch me, I am tainted. All of the damned are now."

"Plank," she repeated desperately, her hands clawed by her sides. "*Is he in the Locker?*"

The king appeared almost uncomfortable.

"Her father," Caspian explained.

"I know," Montcroix answered with a small wave. "No, pirate. I have not seen him in the Locker. He is not there."

Her father wasn't in hell. She should be relieved about that. He wasn't damned. But hell was wide open again, and they could have been reunited if he was. A lump rose in her throat, and as silence fell upon the cliffs, all Ebba could do was fight to not let the black chasm overwhelm her. The jagged clouds threatened to surround her skull. The tiny ember that had ignited when Caspian first mentioned Jagger began to flicker, in danger of going out.

Her being whispered at her to recede to the shell-like state she'd succumbed to before. There, her pain wouldn't be gone, but it would be less.

Ebba stumbled away from Montcroix.

Stubby reached for her, but she swayed away from him, numbness threatening to take over. *Jagger, Jagger, Jagger*, she chanted silently. There would be no end to the hurt inside, no peace. Ever.

But she didn't need to feel peace to save Jagger.

Ebba dragged in a breath and raised her chin, pushing against the weight crushing her.

King Montcroix was speaking.

"I have checked the entrance daily since it first opened. I couldn't be sure of the exact parameters of the light-dark balance that Cannon used to escape, but with what Caspian told me of the pillars, I knew their evil would only grow, which meant there might be another opportunity to leave the Locker," he was saying. "I didn't expect it to be so soon."

Something had happened back in the Caspian Sea.

"Yes, we expect so, Father," his son replied. "In our friend's journals, his grandfather noted that the pillars took over the sea, land, immortals, and finally, the air. We know from that the tainted plague was happening on land a long time ago. The octopi have reported sea creatures are fleeing here because the water is changing. Do you think it's possible the pillars have moved on to draining and tainting immortals? Surely that would give them a huge surge in power."

Immortal creatures, Sally included, had kept their distance from the pillars for fear of boosting their strength prematurely. Though when it came to magical creatures, Ebba could never be sure if they were helping by remaining away or just ignoring mortal plights to obey the call of their nature. There was some definite overlap in motive for most of the immortals she'd met—the powers of Oblivion included.

Peg-leg scratched his chin. "Mayhaps, lad. Remember that all o' the tainted damned who didn't make it across the path in the first wave would've regenerated inside the Locker. That would have boosted the amount o' dark in hell again."

King Montcroix glanced away from Caspian to Peg-leg. "What tainted damned?"

Caspian pointed at the path that was only just visible through the water now. "When the damned stampeded out, not all of them made it across. Some would have drowned and gone back to Davy's."

"Davy's," his father repeated.

"Hell," Caspian clarified.

Montcroix placed both hands behind his back and walked to the cliff edge. He didn't speak, merely stared across the Dynami Sea in the direction of Satyr Island.

Caspian studied his father's back, but he froze, making a sound of alarm. "The damned who perished on the path didn't regenerate in the Locker, did they?"

"No," Montcroix replied.

Barrels stepped forward. "You can't mean. . . ."

The king turned back, lips pressed together. "I don't *mean* anything. All I know with certainty is that the tainted did not return to hell. Which means they remained here or went . . . *elsewhere.*"

Everyone sat in silence, exchanged nonplussed looks. For the life of her, Ebba had no idea what that meant.

"Could it be that those killed outside of the Locker die in truth?" Barrels mused softly.

Ebba's stomach stirred as she turned over his words.

That could change everything. That meant they could kill Mutinous and Pockmark and the others, knowing they'd really die, not just regenerate in the Locker to escape again. The thought struck at a memory—which was surprising, given her recent state.

"Birds," she blurted, straightening.

Locks took her hand. The touch unsettled her purely because her fathers meant so much to her, and now she knew they could be taken away. But her revelation had stolen enough of her attention not to draw away.

"What about the birds, lass?" Locks asked, his blazing emerald eye showing his concern.

Did she really look that bad? Likely.

She brushed the thought away. "Do ye think that be why the Thunderbird gets so angry when a bird be killed? Because he knows his light vessels never come back after?"

"*Yes,*" Caspian said, grinning at her. "Yes, Ebba! You're right. It makes perfect sense. Damned souls only regenerate within Davy Jones'. Once outside of it, they truly die." His grin faltered, and he cast her the same curious look as earlier.

"Aye, aye, that all be well and good, but I want to know what ye're doin' here," Stubby said to the king. "We like Caspian fair well, but that don't extend to ye."

Montcroix didn't appear angered by the comment. Instead, a small smile curved his lips. "My son, a friend to pirates. Who would have thought?"

"They are my friends," Caspian said, setting his jaw. "More than that, really."

His father walked to him. He lifted a hand as though to rest it on Caspian's shoulder before dropping it back to his side. "I know, Caspian. I am prouder of you than you know."

"Proud?" Caspian echoed, complete shock on his face. "Even though grandfather was killed by a pirate?"

"I have always been proud of you. I just wasn't good at showing it." Montcroix inhaled deeply. "How small things seem in death; how small my actions look; how small my emotions feel; how small we all are."

Ebba had never had much in common with the dead king of the Exosian realm, but his hollow utterings struck her deeply. Irrevocably. Was that her future? To become a bitter, twisted shell like him—a shadow of who she'd been when those she loved were alive and well? Everything felt less now. Everything *was* small.

"No," Montcroix said to Stubby, coming back to himself. "I have not come to be saved. In fact, I have come to request the opposite. Mostly, I have come to bring my son an army of the damned."

Quiet reigned.

And then some more. Cannon and Pockmark could've been splashing each other and giggling on the Satyr's island and she might've heard it.

"Well, that be changin' things fair-like, methinks." Locks' eyes narrowed. "But why should we trust ye?"

How easy decisions became when the important things were at risk. "We have his son," Ebba said. "That be why."

Montcroix slid his eyes to her, and a shaded whisper of acknowledgement passed between them.

Ebba approached the cliff edge and propped a foot up on a stone, leaning atop her thigh. "Matey," she hollered.

A tentacle stretched upward from the sea. Coward had turned tail when Montcroix appeared. *Flamin' kraken.* The tentacle stopped in front of Ebba's face and turned sucker-side up in inquiry.

She leaned back to evade a tendril of slime and vaguely registered Montcroix's gasp behind her.

"Can ye transport the damned across the channel to the island?" she asked the kraken. Was she meant to talk to his tentacle? No idea. She recalled Matey mentioning that he could detect some things with his suckers.

Matey's head broke the surface of the black water, the snap of his beak chopping up his words as he gargled, "Are they tainted?"

Blast, she'd forgotten that. They certainly didn't want a tainted kraken on their hands. Matey drew his tentacle back down, and she leaned forward onto her propped leg again.

"Only one entry point to the island." Caspian approached and mimicked her posture.

She hummed. "Aye. And only one tide to get across. Plenty o' warnin' for Cannon. And easy to defend. He'll pick us off."

Matey rose from the sea, the water pouring off him in hissing droves. He peeked nervously at the king.

"I've got scales," the kraken reminded them. "And you'll be going to get the healing part of the weapon, right? The *purgium*. I'd only have time to get a little tainted before you could heal me."

He had no idea what it was like to be tainted. "Nay," she told him. "It ain't safe. The Capricorn, though—when they kidnapped me, they used a wooden raft. We'll need as many o' those as possible."

Matey bobbed his head. "You can count on me, Lady Assembler."

With a monstrous explosion of water that almost reached their perched position, the kraken disappeared beneath the surface.

"Ebba?" Caspian cleared his throat.

She sighed and looked at him.

"Don't take this the wrong way, but . . . were you always this smart?"

What? Ebba shrugged. She didn't know, and she didn't care.

Once again setting her mind to getting Jagger back, she said, "Let's hope the Capricorn can tow loads o' damned across as the others run along the path. Matey can transport all o' us instead. We'll have a better chance if we can attack from a few dir'ctions."

"I'm thinkin' the damned be damned for a damned-good reason," Locks countered.

Barrels tapped his lip, surveying the king. "That is my concern. How do we know your army won't join Cannon?"

"You know, cutthroats and thieves I always understood," Montcroix said vaguely. "They will always choose the easiest route that grants them the most gain. Pirates, however, I never understood. You were not predictable like other criminals. You would not always do as I expected."

Locks grunted. "What be yer point, Forge?"

The king's eyes narrowed. "The point is: the army of damned is made of cutthroats and thieves. Cannon stabbed them in the back. That alone is not enough to deter them, of course. But if they join with Mutinous, they must fight a *war*. If they join with my son, they win freedom after a single battle. That is the prize for an occupant of hell. The only prize. Some have been in the Locker for hundreds of years, some months, and some an entire lifetime. On Caspian's behalf, I assured them that, should they help us defeat Cannon and the tainted, the island where the Satyr gather is theirs."

Wet footsteps sounded at her back. Ebba spun, relaxing when she saw the arrival was Grubby.

Her gaze dropped to the bloodied specks on his hands. A high-pitched ringing filled her ears, and her legs folded beneath her. She landed hard on the black stone.

"Shite, Grubby." Peg-leg lunged forward, hooking an arm under her armpit as she swayed in sitting position. "At least wash yer hands if ye're goin' to eat fish."

"Not a fish," Grubby said, kneeling down to Ebba. "I'm okay, Ebba. Just fine. It ain't my blood."

Some of the dizziness receded. "Not yers," she repeated thickly.

Grubby toed the black stone, dragging his foot in a line.

Her fathers gathered.

"Do ye have sumpin' to tell us, matey?" Peg-leg asked.

Grubby peeked up at them and back down. "Ebba said it would make her feel better if Pockmark died, so I went to kill him."

Her mouth dried. "Ye killed Pockmark?"

"Nay, couldn't find him, but I found his matey, Riot."

Locks stared at Grubby's hands. "So ye killed Riot?"

Her youngest father shook his head emphatically. "I was goin' to. I got a piece o' wood because I weren't allowed to touch him. But then I felt sorry for him and decided not to kill him. Except when I turned on the spot, the plank bopped him on the head anyway, and I thought, 'Well, mayhaps I will then.'"

"So . . . to clarify: You killed Riot?" Barrels answered in the shocked wake.

Grubby thought about that and then nodded. "Aye, s'pose I did."

Ebba blinked three times. He'd gone over to scout with the intention of killing someone to—

". . . Are ye happier now, Ebba?" her father asked her, frowning.

Happier? That wasn't anywhere near what she was feeling.

"How?" she whispered, eyes wide on his face.

"Oh, 'course ye'll want to hear the details." Grubby nodded like that was reasonable. "After I bopped him by a'cident, I bopped him again. Then I attached a couple o' sandbags to his feet and drowned him. I went down to watch, just to make sure. He woke up afore the end and struggled some—I thought ye'd like that part."

Ebba struggled to wrap her head around all of that. "Grubs, I didn't mean for ye to go kill Riot." Did he swim directly there to do the deed? He must be driven mad with worry about her to go to such drastic lengths.

His face fell. "Ye wanted him alive? Oh, Ebba, I ain't sure he's comin' back. His body still be there. Just left him. His breathers be well and truly full o' water."

"I guess that solves the question of whether the damned die in truth when killed outside of the Locker," Barrels said drily.

Locks' brows were at his hairline. "Aye, it will when we check him on the way over anyhow."

"Grubs, that was dangerous," Ebba told him, still trying to assemble her thoughts. "I wish ye hadn't put yerself in harm's way to do that." She might be broken, but that didn't mean she wanted the rest of her fathers hurt.

Tears filled his eyes. "I've made ye sadder."

Sadder? Was that possible? Her insides were empty and cold. 'Sad' didn't seem an apt word to describe her numbness. *Still*, her feelings lingered on the opposite riverbank, out of reach.

"Nay, Grubs," she answered, lying through her teeth. "I'm right happy Riot's gone. Ye've done well, but can ye check afore doin' it next time?"

He cocked his head.

"I'd . . . like to . . . watch," she offered lamely.

His eyes rounded. "O' course ye would. Sure thing."

Locks stood and placed an arm around Grubby's shoulders. "If that be Riot's blood, it's tainted. We need to wash the rest off smart-like. Come on, matey."

Trying to shake off her remaining dizziness, Ebba stared up at the sky, breathing deeply. At least the sun didn't beat down in a relentless and joyful display here. She wasn't sure her flushed skin could currently take it. Here in the Dynami, day was dim, and night was dimmer. She faced forward again, searching for the path, but it was entirely covered by the sea now.

That meant they had six hours until the next crossing.

King Montcroix broke the stupefied lull that Grubby had caused. "Will you take my army, King Caspian?"

Caspian jerked at his father's words, staring.

She observed the dead monarch. Montcroix wasn't renowned for his fair dealings. But in this instance, when on the side of his son, she believed the man could be depended upon.

Glancing up, she caught the gazes of Barrels, Locks, Peg-leg, and Stubby. On their faces was the same realization—plus, what choice did they really have? Would they turn down an entire army? Even if that army was from hell? They weren't fools; they were survivalists. *Pirates.*

"Yes," Barrels told the king when Caspian continued staring. "We'll accept your army."

"But you haven't heard the price yet," the king replied softly.

Stubby exploded. "I thought there weren't no price? Ye're doin' it for yer son."

The king appeared to struggle with that. He glanced at Caspian, and Ebba did the same, just in time to see the rivulet of resignation wiggle across Caspian's face.

Montcroix clearly saw it too. He sighed. "I was. I am. But now I have more information. Call my price a favor, if you will."

"Favor? Price? They sound about the same to me. Don't they, lads?" Stubby hooked his thumbs in his belt as her other fathers chorused "Aye."

"What'll it cost us?" Ebba asked him, tilting her head, eyes narrowed.

The king's eyes rested briefly on his son before flicking to Barrels. "My life."

"I don't know what ye've heard, but we ain't really got magic powers. We can't un-damn ye," Locks said, muttering, "*I ain't sure ye deserve it.*"

"No." Montcroix cut him off with a glare. "I mean that I believe in my son. *He* will restore balance and save the realm. And when that happens, the damned will become the damned again. Good will exist only in the realm. The bad will return to hell."

That seemed to be making some leaps and bounds to her, but Ebba remained mute. There was a reason the king won the Battle for the Seas, after all.

"I will not spend eternity in that place," he said harshly. "I feel the taint creeping within me. To be in a cage is one thing. To be lost to darkness is an unbearable fate. I would rather be ended in truth."

The king's eyes weren't black, so he wasn't contagious, despite his belief. But Ebba hadn't been contagious while tainted, either, so who knew how much he'd taken on.

Peg-leg tapped closer, squinting. "What are ye sayin', royal-lubber? Speak plain."

"You can't mean it," Caspian whispered, stepping forward.

The king smiled sadly. "I am glad we got these moments in hell, son. There was time to explain and gain closure. It is more than most get. But Caspian, no matter that I am standing here, I am dead and gone. If the damned really die when killed outside of hell, I have a chance to be free. Really free."

"But why would you leave Anya, Sierra, and me when you could stay?" her friend whispered.

"I choose to be gone in truth," Montcroix said after a deep breath. "Not from you, not from your sisters, but from an infinity of imprisonment."

Ebba thought he was taking a risk—they didn't know what killing a damned out in the realm actually did. He could go into a smaller prison. Clearly, that was a risk he was willing to take. Montcroix couldn't be blamed for wanting freedom. If Ebba was in the Locker, she'd want the same.

Caspian held his father's gaze as a wave crashed against the cliffs beneath them, sending spray high. None of them interrupted. She watched the quick rise and fall of her friend's chest—saw as he swallowed and blinked.

And in a voice hoarse with suppressed emotion, Caspian said, "I'm glad we had these moments, too, Father."

He turned and walked to the cliff edge. There, Caspian stood gazing out just as his father had done a moment before—his arm resting behind his back and his head bowed.

Ebba contemplated the king again, who stared after his son.

"Ye've promised Satyr Island to those who fight with us," she said, eyes narrowed. "But ye expect them to be dragged back to Davy Jones' when the balance be restored." *Double-crossing weasel.*

Montcroix smiled coldly. "The deal was struck in good faith. As for what I've learned recently, that will remain unspoken in their presence. I was once king of the Exosian realm. The damned shall not roam free there if I can prevent it."

He said that like he wasn't an occupant of hell. But. . . .

"Ye have yerself an accord, King Montcroix," she said, dipping her head instead of spitting on her hand. She wasn't touching anyone tainted with a ten-foot pole. Who knew what it'd do to her in this state.

"I'm glad. I want to be killed by him." The king pointed at Barrels.

Barrels straightened, peering around the rest of them. "What? Why me?"

"You are an Exosian. I will not be killed by a pirate." He dropped to his knees, loosening the neck of his tunic.

Pink flushed the tops of Barrels' weathered cheeks. For a long time, her father feared mainlanders would be unable to recognize him as anything other than a pirate. The king had just paid him a compliment of the highest order.

Locks choked on his laughter, sharing an amused glance with Peg-leg.

"Uh, okay?" Barrels finally said.

The king closed his eyes and spread his arms wide. "Do it then. I am ready."

"Wait!" Caspian turned back, hands splayed before him. "Don't do this, Father. I'll figure out how to free you of the taint. And hell. Just give me time."

Stubby cut him off. "Get up, Forge. We ain't killin' ye—"

Forge wrenched his eyes from his son to Stubby. "You—"

"—until yer army does ex'ctly what they're meant to," Stubby finished. He pivoted toward the rest of them as Montcroix sighed and got to his feet.

"What do ye think, lads?" her father asked them. "Time to cause some trouble for Cannon?"

"Aye," her fathers chorused.

Ebba stared across the channel, mentally studying the ember—still smoldering—deep within her.

"Aye. Time to cause some trouble," she replied. *And get Jagger back.*

When darkness fell, she'd find him.

FOUR

Matey gently deposited Ebba on the western shore of Satyr Island. It was early evening, and they were currently south of Cannon's loading ship. The kraken had circled them east, below the southern tip to avoid detection from those loading the ship.

Ebba's bare feet sank into the dark, muddy sand, and she crouched low as she walked up the beach, knowing Cannon would have scouts everywhere.

The damned that had arrived prior should have taken care of them, but who really knew with people from hell. Their plan could go pear-shaped really fast.

More damned had arrived just before and waited for her and the crew to join them. Another horde of the damned had been dropped along the east coast and were working their way to the northern tip to attack Cannon's pirates guarding the path.

The path between Davy's and the island had been exposed since dusk. The remainder of Montcroix's gifted army were rushing across. They'd arrive in short duration if all went to plan. And *if* all went to plan, they would attack Cannon when night fell.

If.

This wasn't a skirmish in a tavern on Maltu; this was battle. And none of her crew had pistols or cutlasses or daggers. They each had a spear, lent by the Capricorn, who—aside from transporting the damned—would be useless in the land battle due to having the bottom half of a fish and all.

She'd never trained with a spear but had seen the tribespeople on Pleo use them.

The pointy end went into her enemy.

On the way to the island, they'd checked Riot's body was still there. He was dead; gone to wherever those in death passed to when they were doubly killed. Maybe aside from his shell, Riot had simply ceased to exist. The parallels between Riot and Ebba were uncanny, she reflected. But the knowledge that, outside the Locker, Pockmark and Cannon could really die almost stirred her from the numbness that contained her.

Her fathers started forward, spears in hand, and Ebba squelched after them in a crouch. Determination settled heavy in her bones. Pirates and royalty had never mixed well. Not until Caspian. But when the two put their heads together, it turned out entire worlds could be conquered. Between Ebba, her fathers, Caspian, and Montcroix, they had a plan—a plan that even she'd silently decided to put her "save Jagger" mission on hold for.

Wiry shrubs with thorns dotted the gently rolling, dark hills just like she recalled from her last visit. Hoof indents studded the ground from the regular passing of the Satyr. Memories of how the creatures had trussed her up and made her run behind them swirled before her eyes. The Satyr had imprisoned the female Capricorn for nearly fifty years. Was kidnapping women in their nature? Or had the taint made them into monsters?

In Ebba's experience, immortalkind obeyed their nature above all else. Only the truly powerful seemed able to challenge the call and duty of their magic at all, and even they struggled to do so. Sally, the queen of the wind sprites, had managed to oppose the call to lead her people—in the form of a massive bender. Even then, the sprite still lost the battle to thwart her power and position on occasion—like the time when she didn't save the crew from King Montcroix on Exosia because it might have affected future alliances with mortals. Then there was the enormous Matey. Ebba wasn't sure what the nature of a kraken was, except to devour ships. At roughly the size of half of *Felicity,* Matey was the only one of his kind left—so he *said.*

The Satyr struck her as a naturally harsh and dominating race. Knowing more now, Ebba assumed they'd been tainted by Medusa at some point in the last fifty years. That thought might have had her hesitating weeks ago. But the reality was the Satyr and tainted pirates stood between her and someone she needed, someone she loved. In another time or another realm, Ebba might have paused to sort the sometimes bad from the truly bad and everything between, but there wasn't time. And she lacked the will.

She tightened her grip on the spear, ready to plunge it into whomever necessary to get to Jagger.

Ebba strode down the worn track beside Locks.

Her other fathers flanked her in front and behind. Caspian led them while his father, Montcroix, walked with his tainted a hundred feet in front. They had just over one thousand damned in total. Or should if everyone could cross the path. And if not many of the eastern party were lost fighting any tainted pirates guarding the jetty to hell.

Runners dodged through the shrubbery to King Montcroix, slowing as they reached him. Runners from the eastern shore.

Just as planned. Ebba vaguely recognized the red-bearded man at the monarch's side as the one who'd led her and Caspian through the horde of damned just before everything went to shite.

A screech punctured the air.

They all wrenched to a halt, damned and living alike.

"That ain't in the plan," Locks whispered, scanning the darkening skies.

With the dying dredges of the dusk light, and with the ever-present angry clouds in the sky, Ebba's eyes couldn't glean anything. But the screech had come from above.

Barrels whispered low. "The Daedalion? Or spies for Cannon?"

If it was the Daedalion responding to their message, why didn't they approach? The thing was, even after months on this quest, there was so much Ebba and the others didn't know about immortal creatures. That screech could have come from anything.

"That might put seaweed on the rudder," Stubby said.

Caspian joined them. "I'm going ahead to speak to my father."

The damned in front of them resumed walking. Ebba and the others followed, but a shimmer of dissent had interrupted her confident step from before.

"We have no choice but to continue," Caspian said upon his return. "We're not far from our rendezvous point, so everyone needs to stay as quiet as possible."

Before coming, they'd guessed at what defenses Cannon might have in place.

He'd be staying off the exposed beach and would likely use the natural peak of the rolling terrain to plant sentries. His main force had to be waiting in the dunes somewhere. Hundreds of tainted pirates had escaped the Locker in the first wave, and Grubby said Cannon's ship was a man 'o war, fourth or fifth rate from what he could tell by the number of cannons. A warship.

"Where did they get all o' the trees for the ship?" Stubby asked. "That must've taken upward o' a thousand."

Barrels hummed. "Maybe that's why there aren't any trees here."

"They were Medusa's servants," Peg-leg said. "She had trees on her island. The male Capricorn could've hauled them over."

Ebba didn't care how the ship was made, just that it was here and an obstacle.

The ship was tainted, so none of them could get aboard without risking infection. If the ship set sail before their damned could get on board, their chances of freeing Jagger were bleak—if he was even on there. Matey could only do so much to the ship by hurling catapults, after all, especially if Jagger was on board and at risk.

Maybe Cannon was banking on that.

Their party slowed in response to the movements of Montcroix's group ahead. Peg-leg hobbled forward to get an update from the deceased king.

"Ebba, lass," Locks said, gripping her arm. "I'd like ye to stay with us durin' the fight. We stand the best chance o' gettin' Jagger back that way. Let the damned do the grunt work."

That wasn't necessarily true, but Ebba could see why they wanted that. She didn't want her fathers in the fight either. "Sure."

Locks hesitated. Did he hear the breeziness within her reply?

Jagger was here somewhere. Hurting. Tainted. That he could overcome the taint in time meant little. Each time he was subjected to the pillars' method of feeding, he lost more of himself. Being immune didn't make him infallible. The experiences left him with scars, with less of his soul, and with vivid horrors. They'd all been tainted. They all knew. But only Jagger knew what it was to be tainted again and again.

Ebba could sail through infinity and never find someone like him.

Would he recognize her? How she wished she could give him the person she'd been; that joyful, spoiled woman he'd known. Instead, she now knew how hard life could be; how cold. Why would anyone wish to grow up to endure such things?

Dusk had fallen well and truly.

Montcroix's group had stopped ahead and crouched behind the last dune in a long row that blended into the distance, disappearing with the rolling hills and wiry shrubs. The king gestured them over, and Ebba and the others hunkered down slightly apart from him.

He spoke low and fast. "We're close to the ship and surrounding beach. Five hundred feet. You are certain no one was on the beach when you checked before the tide dropped again?" he asked Grubby.

Grubby's eyes were wide. "Aye, no one was even loadin' up anymore. And in nights gone by, the damned would go into the dunes to caulk. But some stayed on the ship. Pockmark and his friends, at least."

"Cannon knows we have a kraken. If he didn't see for himself, surely others did as they fled hell. Cannon won't be on the ship—too dangerous," the king mused aloud.

Yet Cannon never did as they expected. He'd even outsmarted Montcroix in the final Battle for the Seas. In the end, his death was just part of the pillars' ultimate plan to store one of the pieces of the root in the Locker for safekeeping. That was the flaw in their perfect strategy. Their plan considered the counter-strategies of a normal man.

Cannon was much more vile and cunning than a normal man, and he had the help of the pillars.

Caspian crouched beside Ebba as his father left to address the damned. "Won't be long. We attack at nightfall."

Ebba turned to look in the direction of where she knew the ship to be. Jagger was somewhere here. She could feel it in her bones.

"Not long," she agreed in a distant echo.

"We'll get him back, Mistress Fairisles." Caspian took her hand. "Jagger will be okay."

Hope and belief were gone. *On the other side of the riverbank from where she stood.* Ebba couldn't recall what they'd felt like. But within her, Jagger was the river itself, and Ebba could recall the blitz of powerful awareness she'd felt around him.

She wanted Jagger to be okay and safe. He *had* to be okay and safe or the ember would die. And that was it for Ebba.

"The two of you are not betrothed, then?" King Montcroix asked, eyeing their hands. "She is attached to the silver-eyed pirate?"

Ebba's lips quirked in cold amusement at his eager tone. "Yer son be safe from me, Montcroix."

Caspian remained mute, fidgeting. Once, the current conversation would have been highly uncomfortable for her, too. Such things seemed small now.

"You would not have survived in the castle," the king told her. "You are not meant to be caged."

Caspian's grip tightened as he stiffened. Was he remembering saying that to Ebba months before? Those very words.

Perhaps it was because he'd lost so much and she had been the constant, but Caspian had developed a deeper regard for her. She didn't doubt it was real. Just as Ebba didn't doubt that she might have returned it if she'd never met Jagger. She forgot everyone else when she was with him.

Caspian had inspired warmth in her, security and love, but never spontaneous, exciting heat. Jagger was undeniable.

"I wasn't meant to be caged." She agreed. "We would've been at each other's throats within months."

Caspian tore away from his father's heavy gaze to stare at her. "We'll never know, will we?" He dropped her hand and moved away.

"I do know." She turned to look in Jagger's assumed direction once more.

"So do I," Montcroix said immediately. "You would have made a terrible queen, hated by the people. Exosia would have turned into Febribus within months."

Her lips quirked for the second time though her insides chilled. Possessing the same cynical humor as Montcroix didn't bode well for her. "Maybe that's what the realm was needin'. An end to yer tight-ass landlubber rules."

Distantly, she registered how different this was from their first meeting in the castle. Ebba wouldn't have dared to utter those words. How events could change a person. Both of them.

"Those who've never had to rule can never understand what it means to rule. Forming and adhering to the laws that protect and govern a people takes strength and discipline."

"Rules are made to be broken."

"That is exactly what I would expect a pirate to say. In some ways, your kind is predictable."

"That's what ye should expect from *everyone*, Forge. When a person be whittled down to their base nature, they'll break every law to survive. Dressin' them up nice and givin' them manners don't do a thing to get rid o' that. Ye want to see refined people? Look at pirates. They have to survive each day. Tell me: If yer people were reduced to our constant state overnight, what would they do to survive? Would they kill strangers? People they knew? Children? Would they steal an' swindle, ransack an' form cults? I'm thinkin' they'd do a lot worse than the average pirate."

King Montcroix tilted his head as Caspian had done so many times. "An intriguing mindset. I hope you are cured of your cynicism, Mistress Fairisles. The realm needs its birds, and even now, you are surely a bird."

A thin shout carried on the air from the northwest, followed by a faint pop.

Ebba stilled. *Pistol fire.*

Montcroix dipped his head at her, and she nodded back, the disturbing sense of sameness hitting her again.

The dead king stood without warning, roaring, "Damned. Forward march!"

Even knowing the plan, Ebba jerked as the damned erupted from their crouched positions along the dune and climbed the rise in the darkness, heading in the direction of the beach.

Their footsteps only shuffled at first, but as soon as the first two rows reached the top of the first dune, the sound changed to a rumbling stampede. Ebba's gut tightened as coiled energy coursed through her.

When the last of the damned disappeared over the first rise, she straightened, clutching her spear.

"Let's go, lads," Stubby growled.

In the middle of her fathers and Caspian, Ebba pushed her way up the dune, listening as guttural shouts broke through the steady drum of running damned. People from all walks of life who had been condemned to hell—grimy, desperate men, women, and children.

The high-pitched whirring of gunfire soared above the bellowing, screaming mess, and the slap and pop as the bullets met with flesh were loudest of all.

Yells turned to groans of agony. The bitter stench of gunpowder saturated the air.

The moon shone through the thick clouds, and as Ebba reached the top of the dune, she fixed her eyes on the black man o' war in the distance.

"I'm comin'," she whispered quietly enough no one else could hear.

Not wasting her breath further, for fear she'd need every scrap of it before the end, Ebba hurtled down the dune toward shore.

FIVE

From her vantage point atop the last dune, Ebba watched as the damned swept down to the shore, collecting the tainted pirates who had fled from the dunes to the beach. With the full moon bright in the sky, nothing was hidden. Montcroix's army of the damned weren't leaving any alive, taking their revenge on those who'd left them to rot in Davy Jones'. And none of them were killing cleanly.

Perhaps she shouldn't expect mercy from the occupants of hell.

Peg-leg and Barrels caught up, and the group set off down the dune to join the fight.

The tainted pirates and the damned were an indiscernible, throbbing throng that covered the dark, muddy beach as far as she could see. They clashed in a mix of swinging limbs, darting dodges, and glinting iron.

On the other side of battle, bobbing ninety feet out in the water, was Cannon's black ship.

They all slowed at the bottom of the dune, surveying the bloody mess before them.

"Should've thought o' some way to sep'rate ourselves," Locks said.

A strip around the arm would've done nicely. Though separating themselves so they could be identified by their army would also allow Cannon's tainted to spot them too.

"Let's go," she said, taking a step forward.

Caspian gripped her arm gently. "Father said to wait."

And what if Montcroix was already dead? The thrum of battle was in her. Despite her earlier words to her friend's father, *Ebba* was now reduced to her base nature. And her base nature was focused on Jagger. She had to find him. And all the reasons for standing here were fading before her eyes.

She made to shake off Caspian's hand, but the sight of Montcroix striding toward them stilled her tongue.

He called to them, "The forces from the east and north have converged here. None have spotted Cannon or Pockmark yet."

They could be in some obscure corner of the island, but her eyes strayed to the black ship—the ship where none of them expected Cannon to be.

"He be on the ship," she said. Something under her ribs tugged her in that direction, and she had a strong feeling it was Jagger.

Stubby shook his head, sucking in breaths after their jog to get here. "Sleepin' on the ship when we have a kraken? That'd be the fool's thing to do." He reached out a hand to steady a wheezing Barrels.

"We'd never expect it," Locks countered, wiping his brow.

"We can't go *on* the ship. It be tainted," Peg-leg said, panting hard.

Ebba tilted her head. "The perfect place to evade anyone free o' the taint."

They all ducked as a piercing screech echoed across the beach. It was the second screech she'd heard in as many hours, but this time, when Ebba tilted her head back, the owner of the sound was visible against the moon.

Ebba grinned. "Nay, we can't touch the ship."

"Why are you smiling?" Caspian asked, frowning.

She pointed up.

He echoed her smile. "The Daedalion are here."

Ebba scanned the beach anew. Peg-leg's comment had penetrated the battle-fueled craze she'd nearly entered. But if Ebba was tainted, she'd be useless to help Jagger. She couldn't physically touch the ship. None of them could. If she'd had shoes, perhaps, but her feet were all too bare.

Her fathers and Montcroix erupted into an argument over what to do next. Ignoring them, Ebba watched the Daedalion as they circled in to land at the top of the dune she'd just descended.

"We need to flush him off the ship," Ebba muttered.

Conversation ground to a halt.

She continued, "Matey."

"Jagger be on the ship, lass," Locks said. "If Matey sinks it. . . ."

There was no chance of beating Cannon without risk. They weren't battling an idiot. For once, she and her fathers and even the damned king were going to outsmart the notorious captain. They were going to do the unexpected. And that involved using everything —and every creature—at their disposal.

"He's unfurlin' the sails," Grubby said, pointing to the water.

Her cold heart skittered across ice.

Ebba glanced back at the Daedalion as more landed at the top of the dune, illuminated against the night sky. After their parents had willingly met death in each other's arms, the flock had taken to the air. The hawk-man in the middle was the most familiar; he was the son who'd made the protection vow to her crew, but his name escaped her. She needed the *scio* to communicate with the creatures, but she seemed to recall that the Daedalion had understood pirate tongue. Immortals' ability to speak the mortal tongue depended somewhat on their level of power and somewhat on what body parts they possessed.

A one-way conversation would do for now.

"Daedalion," she called, pushing back up the hill. Once there, she half-bowed, and they did the same.

"There be no time for ahoys," she told them. "Ye've come when we need ye most."

All three of the landed Daedalion were males. They towered over her even with their great wings tucked fast against their bodies. Half hawk and half human, their golden eyes contemplated her silently.

"We need to draw Cannon off the ship," she said, feeling more than knowing her crew was listening. "The ship can't leave the bay. Can ye scour his sails for us? Don't touch the wood o' the ship. Nothin' livin'. And watch yer heads. Our kraken friend'll be throwin' catapults."

The Daedalion's eyes widened briefly before the hawk-man in the middle nodded.

Ebba turned back and stood staring at her crew's gaping faces.

Aye, she'd never taken charge like this before. She also wasn't the same person anymore. There was one task on her mind, and it would be done.

"How long until we take the beach?" she asked Montcroix.

He contemplated her with narrowed eyes. He glanced back. "The fighting will continue for some time. The tainted pirates are going berserk as we speak. You know that when they go berserk, the pillars cannot control their actions or minds. I doubt the tainted will turn tail and run into the dunes when that happens, but their frenzied violence will make the pirates easier to overcome. We can fight through the middle. We should claim the beach by midnight. The entire island by dawn."

Ebba listened with half an ear and watched as the Daedalion formed a great V that they aimed at the ship. "Barrels, please signal Matey."

"Ye're sure, lass?" Stubby asked.

Caspian spoke. "She's right. If this becomes an impasse, Jagger will only suffer longer."

Her fathers exchanged a long glance while Montcroix remained mute. Then Barrels pulled off his tunic and climbed halfway up the dune, waving the used-to-be-white material high overhead. Moonlight brightened the beach, but though Matey knew to watch for such a signal, they couldn't count on him alone.

The red-bearded man from earlier approached Montcroix, a bundle under one arm.

"The weapons, sire," he said, dropping the bundle onto the muddy ground.

"We can't touch tainted weapons," Locks said.

Ebba crouched by the cutlasses, abandoning her spear. "The taint can only inhabit livin' things. These be metal."

She reached out, and Peg-leg seized her hand.

"A precaution-like, I'm thinkin'," he said.

Letting go, he tore a strip off the bottom of his tunic and wrapped it around her hand. He repeated this for himself. By the end, most of his rotund midriff was on display.

Ebba took up a cutlass, and one by one, the others did the same, pausing to wrap their hands. It was a small safeguard against the taint but a safeguard nevertheless. She grabbed the spear again, too. Better armed than sorry.

Bodies littered the beach. The throng didn't seem as impenetrable as the damned had culled the pirates' numbers, but still, dodging the tainted remains and piercing through the crowd of Cannon's crew would be a tall order.

"To the shore," she said simply.

Montcroix barked out a string of commands, and a group of the damned peeled away, sprinting back to flank Ebba and her fathers.

Spear in one hand and cutlass in the other, Ebba ran.

The damned either side of her did most of the work at first, but as much as their protection helped, it painted them as a target. Tainted pirates, their eyes flooded with black, spun away from their foes farther up the beach and raced directly for them. Fast. Rage-fueled.

Numbness engulfed her, but the need to get past them made her keenly aware of her surroundings.

The first pirate penetrated the horde of the damned.

A sea of black eyes and foaming saliva covered the beach ahead.

Not slowing her pace, she lifted her cutlass and sliced in an arc, ducking to avoid the spray of blood.

They managed to get another twenty feet before the pirates flinging themselves against their outer ranks slowed them.

Stubby and Barrels pushed ahead to fight beside her, and for a while they appeared determined to save her from fighting at all. But the numbers were too great.

Montcroix roared for more damned to attack the pirates, but there was no possible way for her to see if they were obeying.

She awkwardly thrust her spear forward, grimly satisfied when it pierced the innards of a pirate so starved he could've been buried weeks earlier if not for the dark magic sustaining him.

After a few attempts, she yanked the spear free with a wet squelch and strode to the next obstacle blocking her from Jagger. She blinked into the muzzle of a pistol, lurching forward when the chamber clicked empty.

Barrels leaped from somewhere behind her, swinging his blade in a downward arc, felling the pirate who'd nearly ended her life.

She released a slow breath and prepared herself for the next onslaught. But as Ebba made to lunge, the pirates shied away.

They were falling back. *Parting.*

"What's goin' on?" Stubby said. He'd lost his spear along the way and held his cutlass aloft at the level of his eyes.

Barrels was breathing hard. "Shite, the Satyr."

Her ringing ears hadn't registered the goat-men's stampede, but she peered through the parting pirates and confirmed that the immortals were racing toward them. The Satyr stood between her and the ship. Time took on an odd quality, and Ebba peered past the cantering immortals to the black water glistening in what little moonlight existed. She watched as a boulder the size of *Felicity*'s mermaid figurehead hurtled through the night sky, courtesy of Matey, who'd clearly received their message to commence flinging catapults.

"Spears!" Caspian roared, breaking through her stupor.

He pushed past Ebba and dug his spear into the muddy sand so the sharp tip pointed toward the stampede of Satyr at an angle.

Ebba smirked and did the same with hers, standing aside as three of her fathers quickly mimicked Caspian's action too. Then they scrambled out thirty feet back, their cutlasses at the ready.

"Fall back from the spears," Montcroix shouted at the damned. Those who could hear hastened back to stand behind her fathers.

The Satyr at the front witnessed their ploy. But with their stampeding kinsmen hard on their heels, they had no option except to run.

Most of the front row managed to leap over the spears, but the shrieks of the rows behind were music to Ebba's ears.

"We need rope to trip them, like last time," Caspian whispered.

She heard the fear in his voice. "The sharp o' my blade'll hurt them more than rope, methinks."

The damned at her back swelled around her crew as the first of the Satyr bore down for the kill. The goat-men galloped through the lines of Forge's force, trampling those in their path. But the Satyr twisted as blows from the damned rained down on them from all sides.

Ebba widened her stance, crouching, watching for the moment when the Satyr broke through the damned and attacked her.

A Satyr careened toward her, his face already scrunched with pain. He carried a spear, but this was wrenched from him by one of the damned in the last line of defense.

Ebba sidestepped and held her cutlass low. Her arm was nearly torn from the socket as the blade sliced through the immortal's shins. He brayed high and crumpled to the ground, and she wasted no time leaping after him. The trapped female Capricorn flashed in her mind as she dug the tip of her cutlass into his abdomen before drawing the blade all the way to the bottom of his ribs.

She didn't wait to see what fell out.

The damned surrounded the herd of Satyr.

Ebba checked her immediate vicinity and then peered across the bloodied beach for her fathers and Caspian. Caspian fought a Satyr alongside his father, empty sleeve tucked into his belt. Grime etched the determined lines of his face as he darted quick attacks, working back and forth in sync with Montcroix.

Grubby smiled as he cut down a tainted. Stubby and Peg-leg fought back-to-back against two Satyr.

Ebba sprinted to the pair but halted as a damned threw herself bodily against the Satyr from the other side of her fathers. The woman toppled the larger goat-man. Peg-leg lifted his right leg and pinned the creature with his wooden peg. Stubby then plunged his blade into the immortal's heart.

"That's for takin' my daughter, ye soddin' cur," Peg-leg roared.

Stubby stumbled back as the second Satyr reared, punching wildly with his bunched fists. A scream lodged in Ebba's throat as the creature brought its hooves stamping to the ground only a hair's width from Stubby's head.

Caspian bowled through, thrusting his cutlass through the Satyr's chest. The Satyr backhanded him out of the way before reaching both hands to the sword in his ribcage. Her legs unlocked, and Ebba raced to Stubby's side, dragging him free seconds before the immortal collapsed to the muddy ground.

She left Stubby to stand and jerked Caspian's cutlass free of the dead immortal.

Spinning, Ebba gripped Caspian's arm and hauled him upright, shoving the weapon back in his grip. His eyes weren't focusing. He seemed to be battling to stay conscious.

"Are ye with me, man?" Ebba bellowed at him over the din.

"Always with ye," he slurred.

Shite. "Stubby, watch Caspian. He's broken."

"On it, lass."

Barrels was off to her left. Grubby supported a limping Locks. All around her, damned pulled the Satyr to the ground. The tainted pirates had stood back for the immortals' cantering attack but now pressed in. They dwindled in number, hacked at by the damned who'd responded to Montcroix's earlier shout for reinforcements.

And through all of that, like the steady beam of a lighthouse, a direct path to the shore appeared before Ebba. With the shouts of her fathers behind her, she unleashed the coiled tension in her legs and ran for the beach.

None of the pillars' minions bothered to pursue her because no one could keep up as she weaved between the fighting, leaping over the bodies, feeling the blood-soaked sand ooze between her toes.

They'd all need the *purgium* after this. Yet another reason to win.

The shore loomed, and Ebba scanned the skies, noting the Daedalion circling high above Cannon's ship. The yellow-white sails of the vessel were in tatters, some of them hanging by a thread. She smirked at the sight and scoured the water for any hint of Matey's position.

No catapults came.

Where was he?

Ebba reached the shore and immediately spun to place her back to the water. She held her cutlass aloft as she scanned the beach for any tainted pirates who might be hard on her heels. But only Grubby had managed to stick with her. Her part-selkie father arrived and mimicked her defensive position. Ebba returned to her vigil over the ship, safe in the knowledge he'd have her back.

Where was Matey? More importantly, where was Cannon?

She squinted to the ship's bow, peeking through the haze of pistol smoke. Ebba could just make out three figures standing there. One of them had to be Mutinous.

The yells of her fathers reached her, and she glanced over her shoulder as Stubby and Barrels caught up.

"Hey, look at what Matey's doin'," Stubby said, frowning.

She opened her eyes and then some more. Matey was wrapping his tentacles around the ship from beneath the surface.

"What's he doin'?" Ebba demanded. "He ain't meant to pull the ship under!" He *really* couldn't. Not while Jagger was onboard. This wasn't the time for Matey to answer the call of his kraken nature.

Barrels wheezed, rubbing his eyes and peering at the vessel. "But look. It's working. I think someone is lowering the rowboat."

Ebba swung her gaze to the bow again. She could just make out two figures there. They were grappling by the looks of it. The third had moved to port side to lower the boat. Was one of those figures Jagger? Even with the moonlight, they were too far away to tell.

Her hands curled into fists. Matey's undertow was sucking the ship downward. She had to do something.

Placing two fingers in her mouth, Ebba let out a shrill whistle, waving both arms overhead for the Daedalions' attention.

Several of them dove for her.

She was going to the ship. She'd enter hell again for Jagger, and she was willing to do worse for him, too, by entering the belly of a tainted vessel.

Peg-leg and Locks finally caught up, supporting a stumbling Caspian between them. The prince's eyes rolled back in his head as he lost the battle to remain cognizant. Her fathers lowered the unconscious Exosian to the ground.

"Ye ain't goin' up alone," Stubby said. He nodded at Peg-leg, Grubby, and Locks.

Barrels shook his head, still panting. "I'll stay here with Caspian. But don't kill Cannon without me."

The Daedalion landed.

"Can ye take us to the ship?" she blurted.

In answer, they presented their backs and bent forward. Ebba didn't pause to ask if that was permission. She jumped aboard, clasping her arms around the middle Daedalion's neck. The bony joints of the creature's wings dug into her stomach.

The aggressive beating of the hawk's wings nearly jostled her off as the bird-human climbed in the air. Ebba only had time to look each way and see that her fathers were clambering on to the backs of their own Daedalion.

She bit back on a cry of alarm as her Daedalion banked sharply to the left, circling in to the ship. Ebba exhaled when he stabilized, and she hoisted herself into a better position before peering down.

One pirate sat within the lowered rowboat. From this vantage point, she thought the person might be Swindles. The tainted pirate wasn't heading for shore; judging by his trajectory, he was aiming for the southern tip of the island.

He was running.

A tentacle exploded out of the water, extending high and crashing down upon the tiny vessel. The black-eyed pirate jerked at the sight and flung himself over the lip of the rowboat. Too late. Ebba watched as Swindles went flying through the air. And not just him. . . .

Matey's destruction had also thrown a black chest high into the air. The chest spun through the night sky and a tendril of moonlight caught on a very familiar sword latched to the side.

Veritas.

"Get the chest," she urged the immortal beneath her.

The Daedalion swooped sharply in reply, and Ebba's stomach lurched. She blinked against the wind making her eyes water, desperate to keep both eyes on the box. But as they dove, she could only cling on with no notion of where the chest was and how close they were to the water.

There was a scratch and a thud. The Daedalion wrenched out of his sheer dive, forcing the air from her body. Ebba skidded forward toward the creature's head, and for a few seconds, stared six feet down to the water's surface. *And the chest.*

"Good work," she said grimly, working back to the safer position between the immortal's wings.

The Daedalion climbed in the night sky once more, and Ebba ignored the ruined rowboat below, returning her gaze to the ship. The creature circled them closer. Lower.

Mutinous Cannon stood at the bow of his ship, face impassive and eyes black.

If Pockmark had intended to leave with Swindles in the rowboat, the mutiny hadn't worked in his favor. Mercer Pockmark lay at Cannon's feet, his head turned at an unnatural angle. Cannon loomed over him, hands clasped behind his back, shoulders drawn back and chin high. As though the son of his son didn't lay murdered by his own hands less than a stride away. As though tentacles weren't pulling his ship down to the ocean floor. As though his army hadn't dwindled to naught.

That kind of calm only came when a person had accepted they were about to die, or perhaps Cannon was tainted enough to enter a crazed frenzy after the struggle with his grandson.

But then why was he standing so still? Or was Ebba still making the mistake of comparing him to a normal man?

It didn't matter; he *was* going to die, but not by her hand. Mutinous Cannon was her fathers' prize.

"Take me closer to the water," she called, dismissing Cannon.

Her instructions should have included 'slowly.' She held on for dear life as the creature turned almost vertical for the second time. Her body lost all contact with his, hovering precariously on the point of flipping feet over head. When the immortal flattened again, she braced her stomach, landing against his feathered back with a thump but managing to keep the air in her lungs this time.

Ebba dragged in a huge gulp of air.

"Matey," she bellowed.

The black ship was almost completely submerged. Water flooded the scuppers, and Jagger was still in there. He had to be!

"Matey!" she screamed.

His head popped up from amidst the tentacles coating the deck and hull. "What?" The gargled and snapped word was barely discernible.

"Jagger be in there, Matey. Ye need to find him."

Matey's eyes glowed red, and unease stirred deep in her innards. All immortals had to battle their nature, and she had an unsettling feeling Matey had lost that battle so far.

"Save someone off the ship?" he growled.

Ebba groaned inwardly. "Remember our plan? Ye helped make it. We're goin' to kill all o' the tainted pirates."

The glowing of his red eyes didn't falter. "I made the plan?"

He would remember it that way. "Aye, Matey, ye made the plan. Do ye recall when we named ye Matey? Ye saved us from our ship, and we be right good friends now."

"You're sad all the time. You never speak to me."

Bloody hell. "I wish to speak to ye now. I want to hear o' yer grandfather and . . . the ships ye've sunk."

Matey's eyes blazed, and he bellowed, "I will devour all ships."

"Sink it, Matey. Ain't no one sayin' not to sink it. We're rootin' for ye—truly. We ain't never seen a kraken sink a ship like ye're sinkin' this one. But what'd really show skill is if ye were able to multi-task. I heard a couple o' the damned on the shore sayin' ye couldn't do it."

He roared, snapping his mighty beak. His tentacles tightened, and the ship dropped lower. Ebba hoped she hadn't just killed Jagger.

Matey was lost to his calling. There wasn't anything for it. She'd have to go in.

"Drop me on the deck," she instructed the Daedalion. "Ye need to take the chest to Barrels and my other fathers on the shore. And if ye could ask some o' yer crew to bring me and another off, I'd be thankful."

Really, Ebba didn't expect to make it back to main deck.

The hawk-man hesitated, not erring from his swooping circles over the kraken's head.

"I know the ship be tainted," she said, assuming the reason for his uncertainty. "But if he's dyin', I'm dyin' with him. Ye surely understand. Yer parents' love spanned life and death."

She was mostly gone anyway. What did it matter?

A tear trickled from the golden hawk eye but was swept away by the wind. The creature nodded its great hawk head.

"*Fine*," Matey said with a sigh. "I'll get him."

He would? Ebba wasn't sure she trusted the kraken in this state.

She'd give him one minute before entering herself.

Matey worked his tentacles. The slimy masses writhed over each other, but eventually one slid free of the others. Without preamble, the kraken plunged the tentacle through the deck, sending splinters flying.

"Careful," she cried out. "Don't hurt Jagger. *Please*, Matey. I need him."

Whether it was life or death, she needed him. So close like this, her being screamed for his return. The thought of his silver eyes, his cunning strength, and his unfathomable love for her consumed her.

Matey squinted as he dug around below deck.

Ebba couldn't breathe, couldn't think. Not when the ship was a single breath away from sinking. Her eyes had one job, and that was to watch the splintered opening in the deck where Jagger might emerge.

If she'd been paying attention, she might have seen Cannon rushing for Matey's tentacle, his cutlass held high overhead.

"Nay," she gasped.

Stubby's Daedalion swooped, and Ebba choked on her shriek as Stubby leaned over and plunged his cutlass into Cannon's back.

Her eyes widened as Stubby's shout reached her.

"That's for my father, ye worthless slime," he roared.

Cannon spun on the spot, the cutlass protruding from his back. He looked about as shocked as Ebba felt.

She jumped as Locks executed a similar maneuver, plunging his sword through Cannon's gut. Her father didn't utter a word, but white rage etched every line of his face.

Peg-leg was next. His cutlass found its home just above Locks'. Cannon coughed twice, slamming to his knees on the destroyed deck.

"Two decades of plannin', and look where it got ye," Peg-leg called down to him. "Ye lost, Cannon. All that shite and ye bloody lost."

Mutinous Cannon's eyes flooded black. He coughed again, and blood spurted from his lips. Could he even feel at this point? Could he feel that he'd failed? Despite every attempt to break her fathers, to break his crew and the realm and even hell itself.

Could Mutinous reason that he'd finally lost?

Ebba wasn't sure. But she was certain the pillars were watching every bit of this. *Good.*

Grubby swooped.

"Tell yer pillar masters we be comin' for them next," Locks yelled to the bloodied form of the man her fathers had feared for decades.

Grubby thrust his cutlass forward, sloppy and toothless smile gone and foreign fury in its place. His curved sword entered directly over what remained of Cannon's heart, the force of the Daedalion's flight ensuring the blade met with little resistance.

The cutlass slammed out Cannon's back, curving out through the top of his shoulder blade. Dark crimson dripped from the tip of the weapon.

Ebba's heart thundered in her ears, and as if underwater, she slowly turned her head to watch Matey's tentacle retreat out of the hole in the splintered deck. Her chest couldn't inflate—like an anchor had been dropped onto it.

Nothing filled her. Not air. Not life. Certainly not hope.

Even when Matey pulled a tall, thin man from the ship's belly, Ebba couldn't push that anchor off her chest.

The moonlight caught on the man's flaxen hair, making the strands appear silver. Ebba stared at the limp form of Jagger wrapped in Matey's grip. The kraken extended the tentacle, holding him aloft, and then lowered Jagger to the water, setting his lifeless and naked form onto what remained of Swindles' rowboat.

Matey shoved the raft toward shore.

Her mind could register, but not process. Ebba couldn't blink. She couldn't have uttered a single word.

Her Daedalion extended its wings wide and beat them at an angle, providing a gust to help push the raft holding Jagger inland.

Ebba couldn't look.

She couldn't look.

SIX

Ebba slid off the Daedalion's back, legs buckling slightly as she landed in the muddy sand. Tears slid down her cheeks, the first since leaving Davy Jones' Locker. Dread weighing her, drowning her, she rounded the creature, not interested in the black stone chest and sword that lay upended by his right claw.

Montcroix collected Jagger from the raft and laid him in the middle of her fathers. As she wiped her face, they parted for her.

Or were they afraid of her? She was afraid of herself. Of what she would feel if Jagger was dead. If only because, for one slice of eternity, against her better judgment, she'd dared to hope.

Jagger's back was to her. The nubs of his spine were visible. He'd lost weight. His flaxen hair lay limp across his forehead, streaked with the same dirt and grime that coated his naked length.

Stubby blocked her path, and she dragged her eyes up to his face with colossal effort.

"Ebba," he said hesitantly.

"*Don't say it.*" The words ripped from her. Burning heat scalded her eyes, and a sob tore from her lips.

A snatched growl, like one might expect from a cornered animal, silenced them both.

Her fathers shouted, and Stubby whirled, allowing her to see past them.

The breath caught in her throat.

Jagger did his best to stand, wavering on the spot, his eyes flooded black from the taint. Pus-filled wounds marred the skin on the tops of his shoulders.

He lunged for Barrels and ripped the spear from her father's hands, swinging the weapon wide. Caspian was still unconscious from the Satyr's backhand, and Montcroix heaved him back, falling over the prince and landing on Jagger's other side. Her fathers shied back several feet.

But Jagger stood strong.

A keening noise left Ebba's lips, and she clamped down on the sound. But he heard.

Keeping the same warrior's pose, he cocked an ear in her direction.

She stepped forward, and he lowered defensively. What had they done to him? So little time. Even when she pushed him off *Malice*, he hadn't been so far gone. Could he even come back from this?

She took another step forward. "Jagger," she whispered hoarsely, her very being aching at the sound of his name on her lips.

Jagger turned to look at her, his black eyes showing no recognition.

"Jagger," she repeated, tears flooding both cheeks, nearly obscuring her vision. "Jagger, it's me—"

With a snarling roar, he rushed her. His movements were too fast, too practiced for her fathers to reach them. And Ebba had no desire to move.

Jagger twirled the spear overhead and then planted his feet, hissing as he jabbed the weapon to her throat. Curious, Ebba watched the approach of the sharpened tip. She spread her hands palm-up, staring down the shaft into Jagger's eyes. Tainted they may be, but his were the last eyes she wanted to see. Her only regret was that if he did recover, he'd have to live with the consequences of this moment.

His eyes widened as the spearhead closed in on her neck. The air between the tip and her throat whooshed as he arrested the jab.

Ebba's heart beat wildly. She swallowed, feeling the pressure of the spear tip against the base of her throat. Jagger didn't lower the spear, but he stared at her, breathing hard and blinking as though trying to bring her into focus.

"Jagger," she said again, wincing at the pressure of the weapon against her flesh.

He jerked and, with shaking hands, threw the spear aside, falling heavily onto his knees.

She fell with him, and they stared at each other, two feet of thin air between them.

"Viva?" he whispered, swaying when he knelt.

"Viva." Ebba nodded gently.

"Don't leave me," he begged. Jagger closed his eyes and slid sideways into an unmoving heap.

But he was alive. *Somehow*, he was alive.

Ebba's shoulders shook with sobs she needed to repress. That didn't stop the wetness covering her cheeks or the trembling of her hands. "H-he needs clothes," she said. "H-he—"

A hand rested on her shoulder.

"We've got it, lass," Locks said softly.

Ebba tried again, her voice rising. "He's tainted." They couldn't touch him. Not yet.

Hysteria was working up through her body.

"He can have my tunic," King Montcroix said, drawing his off. "I won't need it where I'm going."

A high-pitched wail left her lips, and finally, Ebba couldn't control the sobs any longer. She crossed both arms over her chest and caved inward, painful, guttural keens wracking her body.

She babbled wordlessly. It was too much. All of this was more than she could bear. What had they done to the man she loved? What had they done to her? To *Plank?*

Why had they taken Plank away?

Peg-leg dropped to one knee and enveloped her in his arms. Grubby wasn't far behind; neither was Stubby. Locks squeezed his arms over the others, and Barrels held them all, only his mouth visible to her from the middle of their cocoon.

They stayed that way, and she gave over to the power of whatever rested dormant within her, almost wishing Jagger's return hadn't forced her to feel such powerful emotions.

In time, her shoulders stopped shaking. The terrible moaning from her lips faded into catching breaths. The arms of her fathers grew heavy, and Ebba straightened, letting their arms fall away.

She located a blood-free part of her tunic to wipe her eyes and face while her fathers did the same.

As they'd mourned, Montcroix had dressed Jagger in his own tunic; he'd even given away his belt. He knelt over his son now, staring at Caspian's slack face. The Satyr must have put some force into the blow.

Barrels slid his cutlass free of his belt and approached the damned king. "If you mean to go ahead with this, it should be done while Caspian is unaware."

Montcroix didn't immediately answer, but as the waves gently tumbled onto the shore, he nodded.

Ebba had experienced enough death in one day. She crouched by Jagger, her back to Barrels and Montcroix. She scanned the beach, watching the damned milling through the fallen tainted.

Had any survived? That seemed to be the problem of the damned; this was their island now.

Peg-leg knocked at the small stone chest with his peg. With his *right* peg. "Ebba, is this what I think it is?" he asked.

She stared at his wooden peg. "Yer wrong leg be gone."

Much had happened to her in recent weeks, but Ebba was sure of that fact.

"Aye," he said drily. "The *purgium* healed my left leg and took the right as payment. Not a bad trade-like. Ye know my knees pained me sumpin' fierce. The *purgium* took away that wear and tear, too."

Stubby made a wheezing sound, cutting off at a glare from Peg-leg.

Sink her, she'd really been out of it. Ebba scrubbed her face with both hands and answered his question about the box.

"Swindles was makin' off with it. I've an inklin' Pockmark was goin' to join him afore Cannon killed him. *Veritas* was latched to the side o' the chest, so it seemed likely the others were inside. Maybe the pillars thought tryin' to take the root o' magic away was best when they saw the ship wasn't goin' anywhere. Open it and find out," she said, glancing again at Jagger.

He was breathing. He was breathing.

Locks and Stubby gathered round as her father used his wrapped hand to ease back the fastening. He pushed back the lid and tilted it to her.

"And there they are," he whispered.

Inside the small stone chest, each in a separate velvet-lined partition, were the five parts. With *veritas* latched to the back of the box, that made six.

Stubby reached down and picked up the *scio.* "All parts o' the root. At last." He glanced at Ebba. "I don't like to trouble ye just yet, but with Cannon gone, I'm thinkin' the pillars'll show up quick-like."

He was right. She should do it now. The end of the realm didn't care if she slept or cried over Jagger.

Ebba stood and walked to the chest and easily picked it up. The square case was only large enough to cram a pair of boots inside, and despite being made of stone, the walls of the box were thin.

"What's the new piece again?" Peg-leg asked.

She studied the parts and turned the one in the middle. "*Fortudo,*" she read aloud. "Caspian said it meant bravery."

Nothing had happened the last time Ebba touched it, and it was no different now. No tingling or exploding white light as with the others. No fullness in her chest or the sudden ability to understand magical creatures.

"Feels weird," Locks grunted. "To finally have all six."

Even in her numb state, she could agree. Recalling her earlier realization, Ebba touched the *purgium* and screwed up her face in expectation of pain. Nothing happened when her skin touched the healing cylinder, and she slowly relaxed. "Didn't get any taint on me."

"We'll be washin' all o' our clothin' regardless," Locks said. "And I'm guessin' we should all touch the *purgium* after ye put the root together."

After she put the root together. . . .

Ebba picked up the *purgium* and *dynami* and brought the flat end of one to the rounded end of the other. She tapped them together. *Clink, clink, clink.*

Maybe if she turned them around?

Clink, clink, clink.

Ebba lowered her arms, staring at the cylinders.

"Bit o' an anti-climax, that," Peg-leg said, grimacing.

Stubby peered into the small chest. "What about the *scio*?" he asked. "It's got a pointy bit. Could that fit into. . . ?"

They stared into the chest. *Fit into what?*

Nevertheless, Ebba dropped the *dynami* and *purgium* into her lap and took the *scio* from Stubby.

Staring into the chest, she selected the *amare*, her heart squeezing at the thought of Jagger. She had to get him washed somehow. Try to get some water into his mouth. That seemed impossible when she couldn't touch him, but she'd figure out a way because he'd figured out how to keep breathing.

"What's Matey doin'?" Peg-leg asked, peering back out to sea.

Grubby laughed. "He's eatin' the ship."

Locks cursed. "Matey's lost the bloody plot. He can't eat the ship. He'll be tainted."

". . . Whatever floats his kraken boat, I s'pose." Stubby scratched his chin. "Ye know he has a hard time controllin' his eatin' when he be in a rage. And I ain't swimmin' out there to stop him."

"I can," Grubby offered.

Locks clapped him on the back. "Best not, m'hearty. Angry Matey doesn't much like selkies."

Aye, that was how Grubby ended up himself again after the *purgium* healed him.

Ebba attempted to jam the two cylinders together without success. She pressed her lips to the surface of the *amare*.

"Meld," she whispered.

Locks snorted.

"I'm open to yer ideas," she snapped at him.

Locks arched a brow and didn't pause before freeing the *veritas* of its constraints. He ran his fingers over it. "Maybe the sword can show us how to do it. It'll confirm if we know the answer, aye?"

"What're the odds of guessin' the right answer to an age-old magic?" grumbled Peg-leg.

"Next to none with that attitude." Locks then closed his eye and pursed his lips, muttering to the sword.

Shaking her head, Ebba placed the *scio* and *amare* in her lap with the others and hovered her hand over the *fortudo*.

When the cylinder didn't give her stomach the token warning stir, Ebba held her breath and picked up the *fortudo*. She released the breath in a whoosh.

"Why is it ye can hold five now?" Peg-leg asked.

No notion. There'd never been any rhyme or reason to how many she could hold. Her last theory was that she had to endure being blasted to Oblivion by holding too many. And that somehow, doing that allowed her to hold more. But she'd never held five before. And there hadn't been any blasting between times. She knew there was an answer to the mystery; Ebba just had no bloody idea what.

"Any luck?" Stubby asked Locks, who still held the sword, muttering.

"Give her a scant bit," he replied with a bite.

Peg-leg grinned. "Ye look like a right eejit doin' that."

Locks cracked open an eyelid and scowled. He tossed *veritas* to the sand. "At least I was bein' helpful."

The *veritas* lay within reach. She wondered if. . . . Ebba reached out.

The warning stir in her gut was immediate and strong. She ripped her fingers back to safety.

"Not that one?" Grubby asked.

"Nay," she answered. And that seemed slightly problematic considering the whole 'Ebba must build a weapon' thing. "Mayhaps that be why Caspian has to carry them to me one by one."

As she spoke his name, there was a loud crunch and squelch.

Ebba wrinkled her nose.

"And that be the end o' King Forge Montcroix," Peg-leg said, staring over her head to where Barrels had met King Montcroix to uphold their end of the bargain.

"Poor lad." Stubby glanced to where Caspian still lay immobile. "What an ordeal to sort through. Yer father be dead. He be alive. He wants to be dead, and then he be dead-dead. Sink me, ye don't think he'll come back *again*, do ye?"

Locks hummed. "No way to know where the dead go when they die again, is there? But I'll be pissy if he comes back a third time."

"Phew, Matey is really chewin' up that ship, ain't he?" Grubby said, chuckling. "Good thing he has six mouths."

At least. It wasn't as if she'd properly paused to count them while retrieving the *amare*.

Barrels stumbled back into view and lowered to a crouch, sucking in air. He was chalk white, his lips pressed tight together. His cutlass was stained with the blood of King Montcroix.

Her other fathers snickered.

"I'm not built for assassinations," her eldest father forced out.

No kidding.

He glared up at the others. "You killed Mutinous without me."

"And ye got Forge. Stop yappin'. And why is killin' one okay, but killin' the other be assass'nation?" Peg-leg demanded.

Barrels waved a hand. "Stop talking."

"Don't ye get high and book-readin' on me." The cook's meat-cleaving hand curled.

"No," Barrels said, peering toward shore. "I mean *stop talking*."

Ebba's jaw dropped as she followed his gaze out to sea.

Matey had abandoned the ship and bobbed around 150 feet off shore, looking directly at them. He didn't call out, and he didn't wave his tentacle in greeting. But the subtle sign that all wasn't well with the kraken was his diamond-shaped eyes.

Glowing black.

"Shite," she whispered.

"I'll double that and take it neat," Stubby said, taking a step back.

As he did, the kraken lifted slightly in the water.

"Don't move," Locks said. "He's tainted."

"I know he be tainted; his eyes are glowin' black," hissed Stubby.

"Aye," Locks answered in a low voice. "But he be tainted and lookin' like he wants to come on *land*."

Blast it all, she hadn't considered that.

Working slowly, Ebba began to replace the pieces of the root into the small chest. "Locks, ye're on the sword, aye?"

"Aye, lass."

She gripped the *scio* and addressed the Daedalion she'd ridden. He stood with his brethren just inland of their position near the water.

"See the kraken?" Ebba called softly to him. "He be tainted and can come ashore. Can ye fly us to safety?"

The Daedalion bowed his head, and when he replied, there was no screech but a simple, "Yes."

"Our friend be tainted, too," she hesitated before saying. If the Daedalion wouldn't carry Jagger, it looked like she'd be fighting Matey on her own. "Can you carry Jagger? I have an object that will heal ye in this chest if ye catch the taint movin' him."

The hawk-man who'd carried her to the ship neared. "I will carry him. The scales covering my claws will protect me for a short while. We'll need to think of something else for the journey across water."

Across water? She hadn't thought beyond washing Jagger. He couldn't survive a journey to the Caspian Sea in this condition. He needed care. So did Caspian, for that matter. They all needed clothing and to wash off the tainted blood, plus check themselves with the *purgium*.

Ebba smiled.

"Uh, Matey be comin' closer," Grubby said.

"How close be close?" inquired Locks, who was inching toward the *veritas* he'd thrown to the ground moments before.

She reached out and drew the lid of the chest closed, fixing the latch of the small case in place.

"Tentacle-on-the-shore close," he said happily.

Ebba wrenched around.

"He's comin' on land, lads. Move, move, move!" Stubby roared.

She leaped into action, grabbing the chest and launching it at the nearest Daedalion, who caught it like a champ.

Swooping down, she hauled Barrels to his feet and beckoned to the closest immortal.

The others ran to clamber aboard the waiting Daedalion.

Ebba dodged to Caspian and Jagger, eyeing the edge of the shore askance. Matey's head had disappeared, but the tips of his tentacles inched their way through the shallows like wriggling worms.

A Daedalion swooped to land on the beach, pausing only to collect Caspian before taking off again.

She crouched beside Jagger, scanning the skies and the shore. The male immortal who'd carried her before plunged into a dive for Jagger but screeched as Matey swatted at him.

Ebba half-stood, prepared to drag Jagger to safety. A kraken with glowing eyes she was prepared to talk down. A kraken with black eyes was another thing entirely.

The Daedalion went for a second swoop and then a third before screeching. Male and female immortals who'd already taken to the sky darted over the kraken, evading his tentacles as he swatted at them.

The immortal dove for the ground and picked up Jagger in a careful grip.

"Go," she urged. "Quickly."

The Daedalion took flight, and Ebba's shoulders slumped in relief. Everyone was safe.

The ground behind her reverberated.

Ebba froze. Why wasn't she on a bird?

Why wasn't she on a bird?

She slowly turned, eyes widening on Matey—the whole *Felicity*-sized, octopus-headed, scaly, tentacled girth of him. He stood on land as the hawks attacked like buzzing flies. He ignored them to focus on her, but she could tell they'd angered him, and that his anger was mounting with each passing second.

Snapping his beak, the kraken whipped out a tentacle, and Ebba jolted as he struck one of the Daedalion from the air.

"Time to run," she announced.

Ebba turned tail and sprinted for all she was worth. Her energy-deprived legs pumped. Her dreadlocks whipped behind her, making her feel like she was moving at an incredible speed.

That was when she learned that though Matey was a water creature who felt fat on land, he could *move*.

Out of morbid curiosity, she dared a glimpse back. In another world and time, she might've laughed at the way Matey moved, like a sea lion with too many parts.

If he hadn't been gaining on her. His eight tentacles gave him speed across the muddy sand. She was slipping through it and losing ground.

"I need a lift," she hollered upward.

A tentacle jabbed through the air on the right side of her body. She yelped, throwing herself to the left, barely escaping as another slammed down where she'd just stood. Ebba rolled underneath another.

This was not happening to her today. Not when Jagger was alive.

Jumping to her feet, she took off north down the beach, angling for the firmer ground of the dunes and beyond.

The air left her as Matey caught her with a blow to the midriff.

Out of control, she circled rapidly through the night sky. Pain lanced through her side, and the landing caught her entirely off-guard, spearing an extra dose of agony through her chest.

Ebba rolled in the sand onto her back, stuttering in her attempt to breathe.

Get up, ye sod. Head spinning from the throbbing wound, she rocked to her good side, staggering sideways in an effort to remain upright.

At least Matey had whacked her in the direction of the dunes.

She clutched her side, blinking as she weaved in that direction. A screech echoed from above.

The ground behind her shook. She wasn't going to outrun him.

Ebba whirled and held up her finger. "What would yer grandfather say?" she yelled at the kraken.

Against all odds, he stopped. Matey *actually* stopped.

Her skull scrambled for more.

"Uh . . . this ain't how a kraken behaves. Not one with journals and the like."

Matey lifted two tentacles to rub his temples. Or where she assumed his temples might be. His eyes were black, but he'd heard her. Ebba recalled Verity saying long ago that the taint affected immortals differently. Those with magic had to be surrounded by the taint and drained of magic before they'd succumb. But what about when an immortal ate a tainted ship?

Ebba tracked a female Daedalion flying low to the ground in her direction.

"Ye know better," she continued. Then she really looked at her friend. "Ye can fight this, Matey. Ye can do it."

Ebba backed away, and as Matey reared up, tentacles lifting, she spun away and leaped for the Daedalion.

The hawk-woman screeched as Ebba nearly slid right off the other side of the flying creature. Ebba twisted to grab hold of the Daedalion's wing. They barrel-rolled in the air three times before Ebba managed to right her position and release the immortal.

"Sorry," she panted.

The Daedalion screeched again, beating hard to raise them up through the air and out of tentacle range. As they joined the rest of the flock, Ebba glanced down at Matey.

The kraken was cantering after them.

She rested her forehead against the female's feathered back, breathing hard.

"Are ye all right, lass?" one of her fathers called from far to her right.

Was she okay? Ebba didn't want to think about that because she suspected the answer was a long one.

She lifted her head and peered through the lightening sky at Peg-leg. She nodded in reply, unsure if he could see.

"To Zol," Locks shouted from farther ahead.

Zol? Nay, they couldn't get that far with Jagger and Caspian like this. With the blow from Matey, she might have trouble with that too.

"Nay," she answered as loudly as her ribs would allow. "Somewhere else. Somewhere closer."

SEVEN

Ebba wrung the excess water from her freshly washed dreadlocks and accepted a flagon of water from a female Capricorn. Her time in the lagoon as a captive of the Satyr felt like another lifetime, yet it was only a few weeks ago.

Each of the crew had washed in the lagoon, touched the *purgium*, and accepted the berries and nuts offered by the female Capricorn to fill their bellies. Ebba had touched the tube again in a hopeful attempt to heal her ribs, but the part didn't heal injuries that would heal themselves.

Her crew's clothes were soaked with tainted blood, and the risk of keeping the garments was too high, so. . . .

Stubby swished side-to-side in a fuchsia gown that was far too tight across the shoulders. He'd cut the dress off at the knees. "I ain't thinkin' these dresses are too bad. No restr'ction in movement, aside from the back."

"Here, this is what I did," Locks piped up from where he was twitching the pleats of his sunshine-yellow skirt into place. Scooping up a jagged stone from the edge of the pool, he strode to Stubby and bunched the front of his dress in a fist. Locks hacked a line through the middle of the neckline on the front and then repeated this on the neckline at the back.

Stubby circled his arms. "Oh, aye, that does give me more space to move. Good notion."

"Mine is too loose," Barrels complained, patting the gaping front of what appeared to be an extravagant nightgown. "I'm quite pleased with it otherwise. Part of me has always wondered."

Ebba glanced away from her fathers at a low groan from Caspian.

She sighed heavily. While it'd been a mercy for his father to go when he wasn't cognizant, Ebba didn't relish delivering the news. And somehow—she glanced at her fathers, who were now accessorizing—Ebba expected that the task would fall to her.

A Daedalion landed on a flat boulder to her left, holding thick vines entwined with its claws. Ebba leaned forward and snatched the *scio* from the stone chest at her feet to talk to the immortal. She stood, dusting off the back of her black ankle-length skirt. With limited wardrobe options, the smallest outfit had immediately become hers. Holding her arm braced against her ribs, Ebba walked to the Daedalion and studied the thick vines the immortal had collected.

"They should work," she said, tapping her mouth.

The hawk-man clicked his beak as he answered, "Two of our flock are gathering more. We will need your help to make a net to carry Jagger. But this should be enough to help us lower him into the water to wash him."

Swallowing, Ebba glanced at Jagger, who was yet to move. None of them could touch him. They'd used cloth-bound hands to prop his mouth open and get water down his gullet, but being incapable of properly caring for him when he so desperately needed help had torn a fresh chasm within her.

"Thank ye," she said.

Peg-leg picked his way over the rocks to her. "These ones for the lad?"

Ebba nodded. "More'll come for the net." She tipped her head upward to meet the Daedalion's gaze. "I wonder if ye could help us with one other thing."

He tilted his head inquisitively. So like a hawk, and yet no less intelligent or compassionate than a human. Probably a lot more of both than most humans if Ebba was honest.

"The female Capricorn were separated from their men near-on fifty years ago," she told him plainly. "The Satyr kept them here to force the men to do their biddin'. I ain't sure if it's pos'ible, but could ye carry them to the sea?"

The hawk-man blinked slowly, opening his eyelids to display keen yellow eyes. "My parents died for their love." He turned to look at where Jagger lay on a bed of leaves and then peered down at her again. "Love sets us all free. And it will always be the Daedalion's task to ensure those who love truly are allowed to do so. So we swore when our parents passed from this realm to the Oblivion. So it will always be. We would be honored to reunite the Capricorn."

Ebba reached out and, after a quick internal debate, hesitantly rested a hand on his wing. "Thank ye kindly."

There was one oath she would keep, and that might mean something to her one day. Despite the darkness within Ebba, she would never wish misery on another. The ember inside still flickered. Perhaps a touch stronger than before. It wanted the Capricorn to be happy.

Ebba crouched by the edge of the lagoon, beckoning at the closest female Capricorn. She forced a smile when three of them swam closer. The horizontal pupils of their eyes had always given Ebba the heebie-jeebies, but she'd spent enough time with them to know they had compassion and intelligence too.

They'd been slaves long enough.

"Are ye ready to see yer men-folk again?" Ebba asked them, still clutching the *scio* tight.

The meaning in their soft bleating was clear this time.

"Does she mean it, the lovely one?" the middle woman asked.

"She cannot say it if she's not truthful. To lie would be to break us," the Capricorn on the right choked.

The left one was shaking. "She swore to us. The lovely one would not mislead us."

Ebba focused intently. They spoke oddly, but the consensus was that Ebba might be lying. "It be no lie, I swear to ye. For a time, I didn't think I'd get back. But I'm here now, and the Daedalion have agreed to fly ye out to the sea. If ye'll go."

The three Capricorn shied back, their eyes wrenching to the sky.

"Those who dwell in the water do not belong in the sky—"

"The lovely one dwells on land and lives on water—"

More female Capricorn drifted closer.

"Look, ye either want out or ye don't, but the sky is yer only ticket to yer men." Ebba said, glancing to where Peg-leg and Barrels were carefully looping the vines around Jagger's feet and under both arms in preparation to wash him.

She dragged her eyes away and startled to find the full attention of the entire lagoon of goat-fish on her. "Will ye take it? Or will ye fester here and die?"

The Capricorn flinched as one, but that was about the size of things. The Satyr had chucked fish down each day to feed them. The Satyr were mostly dead. Any survivors would have scattered to hide, and with the damned now in control of the island, she doubted they'd last long. Without the daily fish, Ebba doubted the women would last any decent measure of time either.

The three in front held hands, exchanging long looks.

"The lovely one's question has but one answer," the left Capricorn bleated on a sigh. "The answer is to accept. And we thank the lovely one as we accept."

Ebba stood carefully, arm against her side again. "Good, and my friends won't drop ye. Ye'll be fine." She hoped. "They'll take ye right now afore we put our tainted friend in yer pool. I'm pretty sure that wouldn't be good for any o' ye."

A tense murmur spread through the gathered Capricorn.

"The sea," one whispered. "Our eyes will love the sea again."

"Aye . . . well, just make sure to stick to the parts that ain't tainted as long as ye can. It be spreadin' through the Dynami."

The gathered creatures nodded frantically. Ebba forced another smile and turned away. That was as much as she could do for the Capricorn. It got to a point where people had to help themselves too.

The Daedalion edged forward, and Ebba left the immortals to their task, crouching beside Jagger.

The sight of him still shocked her. So much less in so few days. Being the immune, he was of immeasurable value to the pillars, whose taint stole the will of all it touched. The idea that the six evil beings would value someone who could retain their wits was odd, but Ebba had seen the violent outbursts of the tainted. If pushed too hard, the tainted could break free of the pillars' control and rampage. The pillars' darkness still needed mortals and immortals to feed on to survive. And if the tainted killed each other, surely the pillars would also die in time.

People like Jagger—and his direct offspring—could prevent that from happening. If the pillars were never stopped, they would always come for Jagger.

Ebba rubbed her temples. She'd only thought as far as saving him, but that wasn't really a simple issue. The quest was still the same in the end. Only her reasons for continuing had changed.

At the base of the path that wound to the top of the lagoon, Stubby, Grubby, and Locks were hard at work, knotting and twisting vines together into the net that would transport Jagger across the sea. Locks was whistling his 'I love Verity' song as he worked.

Without any discussion, they'd all silently assumed the next step was to return to Zol. To Barrels' family and Verity.

"If ye help Barrels at the top, lass, I'll take Jagger's feet," Peg-leg said.

That it would hurt her ribs was a given. But pain was about the only thing she could feel these days, so she'd embrace it.

Ebba avoided looking at Jagger's face and took a tight hold of one of the vines looped around his arms. He still had Montcroix's tunic and belt on. They'd torn the few remaining dresses into strips for the hands to wash Jagger and look after him on the journey to the Caspian Sea.

"One, two, three. Heave," Peg-leg called.

Ebba braced her stomach against her injury, and they all grunted as they heaved Jagger forward. Thin as he was, Jagger was still a taller frame than most. Oversized, she'd called him in the past. Well, Ebba would give what was left of herself to see him restored to that again.

With Jagger strung out like a hammock between them, they shuffled awkwardly to the edge of the lagoon. They paused to wait as a Daedalion picked up the last of the female Capricorn—the one who'd made the call to leave. The woman waved to Ebba, who couldn't find the willpower to raise her hand in return.

"All right, feet in first, then," Peg-leg said.

They managed to sit Jagger on the edge of a rock. Then Peg-leg stepped to a lower rock, paused to wrap his hands, and began to wash Jagger's feet and legs.

"Be careful the water don't soak through yer hand wrappings," she whispered. "The taint might come with it." They needed to be as careful as possible.

Jagger groaned, his head lolling.

"It be okay, Jagger," she murmured. "We've got ye."

He quietened but groaned again when Peg-leg resumed his cleaning.

Ebba bit her lip against the sound and continued speaking. "Ye're a right ripe bugger at the minute. The Daedalion asked that ye wash afore they carry yer stinkin' body across the sea." Her voice caught, and she paused a few moments before continuing. "As it is, they'd prefer to carry ye in a net just in case ye have lice or sumpin'."

Barrels' eyes settled on her, and she blinked away moisture.

"All right," Peg-leg said quietly. "Lower him into the water."

Achieving that without touching him was cumbersome work. Anything living could transmit the taint, and so eventually, the dark would work through the very vine they held. How quickly was anyone's guess.

Jagger's feet touched the surface of the water.

With a roar, he came to life, pushing away from the water to sprawl flat on the rock. She stumbled back, gasping at the jolt of pain through her side. She absently reached out to steady Barrels as Peg-leg windmilled his arms on the water's edge.

In a flash, Jagger was on his feet. His eyes were dark, wide, *wild.* He placed his back away from the three of them, teeth bared as he leaned down to snatch up a rock.

"We ain't attackin' ye," Peg-leg panted as he recovered his balance. He lifted his hands.

Jagger snarled and darted for him, swinging out the rock with vicious strength. Ebba was locked in place, one hand wrapped around Barrels' elbow and the other against her side.

Spittle flew from Jagger's mouth as Peg-leg scurried away over the rocks.

Barrels extracted his arm and lifted both hands in the air. "We were trying to wash you, Jagger. Nothing more."

The weakness of Jagger's body came second to the blind rage fueling him. Ebba watched, breathing heavily, as he lowered his head, flaxen hair swinging forward.

Jagger retraced his steps, charging at her father, the hand wielding the rock lifting high to deliver a crushing blow to Barrels' face.

"No," Ebba shrieked.

In two quick steps, she was between Barrels and Jagger. Ebba shoved her father back when Jagger didn't stop, ignoring the white-hot pain licking her insides. She had no idea if she was there for Jagger or Barrels, but all she could see was the barest trace of silver around the inner circle of his otherwise black eyes—and the damp gray of the rock he held hurtling toward her forehead.

Her fathers' yells were an indiscernible wall behind her.

"Licks," she whispered, closing her eyes.

The rock tapped against her forehead. Gentle. Not even hard enough to bruise.

"Vi—"

Ebba opened her eyes and stared into two orbs flooded with black. The pillars stared back at her through the eyes of the man she loved.

"Viva." His mouth formed the words as though the simple act of moving his lips was a battle. Was the evil within him using him as a puppet? Or was this him?

She had to believe it was him. Or soon would be.

"Licks," she repeated. Ebba had never called him that before. Really, he'd earned the name in the wake of torture. But the name acted as a reminder that he'd fought before and won. Could he even discern the actual word? Or was he simply reacting to the sound of her voice?

The rock trembled in his grip, scratching against her skin.

She looked into his eyes, and he, blinking repeatedly as though attempting to focus, squinted back.

"Where am I?" he snapped.

Ebba's eyes narrowed. "Don't ye take that tone o' voice with me. The taint ain't no excuse to be a brute."

Sink her if he didn't look a scant bit contrite under all that evil.

She softened, bracing an arm against her side again. "We be on the Satyr's island. Mutinous and Pockmark be dead. So are most o' their pirates. Those who ain't'll be gone soon enough. We're headin' back to Zol. Will ye come with us, Licks?"

Jagger swayed and lowered his shaking arm to his side, finally dropping the rock. He fell to one knee and Ebba fell with him, arms outstretched just shy of touching him. The pain from her ribs was nothing compared to the pain in her soul.

"Can't touch ye," he murmured. "Never touch ye. Too dark. Too far gone."

Tears stung her eyes. "Don't ye ever say that," she told him harshly. "Never, do ye hear me?"

Over her shoulder, she called. "Get him the sword."

"Ebba," Barrels said low in her ear, "I don't think we should give him a weapon."

"The sword," she repeated.

Stubby deposited *veritas* in her palm, and Ebba flipped the blade, extending the hilt to Jagger.

"Take it," she told him as his eyes lost focus. "It will make ye feel better."

Slipping to one side, Jagger shook his head the veriest amount. "Nay, Viva. Not this time. This time I ain't comin' back."

Ebba set her teeth, the hand on her shoulder and the presence of the others fading. "Ye don't get to decide that."

Slapping the sword into his palm, Ebba pushed to her feet and brought her face in front of his. "If ye go, I go. That's the new deal. I ain't bein' left here."

His eyes snapped to her and—though it could have been wishful thinking—the silver ring she'd just glimpsed appeared a whisper thicker.

"Stubborn fool," he sighed. His eyes fluttered shut, and Jagger slid into a heap on the rock.

Ebba's throat worked as she straightened, hands on hips. When she could trust herself to speak, she turned.

Grubby and Locks had leaned Caspian against a rock. The rest of her fathers surrounded her and Jagger. Peg-leg's eyes were fixed on the rock Jagger had almost permanently dented her head with.

Except he hadn't.

And he wouldn't.

Flamin' sod thought he could stop trying? Well, he was about to get the shock of his life. Ebba would get him better if it was the last thing she did—and then berate him for the rest of his life. Because he was right about one thing.

She was just about the stubbornest fool she knew.

"Will we be tryin' to heal Matey afore we leave?" Stubby asked the group.

Barrels sighed. "I'm rather worried about what it may do to him. The *purgium* always demands a sacrifice, and Matey *ate* a tainted ship. Not to mention the task of actually getting close enough to heal him. . . ."

The taint was terrible. The thought of leaving a friend in the throes of the evil went against their pirate code—especially when they owed Matey a life debt.

"If we heal him, it'll only be a matter o' time afore he's tainted again with the state o' the realm," Locks said, looking grim. "We be better to save the realm for good afore we bring him back. Maybe then we'll know more on how to heal without killin' the poor sod."

Ebba just hoped Matey didn't hate them for it.

"Get ready to leave for Zol then," she told her fathers. "We leave in an hour."

They had work to do.

EIGHT

There was no Oblivion.

Funny, that word. It had always signified a place she didn't want to end up—the *sorting* room of souls. Yet, oblivion would be bliss. For all pain to be erased. To be a blank slate once more; a person who did not know heartache and suffering and the cynical, dark thoughts that came after.

Was that why Plank chose as he did?

Her very being felt off-balance, as though her mainsail had a great tear through the middle. To the outward eye, she might look normal, but in reality, she was adrift—victim to the currents and wherever they deemed to take her.

Ebba frowned, staring at the Daedalion's shoulder blades as the creature beat his great wings, gliding at intervals. His larger frame protected her somewhat from the wind, and his feathers helped to insulate her from the cold even if the beating of his wings jolted her ribs something fierce.

"Ye alright, lass?" Peg-leg shouted from his Daedalion.

She nodded.

Each one of her crew appeared miserable, especially Caspian, who'd vomited several times. Despite his head injury, he'd insisted they begin the journey back. After a quick stop to grab their valued possessions from the barrels by hell's entrance, they'd started for Zol.

How far they'd come since leaving their secret sanctuary.

How easily the distance was gobbled up on the back of a winged creature. For weeks, they'd sailed through the feared and dangerous waters of the Dynami. Past the Thunderbird, via Medusa, around Calypso, and over Jendu and Capricorn . . . *with* Matey.

When they first set out, she'd figured that finding the pieces of the root would be the hard part. But Ebba could only hold five parts at once. It didn't matter *which* five, she just couldn't hold all six.

In fairness, she hadn't had a huge amount of time to test each part with the others, and her crew would help to figure out the problem. Yet in her heart, Ebba felt a heavy responsibility and awareness that the task would fall on her shoulders and her shoulders alone. She was the assembler.

Then there was the matter of actually *using* the root.

Before, there had been six pillars for six parts for six of her fathers. Now, she was an assembler who could only touch five parts. Who had five fathers, but there were still six pillars.

There had to be something in those numbers.

Numbers could go to Davy's. She was sick of the coincidental lot of them. They still knew hardly anything about the three watchers and how exactly they were meant to save the realm. Caspian and Jagger had hereditary roles. From what Ebba understood from the cavern on Pleo so long ago was that many assemblers could have arrived to claim the *purgium*. Hadn't the Earth Mother talked of the knights of such-and-such, and the sisters of someplace? The Thunderbird had said Caspian and Jagger chose her.

Aside from what they'd learned from the journals of Matey's grandfather, Ebba could only say that she was certainly linked to her fathers more than any mortal was linked to another mortal. There was magic between her and her parents that related to her job as an assembler. When they hurt, she hurt. When they were away, the separation was torture.

Other than that? Nothing.

Her stomach leaped into her mouth as her Daedalion descended.

The *scio* was in the chest latched to the back of one of the Daedalion, but Ebba assumed they were landing for a break. She hadn't known that any more islands existed out here in the Dynami. But then, they hadn't explored much of it, only coming across a few landmasses the entire quest.

Sure enough, she spotted a cliff range a few minutes later. The cliffs were a light gray and formed the middle peak of an island; it kind of looked like a bird with its wings outstretched.

Her Daedalion landed, and she slid off his back, clutching at a rock to stop her legs from folding beneath her. She winced as blood rushed back into her toes, hobbling atop the cliff range to loosen her stiff joints.

The hawk-man carrying Jagger hovered high above and slowly lowered Jagger to rest on the cliff. Barrels was carrying the strips of cloth from the lagoon, so Ebba reached for the bottom of her black skirt and quickly tore off two strips, binding her hands for the umpteenth time. She guided the net to the ground and then, when the immortal landed, she untied the vine from his claws.

The creature stretched his legs and hobbled off, appearing every bit as stiff as she and her fathers did.

"How is he, lass?" Locks asked.

She shrugged. Jagger's chest was moving. "Alive. Not good, I s'pose. But he will be. He has to be."

Locks paused. "And why's that?"

Ebba lifted her chin and stared silently at him. He knew why.

Her father flinched but didn't look away. "Lass, Plan—"

"Don't say his name, Locks," she immediately said. "I know ye're hurtin'. Ye don't understand why I am the way I am about it. But I can't bear to hear his name aloud. With Jagger, I'm hangin' on. With the rest o' ye here, I'm holdin' things together. But I can't bear to hear the truth. Not yet. Maybe not ever. Please don't push me."

"We've never pushed ye to talk," he said after a brief pause. "And sometimes that were a mistake. But we've never seen ye like this. We've decided to give ye another week to keep to yer own head. And then, whether it be us, Caspian, Jagger, or someone ye've never met afore in yer life, ye'll be talkin'. We all need it."

A week. Agreeing now meant he'd leave her be. Ebba jerked her head in a yes, still staring at Jagger.

Caspian saved her in the end.

He crouched on her left. "How is he?"

She studied her friend—ashen-faced, dull-eyed. His lips were cracked and his eyes slightly unfocused. And his father was dead for what felt like the thousandth time. But Ebba knew that having a father leave was a feeling no one could get used to.

How did he bear it?

"He'll live," she replied. "How are ye?"

"I'm all right."

She frowned. "Nay, Caspian. None o' that. How are ye?"

Whatever he'd been about to say froze on his lips. His dull amber eyes lifted and then fell away to the rock they crouched behind. He laughed shortly. "You think I'd be used to my father dying. I just wish I'd had a chance to say goodbye. Or maybe I feel guilty because I'm glad he went while I couldn't see."

A dagger worked its way into her chest. This conversation wasn't such a good idea. She dug her nails into her palms until the pain bit back the infinite well of her grief. "Aye," she managed.

His eyes flew to hers, and she could see he was stricken.

"Nay." She beat him to an apology. "Don't be sayin' sorry. I can understand yer . . . regrets well enough." Ebba thought back to King Montcroix. "Yer father did the right thing by ye back on the Satyr's island."

Caspian exhaled. His frown slowly softened into a small smile. "He did, didn't he? He chose me."

Ebba considered her friend. "He told me that leavin' felt right-like. That notion seemed funny to him, and I asked why. He said the world was in chaos now but what lay between the two o' ye was calm. He told me how backward that was from when he was alive. He'd always had outward calm and inner chaos, but whatever his mistakes, he was glad to know true peace afore the end."

Caspian's amber eyes shimmered, and he dashed the sleeve of his borrowed nightgown over his eyes. He sniffed hard and then firmed his expression. "He said that?"

Nope. "Well, he didn't speak pirate. But aye, the essence was the same. He was candid in his final moments here." Montcroix was damn lucky she was a better person than him. Flamin' bastard.

Caspian inhaled deeply, turning to her. "Thank you, Ebba. Thank you for telling me. I feel . . . more complete than I have in a long time."

"I'm glad. Now help me with Jagger," she said, leaning over to untie the knots confining Jagger. She didn't want him waking up trapped. The vines could be tainted, so she made sure not to touch any of it.

Caspian wrapped his hands, and he and Barrels rolled Jagger as Ebba pulled the vines free and threw them off the cliff. They'd made a second net to transfer him into so the Daedalion would be as safe as possible. Ebba hoped their precautions were enough.

Ebba took a flagon from Peg-leg and carefully trickled some water down Jagger's throat. He choked pitifully, and the sound was like a fist to her gut. His eyes opened, and she rested a covered hand on his cheek, wondering how long was safe to leave it there. Like this, she could pretend they were really touching.

"Ye're okay, matey," she told him. "Just a quick stop on the way to Zol."

"Zol," he mumbled. "Viva."

He closed his eyes.

"Well, that be good, ain't it, Ebba? He's sayin' a few things and. . . ." Grubby trailed off, kicking at a loose stone on the clifftop.

Stubby clapped him on the back. "Just right, Grubs. He's lookin' far better."

Grubby's ears lifted, and his toothy grin appeared.

They passed around the flagon and split the berries and nuts they'd pillaged from the lagoon. Peg-leg offered some to the winged immortals, but they took off east and a quick glimpse told Ebba they were fishing.

Everyone sat in silence. Really, there hadn't been any time to process the battle on the Island of the Damned—as Ebba had now taken to calling it.

"Mutinous be dead," she said at last, surprising herself by breaking the quiet she constantly craved nowadays.

The calmness of her fathers' reactions told her that was exactly where their thoughts had been as well.

"Not that I got to join in," Barrels sniped.

Next to her, Stubby sniffed. "Yeah, yeah. Ye got—"

Ebba dug a savage elbow into his gut and widened her eyes. Sharks' teeth, did they have any tact?

Barrels colored. As did Stubby.

"About that, Caspian," Barrels started.

Caspian lifted a hand, and everyone stopped talking.

Huh, that was a new trick.

"Was it quick and humane?" he asked Barrels, who nodded.

The russet-haired Exosian squared his shoulders. "In that case, my father requested the task of you. It was a mercy you granted, and I bear you no ill will over it. In fact, I thank you for looking past how he has treated piratekind to grant his wish."

Through the cold, a strangled awe struggled within her. She'd known it a long time. From their very first meeting, if she were frank. Her friend was a better person than she. How could he see past all his emotions to forgive his father's murderer? If Caspian had killed Plank, she couldn't one hundred percent truthfully say that he'd still be alive.

Stubby rubbed his stomach, glaring at her. "Where did *ye* find tact anyhow? Who showed it to ye?" He turned his glare on Barrels. "It's yer sister's doin'. Puttin' her manners where they don't belong."

"I don't see a little tact as a bad thing," Barrels countered.

They acted like Ebba usually blurted out every rude and insensitive thought in her head. Actually. . . .

"I'm glad someone brought that up," Caspian said. "Something is bothering me."

Ebba nudged *veritas* so the hilt rested against Jagger's skin. "Does it have to do with how. . . ." Shite. This was venturing into Plank territory again. "How I can only touch five o' the weapon parts? And there are only five o' my fathers. . . ?" She trailed off.

Caspian's eyes rounded. "No, it didn't. But I think it might. Let's work back. I'm not sure if the rest of you have seen how different Ebba is of late."

"O' course we have," Locks exploded. Then he dropped his voice to a mere whisper. "She's *grievin'*."

"There's been less impatience, too," Caspian mused.

Locks' color began to rise.

Grubby wrung his hands. "I think what Cosmo be tryin' to say is. . . . Well . . . I ain't right sure."

"And that," Caspian interjected, eyeing her part-selkie father. "The fretting."

Peg-leg crossed his arms, expression surly. "No doubt ye'll enlighten us in yer own time."

"Less of the moods, too," the exiled king breathed. "I have a theory. It's only half thought through, and it has to do with your connection to Ebba."

Ebba faced him. "They're connected to me magically."

He broke off. "What? You've already guessed?"

"Just put two and two together." She shrugged. "I can feel it. When we be separated, it ain't just that I miss them. Sumpin' drives me to be reunited with them. When they're in danger, it ain't fear I feel. It be doom. Understandin' that what I shared with them was d'fferent didn't hit until I spent time with ye and Jagger. I never really had anyone to compare my life to. Then I just thought that I had aband'nment scars left over from when they ditched me at Maltu. Took me time to see that I wasn't dreamin' things, but I be sure-like now. Some kind o' magic tethers me to my fathers."

The loss of them was a loss of herself.

Her fathers watched her without speaking. Did they sense the words that she hadn't said?

"Which strengthens my own theory," Caspian said.

Locks leaned forward. "Tell us."

Caspian surveyed them. "There's no good way to say this, so I'll just jump in. Since you were all healed, Ebba has become smarter."

. . . Okay.

That she hadn't expected.

"Not only that," he hurried on, "she is more patient, less moody, more generous, and—as we just saw—more tactful." He looked pointedly at Locks, Peg-leg, Barrels, and Stubby.

"Hold yer damn seahorses, landlubber." Peg-leg uncrossed his arms. "Ye looked at me when ye said moody."

"And me when he said generous," Barrels blurted.

Stubby scratched his head. "Aye, well, I can agree with that one. Ye're a tight bugger, Barrels."

"I taught Ebba to be *thrifty*."

"Same thing," Stubby countered. "Stingy as anythin'."

Ebba ignored them to address Caspian. "Ye think that when Cannon healed them with the *purgium* in hell, sumpin' else happened?"

"I barely know what to think," he said, spreading his hand wide.

Her fathers quietened.

"When Grubby was first healed by the *purgium* while on *Felicity*, you showed increased intelligence. That by itself wasn't enough for me to connect everything. I thought the loss of *Felicity* had forced you to mature. It wasn't until four more of your fathers were healed in quick succession that the change in you became more pronounced."

Locks' eyes narrowed. "Watch it."

Caspian's words didn't bother her. He was onto something. They were on the cusp of solving something huge.

She got to her feet, and he did the same.

"Ye think I somehow took on a vice from all o' them," she said, feeling the closest thing to excitement since leaving Davy Jones'.

Caspian shrugged his shoulder. "That's how it looks to me."

"The Earth Mother said I should be more whole, not less, do ye recall?" Ebba said, spinning to her fathers. Another thought occurred to her. "She was shocked that I couldn't hold both o' the parts at once. She said it was my *right* to hold them. It can't be normal for an assembler to have the problem, just me."

One by one, the faces of her fathers settled into horror.

"We tainted Ebba?" Stubby croaked.

They looked devastated.

"Nay," she answered. "I've felt the taint, and I'd have been able to spot the sameness of the feelin' in hindsight. At most, I took of some o' yer traits along with whatever the link is between us. I ain't sure why the taint couldn't come through, but I'm sure as anythin' that it didn't." And that wasn't just her making them feel better.

Peg-leg blew out a breath. "Right, but why? What be the point o' all those links with us?"

"That's where Ebba's comment gets interesting, I'd wager," Barrels put in, arching a brow.

"How?" Grubby asked.

Locks was shaking his head. "There be a hole in yer theory, though. Grubs was hit on the noggin' again, weren't he? So shouldn't Ebba be dumb again?"

Everyone hissed at him to shut up as Grubby's grin faded.

"Everyone was thinkin' it," Locks muttered.

Barrels hushed everyone, fluttering his hands in agitation. "That's of no consequence. We each still possess our vices. The difference is that—"

"The five o' ye were healed o' the taint," Ebba finished for him.

The significance of what exactly that meant hit her. She saw the same awareness in Stubby's, Barrels', and Caspian's faces.

Caspian whirled to face her. "You couldn't hold the *dynami* and the *purgium* at the same time until Grubby was healed."

"When she attempted to hold a third part when we fought the Satyr, she couldn't," Barrels added, his voice rising too. "Because at that point, *no one else was healed*."

Caspian paced. "It wasn't until Stubby was healed in Davy Jones' that she was able to hold three when Cannon attempted to force her to assemble the weapon."

"Cannon *knew* why I couldn't hold the pieces," Ebba breathed. "It wasn't just that healin' ye o' the taint would tip the scale o' light and dark and open the Locker. He must've known I was broken. The pillars must've told him."

Caspian hummed. "Or it was a coincidence. He was averse to hurting you by healing them, if anything."

She didn't believe in coinky-dinks any longer. But that hardly mattered now that Cannon was dead, aside from guessing how much the pillars might know. "The rest o' ye were healed to break Davy Jones' open. That's why I can hold five now."

Aside from Grubby, the others weren't smiling any longer.

The smile faded from her face a beat later.

Stubby broke the disbelieving silence. "Plank—"

Ebba sucked in a painful breath, her hand lifting to her chest as though to pull out the thick icicle that had just wedged in her heart at hearing his name spoken.

"He wasn't healed. . . ." Locks let the thought land.

Before he left. Which meant. . . .

"If we be right." She glanced at Caspian, who was grim-faced.

He finished. "Then you can't hold all six parts of the weapon without the whole and healthy connection to your six fathers."

And she only had five left.

Ebba faced west toward the Caspian Sea.

She blinked at the sight of what appeared to be two oceans

crashing together at first glance. One ocean was oily and darkened with taint. The other was caught between turquoise and the darkness of natural deep sea.

They were nowhere near where the Caspian Sea met the Dynami Sea. And that could only mean one thing.

The taint had reached them. Time was running out. Soon, the sea creatures who'd escaped the taint thus far would have nowhere left to evade it.

After everything they'd gone through. After the father she'd lost. And now that they actually had all six parts. . . .

. . . Ebba couldn't assemble the root of magic.

NINE

Black.

That's what it was to return to the place Ebba had always called home—the Caspian Sea.

The land, black, as though a layer of soot lay upon it. The sea, black, like oil made up the first three feet of its normal cobalt depths. The sky, still mostly blue, was the only thing yet untouched. The sun beat down on her back as fiercely as she remembered, though the rare wisp of cloud possessing a dark tinge sent a heavy feeling into her gut. The taint was attacking the very air around them.

Water, land, air. They were nearly out of time.

The Daedalion had flown them immediately west and then turned south to Zol. They'd passed over Febribus a couple of hours ago and seen not a speck of natural, vibrant color. The innermost forest of Pleo had shown deep green, but maybe that was wishful thinking. Ebba didn't feel beholden to the tribe of her blood parents. She hoped they weren't tainted, of course. But then again, Ebba hoped *all* good people were safe and sheltered from the pillars' evil. Even the bad ones, really.

If things worked out, Ebba would check on her blood parents. Until then, they were on their own.

A big *if* after their recent discovery.

Ebba lifted her head off the Daedalion's back and peered over its beating wings at Neos. Only the tip of the mountain remained free of the soot-like covering. The rest of the island looked as though someone had sprinkled charcoal on the sea and each island and added water and dirt. The slick appearance of the viscous sea around Neos gave her the impression she could plunge her hand into the depths and pull back only to find the sticky water came with her. Ebba wasn't about to check if the taint extended all the way to the ocean floor here—but if sea creatures escaping to the Dynami was any indicator, the Caspian Sea was no longer safe.

The pillars had done this. Verity's words had come to fruition, and the change in the realm was shocking, disturbing. Even within Ebba, the sight triggered a deep-rooted disbelief. Once, this was her home and playground. Now, the Exosian realm belonged to strangers. She'd been shoved out into the cold to look in through the window and watch as the pillars renovated without her say-so.

How could her crew undo all of this? Even if they figured out the problem of Ebba not being able to hold all six parts? How could they defeat the pillars and lock them away without repeating the mistakes of the three watchers hundreds of years ago? Ebba wasn't imprisoning the pillars if the wall would just crumble again, leaving the problem for a future generation to solve.

And all of that came back to *if*.

If they could figure out a way for Ebba to hold all six parts.

She turned from the oily ocean and rested her forehead against the hawk-man's feathered shoulder blades, thinking hard. Could a connection to another person be forged somehow? Maybe with magic? That was the only solution she could think of. And yet her entire being shied away from that notion, and she'd learned to trust that feeling by now.

At this point, she only had something Caspian said to cling to.

There were so many pieces that Ebba was trying to keep track of. Why her? Why her fathers? What did the weapon form? How was it put together? How could they possibly succeed? *Endless* questions. But she'd forgotten one part of the Earth Mother's unhelpful musings.

She shouldn't have because when Sally had left, it was mentioned again.

The Earth Mother had said that she'd never liked the pathway shown for Ebba and her fathers because they were only ever eight instead of the usual nine. Of course, now they knew the assembler required six connections to 'make her more.' Ebba assumed that normally the other two would be Jagger and Caspian, the immune and the bearer. *Nine*.

But Plank was gone.

Eight.

Ebba could no longer blame the Earth Mother for being so hesitant in handing over the *purgium*. She could be furious about it. Actually, she was furious at the powers of Oblivion in general. They were the most formidable immortals—aside from the pillars—in the realm. Where was the help? Why hadn't the Earth Mother sat them down and explained everything? Would doing so have messed with the future? Or were the powers of Oblivion really so literal? *Why* did the Thunderbird make a storm to test them instead of speeding them on with a breeze to find the next part? Immortals were slaves to their nature. Ebba understood that. She'd met enough magical creatures to see that was generally the case. Even Matey had a limit before he'd started eating ships. And Sally, too, at times. But in her eyes, that made magical creatures—in particular the powers of Oblivion—untrustworthy. If they'd helped, maybe the battle wouldn't have needed to begin. Sure, the crew of *Felicity* had taken their sweet time joining the plight. But if someone with the knowledge had sat them down, explained everything, and shown them the consequences, things could be much different.

If Ebba ever saw the powers of Oblivion again, she'd tell them just that.

Caspian thought as she did—maybe even more keenly. However, her fathers didn't seem angry over the lack of responsibility in the powerful immortals. They accepted that nature was to magical creatures as survival was to pirates.

. . . Perhaps, at the end of the day, immortals *and* mortals were to blame for the dank, grim state of the realm. And for Plank leaving.

Ebba gave way to the burning behind her eyes and focused on the tear slipping silently over her cheek before the wind caught it and swept it to nothing. Plank's death was her fault as much as the immortals. And most of all, Plank's death was Plank's fault. That's what she couldn't understand.

In the depths of her misery, the faint trill of a bird reached her. They hadn't seen any life thus far, so the sound stuck out worse than a landlubber on a ship. The trill was different to the Daedalions' screech—melodious and sweet.

She scanned the blue sky and spotted two white birds far off to the right. Not far enough, really, considering there was a flock of gigantic hawk-creatures close by. Did hawks attack other birds? Ebba wasn't sure.

The two white birds flew around each other in happy circles, trilling their clear, crisp song. And the longer Ebba watched, the heavier her heart became until anger churned thick within her. Black edged her vision as she watched the birds' dance, which was almost a celebration. She turned her head away but couldn't block their elated whistle.

It was the first time in her life she'd ever felt an inkling to kill a bird.

Eventually, the two birds fell behind; however, not until the Daedalion began descending did she lift her head again. This time to see Zol in the distance.

She'd prepared herself for black, but the sight of their sanctuary looking so grim was hard to take. Their beloved haven, taken by the pillars.

But the land could be replaced. Hammocks could be restrung. People were a different matter.

To her left, Locks shouted at his Daedalion. The immortal tipped into a sharp dive, angled for Zol. Ebba straightened. What was he thinking? Zol was black. Gone. He couldn't land on tainted ground.

But as her own Daedalion loomed closer, Ebba saw what Locks had before her.

The flat top of the expansive cliff ring that surrounded their inlet was untouched by taint. It was as though white paint had been poured over the top of the cliffs and had trickled down the vertical sides before drying. Previously white in entirety, now only around ten feet of the sheer cliff face remained free of taint. The evil crawled upward from the land below, covering everything in its path in black slime and tar.

On top of the wide cliff ring were a lot of people she recognized. A few days more and the flat top might have been covered, too, leaving their Zol friends with nowhere to escape.

The rest of their Daedalion circled in to land.

In a feat that belied his age, Locks leaped from his Daedalion as soon as its claws touched the clifftop. Verity was waiting. The ex-soothsayer threw herself into his arms as Ebba's Daedalion came to land.

She witnessed their tear-streaked faces and joy, and something akin to peace settled over the space where her heart had been. Ebba could be happy for Locks and Verity. Or relieved.

Happiness and relief blurred together these days.

Jumping from her Daedalion's back, Ebba turned away from the horde gathered as she shook her legs out. Suddenly, seeing others was the exact opposite of what she wanted to do.

Was it that she knew them? Or because they'd known her as someone else?

Her black ankle-length skirt was more of a knee-length skirt by this point, but she tore off two more strips and wrapped her hands in the light material. After, she guided Jagger down as his Daedalion hovered high above. After untangling the vines from the immortal's claws, she set to work easing Jagger out of his net.

Black eyes looked up at her, and Ebba's breath caught, pain spearing through her torso. She stammered as she recovered. "Ye creepy bugger. At least say ahoy afore ye stare."

Jagger didn't say a word, and Ebba lowered her face close. How close was too close? The taint hadn't blackened the sky and sun yet, so she assumed the air between them was safe—for now.

"There be more silver around yer eyes today," she told him, keeping her tone light as she threw off more vines, freeing his legs. "And less yellow, too. Would ye like me to unbind *veritas* from ye?" They hadn't wanted it to be lost during the flight, so Stubby had latched the sword to Jagger's forearm.

Jagger licked his cracked lips and nodded.

"Ye should blink a couple o' times," she added when his stare didn't falter.

He didn't.

"All right, I can work with that," Ebba drew out. "Then I'll fetch ye some water."

Jagger continued staring as she worked. Sink her, that was off-putting. And what kind of knots were these?

"Bloody hell, Stubs," she muttered, picking at knot four of twenty-five.

As she worked, Ebba listened to the crowd behind her, her unease swelling.

"—Caspian!—"

"—Did you get the parts?—"

"—We were losing hope that you would return, brother—"

The excited babble of their shouts and laughter suddenly died down.

"—Where is *Felicity*? Did you leave her somewhere to return faster?—"

Ebba closed her eyes as Barrels replied, "I'm afraid we lost *Felicity* several weeks ago. Without our friends here, we would never have made it back."

All sound died. One moment there, one moment gone. Just like her father.

Marigold was the one to ask, "But where is Plank?"

Those who hadn't noticed his absence yet gasped. Their horror and shock was plain, and the sound drove Ebba back to her own blinding agony; to the exact time when she knew her father was gone. To that second when she lay there, immobile as the entrance of Davy Jones' crumbled, and caught Plank's hazel eyes as he whispered, '*I'm sorry.*'

Ebba's shoulders shook against her will. She squeezed her eyes shut with all her might, but fresh tears pushed out to wet her face.

"We lost Plank," Stubby said finally.

A low moan escaped her, and the air in front of her shifted. Startled, Ebba peered through blurry eyes to where Jagger crouched before her. His hands were raised and hovered either side of her cheeks. His hands shook.

"Oi! Get away, ye tainted bugger." Peg-leg tapped toward them.

Jagger *did* blink then. He peered over her shoulder, and Ebba had front-row seats as his tortured expression snapped to a feral snarl.

He erupted to his feet, *veritas* in hand.

Ebba remained crouched. Her calm voice carried. "Peg-leg, stop."

The tapping ceased.

"Leave me with water and take the others to the far end o' the cliffs," she instructed.

"But lass, it ain't safe."

It was. And she wasn't above using Jagger as an excuse not to see the others. They deserved to know what had happened since the crew of *Felicity* sailed away from Zol. But Ebba was too heartsick to tell them or listen. She feared the pain and what it could do to the tatters of herself she'd scraped together. Ebba was ashamed of what she was now.

"Leave me with him," she repeated as Jagger maintained his position over her, sword raised in readiness to slaughter the world.

But he was too late. The realm was taken. All of them now held on by a thread.

Zol was no longer a sanctuary.

TEN

Ebba perched on the clifftop to watch Jagger sleep. Even in sleep he appeared agonized. She knew his demons well enough to have an idea of what was going on inside his skull. Jagger was battling a darkness only he could see. The pillars would be throwing his worst fears at him and all of his regrets and pains: leaving his tribe behind to pursue the quest; the horrible things he'd been forced to do; being held prisoner in the pitch-black belly of a ship.

"I love ye so much," she whispered to him. "Ye'll fight this, and I'll help ye. Ye know I don't take nay for an answer."

Footsteps approached, and Ebba glanced over her shoulder expecting more food and water from her fathers.

She should've known better.

"Ebba-Viva," Verity greeted her, passing her a flagon.

"Verity," she replied in the same tone, eyeing the other objects in the healer's grip. Unless Ebba was mistaken, that was her scrapbook and the bangle from Marigold.

"Where are ye gettin' the water from?" she asked the healer.

"Wind sprites," Verity replied. "They bring supplies each week.

They transported us up here too. You should've seen Marigold and the Exosians. I thought they'd die from shock."

The ex-soothsayer hadn't changed much. Periwinkle blue eyes and blonde hair concealed insides made of iron. She and Ebba had both been locked in the hull of *Malice* together. Ebba respected her still, yet she felt as if she hardly knew her.

So much had happened.

Verity spoke again. "You know . . . I expected a hug at least."

The rope of her temper frayed. "Not in the huggin' mood."

"I can hardly blame you for that. And I hear your ribs are cracked."

"Aye."

Verity crouched before her. She set the scrapbook and bangle on her other side and placed both hands either side of Ebba's rib cage. The healer closed her eyes, and intense heat seared through Ebba for an instant before the scalding was gone again.

The healer retreated a few steps as Ebba prodded her ribs. "Are they fixed then?"

"They are. All things heal."

Ebba resisted the urge to roll her eyes and changed the subject. "I'm glad ye and Locks are back together."

"As am I." Verity sighed. "Even though I'd seen the possibility of us reuniting."

Ebba grunted. "Can ye see if we'll kill the pillars?"

"No, Ebba. My visions, when I had soothsayer powers, were received from the Earth Mother, and she only gives what is needed or what concerns you. On Febribus, when your crew visited, I saw the only possible future that involved Locks and myself reuniting. When he landed on the Daedalion yesterday, that was the outcome of letting *Malice* take me."

She had no idea what would happen now? When Verity had said she and Locks would be happy, Ebba had assumed that meant both of them would *live*. Their happiness could last mere days.

"I thought you might like to have your bangle and scrapbook," the healer said, leaning down to pick up the two items off the ground.

Ebba took a sip of water and then stoppered the flagon. "I'll take the bangle."

Verity straightened and tilted her head. "Not the scrapbook?"

"Nay, toss it off the cliff if ye like." She didn't want to see it. Didn't want to be near it. Ever since her fathers had gifted the book to her, all she'd wanted to do was devour it—even learning to *read* to do so. And reading through all her fathers' memories of her childhood when the crew was happy and whole? Aye. But the crew wasn't happy and whole. Now, even glimpsing the leather-bound scrapbook made her want to recede into cold, unknowing darkness again.

"Oh?" Verity said with a laugh. "Why didn't you say so?"

The healer threw the scrapbook over the cliff.

"No!" Ebba shouted.

Mouth drying, she bolted to her feet, running to the edge to peer after it.

The book floated a few feet below, high above the water.

Ebba sagged in relief that quickly turned to anger. She faced Verity, demanding, "Why did ye do that for?"

The healer waved her fingers. The scrapbook floated up into her arms again. "You know why, Ebba-Viva Fairisles."

Her hands curled into fists as she met the woman's periwinkle gaze. Yes, apparently a part of her *didn't* want the scrapbook to disappear. But that didn't mean she was ready to open it! And she certainly wasn't ready for people to force her to start healing.

She scowled before resuming her seat on the flat clifftop. "I thought ye were just a healer anyway. How are ye controllin' flyin' books and such?"

"I am a healer. Weak magic only."

Aye, and Ebba was an optimistic dragon with allergies.

She sighed, glaring at the scrapbook again. "Ye can take it away. I ain't lookin' at it."

Verity snorted. "I'm not carrying it. It's yours." She placed the book at Ebba's feet and then reached for her hand. The healer worked the gold bangle—a gift from Marigold and her family—up Ebba's arm until it rested around her bicep.

"There," Verity announced, leaning back.

Ebba grunted, peering the other way to where Jagger slept.

"Do you plan to mope over here forever, or will you join in on the planning?" Verity asked.

Ebba seized the anger that tried to shoot out of her. When she could trust herself to speak, she said, "Verity, don't talk to me like I be a child. Ye may understand more than most, but ye don't understand me because ye ain't me."

Jagger was stirring.

The pause was lengthy. "I apologize," Verity said. "You're right. You are the assembler, and I have no idea of the depth of your connection to your fathers. Or how the loss of one could have affected you."

Ebba glanced back and read the sincerity on her face. Despite the reference to Plank, she nodded.

The healer forged on. "You clearly have a vested interest in Jagger's health. And that of your fathers."

"And all o' ye," Ebba added. "Don't think that ye aren't all important to me too. If I ain't comin' over to talk, it ain't because I don't care. There just ain't enough o' me to go around right now."

Verity studied her for a long moment and then blinked several times in quick succession. "Each day our clifftop gets smaller. We haven't been idle in your absence, Ebba. The immortals and mortals of this world who can fight have been gathering. We've made plans. You have returned with all six pieces, but it is time to decide what must be done."

"—I can't put it together," she ground out, more frustrated at the situation than at Verity.

"And so you won't try?"

Ebba's control on her fraying temper slipped. "Ye see this as not tryin'? I'm carin' for the other half o' me that sacr'ficed his very soul for at least the third time to save us. We need him, Verity. I can only be so many places at once." Even to Ebba, her words sounded weak.

Verity's face didn't soften. "The realm needs you to be in one more. All living creatures need you to spread yourself thinner, Ebba-Viva. *You*. Caspian, your fathers, and Jagger, yes. But without *you*, all is lost. There is no time to mourn or submit to darkness. The realm has chosen you to do the job, so there is nothing else to do but do what must be done—if you have the will to fight."

Jagger was her will to fight.

"Plank ain't to be mentioned in my presence," Ebba said. "If that be understood, then I'll talk about anythin' else."

Verity hesitated. "Very well. Your fathers have already requested as much. But you know that eventually—"

Ebba snapped. "I be knowin' that eventually has nothin' to do with ye. Those be my terms."

The healer's intake of air was sharp.

The trill of a bird rang down from high above. Ebba tipped her head back, glaring at two white birds dancing together in the sky. The sodding things were back. The same ones. Rage exploded in her gut. She couldn't explain why the birds made her feel so bitter, only that if they got close enough, Ebba would try her utmost to hurt them.

But they didn't. The birds swooped down the side of the cliff and disappeared.

"I'll go tell the others," Verity said.

Ebba blinked. What were they talking about? The ex-soothsayer watched her in expectation. Oh, planning. Right.

"Aye, I'll come over once Jagger be sleepin' again." That'd give her time to collect herself. Hopefully.

Once alone again, she tipped more water down Jagger's throat. This time he managed to sit up. She watched as he turned his face into the wind.

"The breeze clears yer thoughts," she said over the slight whistle of the breeze. "Ye told me once. Ye liked the crow's nest best—

farthest from the belly o' the ship. This be a good place for ye, I'm thinkin'."

He turned to her and licked his lips. "Aye, Viva."

Her chest tightened. The first words he'd spoken in days. That had to mean something.

"I thought ye were handsome when I first met ye, did ye know? I was ignorin' such things at the time, but I thought ye were made up pretty well as far as men go. In another time, and as another person, I might've not tried to kill ye twice afore I admitted it."

Did his lips just twitch or was that her mind playing tricks?

"The tattoos *really* caught my eye. I like the way they move when ye use yer chest muscles. It's like watchin' a story—that I don't want anyone else to see, mind," she added.

Unloading all of this was nice. Was this why Barrels used to keep a journal?

Ebba hugged her knees to her chest as Jagger fully turned to her, shuffling closer.

"I can't believe I haven't kissed ye yet, and I love ye," she said, frowning. "That seems back the front, don't it? Guess we'll have to see if we're phys'cally compat'ble later. I'm sick o' ye havin' the taint. If ye mean to keep me interested, ye won't get it again. Am I clear?"

He nodded, and Ebba's lips curved.

"I'll be sure to remind ye o' that. While we're on the subject, I want ye to know this thing between us be exclusive-like. I won't keep a boyfriend on each island, and I expect ye'll pay me the same respect. Savvy?"

This time she was sure. His lips definitely twitched.

"Would ye like to be my boyfriend, Jagger? And would ye like to kiss me when ye be rid o' the tainted shite?" Ebba had an ulterior motive. She just wanted to hear him talk again. Emotional blackmail was just one tool in a pirate's repertoire.

Jagger guided his body down to lay flat on the cliff.

"I'll marry ye," he said in a voice so scratchy she could scarcely make out the words.

Sink her. That was a jump. "I'll consider it. But after thirty, most likely. I don't wish to be tied down earlier than that."

"Month."

"Decade," she countered.

"Week."

He was going lower. That's not how negotiations worked. "We'll figure out the details later," she said. *Much later*.

She continued, "And what about the kissin'?" Right now, that was her major concern. Ebba had a highly cultivated idea of how Jagger's lips might feel pressed against hers. She knew how his body felt alongside her own. She knew his smell, and though there were gaps to fill in, Ebba knew the important parts of his mind.

She'd seen what he would do for others. And for her. But the kissing. That needed to happen sooner rather than later, judging by the unsettling, warm sensation in her innards.

Jagger glanced at the flagon. "Water."

"Shite, sorry." She scooped it up and then crouched by his head, unstoppering the flagon.

He was smiling.

Her eyes narrowed. "Was that a ploy to get me close, Licks?"

How much longer until his eyes would be completely silver? Ebba needed him back—and she didn't use the word 'need' lightly. Truly, if she was to survive what lay ahead, he had to be here with her completely. Loving him was the most selfish thing she would ever do because to love him felt akin to simply being. He was her survival. For a pirate, survival was everything.

"Aye," Jagger said hoarsely. "And I like it when ye call me Licks."

"Are we goin' to change what that word means to ye then?" she asked, genuinely curious.

He nodded.

How like Jagger to turn a weakness into a strength. How did he manage things like that so effortlessly? Was the quality part of his character or part of his immunity? Hopefully she had time to figure that out.

She trickled water into his mouth anyway and then sat back just enough so that they weren't touching. "I've watered ye. Tell me about the kissin' now."

He'd closed his eyes but cracked one open. "A pirate has to have some secrets. How will I surprise ye?"

Ebba had reached her quota of both. They'd do it the hard way. Stretching her fingertips behind, she gripped the hilt of the *veritas* and rested the blade against Jagger's thigh.

"It be a shame ye're too weak to move much," she said in a throaty voice, leaning farther over him. "I be thinkin' it's a prime time to learn a few truthful things about ye, *Licks*. So I repeat: Tell me about the kissin' now."

Eyes closed, Jagger's lips curved.

And he told her everything she wished to know.

ELEVEN

"About time," Marigold hurled at Ebba the moment she came into hearing distance.

Jagger had fallen asleep an hour ago. Convincing herself to walk across the top of the cliffs to join the others took an hour more.

Everyone sat there. Not like there was anywhere else to go.

Caspian sat wedged between his two sisters. They appeared nothing like the well-groomed princesses she'd first met. Dare she say it, even the eldest had gained a feral edge. Good for her.

Verity sat on Locks' lap, his arms around her hips.

Barrels sat next to the gray-haired and seething Marigold. One of her grandchildren—Ebba forgot their names—sat upon his knee. Marigold's sons sat to her left with their wives, their spawn scattered around their ankles. Sharks' teeth, had there always been so many?

A closer look told her that whatever the wind sprites had delivered, there wasn't enough food to go around. The Exosians were chubbier when Ebba last saw them. And cleaner.

Maybe she'd get on better with them now that everyone was unwashed.

Her fathers stared at her, and she stared back. Maybe she really had been out of it. Where were the Daedalion, for starters? Ebba scrubbed at her face with both hands. *All right, time to pretend ye're okay.* A high-pitched laugh slipped through her lips, and two of the children scampered to their mothers.

She slowly lowered her hands.

One of the Exosians' wives, Virtue or something like that, whispered, "Is she okay?"

Okay? *Okay?* Bitter laughter snaked up her throat and Ebba clamped her lips shut, realizing she wasn't doing a great job of appearing . . . with it.

She cleared her throat. "Ahoy."

Everyone exchanged long looks.

Grubby waved. "Ahoy, Ebba!"

And that was why she loved him.

"I'm sorry for the delay. I can see ye're all hungry and ready to be off this here rock. So how about we get down to what happens next?" she said.

Stubby kicked the chest of parts by his feet. "We were thinkin' ye should give assemblin' the root another go afore we start hagglin' ifs and whens. What do ye say?"

That it won't work. Judging by the flatness in his gray eyes, Stubby was of the same mind. But the others who hadn't been in the Dynami Sea clearly needed to see it with their own eyes.

Ebba lifted a shoulder. "Aye, I can do that. Jagger has the *veritas*, though."

Caspian stood and opened the lid of the trunk. He extracted a cylinder and walked over to her.

"How are ye?" he whispered.

"I am," she answered calmly.

Caspian's eyes flew to meet hers. Did he know what she meant by that? Because Ebba had hardly a clue.

"Yer noggin' okay?" she asked her friend.

He nodded. "Mostly better now. Just deep bruising. The nausea is gone at least."

Guilt tinged her thoughts. "I should've been over here to see how ye were."

His mouth twisted, the dimple there flashing. "I have all of these people. Jagger only has you. And you feel you only have him. I can understand even if I don't wish to."

Right. That was oddly forthcoming, considering their audience.

She took the *fortudo* from him and lifted both brows, understanding dawning. "I think the *fortudo* was just workin' on ye, matey."

He frowned at it, rubbing his chest as his cheeks reddened. "Yes, I feel oddly deflated without the bravery it lends me. What do you feel with it?"

She focused on the tube. "Nothin'. Never have since the first time."

"I can't say I've ever known you to lack bravery."

Ebba snorted. "When lookin' at the pillars' shadows. When trapped aboard *Malice*. When Cannon was healin' my fathers."

Caspian's brows drew together. "Bravery isn't the absence of fear, Ebba. You walked into the kraken's mouths. You sailed us through Syraness. You didn't give up when you could have."

"Aye, well, I'm still thinkin' on that one."

The exiled king shook his head. "No, you're not. Not now that Jagger is here."

He was a good enough friend to utter the words. And she was a good enough friend not to hear the bitterness stowed within them. He'd move on one day, and to someone ten times better suited to him.

They walked back to the chest, and Caspian passed her the *dynami* and then the *scio*. Ebba tried each of them end to end, but nothing fit. He gave her the *purgium* and as both of their hands touched it, they looked up at each other.

"What is it?" Peg-leg asked. "Is sumpin' happenin'?"

No.

And yes. She'd just realized something obvious.

"The *purgium* isn't healing you," Caspian said in a vöice just for her.

She blinked back at him. He'd had exactly the same thought, the same memory of when they'd sat in *Felicity* after the battle on Pleo and spoken of her broken heart and the fracture in her soul. Ebba had forgotten that the *purgium*'s healing abilities applied to wounds of the mind as well.

Caspian took her hand gently. "The *purgium* only heals permanent injuries, Ebba. That must mean you can heal."

But she knew that wasn't possible. There had to be a flaw in the *purgium*'s ability because there was no coming back from what she felt. She'd felt fear; she'd been near death; she'd been so lost that it seemed nothing would ever be right.

This wasn't like those times.

How she felt over Plank's absence was a permanent state. There was no fixing it. There was just learning to live with the pain. With Jagger back, she could manage that. Yet the *purgium* hadn't healed her and she'd touched it at least twice since Plank's departure. . . .

"Maybe there be some wounds even the *purgium* can't heal," she whispered to Caspian.

"What's happenin'?" Locks said grumpily.

Ebba shook her head and gestured for the *amare*.

Her clinking efforts to put the tubes together soon drew a frustrated crowd of landlubbers, children-lubbers, royal-lubbers, and an ex-soothsayer.

"Try to put the pronged ends together—"

"That won't work. Maybe we need yarn—"

Somehow, Ebba didn't think that assembling the root of magic involved tying the pieces together with yarn.

Caspian lowered his head to hers. "Can you imagine the pillars tying the cylinders together with yarn?"

Laughter startled from her. She jerked at the rusty sound and dropped her gaze to where Caspian rested his hand upon hers.

He quickly squeezed and let go.

Ebba regarded him, noting the flush in his cheeks. On her side, there were no blurred lines. Jagger was her pirate booty. Caspian was her friend. But he had no one else, yet, and that probably made things hard.

She bit her tongue and instead announced, "This be stupid."

Dumping the cylinders back in the chest, she stood and ushered the others back to their seats. "That ain't happenin'. What be the actual plan?"

"Sally," Stubby announced. "She told the others to send for her when we arrived. We sent the Daedalion to get her."

Verity sighed. "All of them went."

They'd sent their only ride off a tainted island to fetch the queen of wind sprites, who was mostly unreliable.

She turned accusatory eyes on Stubby, who reddened.

"The flock wouldn't split up. It were all or nothin'."

Ebba rubbed her temples. "So there ain't no plan?"

"Sally took Stubby's hobby ship for safekeeping," Caspian said. "I'm assuming that means she has some kind of plan. Without the *scio* she wasn't able to relate anything to the others."

Ebba had spent enough time with the queen of the wind sprites to know that Sally could communicate a whole bunch when she felt like it. Also that during her recovery from alcoholism, she'd chewed up a bunch of wood. Odds were that had become the spare ship's fate.

Stubby crossed his arms, turning up his nose. "Guess my hobby ship got out of the inlet after all. Just like I always knew it would. What do ye all have to say *now*?"

The loudest groan came from Barrels. "You mean to say that you knew the queen of sprites would one day order her minions to use their astounding strength to lift your ship—the one you accidentally made too large to get out of the tunnel—and deposit it in the sea?"

"Aye," Stubby quipped, glaring at all of them in turn.

"As much as I love Sal, I ain't waitin' on her. She's been shady in the past," Ebba said. "We need time to figure out how to get this weapon sorted. And seein' as the air be the only thing left untainted, we need the Daedalion. Otherwise, we just be sittin' ducks for the pillars."

Locks shuddered. "That's what bothers me. Where *be* the pillars? A bunch o' their tainted pirates died—Cannon one o' them. They had to have witnessed it all, bein' entwined in their souls. They know we have all six parts, and they haven't come."

Marigold interjected. "Fear?"

Ebba's weren't the only brows that lifted. Caspian and Verity were right behind her. Jagger's would've been the same.

"Not fear," Verity said. "They won't fear the three watchers until the weapon is formed. Then, and only then, is the playing field evened. We are part of their plans; we just don't know it yet."

Plans within plans within plans.

"*Or*," Barrels countered, "maybe they aren't here because they know we'll fail. If they see through the eyes of their tainted, they would know . . . we're a man down. If the assembler cannot assemble, the weapon cannot exist, and the pillars have nothing to fear."

Everyone stared at him. That certainly put a hopeless spin on everything.

"But they probably just have another plan," he blurted.

Guess when you had six minds merged into one, multiple plans were inevitable. But the realm had more minds than that right here. Sure, most were landlubbers, but still. They could nut it out together. They could—

The trill of a bird drew her furious gaze to the skies. But Ebba's search for the two white birds came to an abrupt halt at the sight of Stubby's hobby ship floating through the sky toward them.

She whistled low. "Heads up. Sal be comin' after all."

That sent everyone scrambling. Those who'd been stuck on Zol for weeks whooped at the sight.

In a trickle, Ebba's fathers came to stand either side of her with Caspian already on her left.

Peg-leg hummed. "Be it strange that I just take a flyin' ship in my stride by now?"

"Nay," chorused the others, Barrels and Caspian included.

"Kind o' nice that it don't have snakes comin' out o' somewhere," Locks said.

"Aye," they chanted.

Caspian pursed his lips. "My least favorite were the Capricorn. That fight in the sea was exhausting with one arm."

"And one leg," Peg-leg put in.

"And one eye," Locks said with an added snort. The three shared a grin.

"It was the kraken for me," Barrels said after a beat.

Stubby grunted. "When the Satyr took Ebba." He stopped. "Nay, make that when she walked through the six mouths o' the kraken. I thought I'd die."

"Oh, aye," her fathers muttered.

They all avoided the obvious: Mutinous Cannon and Davy Jones' Locker. Perhaps, like Ebba, they felt that memory was still too recent to make light of.

Grubby scratched his jaw. "I'm thinkin' the Capr'corn were about the most fun. Near about wet my pants when a dolphin was speakin' to me for the first time."

The men who surrounded her gave over to laughter, drawing the attention of the rest of their Zol group.

Caspian wrapped his arm around Grubby's shoulder, chuckling.

She made certain to quirk her lips for show. Really, Ebba was truly glad for a reprieve in the otherwise grim script of their lives. There couldn't be many more moments like this in what lay ahead, so they had to laugh about as much as possible.

But no one had laughed about Mutinous Cannon or Davy Jones' Locker.

And no one had mentioned the Pillars of Six.

TWELVE

Ebba watched as Marigold finally decided to trust the sprite minion who would carry her to the ship. Not that she could blame the Exosian. Sally's minion was roughly the size of two of her fingers. The tiny immortal clung to Marigold's wrist, expecting the woman to walk off the cliff.

Which she did.

Marigold screamed, plummeting from sight before re-emerging in a steady bob toward the floating ship. The glowing sprite hung on without apparent effort.

Caspian's sister, Sierra, had taken a running leap for her sprite, nearly giving her older brother a heart attack.

Listening to her fathers' sniggers as Marigold continued screaming, and Barrels' waspish request for them to shut up, Ebba searched for Sally. Her minions were everywhere, but the queen of the wind sprites had remained out of sight.

They didn't have to wait long.

"My cat," Barrels gasped.

His flying cat.

From the ship, through thin air, galloped a Pillage who was

noticeably larger than when the queen of sprites had stolen the cat to become her noble steed. Upon his back, stiff-backed and seemingly above everything, was Sally.

The queen rode Pillage through the air all the way to where they were gathered on the cliff.

"Pillage," Barrels cooed, glaring at the glowing sprite.

She ignored him, waving imperiously at her servants, who produced a thick gold cushion. Sally floated off the fat ship cat to hover cross-legged above the cushion. The hovering seemed to negate the need for a soft seat, but Ebba expected Sally took delight in torturing her minions with little details like superfluous comfort.

Without Sally's help, Pillage dropped to the ground and wasted no time bolting for Barrels, who scooped the cat up in both arms, holding Pillage tight as he cooed wordless greetings to the feline.

The rest of them watched for a time until Locks made a sound of disgust.

Caspian held out the *scio* and Ebba touched a finger to the tarnished silver.

"Saliha," she said in greeting.

"I seriously can't believe you remember my name," the sprite said, scrunching her nose.

Ebba would give her that one, but they'd have time later to clue Sally in on how she'd gotten smarter.

"We need off this rock," Ebba told her.

The sprite pointed at the ship, not offering anything more.

Stubby placed a finger on the *scio*. "Still sober, Sal?"

The sprite queen glanced behind her as one of her guards cleared his throat.

"Ye've been chewin' wood," Ebba said, nodding. "Knew it."

"Do you want my help, or would you rather die and plummet the realm into forever evil?" Sally asked, inspecting her nails. "Because I'll do it to prove a point."

Ebba grinned, and the sprite glanced up, an echoing smirk on her tiny face.

The rest of her fathers joined the gathering around the *scio*, each locating a spare inch on which to place their fingers.

"We have a few problems," Caspian informed the queen.

"I know," she answered.

"I—" Caspian cut off. "You do?"

Sally lifted an imperious hand in the air and gestured with one finger. One of her guards floated forward.

"Yes, your royal majesty?" the female guard said, bent at the waist.

That was laying it on thick. Ebba eyed Sally's wolfish grin, shaking her head.

"Fetch the volume from the desk on the ship."

The guard hesitated. "Which volume, your royal majesty?"

"The right one," Sally answered.

It was saying something that the white-glowing sprite grew paler. But the creature zipped off in a fluttering of wings.

Sally uncrossed her legs and floated over to Ebba. Without words, she hugged Ebba's face and whispered low, "I'm so sorry you lost him, Ebba. So very sorry that I wasn't there to help you."

The lump in Ebba's throat rose hard and fast. Her eyes remained dry by the skin of her teeth, but the lump stole her speech. Sally leaned back, and Ebba could only nod, silently beseeching her to drop the matter.

The sprite queen floated back and forth in an immortal version of a pace. "You cannot put the weapon together."

Stubby's jaw dropped. "How do ye know that?"

"Remember why I left?" she asked. "It was to search our archives. They're extensive and span thousands of years. Finding the answer wasn't easy. Well, I assume it wasn't. I just told other sprites to do it. But it took them a long time." She paused. "Maybe they didn't work hard enough. I should make a few heads roll."

Power might have gone to Sally's head.

Caspian leaned forward. "What did you find, Queen Saliha? We have no idea what to try next. Only that we must evade the pillars. Any insight you can offer would be greatly appreciated."

Fear flashed over the queen's face. "Yes, King Caspian. The pillars must be evaded. But the answer to that and of what to do next are one and the same."

The female guard returned and rested a heavy mahogany book atop the vacated gold cushion. She drifted back and fixed wide eyes on her queen.

Sally shot forward and inspected the volume, slowly lifting her gaze to the guard's.

"Correct," she announced.

The guard sagged in relief and resumed her position beside the second guard.

Locks whistled. "Tight ship ye're runnin'."

"But of course," the sprite said. With a twitch of her finger, the wind surged and opened the book. The sprite muttered to herself, reading snatches of the pages and turning the pages with the breeze until she burst out with, "Here, a lodging of a guest who visited our kingdom, dated Dawning Age, year 4561."

"When was *that*?" Grubby asked.

Sally halted. "The Dawning Age began when this realm was first formed after a fight between the Earth Mother and Mortem. The pillars took over after five thousand years and then started the Age of Darkness for the next 4500 or so years."

"Then the Age of Prosperity for five hundred years," Caspian added. "Then the current age, the Age of Kings. Wait, are you saying that two immortals had a fight and created the realm?"

Sally appeared bored. "Correct."

"Who be Mortem?" Stubby piped up.

"A power of Oblivion."

Peg-leg groaned. "Bearded lovers, what does this one do?"

Sally appeared amused. "You've met the power of creation, the Earth Mother. You've met the power of souls, the Thunderbird. Mortem is the final one. The power of death."

They watched her.

Grubby broke the quiet. "Don't think I want to meet Mortem."

"Yes, well, shut up and listen closely," the sprite queen said. "I don't like repeating myself."

No kidding.

Sally's voice swelled. "Blah, blah, blah, ten mortals died. Blah, blah, blah, here it is! The trinity arrived as expected. The immune with her sword, the bearer with the root of power, and the assembler with his anchors—"

That was strange. To think that these three people, with the same responsibilities as Ebba, Caspian, and Jagger, had existed thousands of years before.

"They reported the traditional passage between the islands had gone without incident after the end of the Earth Mother's reign. The selkies joined them from Exosia to Maltu. The kraken from Maltu to Febribus. The Jendu from Febribus to Pleo. Blah, blah, blah, you get the point. This is the important part. *Now, it falls to the sprites to step in as guardians for the final leg of the trinity's journey so the weapon can be dismantled. Tomorrow, we will be led by Queen Tasina*—my grandmother," Sally explained, sticking her tongue out, "*to where paths cross.*"

Sally flicked her finger and the volume slammed shut. "To where paths cross," she repeated triumphantly. "The root of magic can only be assembled in a certain place."

Ebba glanced at Caspian. That had to be why she couldn't put the parts together. They weren't in the correct location.

"That be great." Locks drew out, "Where is that . . . exactly?"

"—That could describe a lot o' paths—"

"—Sounds special-like though—"

"—Someone needs to make a guide—"

A strong gust of wind shot into their mouths. Ebba choked, hacking out a cough as she slapped Peg-leg on the back. They all huddled around the *scio* again, obediently mute.

Sally glowered. "When the immortal realm opened up into this new realm, we referred to the border colloquially as 'where paths cross.' Every immortal knows where it is. Mortals who know of it, usually only seafarers, refer to the same space as the Oblivion—which is actually the name of the immortal realm."

"The Oblivion," Barrels echoed faintly.

Caspian's amber eyes were all but burning holes into Sally's face. "The Oblivion ruled by the three powers: Earth Mother, Mortem, and the Thunderbird?"

Who cared about that? Ebba cut in. "The Oblivion, located through the eye of Charybdis, where souls go to be sorted into the good or bad pile?" The very whirlpool they'd once used to evade capture by Pockmark. "*That* Oblivion?"

The sprite dipped her head, saying cheerfully, "That's the one."

Peg-leg and Locks broke away to take a seat on the jutting rocks on the clifftop.

"I don't suppose the entry gave any specific details on how the sprites escorted the trinity to the Oblivion? Alive." Barrels kept a finger on the *scio* and reached for the mahogany volume.

Sally batted his hand away. "It's written in our old tongue. No touching, aged mortal. And no. But the answer is simple: We'll fly you in. Well, my minions will. I'm above grunt work."

This was crazy. And that was saying something.

As the others spoke to Sal, Ebba turned to Caspian, wishing Jagger was strong enough for this discussion too.

"What do ye think?" she asked.

The exiled king brushed his too-long curls back. "We've always been referred to as the three watchers. I wonder why this entry referred to us as the trinity."

"That's what ye're thinkin'?" she asked him doubtfully. "Not about travelin' through the eye o' Charybdis to the Oblivion and most likely dyin'?"

"Huh? Oh yes, I suppose so. Not much crazier than going to hell, really."

Ebba snorted. "I believe ye just used pirate logic, matey."

He quirked a brow. "Don't tell."

"Only if ye don't say I thought o' yer logic first. I'm seein' one problem with the plan. What about ye?"

"Aye," he said, mimicking her. "I thought that when she said we couldn't assemble the weapon, she knew you needed. . . ."

All of her fathers. Ebba swallowed.

"Want me to handle that?" he asked.

Did she want him to tell Sally that even if they could assemble the weapon in the Oblivion, Ebba couldn't actually do it because Plank was gone? "Yes," she said. "I'm goin' to get Jagger ready."

She disconnected from the *scio* and wove through her arguing fathers, abandoning poor Caspian to deal with the lot of them.

They'd left boarding Jagger until last. Sally had scoffed away their mention of suspending a net from the boom so he didn't infect the ship with taint. Ebba assumed she'd use her glow in some way, but no doubt the queen sprite would reveal that in her own sweet time.

Jagger was sitting up, his legs dangling over the edge of the cliff. Ebba quickened her step. She'd intended to be back before he woke. Had he checked how far the taint was up the side? If he was touching any, she'd be peeved right off.

"I've checked," he said as she approached.

Savvy bugger. "I don't like ye sittin' on the edge," she said, hovering close in a crouch.

"In case I jump?"

Aye.

He tore his gaze from the oily black sea to her. "I wouldn't jump. I couldn't even do it when ye weren't mine. Now that ye are, there's no way."

And yet that sentiment hadn't always kept her loved ones here. Still, something unknotted in her gut. Ebba hadn't known if leaving him unattended was safe or not.

"Ye're the only person who's allowed to kill me," he said, winking.

Ebba shook her head, smiling, and perched beside him on the

cliff. She peeked over to make sure the taint was well below where her feet rested against the vertical edge. "Is that so?"

"Ye've attempted twice by my count. And that ain't includin' the time ye handed me a pistol to shoot myself with when we were anchored at Pleo."

"Wasn't nothin' personal," she told him, grinning. "Just a bit o' mercy killin' from one pirate to the next. Grudges ain't good to hold on to, ye know."

His eyes drifted again to the sea. "Nay, they ain't. Can't say my one against Montcroix came to much. Maybe I should still kill Caspian."

Was this the taint talking? Ebba opened her mouth.

"Don't stress yer head, Viva. I'm just jokin'."

She breathed a sigh of relief. "Okay, it's just that when yer eyes are still partially black and bloodshot, it's hard to tell if it be jest or cold-blooded murder on yer mind."

Jagger adjusted his grip on *veritas*. "My desire to kill Caspian died long ago. Maybe I was never goin' to go through with it. Why else would I have goaded him to a fight? I would've just slipped a dagger in his back as he slept."

That would've been the easiest way; she couldn't agree more.

"But I'm thinkin' I'll just take this sword instead," Jagger said, staring at *veritas*. "Feels right to have it."

Ebba frowned. "Sally just read us a passage from her archives. It said the immune back then had a sword. Do ye think there be sumpin' to the way ye're drawn to the sword?"

"I don't know anythin' right now, Viva. But my father carried *veritas* for Montcroix, so maybe the immune is meant to carry the sword for the bearer."

Or Montcroix stole the blade after he killed Jagger's parents and then realized truth was overrated.

Jagger sounded so forlorn, Ebba would have moved entire islands to take it away from him. Yet this was what destiny had planned for him. To be the immune was to bear darkness for everyone else. But it didn't mean Jagger had to do it alone.

She watched as his blinks became longer, listening to the continued argument along the clifftop.

"What're they fightin' about?" he asked.

Ebba glanced over at her fathers, Caspian, and Sally. "Journeyin' to the Oblivion through Charybdis to put the root o' magic together, I'm guessin'. Could be anythin' by now."

Jagger blew out a breath. "Shite."

"Aye, so lay back, and we'll rest awhile. Ain't long afore we'll be on a ship again and bound for who knows what."

She breathed easier when Jagger lay down, fully closing his eyes. *Veritas* was in his hand, and Ebba eased herself down beside him, two feet of space separating them.

Never close enough.

THIRTEEN

She was back on a ship for the first time since *Felicity* sank. If Ebba thought about it, events had taken a turn for the worse the moment they lost their ship to the Dynami Sea.

Ebba ran her fingertips over the oak bulwark. Oak, not cedar. The ship of her childhood had smelled warm and sweet, like hot rum poured over embers. This ship was a work of art, a fine creation with sleek lines and the stamp of an expert craftsman. The heavy burning scent of the oak filled her nose like pollen.

The smell was wrong.

Or new.

Maybe she should pretend the wrongness was just another *difference*. There were real differences, after all. For one, they were being carried through the air by one hundred of Sally's minions who had a rotation roster so some could rest while the others worked. Their glow was on high to ward off the effects of the taint.

Knowing all of that didn't stop a fresh element joining the pile of things she was mourning. When Pockmark took Ebba prisoner, her innocence died. When *Felicity* sank, she took Ebba's childhood to the bottom of the sea with her. And when Plank left, he'd taken nearly everything else. Trying to keep the loving memories of her past alive was hard when she just wanted to hate the woman who'd taken her father away. Felicity, a woman she'd never met and yet somehow felt beholden to because a ship had shared her name.

She stared at the leather-bound scrapbook by her feet. She had to touch the thing to get it onto the ship. Ebba didn't know what she'd expected to happen when she touched it—for it to explode or sting or scream.

The book hadn't done any of those things. Maybe it really was just a collection of memories. Ebba was finding it hard to access her happy memories . . . could reading the scrapbook be the answer to that problem?

She bent down and grabbed the leather-bound book. Briefly closing her eyes, very much doubting if this was wise, Ebba untied the leather cord. She rested the splayed scrapbook against the bulwark, and slowly began to read:

> *For Ebba-Viva "Wobbles" Fairisles,*
> *Our memories of your childhood could fill one hundred books, but here are our fondest memories of you.*
> *We are better people because of the love we hold for you.*
> *Thank you for being in our lives.*

A burning started behind her eyes as she finished the note, penned in Barrels' looping handwriting.

Thank you for being in our lives.

Yet that hadn't been enough for Plank.

She struggled to keep her tears at bay, gritting her teeth and swallowing hard. If the first page nearly reduced her to a crying mess, there wasn't any way she could get through the rest.

Not right now.

Blinking away the blur in her eyes, Ebba closed the scrapbook again, tying the leather cord tight. Then she stared out over the bulwark. The tips of the craggy cliffs of Syraness were just visible to the north. Past that, Kentro was just a blurry line on the horizon.

"How's he goin', lass?" Stubby asked gruffly, leaning against the bulwark and facing away from the black sea.

Ebba turned toward the mast as well, hugging the scrapbook to her chest. Tipping her head back, she could just catch the barest glimpse of flaxen hair up in the crow's nest. Sprites covered nearly the entire mast and were clinging onto the rigging. Their glow kept Jagger's taint out of the oak wood so the darkness wouldn't spread to the rest of them. The taint within him lessened each day, and once his eyes cleared of black, everyone else would be safe.

She'd be able to touch Jagger.

"He's goin', and that be sumpin'," she told Stubby. "He finds it easier up in the nest than down here."

"Aye, gathered as much. He'll come back in time."

She sighed. "I be more worried o' what the memory o' it will do to him."

Stubby hesitated and pulled one of her hands away from the scrapbook. He held her hand tight. Dark brown against white. Cold against warm. The tiny sympathy threatened to shake apart the fragile state she'd managed to establish in her skull, but Ebba didn't pull away.

"He has ye, lass," he said, swallowing hard. "And so I know he'll be all right. But what o' ye, Ebba-Viva? Tell me how ye are."

Her insides seized. "Ye said I had a week."

"Shouldn't trust the word o' a pirate. We wish to know how ye are. It'd be o' great comfort to us if ye could keep us close."

She released a shaking exhale, forcing away the refusal hovering on the tip of her tongue. "I just tried to read the scrapbook, but I ain't ready for it."

Stubby watched her closely. "Aye, I saw ye open it."

"I read the first page."

He squeezed her hand again. "How about I pop it somewhere safe until all this be over? We could read it together."

Ebba wasn't sure she could do that, ever. The very thought of it made her breath come fast and her chest tighten painfully. But she managed a tight nod in response to her father's hopeful expression and passed the scrapbook over into his keeping.

"I think we should talk about Plank. He was a big part o' ye," Stubby said next.

No.

"I'm fine," she grunted, her heart beating so fast that heat flushed up her neck. Talking of the scrapbook was one thing. Making future plans she could back out of didn't mean a thing.

The vice-like pressure in her chest wouldn't allow any talk of her absent father. She couldn't.

"Nay," Stubby said softly. "We don't do that anymore. One of yer fathers be dead. Ye ain't fine. None o' us are fine."

Dead.

She sucked in a ragged breath and withdrew her hand, turning away to peer over the bulwark again. "*Don't.*"

"Ebba, we all lost him, too—"

Black rage slammed through her with the force of a tumbling boulder from hell itself. "None o' us lost him," she snapped, whirling to him.

The gentle murmur on deck ceased.

"He left," Ebba shouted at him, fist curled so tight she thought her nails might break off. "He left you. He left me. He looked right at us, turned around, and walked into a stampede. He chose to die. So don't be tellin' me that we *lost* him."

Stubby's stricken face barely registered. The rest of her fathers hovered nearby. Everyone remained frozen in place as though the smallest whisper might send her over the edge. But she was already over the edge; didn't they see that?

Why wouldn't they leave her be?

"Plank is gone," she screamed at them so hard her throat erupted in pain. "Plank's gone!"

Peg-leg approached, hands raised. His voice was hoarse and his face wet. "Ebba, love. We'll get through this. Ye can scream all ye like. Better out than in, I say. But we ain't goin' away."

Someone else had told her they'd always be with her too.

But the trill of the bird was her real undoing for reasons she couldn't fathom, other than that the bird sounded so damn *happy*. The scrap of dignity she'd been holding onto burst into flames. The two white birds flew into view, twisting through the glowing rigging.

"Sod. *Off*." She hurled the raw words at the creatures. Scanning the deck for a missile proved useless.

Her brand-new boots would do the job. Ebba hopped, wrenching off her right boot.

Scrunching the soft leather up in a tight wad, she waited until the largest bird came into range and wound her arm back, throwing the boot as hard as she could.

The bird twisted, squawking, and the boot missed it, colliding with the mast instead.

"Ebba, nay," Locks gasped.

She had another boot, and she was going to use it. Those birds had to die. But arms stopped her. She fought, kicking out and hearing a satisfying *oof*. More arms grabbed at her, and she snarled wordlessly at those holding her back, twisting side-to-side to dislodge them.

One of her fists caught someone's face.

"Let her go," Ebba heard Barrels call.

All at once, the arms disappeared.

Ebba landed heavily on the oak deck. The burnt scent of the wood filled her nostrils. She gritted her teeth, rolling onto her feet for another go.

Her fathers stood in a circle around her. Verity and Caspian were there too.

"Leave me alone," she said between breaths, wiping at her mouth.

Someone got her. And she'd got several of them. Her eyes landed on a cut on Grubby's cheekbone, and guilt stabbed through the bitterness.

All of them braced for her attack, but Caspian spoke first, if only because her fathers appeared too upset to utter a single word.

"You can't hurt the birds, Ebba," Caspian said. "We might see the Thunderbird in the Oblivion. You know he won't help if his vessels are killed."

Her gut churned at the word 'vessel.' Right now, she didn't care a single flamin' jot about what the Thunderbird would or wouldn't do. She didn't care about assembling the weapon. Right now, she wanted to submit to the anger within her because in anger, she couldn't feel.

In anger, she was brave.

The birds trilled again.

"Move," she told Caspian, eyes tracking the birds to their position in the rigging by the second boom.

He lifted his chin. "No."

"I'll go through ye."

"You can try," he replied calmly.

That was all the encouragement she needed.

Howling, Ebba rushed him, dropping her shoulder. They fell to the deck in a tangle of limbs, and this time, no one else stepped in. She rolled away from Caspian, searching for the birds overhead as she ran for the rigging.

Caspian swept her legs out from under her, and she landed flat on her back, the air disappearing from her lungs.

In a second, Caspian had straddled her, his knees atop the fleshy part of her arms to pin them.

Fury sparked in his eyes, and he leaned in close, his chest rising and falling. "This is bigger than you or me. I know something is happening within you that the rest of us can't fathom. I know Jagger's hurt. I know you feel we can't win. But you need to be bigger than this. If you can't do that, the rest of us will have to do it for you. But the Ebba I know wouldn't shirk her duty or risk the lives of everyone on this ship, let alone everyone in the realm. We need the powers of

Oblivion on our side. We need *you* to assemble the weapon. And we won't let you force yourself further into darkness by killing the Thunderbird's vessels."

Tears trekked from the corners of her eyes into her hair.

Caspian's face softened and he sighed, running his hand through his russet curls.

"He's gone, Caspian," she choked out. "H-he—"

And then she began to shake. Really shake. As though her rum would rattle right out of her.

He shifted, releasing her arms, but Ebba just lay there crying, no longer putting up a fight, uncaring that everyone she respected was standing there watching her completely lose herself.

Caspian had half-turned, and she followed his gaze to Jagger. He was crouched on the bulwark at the base of the starboard rigging, watching her. Sprites flittered all around him, warding off his taint from infecting the ship.

Then he shifted his gaze to Caspian. "She needs someone to hold her."

The prince didn't waste any time. Crouching down beside her, he pulled Ebba against his shoulder. She buried her face into Caspian's chest, her breath coming high and fast as panicked grief struck her again and again.

He stroked her hair, humming as she cried onto his tunic.

Only when her head was aching did her body begin to calm. The stabbing pain within hadn't abated, but the shaking had stopped at least. As had the tears—though only because she had none left inside her, most likely.

Ebba extracted herself and looked up at Caspian.

He met her gaze and winced.

"That bad?" she whispered, wiping her swollen eyes.

"Uh," he hedged, then shrugged a shoulder. "Yes. But if it helps, I'm almost certain pretty criers practice."

She snorted, sending snot flying onto his tunic. They both stared at the glob.

"I'm going to go change my tunic," he announced. "Also because Jagger might kill me if I hold you another second. I'm not sure he remembers it was his idea."

Ebba peered up where Jagger still crouched in the midst of a cloud of sprites. The others had dispersed, giving her some semblance of privacy during her meltdown. She was too exhausted to be embarrassed.

Caspian left, and she stood wearily, rubbing her temples. Sink her, crying hurt her skull.

When she reached Jagger, Ebba frowned at his trembling form.

"Licks?" she ventured uncertainly.

He was shaking just as violently as she had.

"Are ye okay, Viva?" He spoke low and fast. The jerks of his body added a staccato quality to his question.

"Nay, not really," she said. "But I ain't cryin' anymore. Mostly because my head might explode if I keep on. Why are ye shakin'? What's the matter?"

He was gulping back air and didn't answer.

Ebba neared. "Ye need to tell me."

"I hate this," he admitted. "Ye cryin' like that. Me unable to do anythin' about it. *I can't stand it.* Even now, when I should be carin' for ye instead of him, ye're more concerned over whether I'll lose control than anythin' else. I want to be strong for you."

She lifted her brows. Did Jagger even see himself? He inspired so many to be better by just being. "Oh, is that all? I thought ye were cold."

He scoffed, shooting her a black-eyed look.

"Not my best lie, I'll grant ye," Ebba said, rubbing her temples again.

"What's the matter?" he said in irritation.

She dropped her hands. "What have I told ye about that tone?"

Jagger grumbled, "Sorry."

Ebba sighed. "I'm thirsty, methinks. But I don't want to be away from ye."

"I'm fine—"

"I know ye're fine. I said I don't *want* to be away from ye. I want to be here and not anywhere else, ye dolt." Fresh pain stabbed her temples.

From the corner of her eye, she watched as Jagger's shoulders relaxed.

"Oh," he grunted then spoke to the sprites on the rigging. "Could one o' ye fetch some grog from the hold, please?"

Two of the sprites flittered away. The rest settled around him again, their glow working overtime.

"Do ye wish to speak o' Plank yet?" Jagger asked her. "And don't give me the answer ye think I can handle."

Ebba stared at him through stinging eyes and sighed. "Nah, I don't wish to speak o' Plank. Not yet. Perhaps when this be over."

He studied her with eyes that were half black and half silver. "Okay."

"Okay?" she asked suspiciously.

"Okay," he repeated, his lips twitching.

She smiled, ducking her head and accepting a goblet of grog from the returned sprites. They floated back to Jagger with a second goblet.

The pirate dropped out of his crouch, sitting on the bulwark as he accepted the drink. The sprites squeaked frantically as they repositioned themselves so their glow covered him from head to toe.

"It be past time for ye to catch me up on the goings-on," Jagger said.

Ebba observed him. Too thin and gaunt in the face. His features were usually high-boned, but he still appeared as though large scoops were missing from each cheek.

"Viva," he growled. "I can handle it."

"Aye, don't get yer slops in a twist."

"How can I when ye always twist them for me," he shot back.

Ebba leaned against the bulwark five feet from his spot and grinned. "All right then. Let me see. Would ye like to start with the doom part or the doom part?"

"I live for doom."

Her grin faded. "Ye do, don't ye? Should I be worried about that?"

He regarded her seriously. "Ye should only be worried about how hard I'll hold ye when the black fades from my eyes."

Heat rose into her cheeks. She cleared her throat. "Back at ye, m'hearty."

With a deep breath, Ebba started from the moment Cannon had taken Jagger to the present.

It wasn't until Locks joined them that she realized the sun was on its way down. How many days would go by before it didn't rise again? Endless night. That was what had been promised. Was *this* their last sunset?

"Sally's callin' a meetin' at the bow," Locks said.

He squeezed Ebba's shoulder and turned away without meeting her eyes.

"Locks," she called after him. "It ain't that I don't' want to let any o' ye in. It's that I can't talk o' it without fallin' apart. And I can't fall apart just yet because I'm needed. That be why. Nothin' else."

Her father inhaled sharply.

Ebba's chest squeezed tight. "Can ye understand that?"

Locks glanced back. "I can certa'nly try."

"Could ye tell the others it ain't their fault, please?"

He nodded. "I can, but better hurry along. *Queen* Saliha has let power go to her head, methinks."

The sprites confining Jagger's taint chittered angrily, but Ebba thought their hearts weren't really in it. She probably didn't pay them fair wages.

"Ye comin'?" she asked Jagger.

"Aye, let me get *veritas,* though. I'm okay around ye, but the others get my back up."

She waited for him to retrieve the sword, snorting at the cloud of sprites moving around him in a panic, and they walked over to join the others. The children and one of the Exosian mothers were below deck, but everyone else had gathered.

A few glanced at her when she joined. Otherwise, her earlier exhibit wasn't mentioned. Pretending was good sometimes.

Stubby avoided her gaze, and Ebba strode over to squeeze his hand.

"It wasn't ye that triggered that, Stubs," Ebba told him. "It's been buildin' for a wee while."

He inhaled and slowly released it. "Don't like seein' ye like that."

"I don't like bein' like that."

She remained by Stubby's side, and he held out the *scio* for her to touch. Holding *veritas*, Jagger stood several paces behind her in the midst of his personal sprite cloud.

Barrels and Locks leaned in from the other side to touch a finger to the cylinder.

"Now that you've finished your tantrum," Queen Saliha started, smirking Ebba's way.

There was a reason gas was referred to as wind. And Sally was the queen of it.

"Worst pet I ever had," Ebba retorted.

Sally's eyes narrowed, but she recovered, smiling at the others. "We must discuss our plan of attack for entering Charybdis."

Locks quickly repeated her words for those not touching the *scio*.

Barrels frowned. "I thought it was a simple matter of flying the ship through the eye of the whirlpool." He blinked after, turning to the rest of them. "When did that become simple?"

"So," Sally stated, "the thing is that the pillars will probably be waiting for you to get there. They'll likely attack."

"What?" Caspian asked once Locks had conveyed the message.

Ebba felt Jagger shift. A glance back confirmed he'd frozen.

"That's why the pillars haven't come after us until now," he choked.

"I brought him up to speed," Ebba explained.

Jagger stepped forward, clutching *veritas*. "That be why they haven't bothered. If Cannon had taken everythin' to them, all the better. But if not, they knew we'd have to enter Charybdis to put the weapon together. There weren't no point chasin' us if we'd come to them."

"We're going *toward* the things that have caused all of this?" Marigold asked, dabbing her forehead with a handkerchief.

Where did she even get that thing?

Sally bared her teeth. "I told you that I'd made plans. Friends will join us from the other realm."

The immortal realm? Maybe that concept should have sent Ebba spinning, but her head had stopped spinning around the time seals changed into men and started talking.

"It'll have to be a whole heap o' friends to defeat the pillars," Peg-leg said after Locks translated the sprite's comment.

Except everyone had made it clear the pillars *couldn't* be defeated without the root of magic. Which meant. . . . "Not defeatin'. We just have to get past them, aye?" Ebba said.

Sally floated above a map that had been unfurled on the deck. "The Exosian realm ends halfway down the whirlpool. That is where the paths meet. At that point, the pillars will not follow us any farther. Some immortals have returned to this realm after being locked away, but the vast number would not risk being tainted and are still in the Oblivion. We only need to get halfway down Charybdis' throat."

"But the pillars are immortals. Surely they can cross into the Oblivion too," Caspian said from the opposite side after listening intently to Locks' translation.

Verity cut in. "Only the weapon can defeat them, but fighting *all* of magical kind, including the three powers of Oblivion, is too risky. The pillars are strongest in the mortal realm. They won't leave it."

Ebba contemplated that, tapping her lip.

"And if they do enter?" Peg-leg asked.

"Then I hope the powers of Oblivion do their part," Sally said.

Caspian crossed his arms. "They've failed to do so thus far. We shouldn't depend on that."

"There's nothin' else to depend on," Locks interjected.

This wasn't going anywhere. "Ye said friends were comin'. Who?"

"All sprites of fighting age are with me. The Daedalion are close by. The selkies will wait where the paths meet as a final defense. I sent messengers through the Oblivion two weeks ago to request help from any other immortals capable of fighting. I am hopeful the dragons and griffins will heed my call."

Hopeful.

Her fathers shared a look, and Ebba joined in.

She crouched. "So we have six parts, a whole bunch o' sprites, the Daedalion, and a ship that can go in the air or in the sea."

"My plan isn't good enough for you?" the sprite queen snapped.

Caspian replied, clearly not needing a translation to guess what Sally was worked up about. "There's no way we could pull this off without you, Queen Saliha. But we do have several objects that could prove useful that may not be part of your plan. And, well, a crew of pirates."

The sprite queen glared at him and then dipped her head in a regal nod. "I accept your help in planning."

"There be a whole heap o' people below deck to keep safe. That's my worry," Locks said grimly, studying the map of Charybdis.

Ebba blew out a breath. "How long until we get to the whirlpool?"

"I'd say we have about five hours," Sally said. "Four if my minions stop being lazy."

Panic surged within Ebba at the slithering memory of the pillars' shadows standing on *Malice*. They were coming for her crew, their power exponentially stronger than when she'd last glimpsed them.

Ebba couldn't even imagine what Jagger was going through with the threat of being recaptured lurking overhead.

"Five hours," she said heavily, glancing around the group. "Let's get to it."

FOURTEEN

Ebba stood between Caspian and Jagger on the main deck. Dawn was just starting its feather-light sweep over the realm, and if they sailed in the water instead of flying, Ebba guessed they'd already feel the pull of the maelstrom.

The black eye of the entrance to the Oblivion was in sight. At their current flying rate, it would only be another twenty minutes, if that.

"I know we've been in danger the entire time, but the true danger has always felt distant," Caspian said. "This feels different."

Probably because—if Sally was to be believed—they were soaring directly toward the pillars they'd thus far eluded.

"Where are they?" Jagger asked, gripping the bulwark. His knuckles showed white and Ebba couldn't blame him. The pillars might kill her and Caspian and everyone else on board. But Jagger?

Jagger they'd keep.

On her other side, Caspian said, "The closer we are to the eye, the smaller the net."

Ebba pursed her lips. "Maybe they expected us to be in the

water. Once we entered the current, we would've been trapped. Flying like this makes us harder to trap."

Jagger hummed. "Aye, I don't like it one bit."

None of them *liked* it.

"Everyone is in place," Stubby whispered, joining her. He grinned, and Ebba grinned back despite the lurch in her gut. Her fathers chose the most unusual times to decide they were having a good time.

The pirates of *Felicity* had made some . . . alterations to Sally's plans. It wasn't that the sprite didn't think outside the square, just that she wasn't a pirate. Ebba and the others had thrown everything they had into this plan, but aside from the taint, they'd never experienced the pillars' power. There was only so much planning that could be done.

They had to stall for time. Enough time to get to where the paths crossed, halfway down the throat of Charybdis.

"I'm goin' to give the call for the sprites to start descendin' to the eye," Stubby said, surveying the area ahead.

She glanced back over the deck, checking on each of her fathers. Peg-leg and Grubby were at the mast. Barrels at the opposite bulwark. Locks, Verity, and Sally at the wheel. Marigold with her family and Pillage in the hold.

"I'd better join Barrels," Caspian said as Stubby headed for the wheel. The prince exhaled slowly, running a hand through his russet curls. "Shite."

Jagger snorted and repeated, "Shite."

A smile curved Ebba's lips. "Shite."

"Take care of yourselves, please," Caspian said to them.

"Even me, landlubber?" Jagger asked, cocking a brow.

Caspian pursed his lips. "Even you, pirate."

They watched as the Exosian joined Barrels.

A false serenity followed where Ebba just looked at Jagger and he looked at her. It was a lull where the wind ruffled their hair and clothing—where the quiet murmur of the others speaking faded away; a lying second where pretending they were sailing over calm seas on a normal day was possible.

Her stomach lurched a second time as the ship began a creeping descent for the gaping mouth of Charybdis.

Reality slammed home. They were really doing this.

"Viva," Jagger said, the low timbre of his voice reaching her very soul. "I need ye to stay by me. And not because ye can't take care o' yerself. I ain't sure what'll happen if anyone gets between us. I don't want to hurt anyone ye love."

"I know, Jagger. And I will." She borrowed his words. "Don't worry yer head."

Amusement briefly flared in his dark eyes.

"Look sharp-like," Locks shouted. "Sumpin' comin' up on starboard. Fast."

Turning, Ebba leaned over the starboard side, scanning the sky and sea below. They were about one hundred feet above the surface. With the gradual angle of their descent, the ship would only near the surface of the water just before the sprites began to lower them through the middle of the maelstrom.

"What is that?" Jagger asked, resting a hand on the hilt of *veritas* in the belt around his hips.

Ebba followed his line of sight, frowning at a shimmering light cannon balling toward them. Was it a projectile? She tensed, prepared to launch herself back.

"It be a person," Jagger said. "A woman."

What? The pillars were shadows last time she saw them, but she was reasonably certain they'd been male. Which meant this was either one of Sally's allies or the pillars had brought friends.

Reaching down, she freed a dagger from her belt.

The shimmering form traversed the distance between the jagged cliffs of Syraness to the north of Charybdis and their ship, and an eerie voice slid over her senses.

Handsome warrior, to the rocks I bid thee,

For you are weary, and there you can rest your head.
Come with me, mighty warrior to the rocks, I bid,
Together we will rest, together we will be.

Ebba jolted, recognition splicing her skull.

Siren.

They were passing a fair way south of Syraness! To her knowledge, the Siren didn't usually leave her rocky territory.

Yet she clearly had. And this immortal wasn't on their side.

She boomed over her shoulder, "Siren, ahoy! Jagger, ye need to lash yerself down with rope."

Leaving the baffled pirate, Ebba sprinted to the nearest coil of rope and threw it back at him. "Tie yerself down."

The ship plummeted, and for a heart-dropping moment, her feet weren't touching the deck at all.

The cries of the sprites sounded from beneath the ship, and Ebba was slammed back to the deck, rolling to her feet as the ship straightened once more.

But the vessel had picked up speed. A *lot* of speed.

Sally bolted past in a blur, disappearing over the side of the ship to her people.

No time to figure out what that meant.

Ebba staggered to the next coil of rope, wind whipping around her. "Verity, the men need to be tied down." She raised her voice over the Siren's swelling song and the rushing of wind.

Shite, shite, shite. The pillars weren't alone. Her crew hadn't planned on fighting *other* tainted immortals.

The uncontrolled descent of the ship slowed. Though their downward slide toward the maelstrom was still faster than before. Ebba's eyes rounded as the answer hit her. The Siren was affecting the male sprites. Only the females were holding the ship aloft. And now Sally was helping them.

"You get the ones at the mast. I'll get the others," Verity called.

Those in the hold should be okay for a while.

Ebba gathered up the rope and ran to Peg-leg and Grubby at the mast. She took one look at their frenzied eyes and blanched. The Siren was getting to them!

The Siren's song grew louder, floating over the wind. How close was she to the ship?

Ebba dumped the coil of rope on the deck. Locating the end, she formed the quickest loop knot of her life and she circled the mast. Once back to the coil, she rifled through to locate the other end and began pulling the length through the loop knot. Her hands blurred as the Siren's song swelled.

She called back over her shoulder, "Jagger?"

No answer came.

Peg-leg and Grubby surged forward to meet the Siren overboard, and Ebba pulled the rope tight, shoving both men back against the mast. Keeping the tension, she ran the loose end of the rope to the rigging and secured it there so her fathers wouldn't get free.

Ebba glanced behind her.

Her mouth dried as she spotted Jagger standing on the bulwark.

"No! Get down," she yelled at him, sprinting toward him.

The Siren rose before Jagger, her blonde hair flowing down her back, her skin luminous from the magical glow within. Behind her, glowing male sprites hovered in a thick wall, just shy of touching her.

The Siren sang to Jagger:

Handsome warrior, to the rocks I bid thee.

"No way, ye soddin' bird-lady," she roared. "He's mine."

As the Siren extended a hand to the pirate, Ebba lunged to grab hold of Jagger's leg.

With a ringing slide, Jagger pulled *veritas* free of his belt and plunged the blade up through the Siren's stomach.

Ebba adjusted her course at the last second, catching herself against the bulwark instead of grabbing Jagger's leg. She stared up at the spot where the sword disappeared under the Siren's ribs.

The Siren began to shake, her skin bubbling and rippling from within. Scales appeared on her face, receding and surging. As her hair began falling out, Jagger wrenched *veritas* free and leaped back down on the deck.

Ebba closed her mouth and pushed off the bulwark to join him.

"So that's the Siren," he said.

Ebba crept up to the bulwark again to peer overboard.

The male sprites were shaking off the Siren's song. As they came to, they bolted back to support the ship, which slowed right down to the controlled descent of before. They'd cut the distance to the water in half—and then some. Less than fifty feet remained between the ship and the mouth of Charybdis.

The Siren came into view. Or what was left of her. Hundreds of vibrant blue feathers fluttered down to the sea, the body of the Siren gone.

Jagger stepped past Ebba and untied the rope holding her fathers to the mast.

"How did ye resist the Siren?" she asked him, giving a cursory glance around deck to check on the others.

Locks was already free, and Verity was releasing the rest.

"What happened?" Peg-leg asked, shoving off the rope.

Ebba strode over to help Grubby. "Siren. Jagger killed her."

Her father blanched. "He resisted?"

Jagger replaced the bloodied *veritas* in his belt. "Immune," he reminded Peg-leg.

And maybe *veritas* had something to do with it.

"Ye know," she told him, "even though ye're an immune and were holdin' the sword o' truth, I still feel like it was my a'tractiveness that gave ye power to resist her."

He snorted and leaned over the side to peer down. "Shite, we lost a lot o' height. But we're still a good five minutes from the eye. Do ye think the pillars have more friends comin'?"

"Best to assume they do."

"Unfurl the sails," she hollered to her fathers. "Sal, it be time for that extra gust of wind we were talkin' about."

But the surge of wind they'd discussed earlier never came.

Jagger sucked in a breath, still looking overboard. "She's fallin'."

What? Ebba ran to the bulwark and gasped at the sight of Sally somersaulting through the air, head over tail.

"Get her, ye fools," she hurled at the sprites. She must have exhausted herself replacing the power of the male sprites.

A group of the tiny immortals tore away from the ship, and the effect was immediate. The ship's descent quickened.

Thirty feet, twenty-five feet, twenty feet.

Shouts rose from behind.

Ebba whirled and choked back a scream at their new guest.

Snakes still wriggled from her head with a life of their own, but the immortal had lost every trace of goddess-like beauty. She'd finally transitioned. The gorgon, Medusa, swiped at Peg-leg, throwing him clear to the bow.

Grubby dodged her second swipe, rolling a few times before jumping to his feet.

Medusa glanced at Ebba for a moment, licking her now pointed teeth. Her head appeared more serpent-like than human. Thick scales lined her body, those over her torso like armor.

The gorgon shifted her slitted red gaze to Jagger, who was on his knees, clutching at his head.

"My masters call for you," the gorgon sneered.

Once, Medusa had wanted Jagger for herself.

Her dagger lost somewhere during the Siren's attack, Ebba yanked her pistol from her sash and took quick aim, firing.

Crack!

The gorgon jolted, shoulder thrown back.

Medusa turned her red glare on Ebba.

"Boom!"

Barrels' call went up a scant second before the mainsail boom catapulted through the air. Ebba ducked. But the immortal was too fast to be caught by that particular trick. She dodged the swinging beam with the same blurring speed Ebba recalled from when they'd first met her.

She threw her used pistol at the immortal, who didn't flinch as it struck her in the stomach.

Instead, Medusa tipped back her head and smiled, displaying every one of her pointed teeth. The dawn was steadily brightening the sky, but like a candle snuffed out, any light was suffocated. Shadows took its place. A cloying black stickiness spread over the heart-pounding fear within her.

Ebba lifted both hands to her neck, coughing through the sudden thickness in her throat. What was Medusa doing? The immortal told them that in transition she had neither her goddess nor gorgon's powers. Was this something a gorgon could do?

"My masters are here," Medusa declared.

Cold dread plunged Ebba into its icy midst. A heartless immortal was before her, and she shouldn't turn to look at the pillars. But morbid curiosity could not be denied, and her head turned almost of its own accord to peer behind her.

A mistake.

In a heartbeat, Medusa was on her. Pain exploded across Ebba's back as she was sent flying across the deck. Over the deck. Over the *bulwark*. Off the safety of the ship.

"Nay." Jagger's horrified wheeze echoed out to her from where he knelt.

The ship was gone. Thin air sat between her and the black, tainted sea.

And then Ebba was plummeting through the air beneath the ship.

The choking sensation in her throat grew as she fell. She couldn't scream. And that was the moment when, after months at sea trying to get the weapon to destroy them, she came face to face with a pillar.

Caspian once described the pillars to her as beautiful men who appeared to be carved from stone. He was right, in part. The statue-like perfection of their features was the most immortal thing she'd ever seen. So flawless and smooth that her entire being shied away from it in horror. Because such perfection had to be a sign of poison and death.

Such rigid youth and symmetry could only destroy her in a blink.

As she toppled, the god-like pillar closed in on her. And in his eyes, decay—the end. Ebba knew she was physically falling toward the currents of Charybdis, but with his proximity, her very soul had flipped directions. Now, her mind believed she was hurtling toward the pillar. To what she saw there—darkness, death, destruction.

The blackness suffocating her turned to lightning-sharp agony as her very insides split in two as though her innards were being drawn out of her body like linked sausages.

Five feet away.

He was going to catch her, and when that happened, she would be gone. Taken. Unaware of anything but endless horror.

Three feet.

Ebba couldn't be gone yet.

Her fingers inched toward the object on her belt. She took hold of the *purgium* with colossal effort and tugged. It was her only weapon. She had no idea if the pillars were tainted themselves, but the tube might heal the pillar, and the sacrifice demanded could hurt him.

She'd still fall into the currents of Charybdis, but at least there, she stood a miniscule chance of survival.

The pillar surged before her, and Ebba yelled wordlessly, wrenching the cylinder free.

This close to him, her pounding heart wanted to seize in terror. Darkness stuck to the immortal's white skin like wisps of smoke that constantly appeared and were blown away. Ebba stared into his eyes, feeling her horror slipping away even as she noted the pillar's skin appeared dead, not carved of white stone at all.

How curious.

His eyes were entirely black, but she wasn't afraid any longer. Why was that? From the folds of the smoke that enclosed his sculpted body like a cloak, the pillar withdrew a jagged dagger the length of her forearm.

Ebba's grip loosened on the *purgium* of its own accord as she stared into the chasms that were the pillar's eyes.

Death.

Death.

Your will is mine.

Her will was his.

"Viva!"

She jolted at the roar, breaking free of her stupor. Ebba screamed at how close the pillar was. Throwing her arm out blindly, she felt the *purgium* make contact with the smoke cloak creeping over the pillar.

White light exploded, and Ebba cried out, lifting a hand to shield her eyes as she was thrown backward by the blast. As she spun blindly through the air, the pain splitting her insides dissipated. The pressure on her throat eased though the wind tore at her hair and snatched away her breath.

Where had the pillar gone? And where was the sea?

A screech sounded a scant second before what little air she'd retained was forced from her lungs. She'd landed on something warm and hard, but her shocked mind could only focus on sucking in air.

After a minute, she relaxed, processing the beating motion under her. She was on a Daedalion. The pillar was gone for now.

"Ebba-Viva! Are ye okay?"

Ebba adjusted her hold on the creature and, with no small amount of effort, peered behind her.

Stubby.

She managed a weak nod. She was okay. At least Ebba thought that was the case. But she'd been right by the pillar; so close she'd felt his evil sliding into her, sucking away her very will without her realizing, even as she stared at him, knowing it would happen.

The Daedalion landed on the deck with a heavy thud that she hadn't expected. Powerless to stop her slide from the creature's back, she landed in a heap on a hard and mostly familiar surface.

The ship.

Her people.

The pillars were here. She had to move.

Stubby dragged her up, and Ebba struggled to get her bearings as the Daedalion took flight back the way they'd come.

"W-what happened?" she said.

Her father looked into her eyes and shouted, "She ain't taken by taint!"

No, the *purgium* had saved her. Somehow.

"The pillars be surroundin' us, lass," he said. "We're hoverin' right above the eye o' Charybdis, but the pillars have stopped us from movin' farther. Barrels got the landlubbers out on the Daedalion afore the pillars closed their ranks around the ship. I was only able to get down to ye when ye touched the *purgium* to the bastard. It broke through the black sphere they've erected around us."

The *purgium*. Ebba frantically searched herself before realizing the cylinder was still firmly in her death grip.

The clanging clash of blades rang, and Ebba stared at the wheel before her and then out past to the main deck.

Caspian and Locks still fought Medusa. The rest of her fathers stood in a ring facing outward, useless in the small space.

Immediately around their ship was a glowing circle, fiercely bright. She tracked the source of the light to the crow's nest where Verity stood, Sally on her shoulder. The sprite's arms were outstretched. The bulk of the light burst from her, but Verity shimmered as her lips moved, her eyes not shifting from the orb around them.

The orb that was shrinking.

In sharp contrast to the glowing orb was the inky black sphere encompassing the entire ship and Sally's efforts to keep them out. It was a void darkness. Not night, simply the absence of all light and hope. In the air, Ebba could taste the soot of the pillars' power on her tongue.

A gap in the dark sphere around the ship was steadily closing.

That must have been where the *purgium* had just blasted one of the pillars.

Ebba held her breath at the sight of the Daedalion who'd saved her frantically beating its wings to escape the spreading black and join the rest of its flock.

It screeched long and high as the dark orb snapped shut. Both she and Stubby stared in horror at where their friend had been. But the Daedalion didn't reappear.

Her hands curled to fists.

Ebba spun in a full circle, her mind taking stock of the five pillars spreading out around the ship. *Five*, not six. Whatever the *purgium* did to the last pillar, the immortal wasn't currently in a state to fight alongside its brethren.

"They strike panic right into the heart o' me," Stubby wheezed, glancing around the five pillars. "I can barely breathe."

The pillars' sphere around the ship was complete. As one, the five immortals lifted their arms. Black smoke poured from their palms, shooting at Sally's orb.

"How far above the eye are we?" she rushed.

Stubby drew his cutlass, moving to the main deck. "Floatin' in the air right over it, lass."

Right over it. So very close.

Medusa lunged for the rigging, her gaze on the crow's nest where Sally and Verity still worked to combat the pillars.

Caspian was close on her heels, swiping at Medusa's exposed back with a dagger. The *dynami* glistened from his belt.

"Where be Jagger?" she asked, sweeping the deck.

Stubby pointed to the far corner.

He crouched, hands held in a rigid clawing position either side of his head. His eyes were flooded with black and wide open as though locked in a nightmare. Locks stood in front of him, lashing out whenever Medusa came his way.

Ebba sprinted for Jagger, but a sickening crunch reached her ears as Caspian punched the gorgon in the face. Medusa reeled away, shrieking. Ebba whirled toward the fighting pair, cylinder in hand. Clearly, the *purgium* could affect the pillars. That was the only defense she could think of right now. But they were being attacked from the inside, too. She'd heal the gorgon first. Full of taint as she was, the *purgium* would take Medusa's life in payment for the healing.

Caspian stood over Medusa, however, and no sooner had Ebba had the thought than the king plunged his dagger into her heart.

The gorgon twisted like a dying fish, and the power of her movements flung Caspian across the deck and into the mast.

Ebba ran for him.

"Caspian," she said, dropping to her knees.

"I'm okay," he wheezed. "Jagger. They're getting to him."

Her next stop.

Locks stepped aside as she hurdled Medusa's twitching body and barreled toward Jagger. Black slammed into the glowing orb around them, and then it was shrinking, shrinking. The orb was barely covering the ship, and the sprites—still coating each side of the ship—fled up onto the main deck to join them.

Her crew were trapped in the confines of the ship deck. Where were Sally's friends? Where was help?

There was none.

She crouched. "Jagger. I'm here."

Tears ran down his cheeks, and blood was smeared across his face, but Ebba couldn't tell if the blood was his or someone else's.

"Can't let them," he muttered. "Ebba, whanau, Ebba, whanau. Kia kaha. Strength." The rest of his words faded into nonsense.

"Licks," she said sharply over the howling wind.

He stilled, and then he was in front of her.

She gasped at the bloodied whites of his eyes. The black rim had thickened. None of the outer silver ring remained. Ebba tore her gaze away and stared up at the five pillars. All of them faced Jagger.

They *were* going for him. Only him.

"Jagger, fight them," she begged.

The pillars were attacking Jagger, and she had no idea how to stop them.

"They're inside, Viva," he panted, clawing at the deck. "Ye're dead. Everyone be dead. I'm on a throne. My children are tainted when they're born. I'm tainted. I want to die."

She winced as one of his fingernails tore free. "None o' that's goin' to happen, Jagger. That's what they want ye to think."

Where was *veritas*?

"Someone get the sword," she yelled over the chaos on deck. "Jagger, don't ye dare leave me. Ye said ye'd stay. That's why I'm still here. Ye don't get to decide otherwise. If this be it for ye, then that's the end for me too."

He blinked, and everything within her screamed for her to take hold of him and hold him to her.

"Ye heard me," she snapped at him. "Ye better fight this because ye're fightin' for both o' us. I need ye to fight for my life, too; I ain't strong enough to do it without ye."

He shuddered.

Someone touched her shoulder. She held out a hand. They deposited the sword in her palm and she slowly drew it forward, not wanting to set Jagger off.

The ship jolted and pitched beneath them.

"*Veritas*," Ebba told him. He shook so hard she could hear his teeth rattling. "Take it."

"I can't."

Her fathers were shouting and running across deck, but she couldn't spare a thought for anything else right now.

"They don't want ye to," she exploded. "Don't let them decide. If ye don't take the damn sword, Jagger, I'll be touchin' ye and taintin' myself to get it done."

His face darkened, and Ebba froze, ready to throw herself out of the way.

Jagger's voice was harsh. "Ye can't be tainted."

"Ebba, far-no, Ebba, far-no," she repeated, attempting to continue his earlier chant. He took up the chant, and she offered the sword to him.

The words caught in his throat as he stretched his fingers toward it.

Ebba bobbed down to catch his gaze, the wind whipping around them. "They don't beat us, Jagger. Do ye hear me? This ain't how this ends."

Yet how neatly the pillars had derailed their careful plans. How pitiful their crew's attempts looked. All of their clever strategies lay useless and unused because the pillars had struck too fast for them to do anything but react.

She jerked, realizing Jagger had stopped shaking and was focused on her. What had she just said? Ebba scrambled.

"We're the three watchers," she hurried to say as his fingers hovered over the sword. Ebba spoke loudly as the bellowing anarchy on the shaking ship soared. "This is what we're here for. And if ye can't do it, no one can. Yer family on Neos, m'hearty, ye've been there for them always. More than any o' them could've asked, but if there was ever a moment when they truly needed ye, it be now. We all need ye, Jagger. Please, ye have to fight back. Don't let them inside. I love ye too much. I can't bear this to happen again. *Please* take up the sword and fight back." She brought her face within a mere whisper of his, their lips almost touching.

He wrapped his fingers around the sword, and she felt the weight of the blade disappear from her palm. The silver ring in his eyes widened slightly.

Tears stung her eyes, and Ebba choked on a sob working its way up her throat. "Fight, Jagger," she whispered. "This be yer birthright. Like yer father and his afore him. Don't let them trick ye, m'hearty. *Ye* were born for this."

The silver ring thickened again, and Jagger dropped his head.

It was working. Just. There had to be something else she could do.

Ebba peered up and away from Jagger. Verity was sliding down the rigging, Sally in her grip. Now, only the deck remained free of the black sphere. Ebba yelped at the pillar looming ten feet to her right, just outside the bulwark.

The tip of Grubby's cutlass was pointed directly at the pillar's throat, and as the cutlass pierced the border where light met dark, the steel disintegrated to dust. The bulwark began to disintegrate, too, as the black net tightened—the very ship disappearing.

The lips of the closest pillar curved.

They needed more glow. More light to combat the pillars' power. They had to boost Sally somehow, but how that might be achieved was way out of Ebba's know-how.

She glanced at the *purgium* in her belt and then to the *veritas* in Jagger's hand. They were part of the three watchers, and yet there were only two of them here.

And when they all touched. . . .

Shite.

"Caspian," Ebba yelled.

It took two more bellowed roars of his name until he kneeled beside her.

"What?" he panted, eyes everywhere but on her. The *dynami* was in his belt.

No time for questions.

Ebba reached out and gripped his forearm, and then, taint be damned, she stretched out a hand and pressed her fingers to the back of Jagger's hand.

White light exploded, and Ebba closed her eyes, a deep calm encasing her heart and chasing away the bitter soot on her tongue that had already begun to work on her.

She opened her eyes, knowing even as she glanced down at Caspian that he would be gold, that her skin would be bronze, and Jagger's an ethereal silver.

Jagger lifted his head, and Ebba gasped as the black in his irises shattered and dissolved as easily as Grubby's cutlass against the pillars' strength. Only silver remained.

While she and Caspian remained luminescent, the blare of Jagger's silver aura grew brighter and brighter until Ebba's eyes watered from the blinding flare.

She fought the overwhelming urge to shield her eyes while every fiber of her being screamed at her to hold on. The air between the three of them heated, increasing, building. Caspian cried out beside her, and she gritted her teeth. It was like having her eyeball pressed against a flame, and yet Jagger didn't appear affected.

He stood, lifting *veritas* high. Ebba gasped at the silver flames licking the weapon from hilt to tip.

What was happening?

The shine around Jagger surged, and if she'd thought the glow was bright before, now it was all-encompassing.

The silver light detonated.

FIFTEEN

Ebba's stomach dropped into her boots, and she bodily left the deck. The ship was falling again! The sprites, trapped in the sphere of the pillars' power with their crew, couldn't move to the underside of the vessel to slow them. Instead, the sprites zipped underneath the lowest boom to try to temper their rapid descent.

The sprites strained, squeaking frantically.

Without warning, Ebba hit the deck between Caspian and Jagger again as the ship jerked out of its freefall and into a barely controlled drop.

The boom wouldn't take that kind of pressure for long.

Though still gripping Caspian, Ebba had lost contact with Jagger, but the fierce, overwhelming silver shine around the pirate hadn't abated. Squinting through blurry eyes, she saw the same was true of herself and Caspian—though they were nothing in comparison to the radiance pouring out of Jagger.

"He's forcing back the pillars," Caspian called over the rushing wind.

Ebba didn't dare release the grip on his forearm, but she struggled to her feet and saw he was right.

The pillars were on the starboard side of the deck. Everywhere their darkness touched had vanished, the very ship disintegrated to dust.

Her fathers, Verity, and the sprites huddled around the mast. But as Jagger strode past them, the pillars were forced away by his blazing silver light.

The pillars' taint began to recede from the deck, but then a new darkness surrounded them.

The ship rocked and pitched, and the sound of rushing water filled her senses, disorienting her for a few seconds.

"We've entered Charybdis," she shouted at a wide-eyed Caspian.

The sprites were still working overtime ahead. Her crew would have to trust in them to deliver the ship safely to the bottom. There were too many other threats to deal with.

Jagger roared, and she choked in fear as he circled *veritas* high above his head and delivered a ringing blow to the border of where the taint sphere met his blaring beacon of silver.

Five cloaked pillars surrounded them—the shortest of the male immortals several heads taller than Jagger—but all five of the god-like immortals were flung away by the blow. The orb of darkness encasing the ship disappeared for the briefest, tiniest breath, and then the five smoke-shrouded pillars rose in a wall immediately before Jagger, no longer bothering to encase the entire ship.

In unison, the powerful pillars lifted their hands, black pouring out. They focused all of their taint on the silver warrior in their midst.

"*Jagger*," Ebba whispered, her nails digging into Caspian's forearm.

Jagger swung his sword, attacking the taint sphere between him and the pillars in sweeping strokes. He never gained ground, but he was keeping the evil at bay as the sprites guided the ship through the throat of Charybdis as well as they could.

"How close are we to the bottom?" she heard Caspian yell.

Her fathers yelled back, their words lost to the roaring of water, wind, and the hissing song of *veritas*. The shouts came again, and Ebba darted a gaze at her fathers to satiate her worry.

They were at the opposite bulwark, clutching on to whatever they could and pointing over port side.

Caspian dragged her over, and Ebba tripped after him to maintain contact. She stared back at Jagger, who hadn't paused in his swinging strokes. Whatever magic was happening didn't require the pirate to be touching them, but she wasn't willing to let go of Caspian in case that broke the connection.

"What is it?" she asked brusquely. Ebba glanced up at the boom as it gave a mighty *crack*.

That didn't sound good.

"It's help," Caspian said on a sigh.

Help? Ebba *did* look overboard then and reared back as a man catapulted past them, nearly taking off her head with a fierce-looking spear. In the air, the man transformed to a huge, black seal.

It was Kahree, the leader of the selkies.

The selkie barked, and his kin zipped past from beneath, aiming directly for the pillars.

Two pillars split their attention from Jagger to turn their backs to the other three. They resumed pouring their power into the air.

But the selkies weren't alone.

A deep rumble emanated from underneath.

The eye of Charybdis seemed endless; the great funnel they descended through grew increasingly dark. Droplets parted from the outside edges of the whirlpool wall, drenching her. The roar of the churning water bordering the air they dropped through shook her senses apart.

The wind surged, and their ship slowed abruptly.

Ebba's legs buckled underneath her.

Caspian was ripped from her. She rolled, ready to pounce on him and restore contact, but Jagger was still going strong, his silver inferno not dimming in the slightest.

Only her sea-legs saved her from sprawling on the deck when the ship connected with solid ground with a jarring force. Something had slowed their careening fall. Ebba wasn't left guessing who when the Thunderbird soared overhead, spreading his wings wide. He'd used his wind to slow them before they landed.

Were they at the bottom of Charybdis now?

The power of Oblivion now channeled his wings toward the pillars, a funnel of wind visible to the naked eye blasting directly for the dark immortals. The pillars hunched against the gust, and the inner walls of the whirlpool buckled outward from the sheer force. If the gale hadn't been aimed over their ship, Ebba had no doubt she'd be somewhere in the vicinity of Portum.

Ebba edged nearer to Jagger, desperate to help and desperately *aware* this was his battle. Her earlier words, though uttered frantically and instinctively, were true. Jagger had been tainted time and again. Jagger held the most demons of any of them. *Jagger*, whether for himself or because he was the immune, was given the task of keeping the pillars at bay.

He continued his fighting vigil by the disintegrated edge of the deck, and she lingered back by the mast for fear of putting him off.

The beating of the Thunderbird's wings continued, throwing the eye of Charybdis into anarchy. Water poured down onto the deck, and Ebba buckled under the bucketing downpour.

The air crackled, and five bolts of lightning struck the pillars in the chest, the *snap* making Ebba shriek.

Jagger continued swinging, and she glanced back to confirm the source of the lightning.

The Earth Mother had joined the fight.

Ebba smiled grimly and then noted the third immortal with them. That had to be the power of death.

As she watched, the third power lifted his hand, palm-side up, and curled his fingers in a tight fist.

Ebba whipped back to watch the pillars, who'd now doubled over, a shimmering speckle of dots exiting their mouths, drifting to where the power of death held his fist aloft.

Two of the pillars still faced the selkies along with a brown-feathered immortal Ebba couldn't identify. Two more had abandoned the efforts on Jagger to direct their black smoke at the powers. As she watched, one of the pillars attacking the selkies split away to join them.

Jagger was gaining on the black sphere now, but Ebba trusted the pillars about as much as she trusted an injured snake. What happened when he reached the pillars in front of him?

She cupped her hands around her mouth to be heard over the screaming and bellowed shouts. "Jagger!"

But he didn't stop. Ebba left the relative safety of the mast and crossed the gap. She'd just closed her hand around Jagger's belt when all five pillars abandoned their battles and spun inward to meet each other.

Holding hands to create a circle, the pillars stooped as one and then straightened in a burst that sent a shock wave hurtling outward.

Jagger smacked into her, and the wave carried them across to the other side of the deck. Ebba's hip bounced on the oak wood, and she yelped, tumbling twice more before colliding with something far softer.

The shock wave was gone as soon as it had come, and she groaned, hand going to her throbbing hip.

She opened her eyes and stared at the underside of *veritas*' blade. The blade had stabbed into the bulwark *right* above her nose.

"Get off me," came Peg-leg's muffled voice.

"Shite," Jagger said, looming over her. He gripped her arm and pulled her from beneath the sword. Propping his foot against the side of the ship, he yanked free the sword that very possibly could've killed her.

Ebba glanced around as the others got to their feet. The dark sphere had disappeared. The pillars were nowhere in sight. "They fled?"

Jagger craned his head and stared up through the funnel. "For now, aye. They realized they were outnumbered, like Verity was sayin'."

Outnumbered, perhaps, but the pillars had managed to hold them all back. Even against whatever juju Jagger had found and the powers of Oblivion, the pillars had held their own. What if the sixth had been present?

She shook her head and looked up at him, remembering the pillars' attack on him. "Jagger, sharks' teeth, are ye okay?"

He met her gaze, and Ebba gasped.

"What?" he demanded.

"Yer eyes. They're silver even though ye ain't blazin'."

"They are?"

She inhaled. With shaking hands, she clasped both sides of his face.

"They are," she said jubilantly.

His eyes were wide. He dropped *veritas*, letting the blade clang to the ground, and placed his trembling hands atop of hers. The pirate closed his eyes, leaning into her touch. A peal of joyous laughter left her lips before she stepped closer to him and slid her hands free to hug him tight against her.

His hands fell to her shoulders where he gently squeezed before sliding his palms down her arms.

Then Ebba was encircled in his warm embrace. One of his hands was around her back, and the other bunched in her dreadlocks. She couldn't have moved a single inch in his boa-constrictor hold. Then again, she didn't want to.

"What happened to ye?" she mumbled into his chest, letting her hands roam up and down his back. "Ye turned into an inferno back there."

Disbelief colored his voice. "I ain't rightly sure, Viva. Just that when we touched, I looked over at the pillars and sumpin' fierce rose inside o' me. I knew I had to attack them. I just felt it in my gut. As though someone was walking alongside me, telling me exactly what to do."

Like the instinct that warned her not to touch the sixth part? Ebba moved her hands down his back, over his butt, and to his thighs. "Ye think the immune is meant to fight them?"

He squeezed her tighter. "It was as though my body wasn't completely my own. Does that sound crazy? I just knew what to do."

"Nay, not crazy at all," she mumbled against his chest.

"Viva? How long are ye goin' to feel me up for?"

Well, considering they still couldn't kiss yet, she'd planned to continue for a while. Jagger's eyes weren't black any longer, so he wasn't contagious. But the taint could still be spread through blood—and they had no idea if that same concept extended to include saliva. Jagger wouldn't kiss her until every single trace of taint was gone from within him. And only time would rid him of that. She craved his kiss more than anything else in the realm. Resisting the urge to kiss him was borderline excruciating.

Ebba stilled her hands, which had started a return journey. But thinking about it again, she completed another groping sweep of his back and then patted Jagger to let her go. "All done."

His body shook. "Anytime. And just between us, I don't know when I'll be able to kiss ye—be it a week, a month, or a year—but I want ye to know it's all I've thought about for months."

A *year*? She swallowed her panic at that thought. "Aye," she said to him, tucking her dreads behind an ear. "I'm lookin' forward to it too. A lot."

The air between them crackled. For fear of jumping the pirate and accidentally tainting herself, Ebba glanced around.

Locks was helping Verity up.

"Are ye both okay?" she called to them.

"I have no idea how we got through that alive," Locks whispered after a beat, pulling the healer into his arms.

"Sally?" Ebba asked Verity.

The healer pointed over the bulwark to where the sprites were gathered off the ship. The Thunderbird had slowed the ship to land at the bottom of Charybdis. And apparently . . . the base of the whirlpool was a beach . . . of sorts.

"Go check on her," Caspian called to her, averting his eyes. "The others are okay."

She threw him a grateful glance, giving Stubby, Barrels, and Grubby a quick once-over regardless.

Leaping over a drunkenly weaving Pillage, Ebba jumped down from starboard side, which no longer had a bulwark, and landed on the rocks their wrecked ship now rested upon.

She looked around Oblivion for the first time.

The rocks underfoot and dotting the beach were black. Not just any black stone, but the dark stone with the embedded-red hue that had formed Davy Jones' Locker itself. The ankle-deep water was the same vibrant purple as the boiling river in hell, except the water here was cool and fresh. Which was lucky—because she was already standing in it. But for those *teensy* details, the bottom of Charybdis was like any old rocky shore.

Jagger landed beside her, *veritas* back in his belt, and they shared a long look that conveyed concern over the general sameness of the scenery to hell.

A thought for another time.

They waded up onto the black stones, and Ebba broke into a run across the blue-tinged sand toward the whirring flock of sprites.

"Sally," she puffed.

The sprites parted for her, and Ebba located Sally lying prone on the sand in their midst.

"Sal!" Ebba gathered the sprite up. She stared intently at the sprite's chest and turned to Jagger. "I think she's still breathin'."

"She is severely depleted," an age-old voice answered.

Ebba turned to look at the Earth Mother. The sprites scattered, and she couldn't blame them one jot. The Earth Mother still had that swirling-rainbow-eyes thing going on that gave her the willies. It gave her the feeling like one thousand people were looking out at her instead of one.

"Her magic be depleted?" Ebba rushed.

The Earth Mother nodded.

She sighed. When they'd first met the power of creation, her literal nature hadn't been so apparent. Probably because their crew knew nothing then.

"Will Sally recover? In health and in magic?" she pressed the power.

"Of course," replied the Earth Mother, a frown creasing the space between her brows.

Jagger stepped forward. "Papatuanuku," he said, bowing slightly.

"You know my true name, child of my children," the Earth Mother noted, her frown easing.

"I was raised by your original children," he said.

The Earth Mother smiled. Flowers bloomed at her feet.

Ebba squinted at the metallic petals and added that to the general weirdness of the scenery along with the blue-tinged sand. "Is there anythin' I can do to help Sal heal?" she asked.

"Yes."

Jagger glanced at Ebba's mounting scowl, and asked, "What can we do to help Sally heal?"

"I can help her heal, but her magic will only be restored with time and rest."

Already, Ebba had the notion the powers of Oblivion might drive her up the wall.

She gently transferred the sprite queen to the Earth Mother's hand and turned back to look at the ship. A low whistle left her lips.

Sink her. She really hadn't noticed how torn-up their vessel was.

Great gaping holes dotted the sides from where planks had torn away. When that happened, Ebba couldn't say. A lucky thing they hadn't landed in more water down here. Drowning after fighting the pillars would've been shite.

The selkies were transforming in the shallows and wading up onto the beach. Ebba's eyes landed on several unmoving naked forms being carried between them.

The sprites had reconvened farther down the beach, and a row of tiny bodies had been lined up—also unmoving.

The Daedalion who'd flown her most of the way here from the Dynami Sea had been swallowed by the pillars' taint, saving her life. Was he still alive?

Stubby and Peg-leg strode toward them, and Ebba ran to her fathers, flinging herself first at the cook, who groaned but quickly returned her hug, squeezing her close.

"We were gettin' the princesses, Marigold, and the others onto the Daedalion to leave, like we'd planned. Caspian yelled that ye were overboard. I thought we'd lost ye. We all raced over, but the pillars' power separated ye from us. Jagger lost it. Medusa was attackin' us. So we got Sally and Verity up to the crow's nest to fight back. Ye were just suspended in the air below us for a full five minutes, surrounded by black. It was terrible," the cook whispered.

Five minutes. It only felt like thirty seconds at the time. "It didn't feel that long," she admitted. "I thought I was fallin' to the sea."

He let go, and she gripped Stubby's hand.

"If ye hadn't have used the *purgium* on him, I can't think o' what might've happened." Stubby shuddered.

She hugged him. "But it didn't happen. Ye got to me. Thank ye, Stubs."

He dipped his head in a curt nod, clearing his throat.

Ebba would never tell them how only one second of distraction had saved her life. They didn't need to know how close the end had been. *She* didn't want to know how close it had been.

"What do ye think happened to the sixth pillar? He just disappeared."

A thud sounded to her left. She peered across to see the power of death had landed there. The Thunderbird joined them in short measure, the ground reverberating with his landing. Jagger and the Earth Mother completed their group.

They were in the Oblivion. They'd really made it.

Ebba accepted Sally back from the Earth Mother. The sprite's color seemed a little better. She tucked Sal under her jerkin against her heart, hoping that doing so didn't degrade the queen in front of her people. Everyone needed comfort sometimes. Including royalty.

"You touched Pravitus with the *purgium*," the power of death stated. "We watched you do it."

"If that be one o' the pillars, aye. Does that mean he's dead?" she replied, holding her breath.

"The taint is inherent to the pillars. They do not need to be healed of it, but the *purgium* cannot understand that they should want to keep the sickness inside. When the root of magic is whole, that urge is regulated by the other parts, but separated like this, the *purgium*'s confusion cannot be tamed." The power of death observed her and her fathers. "You greatly weakened the pillars with your act."

She should've known better. "I did?"

"They are a hive mind, assembler. To hurt one is to hurt the others."

That seemed like a weakness she should keep tucked away for a rainy day. Actually, it seemed a lot like the weakness between her and her fathers. When one of them was hurt, she hurt.

"I am Mortem," he said, dipping his head. The power of death turned to Jagger. "The immune is here. I see the bearer. Tell me, have you brought all six parts of the root of magic with you?"

Peg-leg pushed forward. "Aye, the others are just gettin' them. We were told we'd have to come here to weld them together."

"Not that the three o' ye were any help gettin' the parts together or givin' us any guidance on what to be doin'," Ebba withered.

"That the root must be assembled here is common knowledge," Mortem replied, his eyes narrowing.

Caspian stepped up beside Jagger. "No, it isn't. Mortal history makes no mention of magic or immortals. And the Earth Mother and Thunderbird both knew of our ignorance. We barely got here alive. The three of you could have left Oblivion to help us fight just now. Instead, you waited until we were inside before lifting a finger. You could have just saved the lives of selkies and sprites, but you stayed hidden in here. Why did you not help us or your kind?"

Everyone stared at Caspian, who was breathing hard, jaw clenching.

"I agree," Ebba stated. "If the realm was lost to the pillars, it would've been yer faults, not ours, because ye didn't lift a soddin' finger until we were right in front o' ye."

Lightning struck the rocks at their backs. "I checked in every so often to see how you were going," the Earth Mother said. "When my powers were fully restored, I saw that we would eventually meet here."

That. . . . Ebba couldn't even put words to the anger she felt at that.

Luckily, Caspian appeared to have been holding things in for a long, long time. "*You knew we'd eventually meet here,*" he whispered. "I lost my arm. I lost my father and my kingdom. The entire realm is probably tainted right now, immortals and mortals alike, and you're telling me you saw we'd get here and had better things to do than beating the greatest evil to have ever existed." Caspian drew himself up and unleashed a string of words that even had Stubby wincing.

"Tell them how ye feel, lad," Peg-leg said, nodding in approval.

He wasn't done. Caspian turned to the Thunderbird. "You almost killed us—*us*—the realm's only chance to survive, because Jagger killed a handful of birds. Are you *insane*?"

The Thunderbird's rainbow eyes flashed. His great wings, formed of pearly feathers, were tucked tightly against his body. "I wasn't testing you. I pushed you toward where I knew the next piece to be—in Medusa's lair."

"You nearly killed us," Jagger said. "If not for Sally combating your wind, none of us would be here."

Mortem grimaced. "He gets carried away sometimes. We all do."

Ebba inhaled sharply. "Ye're blamin' the fact ye can't control yer nature for almost destroyin' this realm and everyone in it?"

The Thunderbird snapped his beak an inch from her face.

"No, you don't get to be angry," Caspian said firmly. "You get to listen. The Earth Mother and Mortem totally neglected us, but you went one step further. You could have ruined all hope with a single beat of your wings. And while we're at it, your system of sorting good and bad souls is completely subjective."

Ebba's brows shot into her hairline.

"I *do* agree with the last point," the Earth Mother put in.

"And me, king?" Mortem said lazily. "What have you to say to me?"

Caspian turned on him. "Where were you? Are you scared of the pillars? Is that it?"

"Yes," replied the power of death. "Entirely. To leave the Oblivion would be to risk capture and the draining of our powers. What use would we be then?"

"The three o' ye could've united as ye did today?" Peg-leg shot at them.

"Today," Mortem stressed the word, "the immune was here to help. Today, the six parts of the weapon and the three watchers and the assembler's soul links were in our midst. Today, the risk was worthy of being risked. You forget, king, that we are responsible for the immortal realm too. Right now, the pillars do not dare attack us, but if they managed to drain a single one of us, they would have the strength to break our defenses. Most of magical kind have fled here for refuge."

"But they wouldn't have had to flee if ye'd done sumpin'," Ebba countered.

Mortem's skin crackled, but she crossed her arms, holding her ground. Verity's skin used to do crazy things, too. Ebba wasn't afraid of skin tricks.

"You forget that one of us can see all future paths, assembler," he said. "Plus, I have kept close track of you since you attained the *dynami*. I even deposited a map of the Dynami Sea in Barrels' office for your crew. I erased all of the islands from it that weren't safe to go to."

Did Mortem just purr when he said, 'Barrels' office'? And that explained why none of the islands they'd gone to had been on their map.

Caspian stared mutinously at the power of death.

A thought occurred to her. Ebba asked, "Doesn't it bother ye that everythin' ye've made is now tainted?" she asked the Earth Mother.

The immortal woman appeared baffled. "Creation is my job. Not death. Though I admit I carry a soft spot for my original children's longevity."

The Thunderbird grumbled, and Ebba gasped at the pain under her ribs from the sound. Sink her, she forgot the Thunderbird's little trick. Whenever he spoke, it was to a person's soul.

Mortem quirked a brow. "And they are not really dead, just without will. So out of my jurisdiction."

Just without will? They had absolutely no idea—absolutely none.

Heat crept up Ebba's neck, and she inhaled deeply, sharing a look with the others. This was a whirlpool conversation, and she wasn't willing to go around and around. They'd come here for a reason.

Jagger took one look at her face and spoke. "We've come here to assemble the root o' magic. After what we've been through to save the realm, we'd like to get it done as soon as poss'ble."

She seconded that.

Weariness piled upon her now that the immediate danger was gone. The thought of entering into another fight with the pillars so soon was exhausting. There seemed to be so many impossible things to do before that could happen.

"Of course," the Earth Mother said, gesturing up the blue-tinged beach. "We have many things to discuss."

Why did getting here alive suddenly feel like the least of their troubles?

SIXTEEN

The powers of Oblivion had led their crew from the blue beach and through a long tunnel. Charybdis was no longer visible in their current location, which the powers had referred to as *the landing*. The landing was a flat, sprawling space consisting entirely of open-ceilinged ruins.

With the energy of the recent battle pumping through her body, Ebba had been ready to assemble the root of magic then and there. But the powers had insisted otherwise, assuring them the pillars couldn't enter the landing and that there was much to talk about prior to taking the next step.

The powers had ushered each of them off to bathe and eat.

She might have been angry at the time, but a long soak in a bath amongst the rustic ruins of this place had her feeling almost mortal again. Being clean felt better than a cool breeze under a beating sun.

The water she sat in was purple like that on the other side of the tunnel. And the water she'd drank earlier had been the same. It *tasted* like normal water. . . .

The open-ceilinged ruins of the landing were built right up to the bank of what appeared to be a sea or lake. The fiery black stones she recognized from Davy Jones' Locker separated the ruins from the water's edge in a thick band. Unlike the bath she sat in and the beach they'd just left, the water on the other side of the black rocks wasn't purple but the brilliant hue of a red apple. The bright red stretched out as far as the eye could see.

Ebba had no idea why it was a different color, but Davy Jones' had the same fiery stone and a boiling purple stream. Should she be worried about the similarities?

Ebba submerged herself once more in the sun-warmed bath—thankfully, the sun here was the same yellow color she'd always known—and clambered out of the large pool. Verity had joined her but washed and quickly disappeared through the ruins to find Locks. Hopefully tea didn't exist down here because the thought of wandering through the ruins only to find an energetic tea party going on would be the last thread on a very worn rope.

Clean and with a full belly of rainbow fruit and star-shaped nuts that tasted like chicken, Ebba was ready to face the next hurdle: How to put together the six parts to form the root of magic. Stubby was looking after the chest, and really, she wanted to sleep, but the thought of Matey and the mermaid-like Jendu and the Capricorn out there watching as the tainted water surrounded them spurred her onward.

A woman with one huge violet eye and about the height of a desk had whisked away Ebba's discarded clothes and left fresh garments.

Ebba picked up the bronze dress. The material was thick. The sleeves were wide. It kind of looked like a robe. She untied the cord, which acted as a fastening, and slid one arm in and then the next before securing it tightly. The neckline of the dress was a deep V. The bottom hem fell to just below her knees.

"Comfy," she decided, patting her front.

Ebba didn't bother with the matching bronze sandals and set off through the dilapidated mud-brick ruins to find the others. Heading back the way the one-eyed woman brought her seemed a good place to start.

She hadn't passed through many tumbled ruins before she heard Barrels' baritone.

"The others haven't made it down the funnel yet," he was saying. "The Daedalion were meant to hang back and then bring them straight down."

Stubby answered, "They'll wait until it be safe. The pillars could still be lurkin'. Or their cronies."

Ebba passed underneath a mud-brick archway covered in black, glittering wisteria.

She scanned the large open space on the other side. Everyone was gathered, barring Locks and Verity. The flooring was uneven brick, and large cushions were scattered through the room under the naked sky.

The others hadn't noticed her arrival.

"I can have someone put on watch for your family and the Daedalion," Mortem purred.

Ebba stopped in her tracks. Had he just purred again? She located the power of death on one of the cushions . . . hugging Barrels close.

Her father sat ramrod straight in the power's embrace, eyes beseeching her other fathers to intervene. He should know better.

Ebba shoved aside that development and focused on what Mortem had actually said. The temptation was to slap away the power's offer of help, seeing as she guessed his offer was born of guilt for barely lifting a finger otherwise. But they needed the assistance of the three immortals in the near future, and they had to at least play nice until the pillars were gone. The thing was, Ebba didn't trust the immortals to do anything properly. What if the Daedalions with Barrels' family members bolted for Charybdis and were attacked? Would Mortem's lackeys help them?

"Thank ye," Stubby replied smoothly. "We accept. We'll also ask a few o' our sprite friends to stand vigil with yer people."

Ebba held back a grin. Problem solved.

Grubby smiled at Barrels. "Sendin' yer kin off was the right thing to do, matey. We had a big X painted on us like ye said afore."

"Easy to say when your entire family isn't out there." Barrels stiffened as Mortem nuzzled his neck.

After a beat, Locks turned to Mortem. "Ye're sure there ain't no way the pillars can get in here? We're exhausted, aye, but if it be between sleepin' and winnin', I'd rather we win."

"I assure you," the power of death said, the same purr rattling his words, "the pillars are not yet strong enough to pierce our defenses. If they do become powerful enough, I will feel it—as will the Thunderbird and Papatuanuku. Even if the pillars reach such strength, they are unlikely to risk such a move against the immortal realm. The source of their power is in the mortal world. By entering this place, they would not only have an immortal army to face but would be at their weakest. So again, I assure you, they will not enter the landing."

"All right, all right," Locks said. "I just don't want to be caught with my slops down."

"I understand, mortal," the power replied calmly. "But assembling the weapon is not as easy as you might think. Going into it hungry and deprived of sleep is not a good idea. Believe me, I have lived to see the process many times."

With that, the power of death nuzzled into Barrels' neck again.

A wheezing laugh escaped Peg-leg. Ebba tore her eyes from the power of death to survey him. Peg-leg's eyes watered fiercely.

"Ebba," Grubby said in a high-pitched voice, spotting where she still lurked in the archway.

Her fathers and Caspian called out greetings.

One person didn't greet her, but the heat of his gaze on her from across the room was all Ebba could feel.

"Mortem here was tellin' us afore that *cats* be his way of keepin' track o' the mortal realm," Peg-leg continued, coughing and thumping his chest. "Seems he was usin' Pillage to watch us for months."

Her eyes rounded, and she looked back at Mortem wrapped around Barrels.

"Pillage is so fond o' Barrels an' all." Peg-leg stuffed a fist in his mouth as Mortem purred again, rubbing his face against her eldest father's shoulder.

Stubby's shoulders began shaking, and he erupted into hoots as Barrels glared at him.

"That's why Sally took Pillage away," Jagger said over the noise.

Ebba had avoided returning his gaze until now. She couldn't even say why she was avoiding the contact; except that the desire to touch him was so strong she felt like she couldn't. Like doing so would mean too much for her to feel in the midst of their quest.

And that was ridiculous. Ebba met his gaze across the open-ceilinged chamber. The red water was still visible to the left, but she thought they had to be somewhere near the tunnel they'd passed through when leaving the bottom of Charybdis. Honestly, the uniformity of the sprawling ruins made it hard to tell.

"Sal took Pillage away so Mortem couldn't spy on us?" she answered. Or the queen sprite just wanted a noble steed.

Mortem lifted his head from Barrels' shoulder. "If I'd known you were all condemned to hell, I certainly would have come to collect you."

Easy to say now that they were here.

"How is Sally?" she asked everyone, venturing away from the archway.

Caspian appeared mostly asleep where he reclined. He shifted off the edge of one of the scattered cushions so she could squeeze in between him and Grubby.

"She's still sleeping. Verity said it will be days, if not a couple of weeks, until she wakes, but that she will in time," Caspian mumbled.

Ebba nodded. "We'd be goners if not for her."

"I don't know, Mistress Pirate. That was some quick thinking of yours on the ship. Made me regret not doing the same when the Satyr had us captive. Surely their taint wouldn't have been able to penetrate our glow either."

Aye. "Well, we had to go to Davy's anyway to get the sixth part."

She hastened to change the subject, realizing they were edging in on dangerous Plank territory.

The Thunderbird and the Earth Mother were absent, so she turned to the power of death. "Mortem, I don't s'pose any other mortals made it down here?"

The power detached himself from Barrels and picked up Pillage, whom Ebba hadn't noticed was curled around Mortem's feet.

"Any mortal free of the taint is welcome," he answered, then frowned. "But none ever seem to come here."

Beside her, Caspian muttered under his breath. Ebba couldn't hear his exact words, but she could guess what they were by the tone. No mortals were here because the only reasonably safe refuge from the taint was situated down the middle of a whirlpool. No mortal would survive the fall. Her crew only did because they'd had sprites and the Thunderbird to slow the descent of their ship. 'Detached' would be the word she'd use for the immortals. At least the powers. Detached. And frustrating. Highly frustrating. She supposed they *were* locked away for a long time.

"Ye only let people free o' the taint down here?" Jagger asked, standing quickly. "I apologize. I thought because my eyes ain't black and I wasn't cont'gious any longer, I'd be okay. I'll go out and wait on the beach and—"

Mortem studied him. "There's no need, immune. We can sense the taint, and none of you bear it."

Ebba's mouth dried. She straightened.

"What?" Jagger asked, clear silver gaze on the power of death. "*None at all?*"

Though Jagger was obviously no longer contagious, Ebba had assumed they'd have to wait weeks to ensure the rest was gone. Or that the pirate would've forced her to wait that long at least, just like in Davy Jones'. He had the notion that anything to do with blood and saliva could still spread the taint—which, considering Cannon had spread the taint to her fathers by blood, wasn't so far-fetched.

When they'd embraced earlier on the ship, she'd believed they still couldn't kiss.

"None," Mortem stated. "Not a speck."

Jagger tore his eyes from the power and slowly turned to face Ebba. She found herself standing in a daze, a desperate urgency building within her.

"Ye're sure," Jagger asked one more time. The strain in his body and voice was evident.

Mortem blinked. "I'm not sure how else to phrase it, mortal. *Yes*."

Ebba stepped toward him, stumbling over a cushion because she couldn't take her eyes off Jagger for a single instant.

"There ain't no way ye're gettin' out o' it now," she whispered to him.

His growled reply sent shivers skittering down her spine. "Had to be sure, Viva. Once I start, I ain't stoppin'."

"Stoppin' what?" Grubby asked.

Peg-leg shouted. "Cover yer eyes!"

Ebba and Jagger ran for each other, covering the ten feet between them in a matter of seconds that were so desperate they were almost painful. His face was determined, and he moved with the predatory grace she'd seen in him from the first moment she laid eyes on him. So much darkness. So much hardship. And yet, now he was here, and she was here with him, and once she was in his arms, everything would be okay because right now, deep in the blackened, charred remnants of her heart, Ebba could feel the searing rightness of love again. It was no teenage fling; no childish notion of attraction mistaken for love. What lay between them was no mere mortal love because whether they knew it or not, they'd circled each other from the moment they met, not as lovers—as equals. As sparring partners who had to fight and test the limits before they could trust and respect each other. And if they died, still their love would circle around and around, going beyond what mortal standards dictated into the land of the dead.

Ebba knew all of that before kissing the man she loved.

She quickly covered the last of the agonizing distance separating them and, breath catching, she threw herself into Jagger's arms. He caught her, not managing to arrest both of their movement. They stumbled together, hardly put off by the notion of falling as their hands found purchase on the other. His silver eyes were wide, his breath coming as fast as hers as Ebba searched his gaze right back.

His hands roamed, seeking the same desperate grip hers did.

She found it first. One hand against his chest, she lifted her other hand to the back of his neck and pulled Jagger's head down. He needed no encouragement. His hand splayed against the side of her head, his thumb resting on her jaw as he covered her mouth with his.

Hot air, warm lips, *right*. Home was what she felt as their lips touched for the first time.

Jagger groaned deep, his other hand slipping down to hold her firm against him. She crushed her lips against his, enduring the bruising pressure as a simple acknowledgement that they wanted to be closer to one another than these bodies would allow them. Ebba twisted to free her other arm, complaining when Jagger mistook her struggle and loosened his grip.

Part of her expected him to smirk at the sound she'd made, but he didn't.

She wrapped both of her hands around his neck, and her fingers quickly seized the opportunity to explore his shoulder-length flaxen hair. He broke off from her lips to press kisses down her jaw as she wound her fingers through his hair. Tears stung her eyes, and the breath choked in her throat as she marveled at the *feel* of him.

Jagger froze at the sound and pulled back. Not enough to make her hunt him down again. Or for him to hunt her down. Ebba wasn't sure who'd been hunting whom from the start, really.

She'd tried to kill him twice, so she was the best hunter.

Tears balanced on her lashes as they looked into each other's eyes.

"I know, Viva," he hushed in a low voice that rumbled through her.

She sighed at the sound. "I just never thought we'd get here."

He pulled her in and rested his head atop of hers. "Ae, *toku wairua.* Aye. But we be here now."

Ebba blinked, and her tears were dislodged as they swayed together. "What does that mean?"

"My soul."

"Toe-koo why-roo-ah," she tried, snorting as he winced. "Sounds better when ye say it. I'll just stick to 'I love ye, Licks'."

He tightened his arms around her to the point of pain. "I love ye, too."

She planted a soft kiss on his tattoos. Finally.

He groaned again. "That settles it, then; I'll never let ye go. Kissin' ye defied my best daydreams."

She laughed against his cheek, inhaling his rope and sea salt smell. "Been daydreamin' a lot, have ye?"

"Ye have no idea," he whispered in her ear. "But I'd be happy to tell ye o' them when this war be done."

They continued swaying together, and slowly, as though waking up from a golden nap, awareness of their surroundings crept over her.

Her fathers' presence wouldn't make her pull away from Jagger. Nothing could. By now, it should be clear to her parents that Jagger was here to stay. Just as it should be clear to Jagger her fathers would always be part of her life. But they were uncharacteristically silent.

"Jagger?"

"Mmm?" His hands moved up and down her back, and she took that to mean that hands moving were fair game. She slowly worked her hands down his front, over his firm stomach to the area above his trousers.

"Viva?" he asked, amusement coloring his voice.

"Hmm?"

"Ye were about to ask me a question."

Ebba moved her hands around his sides and worked up his back, feeling the firmness of his muscles and spine. "Aye, I was."

His lips moved against her temple. She knew his smirk wouldn't be far away.

"The question was. . . ," she stalled, then remembered. "When did everyone leave?"

Jagger's smirked. "Never seen yer fathers move so fast."

Ebba moaned, burying her face in his chest mostly because it seemed a good excuse to be there.

"The others? No idea," he said. "I got distracted after that."

"Oh, aye?"

He put his lips against her ear. "Aye."

She forced a serious expression into place. Pulling back, she regarded him. "Would ye like to be distracted again?"

His smile faded, his silver eyes burning with the same roaring fire lit within her chest. "I tol' ye once we started, I was never stoppin', *toku wairua.*"

Ebba's heart stuttered as he lowered his lips to hers.

SEVENTEEN

"Excuse me, Lady Assembler." The one-eyed immortal from the bathing area shuffled through the archway.

Ebba paused in the act of stroking Jagger's hair. They were back on the cushions, his head on her lap. The entire concept of them being able to touch felt so foreign and temporary that she was in a state of semi-shock.

"Aye?" she replied, trying to focus on the woman's single eye. Ebba wouldn't have said she usually focused on both of a person's eyes, but focusing on just one was messing with her skull.

"Your fathers would like to inquire as to whether you are . . . still drinking tea."

Heat flooded her cheeks. She hadn't drunk any tea!

Jagger sniggered and shifted on her lap. She glared down at him, daring him to say anything.

"Where are they?"

"Outside, Lady Assembler."

She stilled. "How long?"

"An hour."

Ebba flinched, yanking hard on Jagger's hair.

He reached up and freed his flaxen locks from her fingers and sat up, grinning far too broadly for her temper's liking.

"Tell them we just finished," he told the servant.

"Nay," Ebba hissed. She called to the woman, "Not that. Tell them we've just . . . we have . . . that we ain't busy no more. No wait! Tell them they can come in."

The woman shuffled off, and Jagger snaked an arm around Ebba's shoulders. She stiffened, her eyes on the archway that might fill with her horrified fathers at any second.

"Ye ain't ashamed o' me are ye, Viva?" Jagger asked. "Ye're blushin' sumpin' fierce." He stroked her cheek with the back of his hand, tracing the heat down her neck. Or causing it.

Ebba glanced at him then back to the door. "I ain't ashamed o' ye, but I can't say the thought o' touchin' and feelin' around my fathers floats my boat."

". . . Does stickin' yer tongue down my throat count as touchin' and feelin', *toku wairua*? Because they already saw that."

She rolled her eyes. "They didn't see anythin'."

"They did."

"Aye, I know. But they *didn't see any o' it.* Just watch."

Grubby stumbled through the archway. He glanced back over his shoulder and tried to leave, but several arms shot out and shoved him back through.

Verity entered through the archway, shaking her head. "It's fine," she called back.

The rest of Ebba's fathers burst in. Their eyes sought her, and Ebba forced herself to remain still in Jagger's embrace.

"—Did you get the numbers tallied—"

"—Find what ye were lookin' for?—"

"—Couldn't find ye anywhere—"

Ebba slid a look at the silver-eyed pirate beside her. His lips trembled before he pressed them together.

"Are ye sure ye wish to be a part o' all this?" she asked softly.

"They'll keep life entertainin', that be for sure."

Her fathers resumed their seats in the open-ceilinged chamber, and a heavy tension fell upon their gathering. Each one of them was peering up to the sky.

"The numbers and all o' the other stuff be done," Ebba announced.

Her fathers leaped on the comment, turning to talk to each other more enthusiastically than she'd ever seen.

A win; she'd take that over them killing Jagger.

The Earth Mother and Mortem entered either side of Caspian.

Ebba winced, recalling her friend was present during the kiss-to-end-all-kisses. Sink her, how had he taken it?

Caspian took a cushion about as far away from her as possible and didn't meet her gaze. *Bad.*

She jumped at a vibrating boom from behind. The Thunderbird landed—upsetting more of the ruins. Mud bricks toppled, scattering across the stone ground.

"We're all tired," Caspian announced. "We've agreed to tackle the task of putting the weapon together after we rest, but the powers of Oblivion have agreed to sit down and answer our questions."

They were resting first? Ebba supposed that was decided while she was exploring Jagger's body for pirate treasure.

Mortem shot a hooded look at Barrels but took a seat opposite him, saying, "It occurred to us that the trinity believe we've been remiss in aiding the Exosian realm."

"Mortals always need to know why, why, why? Life already knows what's in store for you; just experience it," the Earth Mother interjected with a sniff.

Mortem cut her a stern look. "We'd like to mend bridges between mortals and immortals. If the pillars are to be thwarted, both races need to unite."

"Let's start there," Jagger said. "Why do ye refer to us sometimes as the three watchers and sometimes as the trinity?"

Mortem arched a brow at the Earth Mother, who huffed.

"They were really annoying," she shot at him. Turning to the rest of them, she said, "Your proper name is the trinity. When I took my turn ruling the Exosian realm, the trinity who regulated my rule were overbearing to say the least. So many questions."

Caspian's face smoothed. "So you changed the name?"

"I did a little shifting, yes. I altered the name in mortal history to the three watchers. Gave the trinity more of a supervising role. Two generations later and success. Much less bothersome."

Mortem's skin crackled with black energy. "It used to be that the watchers guarded the assembled root, which was only used in dire need. After the change from the term trinity to the three watchers, the ruler held the root at all times. *Your* actions were what locked us all away the first time," he snapped at the power of creation.

"*Do not* start with me," the Earth Mother warned, her deep voice echoing through the ruins, and her eyes swirled dangerously. "None of us saw what the pillars would become. You agreed to let them rule as surely as I did. *You* were the one to link their minds together."

Mortem's mouth snapped shut.

She guessed that Sal's archives had only mentioned the trinity because they were immortal books. Yet even the sprite queen had referred to them as the three watchers the entire time. Ebba was inclined to agree with Mortem over the Earth Mother's actions. Who knew if the pillars would have caused the same destruction if the root o' magic hadn't been in their immediate grasp.

Caspian straightened. "The pillars weren't always bad?"

The ruins shook as the Thunderbird circled in front of them, pearly wings tucked against his body. He spoke. "The three of us took turns ruling for a millennium here and there, but the responsibility is a large one. When a group of immortals approached us after one of Papatuanuku's reigns and mentioned a council, we all decided that such an idea should be tested. If it didn't work, what was the harm? Four of the six immortals on the council had been our underlings since before the Exosian realm even existed. We knew them well. The other two came after—one full-blooded immortal and a half-immortal."

"One o' the pillars was half-human?" Ebba asked, ignoring the uncomfortable sensation the Thunderbird's voice always gave her.

"Yes," the Thunderbird answered. "You came into close contact with him—Pravitus."

That *thing* was once someone like Verity? She couldn't correlate the two images.

"I want to know how this all began," Peg-leg said. "How are there immortals and magic and a root of magic to start with?"

The Thunderbird exchanged a look with the other two. "*Our* realm, the Oblivion, is magic to its core and is much older than your world. The root of magic only came into existence when Mortem and the Earth Mother created the Exosian realm."

"A fight," Locks said, clearly recalling the words Sally read from the archives.

Mortem colored. "Is that what they're calling it?"

The Earth Mother smirked. "The creation was strong that night."

Ebba glanced between them. *Oh. Ohhhh.*

"Just a one-time thing," the power of creation said flippantly.

The Thunderbird shuddered. "We believe, knowing that immortals would not otherwise be able to exist in the new realm because it did not contain a magic core, the root o' magic came into existence."

"Where does magic come from?" Jagger asked.

"Even our scholars do not know the answer to that question, immune. Some theorize that the two largest volcanoes in the Oblivion exploded, and the resulting collusion of the magical lava created the three of us. From there, Papatuanuku got busy."

Ebba glanced around the ruins, absorbing the unusual palette of colors anew. "So, we're in the Oblivion right now?"

The shaking of Mortem's head surprised her.

"Immortals cannot exist in the mortal realm without the root of magic. Once on red water, you are officially in the Oblivion, but where we sit, where the water is purple from mixing with the blue of your realm, we are still where paths meet. That is why we call this location the landing. It is trinity tradition to only go this far with the root, so immortals in the Exosian realm are not dragged back to Oblivion against their will."

Her eyes rounded. Shite, she hadn't considered that. It was one thing if immortals were dragged back. Another thing entirely if the immortals were tainted and dragged back. None of them wanted that.

Pillage butted Barrels' thigh, and her father scooped up the black cat. Across from her father, Mortem purred then thumped his chest, a faint gray blush covering his cheekbones.

"What I want to know is where it went wrong," Barrels said. Then, he shook his head, clearly realizing who he was talking to. "I mean to ask, when and why did the pillars turn evil?"

The powers of Oblivion fixed their eyes on him.

Barrels fidgeted. "It's obvious?"

"The root of magic corrupts mortal flesh," Verity answered.

The Earth Mother pouted. "You were my favorite. I really wish the pillars hadn't drained your powers." She brightened. "I'd be willing to re-instate them if you wish?"

Locks blanched, and Verity quirked a brow at him.

"I thank you. But no," she told the power of creation. "I am on a different path now."

The Earth Mother's eyes flashed, and lightning struck red water in the distance.

"Prior to the Pillars of Six, a mortal had never held the root for a long period of time. The trinity would guard the weapon, yes, but only to assemble and dissemble it. In later years, the root was passed directly into our hands. So until the pillars we didn't know that the root of magic corrupted mortal flesh."

"Pravitus is half-mortal," Ebba whispered.

Mortem nodded. "Over several thousand years, the root of magic corrupted the Pillars of Six through Pravitus," Mortem said. "Even then, the taint took them slowly because of their immortal nature. We believe that the mental link I forged between the six was their undoing."

Jagger fixed the power of death with a flat look. "Thousands of years and ye didn't notice anythin' was amiss."

The power blew out a breath. "The three of us enjoyed the reprieve in ruling. The council system worked so well for so long that, in part, we saw what we wished to see. The trinity did not seek our aid, which had always been the way. Of course, they were succumbing to the taint as well. There was no safety net if the trinity failed to alert us."

Ebba had always wondered how the pillars were so completely evil. They thirsted for power and to dominate the world, but Ebba had struggled to understand their mindless depravity. She'd never met a mortal or immortal who wasn't gray. Some were light gray, some were dark gray, but no one was pure white—everyone made mistakes. The opposite was also true, in her experience. No one was solely black. Everyone possessed some grain of good within them. The fact that the pillars were solely black had given them an almost fabled presence in her mind.

But from what the powers and Verity had said. . . . "So ye're sayin' the pillars weren't bad aforehand? They were corrupted by the root itself?"

"Correct," Mortem said. "It twisted their bodies and minds into darkness, leaving them with only one objective—"

"Power." Ebba finished for him.

He nodded.

She shook her head. "Even if they'd wished to stop when they realized what was happenin', the nature o' their taint would've made that impo'sible." The taint couldn't be controlled. It spread unchecked.

She almost felt sorry for the pillars. Had they felt remorse back then? Had they panicked upon realizing the root had slowly corrupted them and turned them against mortal and immortalkind? Ebba could only imagine the horror of discovering her power was to steal people's will with no possible way of containing it.

Except, if she discovered *that*, Ebba would choose death to protect her loved ones. The pillars hadn't. Or maybe they'd been too far gone by then.

"The council's taint began after three thousand years or so, and as the trinity had the most contact with the pillars, they were the first to succumb," the Thunderbird clarified.

The Earth Mother nodded. "We sensed when the taint entered the realm, and the three of us left for the mainland to confront the council. They were ready for us, and we barely escaped with our lives. But we did manage to save the children of the bearer and the immune—the hereditary lines of the trinity. They were yet to be tainted. We removed them to an island in the Dynami Sea to mature into adults."

"What island?" Ebba butted in.

The power of creation started. "Uh . . . I shaped it like a sun and threw in some inland rock pools containing acid-water." She grinned. "I was drunk when I made it. Good night."

"Ye mean Medusa's lair?" Ebba replied, jaw dropping.

The Earth Mother hummed, eyes squinting. "In later years. Correct."

"It was Medusa who eventually found the bearer and immune on behalf of the pillars, remember?" Mortem asked the Earth Mother. "We had to keep moving them after that. We had no understanding of the pillars or their taint. We didn't know how their darkness spread. The pillars were still six separate entities then, and their taint had spread slowly over hundreds of years, not like your experience with them in this age. The taint didn't spread to the islands neighboring Exosia until the second millennia of their rule. We thought we had time. The immune and bearer of the generation took fifteen years to mature enough to fight, and we located an assembler. We thought we had a handle on just how the pillars' taint worked and how to avoid it ourselves, but just before we attacked, things took a turn for the worse: The pillars merged their souls and minds into one."

A hive mind. They knew that part.

Mortem sighed. "Their powers were amplified exponentially by the act. One never attempted before by immortalkind. I still remember first feeling it."

The other two powers hummed in agreement.

"So the taint spread quick-like after that," Jagger said in the quiet wake. "And ye found yerself in a position like we are now?"

The powers dipped their heads.

Mortem spoke. "Immortals and mortal-immortal mixes began to succumb. Something that hadn't previously happened. It became clear that if the pillars' power was more than that of an immortal's magic, they could trap the immortal or half-immortal and slowly drain them. Each day, the pillars' power amplified, slowly choking the realm. We were scrambling to understand the changes. Then, hell broke open—the balance of dark outweighing light. Immortals fled here. Many mortals fled here, too. Magic and non-magic co-existed in that time. Despite not understanding many elements of the pillars' powers and how it was affecting the Exosian realm, we had to attack. . . . We failed five times to defeat the pillars. Each of our efforts was delayed by the aging time for the bearer and immune in those days." He cast a look at Jagger and Caspian. "I'm afraid it wasn't the most secure job. Your ancestors were raised knowing they were likely for the slaughter. But on our sixth attempt, through learning what we'd done wrong prior, and through no small amount of luck, that particular trinity were successful. The pillars were finally defeated."

The Thunderbird interjected. "The first two times we just sent them out there. In hindsight, that was always going to fail."

"Then we sent our immortal underlings with them instead of going ourselves," the Earth Mother admitted.

Why wasn't that any surprise?

Mortem's skin crackled. "Attacking the pillars on their grounds turned out to be the wrong move. They were most powerful there. But we drew them away on the fifth. Best to get them where they don't have many friends, too. That's how the last one failed."

"And the sixth time?" Caspian asked. "What happened then?"

Ebba leaned forward, studying the powers. "Do they have a

weakness we should know about? Or was there a trick that won the day?"

"Some edge?" Jagger added.

Each one of the powers of Oblivion shook their heads.

The Thunderbird tilted his head. "Our job was to hold off the pillars' army. We were not there when the trinity conquered the pillars. And they never made mention of what was done."

"They did keep a record, though," Mortem said. "All trinities did."

"A record that disappeared with the rest of immortality seven hundred and sixty-nine years ago, I'm guessing, like all other mortal traces of magical history." Caspian tipped his head and released a long exhale.

"This is likely," the power of death agreed.

Ebba mulled over what they'd said. To have massive gaps in their knowledge filled in was one noggin' ache over, but did any of this really help them? There was no manual to how their trinity powers worked. Or there was, but it had disappeared with all trace of immortals. They'd only discovered Jagger's sword lit up in the presence of the pillars by accident. And that the three of them glowed when they touched was discovered by accident, too.

What else could the trinity do that they had no idea about? There wasn't time to find out, and that worried Ebba greatly.

She chewed on her lip, releasing it to ask, "Jagger's sword lights up, and he can attack the pillars' taint with it. What else do ye know that we can do?"

"Very little, I'm afraid," the Earth Mother said. "The trinity were the regulators of immortal rule. Their workings were secret because knowledge of their power could be taken advantage of by immortals. Everything we know about them has to do with the assembling of the weapon—because that was a ceremonial event."

Peg-leg grumbled, "That be something at least."

She murmured her agreement.

"I keep rounding back to this, but if you knew so much after the last war against them, why didn't you stop the pillars as soon as your powers were restored?" Caspian asked.

The Earth Mother's eyes flashed. "Our powers were restored mere weeks before the pillars regained their shadow forms. We immediately sent out messengers to the immortals who'd re-entered the realm, bidding them to return. We set to fortifying the Oblivion's defenses against the taint next. They were significantly depleted after the crumbling of the wall. That necessitates a constant source of power. The Thunderbird was occupied with putting as many mostly good souls into his vessels as possible to keep hell from bursting free once more, buying us more time. Mortem was delaying death to help the Thunderbird."

"*Subjective Thunderbird*," whispered Caspian.

The Thunderbird straightened and snapped, "What did you say, mortal king?"

Barrels gripped Caspian's arm tight. They all knew he had problems with the Thunderbird's sorting system. They all did. In Ebba's eyes, Caspian's father had deserved to be cast to Davy Jones', but she couldn't blame her friend for feeling otherwise. She'd feel the same to learn that Plank was there.

"Our problems are not your problems, king bearer," Mortem boomed, obsidian glass coating his skin before it cracked and disappeared to dust. "We had our own people and realm to safeguard first. The pillars merged as one entity are *much* more powerful than the pillars we initially knew. Thousands of years ago, there was time to make plans. As it was, the pillars had a fifty-year head start on us this time. The trinity is a power of its own and has always been. The root of magic was your problem to bear. And even then, on behalf of the others, I kept track of your progress. Do not judge us until you have ruled yourself."

So they hadn't been completely incompetent. But if Ebba had their power, she would've done a lot bloody more to help out. The Exosian realm ranked too far down the immortals' priority list. Perhaps caring for their own realm was on an even par with obeying the call of their nature, but the mortal realm was firmly beneath both.

Jagger caught her gaze, his mouth grim. They glanced at Caspian, who was clenching his jaw. Perhaps there was a good reason the trinity had kept autonomy over the root of magic. Ebba didn't think the immortals truly meant to neglect the realm they'd accidentally created, but nevertheless, they had. And continued to. Understanding how best to work with the three powers would take time—and a patience level that Ebba didn't possess.

"What were ye doin' all this time then?" Grubby asked the Earth Mother. "Nothin'?"

Lightning struck the water closer to shore, and Stubby whacked her selkie father.

"I was exploring the pathways of the future," she answered. "To see if there was another assembler. . . ." The Earth Mother trailed off with a hasty glance at Ebba.

"Just what are ye sayin' about our daughter?" Peg-leg asked, rising.

The Earth Mother arched a brow, and his arms were snapped to his sides. His legs were bent, and he promptly sat again.

"Nay offense meant," he puffed.

The power of creation flicked a finger, and he relaxed.

"How do you mortals say, 'It is not a personal thing,'" she answered. "I never liked your path for one simple reason."

Dread unfurled through Ebba. A dread she'd managed to force down for an entire day.

"For the weapon to be assembled, nine must be present. One to protect." Her eyes shot to Jagger. "One to bear," she said, glancing at Caspian. "Six to strengthen and one to assemble." Her eyes ran over the rest of them, landing on Ebba.

"You do not have nine," the Earth Mother stated.

No they didn't. *Plank was gone.*

Jagger gripped her hand as the burning started behind her eyes, and a wave of thick cold coated her insides.

"I can taste her grief," Mortem whispered.

In a shattering and dusting of glass, he was crouched by her side. He hovered his hands over her, and goose bumps erupted on her skin underneath. His skin crackled, and he shuddered, eyes fixed on her arm. Apparently the power of death had a thing for grief.

Good for him, she had plenty to spare. *Take it all.*

"As much as I'm tempted to take your offering, assembler, we feel grief for a reason, just as we feel anger or joy or fear. Grief tells our heart it once loved and that the love was real." Mortem spoke low.

A tear dripped over her cheek, and her reply was hoarse. "Too real."

"The truest loves are."

The eyes of her fathers were on her. Ebba closed hers, better to hide away from the sorrow and knowledge held there. Jagger's hand squeezed hers again, and her mind latched on to that as an anchor. His presence was like a handhold on a sheer cliff. Without him, she would fall and fall.

Emotion made Stubby's voice husky. "So what do we do about only havin' eight? Back on Pleo, ye said there was still a chance. And ye're actin' awful calm-like if that chance already be gone."

"That *is* one question," the Earth Mother said, her tone off. "I have a question for the assembler, though. With one of your soul links gone, how are you still alive?"

EIGHTEEN

The Earth Mother's question was enough to convince Ebba to open her eyes.

"What do ye mean, 'how is she still alive?'" Locks asked. He shared a glance with Verity.

The power observed him dispassionately. "The assemblers are always so, so—"

"Weak," Mortem supplied.

She hummed. "I was going to say annoying and complicated."

Jagger bit out. "She's sittin' right here."

All three powers looked at him, baffled.

"I am standing right here?" the Thunderbird answered after a beat.

A wrinkle appeared between Mortem's brows. "Are we announcing our position?"

Ebba muttered under her breath. "Don't bother, Jagger." She raised her voice. "Why am I weak, annoyin', and compl'cated?"

"Not *you* as such," the great bird said. "Your kind. To assemble the root, you must possess more mortality than the average human. Having an immortal assembler would be the logical answer . . . except the trinity must be mortal to balance the presence of immortalkind. For an assembler to become more mortal so they can complete their tasks, they forge soul links to six other humans, taking some of their mortality. That comes at a price, however. If any of the soul links are killed, the assembler dies."

The powers studied Ebba.

"Usually," the Thunderbird amended. "And they do tend to die a lot. That is why many sets of assemblers exist at one time and why that role isn't hereditary. The root o' magic recognized the precariousness of such a position."

Jagger had frozen beside Ebba.

Stubby turned to the Earth Mother. "When ye spoke o' the knights of such-and-such and the sisters of wherever, that's what ye meant? Any o' the assemblers and their links could've turned up to the Pleo cave at that time?"

The power dipped her head. "If their paths were chosen by the root. Which they were not."

Ebba studied her fingers. She contained more mortality than others and yet felt so, *so* much less than those around her. "How do we figure out how I'm still alive?"

"I'm going to pull some of my power from our defenses," the power of creation told Mortem and the Thunderbird. "Just for a second."

"If you must," the Thunderbird said tightly.

Jagger leaned forward in front of Ebba. "Look for what?"

The Earth Mother ignored him, peering at Ebba's chest in a way that took her right back to Pleo.

"Ahh," she said, straightening. "Well, that makes perfect sense."

"Get back in; the defenses are crumbling," Mortem said, jaw clenched.

The Earth Mother blinked, and the other two powers sagged soon after. Keeping the taint from the Oblivion really *did* appear to be sapping all of their strength. . . .

"The assembler has created another soul link to replace the sixth.

That is how she still lives," she announced, jerking her head at Jagger. "This man is your lover?"

Ugh. "Nay, he be . . . uh, he's—"

"Aye, I be her lover," Jagger announced, leaning back to wrap an arm around her again. "All the lover she needs."

Flaming. Sod.

"Not at the rate ye're goin'," she hissed in his ear.

Ebba didn't need to face him after. She knew the smirk was there.

"Unfortunate that he's the immune," Mortem said, studying them. "He could have acted as the replacement even though the bond you share is not magical."

And there they were. Back to how she couldn't assemble the weapon without Plank.

At least Ebba had an explanation for the emptiness within her. That answer made the pain a scant bit better to carry. She hadn't made up or dramatized her grief after Plank's . . . death. She hadn't been weak and overreacted. Ebba had felt as if she was dying because she nearly did. Her body had taken the matter into its own hands, ready to perish once the sixth link was gone.

If not for Jagger. . . .

She sucked in a breath and turned to him. He reached for her, drawing her in against his chest.

Caspian's eyes flittered to them and away. "There are other things we've noticed with Ebba's connection to her fathers. She almost seemed to have taken on a trait from each of them. Is that normal?"

The Earth Mother shook her head. "No. But her soul was injured when I first met her. I didn't have the power to look closer back then, but there were several cracks in her soul at the time."

"How many?" Jagger asked.

"Six. One for each father."

Caspian stared around the group. "We were right. That's why she couldn't hold multiple parts until each of you were healed by the *purgium.*"

The Earth Mother smiled at him faintly. "Yes, king bearer. Quite right. I'm pleased to see that most of the cracks are now healed."

"Just the one left?" Stubby asked.

The power nodded. "I've never seen an assembler with tainted links, but I'm assuming when the soul bonds were forged, the taint upset the exchange. She needed part of your souls to make her an assembler, but your souls were partially claimed. So she simply took some of your bad into herself—a vice from each—just as you described it, king bearer."

Ebba blinked, trying to think back through her childhood to identify all of her faults. Except, she'd always been that way. Sure, *now* she could see how she'd changed. And how suddenly.

The Earth Mother said. "For your lover's sake, I'm glad there was a reason for your vices and that they are now gone."

Ebba frowned at the power of creation. "I guess I didn't feel like all o' the changes in me were an overnight thing." The confirmation of Caspian's theory bothered her a little because she had changed so much from the girl who navigated *Felicity* through the Siren's nest.

"We carry the wisdom we are born with through life," Mortem stated.

She stared at the power of death. "What now?"

His lips twitched. "When your fathers were healed of the taint, your natural wisdom was reinstated. We do not get wiser in life, Lady assembler. *Knowledge and experience*, however, we never stop collecting. Your growth in those areas has nothing to do with the healed soul links. Those changes were all you."

Caspian straightened, expression stricken. "I didn't mean to belittle you, Ebba. You've changed during this as much as all of us. I was only referring to the instant changes. They're a small piece of who you are overall."

The knot in her chest loosened at their words. She fixed her friend with a small smile. "Ye'd never seek to belittle anyone, I'm knowin' that. Thank ye both."

"That be enough for one night," Jagger announced. "I don't doubt there be more to hear, but we've got a lot to think on afore tomorrow comes."

"Aye," Peg-leg said. "I ain't sure I can keep my eyes open a second longer. And one o' my legs has gone dead."

Ebba groaned with the others.

"Te'rible joke," Locks said. "Never, ever gets better."

Peg-leg cackled to himself, waking Grubby, who'd fallen fast asleep. She envied her selkie father. As tired as her body was, her skull pulsed with information and revelations.

Mortem shot to his feet. "Intruders," he stated.

The Thunderbird immediately spread his pearly wings and took to the air. The Earth Mother blinked into existence beside Mortem, and they held hands.

"The pillars?" Barrels asked, glancing over his shoulder. His face was ashen, and Ebba realized she'd completely forgotten about their friends on the Daedalion.

Mortem relaxed. "No. Not the pillars. The Daedalion have arrived."

"Thank the realm for that," Barrels said, his shoulders sagging. "I'm going back through the tunnel to meet them on the beach."

Her father disappeared in a rush, clearly more oriented in this place than she was to know where the tunnel was situated.

Ebba dragged herself upright, preparing to join him and ensure the others were okay.

"Nay, lass," Stubby said. "We've got this. I'll bet a manta ray that tomorrow'll be a tryin' one for ye. Best get some rest." He looked pointedly at where the one-eyed servant had appeared.

She hugged him tight around the middle. "Are ye sure, Stubs?"

"Right sure, lass. Get off with ye."

He pulled back and bumped her chin up with his hand before trailing after Caspian and the others.

The powers were long gone. Only Verity remained.

"Could I have a word, Ebba-Viva?" she asked.

Whenever people over thirty asked for 'a word,' it was bound to be about something uncomfortable. And more than one word.

Jagger dropped a kiss on her forehead. "I'll wait outside the archway."

The significance of his comment smacked her between the eyes. He expected her to sleep in the same place as him? Her jaw dropped. Now she thought of it, that was exactly what she'd expected too.

Was that weird? They'd slept in neighboring hammocks before.

Her gut twisted. Aye, it was different all right. His body would be against hers. Sprites erupted in her innards, zipping around. Well, call her a headless sea captain, maybe her body wasn't that tired after all.

Verity stared after Jagger, ignoring the servant.

"Your fathers asked me to talk to you," the healer said, folding her arms. "Though why this should be my job, I have no idea. Bloody cowards, the lot of them. If I didn't know they'd screw things up, I wouldn't be here. As it is, I'm tired, so I'd prefer to make this snappy."

Verity didn't mince words. That was why Ebba liked her so much. But she'd definitely spouted more than one word already.

"Firstly, we asked the powers more about how Jagger healed. When he lit up like he did on the ship, that is called the Immune's Cascade and it's triggered by the pillars' presence when the three of you touch. It's a way to protect yourselves until the root is assembled."

Ebba absorbed that. "Good to know." That hadn't been so bad. . . .

"Secondly, if you need me to mix up some herbs to ward off pregnancy, just let me know. Your fathers said they'd talked with you about sexual intercourse when in hell, but they wanted to make sure you knew how to protect yourself."

And there it was.

Her fathers hadn't spoken to her about sex! They'd just mentioned the words 'sexual intercourse.' They'd been much more focused on steering her away from Jagger entirely. And thank small mercies for that. Having the conversation with Verity was bad enough.

"Pregnancy?" she asked weakly. "Little Jaggers?"

"Little Jagger-Ebbas," Verity said, pursing her lips. "And let's not talk about how babies come from pelicans."

Ebba shut her mouth with a click of teeth. Well, okay then. There went her pelican decoy idea. "Thank ye kindly," she managed. "But I won't be . . . drinkin' tea with Jagger anytime soon. I'd have to see how the notion sat with me first."

"Your tribe-pirate-female identity?" the healer asked, her face poker-straight.

"Aye," Ebba said seriously. In truth, she'd been so occupied with touching Jagger and then kissing him for weeks. She planned to enjoy doing just that. Plus, she didn't want to take advantage of him. He was in a vulnerable place, and Ebba had to treat him right. Aye, they could die within the week, but what they had was perfect just like it was.

As much as her eyes had been opened in recent months, the youthful parts of her still clung to the threads of her childhood. If Ebba hadn't been forced to grow up by this pillars business, she might not have for years. But she had, and that involved contemplating things ahead of time. Not to say the new parts of herself she'd explored weren't good in themselves, but the thought of exploring her femininity was the most recent of her self-realizations. That was territory that had to be explored with Jagger.

Slowly.

"I have a notion that Jagger wouldn't be happy with bein' a mistress," Ebba finally decided. "I'd have to make a mostly honest pirate out o' him first or he'd kick off. But there ain't no rush to anythin' serious, Verity. That ain't in my mind, and ye can tell my fathers just that if it'll calm their seas. Bein' with Jagger is enough." She couldn't imagine that changing anytime soon.

A wide smile spread over the healer's face. Her periwinkle blue eyes crinkled at the edges. "I hear you, Ebba-Viva Fairisles. And if you do decide to take Jagger as your mistress, you know where I am. For those herbs. Unless you want children."

Ebba screwed up her face and spat to the side.

Verity snorted. "That's what I thought." She turned away, throwing her arms in the air. "Men."

Ebba watched the ex-soothsayer go, grinning to herself. Then she winced at what Verity would soon be saying to her fathers. Best not to think about it.

She faced the servant, who still waited in the same spot. The short, stout woman didn't show any reaction to what she'd just overheard.

That was Ebba's kind of person.

Jagger was leaning against the other side of the archway, *much* closer than what she'd expected. Ebba glanced back to where she and Verity had just spoken.

"Did ye hear anythin'?" she asked.

"The stuff about me bein' yer mistress?" he asked, then burst out laughing.

She whacked him and, face burning, asked the servant to lead the way.

Jagger laughed all the way through the ruins, his whoops shooting through the crumbling brick columns and half-walls they weaved between.

"I'm glad someone be laughin' when the end o' the realm be nigh," she snapped back at him.

He snagged her around the waist. "Don't be emba'rassed, *toku wairua.* I'd be a mistress for ye."

She stopped. "Really?" That could work.

"A man sayin' he be the mistress o' a pirate woman? Aye, no skin off my back."

He *would* flip that on its head to be a compliment to himself. "Ye've no shortage o' ego, Jagger."

"Aye, and neither do ye."

She chuckled. "Can't argue with that. A full sail is a happy sail."

The servant stopped beside an archway and gestured them inside.

They traipsed through the wisteria-draped entrance into the chamber. Like the bath chamber she'd been in earlier, this room had no ceiling and only two and a half of its walls. A low bed built up on bricks was the only feature of the room.

"Guess the immortals don't spend much time at the landing," she said to the servant.

. . . who was gone.

"Right," Ebba said, staring at the bed. "It ain't no hammock, but it be a sight more than the rocks we've slept on."

She climbed onto the bed and crawled into the middle. Heaving onto her side with a grunt, she tucked both hands under her face and closed her eyes. Luckily the dress was comfortable. Stripping off to sleep with Jagger was a sight more than she was comfortable doing. Ebba wondered what he'd think of her body. Was he as eager to see hers as she was to see his?

And where was he?

She cracked open an eyelid and caught him staring at her. "What're ye lurkin' at the edge like a creep for?" A yawn assaulted her, and she broke off to give it the proper attention.

He still hadn't moved. Jagger's eyes roamed over her frame and face.

Ah. She sat up. "Don't be afraid, Jagger. I won't touch ye. Ye're safe with me, all o' that mistress talk aside. Until ye're ready, I won't lay a single finger on ye. And if it be marriage that ye want first, I can't say I'd want it immediate-like, but we're already fastened at the soul, so I haven't got any strong obj'ctions *after thirty*. I know ye well enough to see bein' with ye most times won't cramp my style." Ebba trailed off as Jagger doubled over. "What're ye laughin' at now?" She smacked the bed, anger bubbling within her.

Still laughing, he straightened and set *veritas* beside the bed. He drew off his wide-sleeved tunic. The tunic was a match for her dress except his outfit was two pieces, the trousers tied off to one side like her dress.

Ebba stared at the expanse of exposed golden flesh.

"That be a whole lot 'o Jagger," she whispered, wetting her lips.

His laughter faded to intermittent chuckles as the pirate crawled toward her over the bed. She bounced with his movements, entirely focused on the way her heartbeat and body heat had just ramped up to seventeen knots.

Jagger lay on his side facing her. "For the record, those moss-green eyes o' yers struck me in the gut the first time I saw ye."

"And when was that?"

"I first saw ye when yer fathers brought me aboard, but I'd heard the *Malice* crew talkin' o' ye."

She blew out a breath. "The fish-lips thing."

"Aye, they may've said that to yer face. But it were common knowledge that ye had lips for kissin'. The only pirate female, Viva. And guarded by six fathers. Forbidden and rare. An enigma for any young man. Then I saw ye, and ye outdid all o' the songs about ye."

She groaned. "Songs?"

"Aye. Songs."

Ebba didn't want to know. Her skull rum caught on the word 'enigma' instead. That's how she'd always seen Jagger, too.

Jagger's smile faded. "O' course, then ye opened yer mouth and ruined my fantasy."

Ebba narrowed her eyes and snorted as he slid a mischievous look her way. "I thought ye were strong and myst'rious when I first saw ye," she admitted, half rolling onto her back. "Sad. Connivin'. Sullen."

It was his turn to snort.

"Ye were tainted," she said, rolling back to face him.

His eyes lifted quickly.

"What were ye lookin' at?" Ebba asked. She glanced down, and her jaw dropped. "My chest."

He waggled his brows, and laughter burst from her lips.

"Best turn yer back to me to sleep, Viva," Jagger said eventually.

"Why? Ain't my fault woman parts disturb ye. Says more about ye than it does o' me."

"I grant ye that, but all the same, I'd like some sleep tonight, and it'll be bad enough knowin' ye're in the bed."

She grumbled as she worked around onto her other side. "Fine. But only because staring at yer muscles makes my stomach do funny things."

Ebba yawned again as his arm slipped around her waist, drawing her back against him.

"Night, Jagger."

"Goodnight, *toku wairua*."

My soul.

Ebba smiled, forcing down the full feeling within her that wanted to exit her mouth as a squeal—pirates didn't squeal—and closed her eyes.

NINETEEN

Ebba lifted both hands to rub her face. Then, lifting her arms overhead, she arched backward in the stretch to end all stretches, pointing her tiptoes in juddering bliss.

"And it still won't go," someone whispered.

Her eyes flew open, and she dropped her arms down, staring up at Jagger. Ebba's heart thundered in her chest, now totally awake. "I forgot ye were here."

His silver eyes were molten. "I didn't have the same luck." His hot gaze dropped to her chest.

Glancing down, Ebba saw the V neckline of her dress had loosened in the night. A lot. The side-tie was the culprit.

"I like the ease o' this dress," she told him. "But it be fallin' off too easy for my liking."

Jagger bunched an arm beneath his head and rested there, staring at her chest. "All night, I waited for the tie to go. And it just wouldn't."

"Ye were awake all night?" She reached for the tie, sliding him a glance.

His eyes were red-rimmed. "Oh, aye, Viva. Sleep was always unlikely with ye in the bed next to me."

Heat swirled low in her gut. Ebba leaned up and kissed him. When Jagger moaned and returned the kiss, she pulled away.

His gaze dropped again, and she whacked him.

"Do that again," he whispered. "I think it's goin'."

Ebba snorted. Tightening the fastening again, she said, "Ye could've retied it durin' the night instead o' watchin' me."

He grinned, showing every one of his teeth. "But I'm a pirate."

Holding his gaze, she looped the ends of the tie into a firm double knot. "Aye, Jagger. As am I, so don't be lookin' anywhere ye oughtn't, or ye'll find yerself at the pointy end o' a cutlass."

Jagger's flaxen hair swung forward. "Aye? And what cutlass be that? Far as I can tell, I have the only weapon in the room." He tilted his head to where *veritas* gleamed on top of his tunic.

He was a true pirate.

She'd never make the mistake of treating him as a landlubber.

Ebba pushed him onto his back and straddled him in one fluid movement. She bent down, her dreadlocks shifting forward in a rattling curtain. "But why are we talkin' o' all this? Seems like we'll have to join the others soon, and ye're wastin' time. Is that what ye be, Jagger? A time-waster?"

He freed the arm beneath his head and trailed his fingertips over the beads in her hair.

"I put them back in for ye," she told him, suddenly serious.

"I know," he replied. "That's when I began to breathe again."

Closing the gap to kiss him, Ebba waited until he'd shut his eyes and then recalled her plan to dive for *veritas* and turn the blade on him.

Sod it.

Ebba met him, pressing her lips against his. They both smiled, but the joy of kissing Jagger quickly faded into something that felt huge, larger than life or death. The love she felt for him was desperate.

Jagger pulled back and stroked her cheek. "I'll never get enough o' ye."

She sucked in a breath. Apparently breathing was optional when kissing. "I know what ye mean."

A beat passed.

"Would ye like to get the sword now, Viva?"

Scowling, she bounced off the bed and swiped up *veritas*. Ebba studied it in the dregs of dawn and whistled. "What does it mean that there be great cracks all through the blade?"

"My thought exact-like," Jagger answered, sitting up on the edge of the bed. "I didn't want to worry anyone last night. We were all exhausted-like."

She sat next to him.

"Shouldn't *veritas* be able to handle a run-in against the pillars?" she said slowly.

"Ye think the pillars know sumpin' we don't?" he asked.

Clearly Jagger did.

Ebba ran her eyes from the tip down the length of the blade to the hilt, worry churning within her at the chips, dents, and scratches covering the blade.

"They've always known more than us," she granted him. "Mayhaps *veritas* is only so much use by itself—without the other parts."

"Surely the sword has been used against their powers afore, though. Shouldn't it have shown some wear when we first found it?"

There was no 'we' about that, but she wouldn't be petty. She turned the blade over in her hands, studying the hilt. Were the pillars now stronger than before? Jagger was right. The heroes who took the pillars down surely used the sword against them at some point. But until now, *veritas* had always been a faultless weapon.

A large crack where the hilt met the hand guard snagged her attention. Ebba brought *veritas* closer, squinting through the tiny gap.

She froze.

"What is it?"

"Uh," she stuttered, lowering the sword to look at Jagger.

He took the weapon from her and studied the crack intently. He, too, lowered the sword, returning her stare.

"Did ye see a swirly sumpin' movin' under the surface just now?" The gap was small, so she wanted to be sure.

Jagger nodded. "Shite. Does that mean. . . ? What does that mean?"

They both peered at the sword resting on their laps. Now that she knew, Ebba almost wanted to laugh at how much she'd dwelled on this particular part of the puzzle.

"The sword ain't *veritas*, m'hearty," she said, her voice tight with excitement. "It's just the casin'. *Veritas* be concealed in the hilt."

Jagger studied the gap again, and his jaw dropped. "It is." Laughter choked in his throat. "We have to tell the others."

Pausing only to allow Jagger time to shrug on his tunic, they sprinted back through the ruins, only losing their way three times before bursting into the room from last night.

Only two of her fathers were awake—Stubby and Grubby.

"Ye'll never guess what," she puffed, slowing to a walk.

She studied their drawn faces. Her elation plummeted into dread with icy suddenness.

"What is it?" she demanded. "Who died?"

Grubby's eyes welled up. "Barrels' kin didn't all come back. Some o' the Daedalion made it in, but not the others."

Ebba glanced from him to Stubby.

"All true, lass. Three o' the children and their parents were taken by some o' the pillars' immortal lackeys as we fought the pillars. The remainin' Daedalion waited half a day after to come down," Stubby said.

"Are Caspian's sisters okay?" she said, stomach twisting.

"Aye. Shaken up and scared, but they'll recover."

Jagger paced. "Ye don't know any more than that?"

"Nay, lad. But if I were the pillars, I'd be keepin' the kin o' my enemy real close-like."

Shite. So would she.

"They be hostages," Jagger said flatly, sitting heavily on a cushion.

Grubby nodded.

If the pillars had taken the five landlubbers, they'd all be tainted by now. Easily. Ebba wouldn't wish that fate on her worst enemy. The children were already demons, but the taint was a horror none should ever experience. There had to be countless children already tainted. To know such darkness existed in the world was hard for *adults* to comprehend.

"We'll get them back," she and Jagger chorused.

"Aye," Stubby said, his lips flattening into a thin line. "That we will."

"Is Barrels okay?" she asked, adding, "And the others."

"Holdin' up," he answered. "Marigold and the other parents be distraught. Peg-leg and Locks be with them, tryin' to convince Marigold she should wait for the root o' magic afore she storms the castle gates."

Ebba grimaced. Woe to any person silly enough to be on the other side of those gates. Marigold was not a woman to be trifled with.

"Then what we've found will help," Jagger said, holding up *veritas*.

"The part be concealed in the hilt," Ebba blurted. She grinned at Jagger's glare. "Gotta be quick around here."

"Ye're kiddin'," Stubby said. "All this time? Bring it here. I want to see, but I ain't sure my body can move after the last few months."

Ebba took the sword from Jagger, passing it to her fathers.

A breath later, Stubby sighed. "And I'm too blind to see through that crack. Grubs?"

"Sumpin' swirly in there, no doubt," her selkie father announced.

"How do we get it out, though?" Jagger asked. "It took the pillars' combined power to damage the blade that much."

"That's easy," Mortem whispered.

The four of them yelped and turned to where the power of death had appeared.

"What do ye mean, it's easy?" Jagger replied, the first to recover. His face slackened. "Ye knew the part was in here."

"Of course." The power beamed.

Of . . . course. Ebba closed her eyes so the immortal didn't see them rolling.

"We need to assemble the weapon as soon as we can and save Barrels' horde o' lubbers," Stubby said, squinting at *veritas* again.

Mortem paused. "And the realm."

Stubby started. "Huh? Oh aye, aye. The realm and all the other lubbers."

Beside her, Jagger snorted.

"I'll go get everyone," she said. Nerves punched her in the gut. "No time like the present to save the world."

Jagger caught at her hand. "But we still haven't discovered how ye'll manage to pick up the sixth part. Ye're linked to me, too, but me bein' the immune renders that useless."

Mortem tapped his bottom lip. "Immune, your powers ensure that the root can be protected until it is assembled, but aside from protection, you have no role in the actual assembly of the root. My fellow powers and I are *hoping* that with your added mortality, the assembler can handle the sixth piece."

Ebba regarded him. "I couldn't pick it up a week ago, and Jagger was there."

"The immune was tainted then."

True. And it was all they had to go on. Ebba glanced around the large brick chamber. "All right then. I'll bring the others back here."

Jagger turned to look at her. She avoided meeting his eyes, knowing he'd never be in favor of anything that risked her life.

Mortem laughed lightly. "Dear, dear assembler, you think that we would carry out the ceremony amidst cushions and ruins?"

Seemed okay to discuss saving the realm here.

. . . "Nay?" she answered.

He arched a brow. "Follow me."

EVERYONE, barring the three powers, the trinity, and Ebba's fathers were told to remain behind in the ruins. Naturally, Marigold and Verity had refused to obey, so only the princesses and Barrels' other kin had stayed back at the ruins.

The rest of them had walked for at least fifteen minutes through the ruins and then entered onto a bridge that spanned across an expansive swamp of purple water and orange reeds. It was the prettiest swamp she'd ever seen. And the strangest.

Ebba guessed from the color of the water that they were still somewhere in the landing. And the absence of tainted immortals raining down on their heads probably indicated the same. Magical beings were only dragged back to their home realm if the root parts were taken *into* the Oblivion.

The path roamed over the marshy expanse until those ahead—the Earth Mother, Mortem, Verity and Locks—descended out of view.

Speeding up, Ebba found the bridge ended in a set of narrow wooden stairs leading directly down.

"An amph'theater," Locks called, already making his way down the narrow steps.

Ebba's jaw dropped as she gazed at the stadium. The stairs alone would take five minutes to navigate to the bottom.

Tiered wooden seats extended from the tiny stage below all the way up to the top of the stairs. The area was circular, *huge*, and inlaid in the marsh.

Purple water poured over the tops of the stadium, disappearing through magical means into non-existence before reaching the top-tier seating.

"Wow," Ebba said, duly impressed. "What game did ye hold here?"

The Earth Mother glanced back. "This was made for the assembly of the root."

Her eyes widened. What? But there were thousands of seats.

"People watched?"

"Oh yes. From the farthest corners of the Oblivion. The lower castes of both realms would save for years in readiness for an announcement the root was being constructed or deconstructed."

Jagger grumbled behind her. "Nice to know it was just play for ye all."

Ebba agreed with him. This was life and death for so many people, and the powers just made everything sound like a game. Perhaps to beings as powerful as them, it was.

"You mistake me, immune," the power of creation said, lightning striking the area off to the far right. "In millennia gone by, there was no danger associated with the root of magic. The pillars were the first to abuse the honor. The ceremony was an exciting time for both realms. The festivities spanned an entire week: games, duels, displays —it brought mortals and immortals together. Those centuries were filled with joy."

Okay . . . that did sound fun.

Ebba continued down the narrow and steep stairs, half of her already set on the problem of getting all of her fathers back up again. Reaching the bottom, she inspected the circular floor, which was much larger than it appeared from high above.

In the middle of the circle was a marble stage.

"Ah," Mortem said, smiling widely. "Many good memories in this spot."

The Earth Mother winked at him. "Let me know if you're ever interested in creating another realm."

Caspian stared at the ground, rings beneath his eyes. He'd stayed up all night with his sisters and Marigold's terrified family. He wrinkled his nose. "This was where Exosia was created?"

Mortem nodded. "The root must be assembled where the root first came into being. A good way to commemorate the dawning of your world, no?"

That wasn't the first thought that came to mind. No one answered the power.

Caspian joined Ebba and Jagger, standing to her left.

"So how does this work?" he asked once the Thunderbird landed.

The Earth Mother pointed to the stage. "In the past, the trinity would go up there. And the six links formed a circle around the stage. They each have a wedge to stand in. See?"

Ebba glanced behind her and saw what the immortal meant. Time had worn away the detail, but she could still see the grooves separating the circle into six wedges.

"The soul links stand at the outer edges of the circle," Mortem said.

"Here?" Stubby asked, moving to the very outside of the wedge to where a circular carving disturbed the otherwise smooth, marble surface.

The Earth Mother dipped her head.

"The trinity touch once everyone is in place," the Thunderbird said. "And then the immune stands back on the edge of the platform above and the bearer would move in and out collecting each piece."

That sounded like a whole heap of simple.

"Too good to be true," she chorused with Stubby.

Barrels strode up to the platform, inspecting it. "What happens if Ebba can't put the weapon together? Not being able to touch the sixth part."

Mortem hummed. "I've never seen the root mostly constructed and then deconstructed. The process takes a lot out of the assembler. . . ."

"How much?" Jagger cut in.

Verity threw a smirk her way and Ebba grimaced.

"All of her mortality, of course."

Time screeched to a halt.

"Hold yer seahorses," Ebba croaked. "Are ye sayin' I *die*?"

The Thunderbird tilted its head. "Just for a few moments. The assembly of the weapon takes your mortality and the borrowed mortality from your soul links, if you recall."

She recalled that fine. But there hadn't been any mention of dying. Until this point, all she'd wanted to do was find some excuse to be away from the pain of losing Plank. And yet now, with Jagger's help, she'd seen that there was so much more to live for. The pain of losing Plank was still unspeakable, unfathomable—a void within her that was both real and magical and something she'd never heal from. Living would be hard, but that was what she wanted now.

"The bearer used to put his hand on the assembler's chest after and bring her back from death," Mortem said, shuddering. "I hate that feeling. Someone dies, and then they're taken away from me just as quickly." The power shuddered again.

"If assembling and disassembling the root requires all of Ebba's mortality, how will she survive deconstructing the weapon again if she can't handle more than five of the parts at once?" Barrels asked.

The powers shared a long, baffled look.

"I should suppose that she wouldn't," the Earth Mother said, shrugging. "As Mortem said, the trinity only ever did one or the other."

"I don't like it," Jagger exploded. "It be bad enough that she could die if any one o' us is killed at any time. She isn't walkin' into certain death as well."

Grubby announced, "Nothin' be worth Ebba's life."

Except there were many things worth her life. And most of them were standing around her. "Only one way to go. Hop'fully the link with Jagger'll be enough for me to manage. It's got to be done, mateys." If only her palms weren't slick with sweat at the thought of being drained of mortality until she died and was *maybe* revived.

Her fathers folded their arms, one after the other. Marigold was next, then Verity, and finally Jagger.

"It's my choice," she insisted.

"And were we landlubbers, we'd listen," Locks said.

"I know my children and grandchildren are in danger, but the answer to that doesn't lie in killing yourself," Marigold said softly.

Ebba disagreed. "We have to head further into danger if we wish to get out."

"Whatever else you lack, assembler, courage you have in remarkable amounts," Mortem said.

"She took courage from all six of her fathers," the Earth Mother said to him in an aside.

That stole her fathers' attention.

"She did?" Grubby asked.

The Earth Mother dipped her head. "Whatever happened when the cracks in her soul from your tainted bonds were healed, she decided to keep a little something."

Stubby's cheeks pinkened. He puffed out his chest. "Well, wouldn't expect nothin' less. She be a pirate."

Caspian frowned at the chest Peg-leg had carted down. "Is that why *fortudo* never affected her?"

The bravery part? True, she'd never experienced the same feeling that her friend did when touching it.

"Interesting," the Thunderbird stated.

Caspian faced her, grabbing her hand. "Are you sure about this, Mistress Pirate? If you don't wish to do this, none of us will blame you."

The lives of his sisters depended on this, too, though. "I'd blame myself," she answered.

He held her gaze, and she saw the same quality she'd always seen in Caspian. Understanding. Dropping her hand, he turned to the powers.

"Okay," he said, exhaling. "I need more details on how to bring her back."

"More?" the Thunderbird said, blinking his huge eyes. "You hold the root o' magic with one hand and then place one hand on her chest. No one but the trinity knows what happens then. We can see you all during the ceremony, but nothing can be heard."

But there was another problem.

Ebba caught Jagger's eyes. They both turned to Caspian.

"I need two hands," he said. His face screwed up and his right hand balled into a fist.

"Yes," Mortem said uncertainly.

Peg-leg snapped at the power of death. "He only has one."

Mortem blinked at Caspian. "Oh, I see what you mean—"

Ebba gritted her teeth, hackles rising swiftly.

"So how do we get around that?" Caspian mused, pursing his lips. "There has to be a way."

"—you only have one mortal arm," Mortem finished.

Ebba wasn't alone in turning to stare at the power.

"What?" Grubby muttered.

But Verity was approaching Caspian, her mouth slightly ajar.

"Of course," she exclaimed, staring at the space where a second arm used to be.

Locks grumbled. "Feel free to explain whenever ye damn well like!"

Verity shot him a glare, and he quietened.

"The *purgium* healed you, yes?" the Earth Mother asked.

"And took my arm as sacrifice," Caspian said.

"Nonsense, it just gave you an immortal arm instead." She gestured to herself and the other two powers. "We can see it. As clear as day."

"Had to turn on my mortal eyes to see what you were talking about one arm for," Mortem added.

Caspian stared at his empty sleeve. No one made a sound as his mouth moved wordlessly.

"That's impossible," he eventually said.

"You are making a fist right now," the Thunderbird said.

Caspian jumped and lifted his gaze to the power of souls. "You saw that? But I . . . I thought feeling my arm was normal after losing it."

Her friend had always spoken of how he could still feel his arm. Peg-leg got phantom sensations sometimes, so she'd just pitied Caspian the pain and odd sensations that went hand-in-hand with losing a limb.

"What was the sacrifice then?" Jagger suddenly called out. "The *purgium* demands a sacrifice."

The Earth Mother turned to him. "The king did not suffer?"

Right. Good point. He'd suffered plenty.

"But I can't do anything with my arm," Caspian stuttered, face ashen.

"Nothing mortal, king bearer," the Thunderbird corrected, tilting his head to the other side. "Everything immortal."

"I . . . ." The left side of Caspian's chest moved, and his eyes lifted until he was gazing directly ahead at his invisible and apparently immortal hand, if Ebba had to guess.

He gazed at the powers. "I don't even really know what it means." He cleared his throat and glanced around at the rest of them. "But I'll have time to explore that later—"

"Wait, wait, wait," Peg-leg interrupted them. "Does this mean I have an immortal leg?" He stuck out his peg.

The powers stared at the wooden peg.

The Earth Mother hummed. "No, but that intrigues me greatly."

Mortem and the Thunderbird echoed the sound.

"I have never known the root to replace mortal flesh with immortal flesh before." The Earth Mother turned to the other powers in question, who added their agreement. "The root will always have a vested interest in protecting the trinity, but to specifically replace the king bearer's arm with one able to hold the assembled root. . . ."

Jagger stepped closer to her. "What do you think it means?"

The powers exchanged a long look.

Mortem answered Jagger. "It could mean nothing. Perhaps the *purgium* simply demanded a mental sacrifice that day. I'm sure that the king bearer losing his arm—without realizing he had an immortal limb instead—was a great challenge to overcome. We cannot know for sure."

Peg-leg glared at his stump. "The root o' magic be a load o' shite, that's what." But there wasn't any heat in his voice. Her father had lived a long time with only one leg.

Caspian took a deep breath. "All that matters right now is that I'll be able to hold the root of magic in my immortal hand and heal Ebba with my mortal one. Is that possible?"

The powers nodded in unison.

"Hold yer seahorses," Stubby said. "Ye're sure on that? Ebba's life, if she's determined-like to risk it—" He glared at her. "—depends on ye bein' right."

"We would never risk the assembler at this dire stage," the Thunderbird said.

And what about when he'd last seen them? Ebba narrowed her eyes.

"Okay, so I just put a hand on her chest and . . . she lives again," Caspian said, glancing at her.

She smiled wryly despite the leaden weight in her gut. "I'm glad one o' ye finally has an actual job to do. Here I was thinkin' I'd have to do the whole thing. Figurin' out which pieces go where and all."

Mortem held up a finger, his skin crackling with black magic. "Actually, that's the bearer's job, too. He is the one who goes out to the links and returns with a piece."

"Ha! Shame," Ebba exclaimed, grinning at her friend, whose eyes had widened. She patted Caspian on the shoulder. "Ye're much smarter, matey. This be for the best."

Barrels hummed. "So that's most of the hurdles sorted, but there is still the issue of only five links being present."

"I hardly think the other hurdles are *sorted*," Caspian butted in.

Mortem regarded them and then glanced at the other powers. They all nodded in unison again.

"What're ye doin'?" Locks asked, ambling closer, his face alight with suspicion.

Mortem's charcoal eyes widened. "Nothing, link. Just conferring with my colleagues to make sure we haven't missed anything. That's it. All we know."

Mmm, why did something suddenly smell fishy? Ebba thought.

"Ye're sure there ain't anythin' else?" she pressed them. Her fathers circled inward.

The Earth Mother shook her head. "There is nothing else we know."

Caspian joined them. "And what about things you don't know?"

That was a good question. "Yeah," Ebba echoed aggressively. "What about that?"

"There are many things we don't know," the Thunderbird said. "But nothing that will hinder the ceremony from taking place."

The fishy smell didn't dissipate.

Ebba caught Jagger's eye. He lifted a shoulder in a shrug that she interpreted to mean 'they're bigger and badder than us without the root.' She caught Peg-leg's eye and grimaced. He gave a tiny shake of the head to Locks, who squeezed Verity's hand, who eyeballed Marigold, who crossed her arms. Barrels tilted his chin to Stubby, who shook his head at Grubby and Caspian.

"All right, then, let's get to it," Ebba said brightly.

"Nay, let's not get to this," Jagger countered. "Did ye hear them? To put the weapon together, ye have to die. Ain't nothin' worth that."

Anger surged within her, but she tempered it, knowing Jagger's comment was born of fear.

"We're all dyin' anyway," she said, approaching him. "Whether tomorrow, when the taint comes down to Oblivion, or by sheer dumb luck, we'll die if we do nothing. At least this way, we'll be doin' sumpin'."

"*We* won't be," he said, turning his face away.

Ebba placed a finger under his chin to bring him back. "Aye, I guess I'll be doin' the leavin' this time," she said. "Twice I've watched ye depart for what we both thought was certain death. Once on Pleo and again when Cannon took ye from the Locker. I know what it be like to watch and wait. But now it's yer turn, Jagger. And ye'll damn well do it because sometimes the hardest thing be to remain behind."

"I won't remain behind without ye," he said, taking her hand.

"Ye won't need to," she said calmly, hoping against hope that wasn't a lie.

Jagger took a deep breath and sidestepped her. "Caspian."

Uh-oh.

"Jagger," the Exosian replied warily.

Threats, she expected.

Jagger kneeling, she did not.

He bowed his head, and his voice strained. "Do ye understand what she means to me? I need to know that ye'll do everythin' ye can to bring her back. She is half of me."

Ebba supposed that to the powers, it would sound as though Jagger didn't trust Caspian. To her, Jagger's words illustrated just how much he *did* trust the Exosian.

With her very life.

Her chest tightened as Caspian reached down and pulled Jagger up. She'd never seen him more serious.

"You know I would give my life for hers, Jagger. And that is because I know what she means to *me*. What the two of you share is the love of legends and something I can only hope to experience one day. I will do everything in my power to ensure she lives. And if I fail, rest assured, you're welcome to put an end to me. I've lived with guilt before, but I couldn't live with myself after that."

Jagger contemplated him, squeezing his shoulder. "I might take you up on that."

The two smiled grimly at each other, and Jagger pulled Caspian in for a hug. One of the back-slapping ones that males tended to do.

Someone sniffed, and Ebba bit back a smile as Verity handed Locks a handkerchief.

She strode to stand with the other two-thirds of the trinity, and they stood staring at each other for an immeasurable amount of time. If she lived, Ebba knew she would never forget it. How Caspian looked at her with one million questions and uncertainties in his amber gaze. How Jagger squeezed her hand, wordlessly telling her that even if she died and Caspian failed, he'd come to drag her back from Oblivion.

Her stomach churned. The sense that the realm was about to crash down around them had never been more prominent.

TWENTY

"I'm glad there ain't no crowd," Ebba said, standing up on the marble platform and gazing at the empty tiers. "Imagine that pressure."

Jagger hadn't let go of her yet. His arm was tight around her waist. "Ye'll do just fine, Viva."

Just like him to uncover the nerves beneath her words. "I have no idea what to do," she told him. "I'm scared, matey. And I'm s'posed to have barrels o' courage."

The stage they stood upon was twenty feet in diameter. In the middle was a hole where the first piece of the root went to help her as she added the successive pieces. Apparently.

"I can feel yer hand shakin'," he said. "But fear don't change a thing. When ye believe in sumpin' more than yerself, a level above fear be born. I always thought o' it like the air bubble under a capsized rowboat. In that air bubble, there ain't nothin' such as fear. There ain't nothin' but the knowledge that, one way or another, the job needs to be done. Embrace yer fear, *toku wairua*. Look at it as you would a small bug; something that *is*, something that you must co-exist with but whose existence will never define you."

Her eyes were wide as she soaked up his wisdom.

"Ye're right," she eventually said. "We'll be doin' this whether I'm scared or not. I just don't want to kill everyone in the realm. Or even in this stadium."

"Caspian be far more likely to screw up," Jagger said, sliding her a look.

She snorted. "Then I'll be dead, but the end o' the realm won't be my fault." That did make her feel better. Oddly.

His face dropped into a scowl. "I meant figurin' out which pieces to give ye."

Ebba shot him a sheepish smile. "Oh."

Caspian walked up the three stone steps and joined them in the center.

"I had a look at the pieces," he said to them, shaking his head. "No idea how they fit together."

"Let's hope ye figure it out," Jagger replied flatly.

"I'm just goin' to go down there and say. . . ." Ebba trailed off, glancing over her shoulder at her fathers, who each stood in a wedge. Her stomach dropped at the vacant wedge where Plank should have been.

She walked down the stage steps and approached Locks first. She smiled at Verity by his side and hugged him tight. "See ye soon."

"Aye, lass," he said brusquely. "In a few minutes."

Verity rubbed his back, and Ebba moved to Barrels, who stood beside Marigold.

She stood on tiptoe and kissed his weathered cheek. "Thank ye for the readin' lessons, Barrels."

"Yes, well. We still need to put them to good use." He cut off and swallowed hard, pulling her in for a tight hug.

Grubby was crying when she reached him, and it drove a dagger into the space where her heart had only recently regrown.

"We'll be done in a scant second, Grubs," she said, forcing her lips into a smile.

He hugged her tight. "I love ye, Ebba-Viva."

A lump moved into place in her throat, and her reply was hoarse. "And I ye."

Stubby was blinking furiously.

"This just be the tip o' the iceberg on the work that needs doin'," he told her sternly. "So get along and do this, and then there be ship repairs aplenty to be done. Probably take the rest o' yer life."

Ebba squeezed his hand. "Aye, I'm thinkin' the selkies can help us with the labor."

"Good notion, lass. Good notion."

She walked away.

"Ebba," he called.

Glancing back, she saw he, too, had sprung a leak.

"I love ye more than me own life, lass."

Ebba nodded, unable to speak.

Striding past the empty wedge where the *amare* lay on the marble ground, she reached Peg-leg, and just fell into his arms. She rested her head above his big gut.

"It be a frightful bus'ness," he said.

"And it needs doin'," Ebba managed to say.

He pushed her back and stared into her eyes. "Ye go now and save the realm, Ebba-Viva, but be back for dinner. I'll m-make yer favorite."

A smile graced her trembling lips. "Ye have an accord."

Ebba stumbled back to the stairs and joined the others once more.

"Ready?" Caspian asked her.

Nay. She nodded curtly. "Aye, royal-lubber. Do yer bloody worst."

He moved away, and she listened as he alerted the others to get ready.

"Viva," Jagger said, gripping her chin.

She gazed up at him, and he lowered his mouth to hers. The kiss was a whisper and a promise; a plea for her to come back and get the rest.

Jagger traced her face with his fingers, and both of them ignored the tremor of his hands.

Silver eyes held hers, and Ebba wouldn't have been surprised to learn and eternity had passed by in those few seconds.

Jagger released her and stepped back.

Caspian joined them, and they all started speaking at the same time.

Ebba grinned with the others. Strength filled her very boots, seeping upward through her.

"I cons'der myself right lucky to have met the both o' ye," she told them.

"I've never had greater friends," Caspian said, the grin fading from his lips. "And I never will again. Whatever has happened, whatever *will* happen, thank you both for. . . ." He frowned.

Jagger finished for him. "An adventure."

The king nodded. "That's it: an adventure."

"So." Ebba blew a dread out of her face. "What do we do now?"

"Touch hands," someone called.

They turned to find Mortem sitting behind the empty wedge, hands cupped around his mouth. The Earth Mother and Thunderbird were positioned either side of him.

"You all touch hands to start it," Mortem shouted again. "It's my favorite part."

Caspian grunted. "Do they have snacks?"

Jagger muttered something under his breath that sounded a lot like *immortals*.

"Here it goes," Ebba said, holding out her hands.

Caspian was the first to take her offered hand.

Her right hand remained without a companion as Jagger stared at it.

"Do it," she told him.

He glanced up at her, the breath catching in his throat. "I can't, Viva."

Well, she could. Ebba slapped a hand on his chest and the world exploded.

The glow wasn't just emanating from them this time; it overrode all of her senses. The sheer power was a roar in her ears that obliterated all sound, a buzzing in her fingers, a blare of silver, gold, and bronze that momentarily blinded her.

The root knew its home.

Ebba dragged in a breath, freeing her hands from the others to look around. Something felt different, not just the amplified power of their glow.

It didn't take long to see what was new.

Six beams of light shot toward her, one from each part. Her fathers were wide-eyed, and Ebba got the sense that they were shouting, but their shocked exclamations were lost to the tidal wave in her ears.

A hand rested on her shoulder.

She spun to Caspian, who pointed.

It was happening again. Jagger was burning with an inferno of silver, but this time, *veritas* was nowhere to be seen. He slammed a hand down in the middle of the circle and a wave of silver shot outward, spreading across their twenty-foot platform through the lower circle, and then up through the tiers.

On the edges of their platform, a transparent silver wall began to form, inching upward until the three of them were enclosed in a dome of Jagger's immune powers.

Jagger strode to the outside then and sank into a predatory crouch, eyes fixed on her and Caspian.

Ebba reeled away from Caspian as his golden glow, already fiercer than ever before, began to build—a crescendo of molten brilliance. His eyes deepened from amber to liquefied pirates' gold. Radiance covered his skin, the rays bursting through his clothing.

He glanced down at her, his mouth moving. But the power the parts shot at them was too strong. She couldn't hear a thing.

Almost mechanically, Caspian turned and descended the steps.

Ebba glanced at Jagger, seeing that he'd shifted and followed Caspian around the perimeter of the platform. He remained inside the silver dome with her but stuck as close to the bearer as possible.

Without hesitation, Caspian strode to Grubby's wedge and plucked the *dynami* from her father's hands. He walked back, and as soon as her friend reached the edge of Jagger's silver barrier, something ancient began to build within Ebba.

Her breath choked at the hot sensation growing in her gut, bordering on too warm. Her gut continued to increase into a tight ball until Ebba nearly cried out, and then it began to spread outward. To her toes. To her fingers. To the crown of her head. Through her senses. Through her soul. An awareness that was older than her and older even than the powers outside the barrier. That awareness was the warning in her gut that told her when to touch the parts and when it wasn't safe.

That awareness was magic itself. Pure, ancient, knowing magic. Ebba's heartbeat slowed to a thud that was audible even over the continued roaring of power.

She glanced down.

Her dark brown skin was bronze as she'd never seen it. Not awash with the glow as before but as though Ebba truly was made of bronze, a living statue. Her dreadlocks had lifted off her shoulders. Her feet didn't feel to be on the ground. Both Caspian and Jagger were watching her, and she saw the same awareness within them.

The root was telling them what to do, helping them.

Without realizing she'd started moving, Ebba found herself crouching before the hole in the middle of the platform, a narrow, circular hole the length of her hand.

Caspian was before her.

She accepted the *dynami* from him and barely took notice of him returning to the stairs before she turned all of her attention to the *dynami*.

It all seemed so obvious to her now, filled with the root's knowledge as she was. Ebba was about to build the weapon from the bottom-up, and what quality could be more apt to build anything from than strength? Perhaps not always physical but strength of the mind, of the heart, and of integrity.

Ebba's chest filled to bursting, and she stroked the *dynami* fondly, thanking it before inserting the part in the hole, rounded end first.

The other end was flat, but Ebba felt no panic though she'd failed to connect any of the pieces before.

Caspian returned with the next part, handing it to her and walking away.

Purgium.

Where would any of them be without that? They'd be tainted and at each other's throats long ago.

With her hands moving of their own accord, Ebba hovered one of the flat ends of the *purgium* over the *dynami*. She closed her eyes to shield them from the bronze flash of light between her hands.

When the flash dissipated, Ebba glanced back.

She blinked at the pole before her. The two parts had lengthened. As she crouched, the top of the *purgium* was in line with her eyes. They were the same shape overall though they'd now melded so tightly there was no discernible joint. But the parts were definitely much longer.

Ebba lifted her head as Caspian walked back through the barrier, *veritas* in hand. Her mouth dried at the sword casing still around the part, but her friend showed no doubt and the awareness within her did not falter.

She stretched out a finger to touch the tip of the blade, jolting as it pricked her. A bead of blood formed there. As quickly as *veritas* had pierced her skin, the sword began to disintegrate, turning to powder before their eyes.

Caspian rested the disappearing sword down at her feet, and they both watched as the hilt turned to dust with the rest, revealing a tarnished silver cylinder she knew all too well.

Ebba picked up the *veritas* for what felt like the first time.

It was flat on one end and with three openings on the far end: one on the top and two on opposite sides of the tube.

Standing, she placed the *veritas* atop the *purgium*, closing her eyes in readiness of the flash that followed seconds later. She'd been right to stand. The three parts combined now formed a straight pole that extended to the height of her shoulder.

That wasn't her main concern.

With the first two, she'd only felt the awe and jubilation of success. Now, Ebba felt weak with a sensation she could only describe as draining. As though someone had pulled a plug within her and her very soul was leaking out in a torrent onto the marble stone. She gasped, pressing a hand to the middle of her chest just above her ribs.

She sucked in a painful breath.

Guess that was what losing her mortality felt like. The pain of growing old and dying accelerated and compacted into a few seconds. Ebba wheezed, sucking in another drag of air.

Caspian re-appeared, and she accepted the *scio* from him, already dreading the aftermath of fitting the fourth piece to the half-finished root of magic.

Bracing herself, Ebba held the *scio* over the hole on the left side of the *veritas*. This time, through the flash of bronze, she could feel it as her essence drained away.

Her knees shook and she nearly collapsed in a heap.

Only her grip on the top of the root kept her upright. If it was willing to kill her, at least it was willing to act as a crutch until that time.

She cried out against the weariness whispering to her to just drop to the ground. He couldn't possibly hear her, but Ebba shouted anyway. "Hurry, Caspian!"

She squinted through the blurriness of her vision.

Another part.

Fortudo.

Her leaden arm lifted, not from any strength of her own, and held the piece over the right side of the *veritas*. She was too weary to guard herself against the flash of bronze, already falling to her knees as the root drained her of life.

Without her fathers' mortality, she'd already be dead.

Air wouldn't fill her lungs. Ebba dug her fingers into her chest, panic filling her as black crowded her vision. She went through the motions of breathing, hoping some wisp of air was making its way in.

There was still another part.

Tears fell freely from her eyes because despite knowing before she agreed to this that her life would be lost, and despite knowing that there was a chance she might come back, the absence of mortality never made life so sweet. Here, on the edge of her end, the desperate freedom, the singular precious gift of life was tangible. And if she hadn't been about to lose hers, Ebba would have felt unadulterated joy at the realization.

She closed her eyes, accepting that her breathing wasn't going to get better. When she opened them, Caspian was before her, his lips moving again. In his hand sat the *amare*.

Of all the parts, the *amare* had caused her the most trouble. It had forced her to face her feelings for Jagger, but it also had confirmed to Plank that he'd never love another. If not for this part, would her father still be here?

Ebba had nothing to fear from this part anymore. She knew that inherently.

Just as she knew she couldn't touch more than five parts. If she touched the *amare*, they would fail.

Determined to try, Ebba still stretched her hand out to the part. The tell-tale warning flared under her ribs stronger than ever before.

. . . But there wasn't any other way.

Ebba gritted her teeth and looked at Jagger, thinking of all she felt for him. He was crouched again and facing outward, taken over by the root's awareness within himself as they all were.

She loved him more than herself.

But as Ebba hovered her fingers over the *amare*, it was plain from the swelling alarm in her chest that though she shared a soul link with Jagger, what they shared was not born of the specific magical bond the root of magic required.

Which meant failure. But they were so close.

The root of magic was all but assembled.

Frustration edged in as she glanced between the root and the *amare* resting in Caspian's hand.

But he wasn't focused on the same things. Glancing over her shoulder, Ebba frowned at the sight of Mortem right up against Jagger's barrier, staring at them.

The power of death gritted his teeth, glancing to the sky in exasperation.

Ebba blinked away the momentary blurriness that she strongly suspected wasn't momentary at all but her final slide into death.

Desperation clawed up through her throat, but the oddity of Mortem's behavior from earlier struck her. The awareness within her paused, and so did she.

Caspian was backing away from her, his molten gold eyes widening. Ebba swayed in her crouch, leaning forward to rest both fists on the marble floor.

Sweat trickled over her brow, dripping off her chin and onto the floor. She blinked through the salty torrent at Mortem again. He stood in the sixth wedge that had lain empty. She focused on the five soul links connecting her to the other wedges.

The power of death wasn't alone. Someone was with him.

Shock strangled her in its cruel iron grip, but her mind hadn't even processed what her eyes were telling her before Caspian rested the *amare* on the ground and reached for her.

A thin bolt, a whisper compared to the other five soul links, shot out from the person at Mortem's side. The bolt shot at her, and pain struck her in the chest and erupted.

Ebba screamed with what little breath remained within, energy draining in a rush as she crumpled to the ground.

She stared up at the yellow sun, the blue sky. And though her insides seared with white-hot fire, she could not inch her hand up to cover the place where her heart had been before Plank. Where he was again now. He was here.

Ebba's eyes began to close.

So heavy.

Like the slow, warm mornings in her hammock when sleep wouldn't let her leave. Like the early morning hours when Stubby's brandy was passed around, and they'd sung every shanty in their arsenal, and everyone was just sitting in tranquil silence under the night sky.

Death.

She smiled.

And then frowned as the descent into loving slumber was rudely interrupted. Ebba was dragged upright. Her head lolled back, and she saw that Caspian propped her up under one arm and Jagger under the other. They were both shouting at her.

Didn't they hear the roar in their ears? Actually, Ebba smiled again; the roaring was gone. The trill of birds and the gentle rush of a calm tide had replaced it.

She jolted slightly at a stinging slap from her left. Her cheek smarted, and she scraped the energy together to glare at Caspian.

He shook a silver tube in her face.

The *amare*.

But there was still a crack in her soul. Plank hadn't been healed by the *purgium*. Or was Plank's presence here, the weaker soul link they shared, enough? Or was he here at all?

Maybe she could only see him because she was dying.

Jagger directed her arm to the strange two-pronged object immediately before her. She willed her eyes to focus on the blurring object.

The root of magic.

The last part.

Caspian held the flat end of the *amare* over the middle hole of *veritas*. Jagger wrapped her hand around the root of magic, holding her fingers there. He began to lift her other hand toward the *amare*.

Ebba had to put the last part in place. Or everyone would die. And as warm and fuzzy as death felt, she'd also felt the exhilaration of the living. She wanted her loved ones to live for as long as possible before they joined her.

She strained to help Jagger lift her arm but was confined to sluggishly staring at the tube in Caspian's hand.

When her hand was close to the *amare*, Caspian and Jagger nodded at each other.

They both released their hold at the same time. Her arm fell heavily. Ebba couldn't have stopped the limb's descent if she'd tried. Her hand barely gripped the *amare*, but the tube contacted the rest of the root.

Jagger and Caspian were ripped away from her sides.

Sunshine and lazy hammock days obliterated everything else.

Ebba's eyes closed.

TWENTY-ONE

Arms were wrapped around her.

Someone was rocking her and kissing the top of her head.

Fire pulsed in her heart. And for the first time in what felt like a long time, Ebba's chest wasn't filled with darkness. She didn't feel like she was one misplaced brick away from caving in.

Air filled her lungs in a rushing burst, and she opened her eyes, her entire body jolting to life.

Before her, Caspian's tear-streaked face loomed.

He dropped the long silver object in his hand and took her face in both hands. "Ebba, y-ye're back. I did it. I didn't think it was workin'. I didn't know how to use it."

She covered his hands, stopping his fear-fueled pirate babbling. He'd brought her back. They'd assembled the root. "Ye did it, Caspian," she whispered, still trying to get a grip on her shock.

"How do ye feel?" he said, slipping his hands away and drawing his arm across his face.

Ebba took stock, breathing through the galloping energy filling her. Emotionally, she felt heavy. Full but heavy. Like she needed a few days to process everything that had just happened.

The arms around her tightened, and she craned to look at the person.

Silver eyes met hers.

"Ahoy," she greeted Jagger, feeling the shaking of his body.

He pressed a lingering kiss to her forehead. "Are ye okay, Viva? Ye need to tell me if ye ain't. I'll fix it."

Ebba lifted a finger to his lips, tracing them. "Nothin' here to fix. I feel good for bein' dead a minute ago. Whatever Caspian did, he did a good job."

Jagger shuddered and lifted his head. "Thank ye, Caspian. I owe ye a debt."

The Exosian contemplated him. "I was playing my part. I couldn't have done less if I'd tried. This . . . knowing feeling filled me as soon as I began to glow."

"Aye, me too," Jagger replied.

"The root's power, I'm thinkin'," Ebba added.

They sat in silence.

"But I'll take that debt," Caspian added.

She grinned at him. He'd never be a pirate-pirate, but he'd learned a few tricks along the way.

Ebba glanced at the gleaming root of magic at Caspian's feet. "So that's it then?"

The tubes had always possessed a tarnished appearance. That was gone. The silver of the weapon gleamed so fiercely it appeared almost white. Squinting past the white to see the rampant pearly swirling beneath its surface was near impossible.

"What shape is that?" she asked. The weapon was about her height, but she'd expected it to reach the height of Caspian's shoulder.

Other than that, she had to admit it looked like a giant fork.

"I believe it's a trident," Caspian said, glancing at the root. "Beautiful, isn't it?"

A true treasure.

"How did it feel to wield the root on Ebba?" Jagger asked.

The Exosian stared at his right hand. "Like . . . I was thousands of years old. Like I'd lived my life and had all of the wisdom that comes with it but was able to go back through my life and use that wisdom in real time. I was part of something greater than myself. I felt . . . certain."

"That sounds great," Ebba lied. She freed herself from Jagger's arms and sat. "How did we put the root together in the end?" She could only recall sunshine and hammocks after the *fortudo*.

The two men shot her a glance.

Jagger squeezed her hand. "Do ye recall Plank showin' up?"

Ebba stilled. She shut her eyes, frowning. "The thin beam o' light hittin' me. That really was him? But Plank was never healed, so how did that work?"

"Yes," Caspian said. "My thought exactly. Was Plank's unhealed bond with you, added to Jagger's soul link, enough to do the job? Or was it that we forced you to connect with the *amare* at the end, knowing you would die?"

"Hey," she complained. "I don't recall ye doin' that."

"Ye were dyin'," Jagger said hollowly. "We couldn't think o' any other way."

Ebba squeezed his hand and then reached out to do the same with Caspian's. "I know. And I owe ye both my life. I'd be dead if ye hadn't. There ain't no way I could've taken it apart to get the *purgium* to go heal Plank."

Caspian studied her. "Are you okay about Plank's presence?"

She shook her head. "My head be spinnin'. I can't think about that yet."

The two exchanged a quick look. She peered between them.

"What?" she asked and started to twist.

"Wait," Jagger told her. "Afore ye turn, there be sumpin' ye have to know."

"Are my fathers okay?" Ebba jolted. The overwhelming and nearly crushing surge of terror that usually accompanied that question was gone. She felt concern and fear, but her mind hadn't leaped to panicked conclusions.

Interesting.

"Yer fathers be okay—" He hesitated. "—but, well, Plank is still here. He has a shimmering quality to him. But he be here."

She stared at Jagger, lips numbing as she sifted through all of that. Her heart twisted inside. *How?*

"Why?" Ebba whispered through numb lips.

"We were kind of busy," Caspian reminded her. "But we can all go down and find out together."

Something built within her. Tiny cracks of irritation joined into frustration that mounted to anger that erupted as black rage within seconds. Ebba launched to her feet and whirled to look behind them.

"Ye flamin' sod," she shouted, spotting her deceased father beside Mortem.

Plank appeared just as she remembered him, raven curls held back with a bandana, soft hazel eyes dreamy—aside from the shimmering quality to his skin.

Her stomach lurched at the familiar sight of him, but she knew better than to believe he was really here. She jumped down from the platform and ran to him, drawing back her arm.

"Ye left us, ye bastard," she shouted at him. "Ye chose death over yer crew, ye flamin' coward."

Ebba punched Plank as hard as she could.

Pain erupted in her knuckles.

"Ouch," she gasped, clutching her hand. Ebba stared at her throbbing knuckles and then lifted her gaze to Plank, who was moaning and rubbing his jaw.

"All right," Ebba mumbled, glancing at Mortem. "Explain."

Jagger and Caspian joined her. She glanced back and noticed all of her other fathers were immobile in their wedges.

"Wait," she interrupted the power of death. "Are they okay?"

Mortem dipped his head. "The links usually recover after the assembler is revived. They'll be fine." He tapped his temple. "I can tell."

She stared down the power of death, who'd clearly been keeping his own very important secrets.

"I'll go and check on them," Caspian offered.

Ebba threw him a grateful look, and still ignoring shimmering Plank, she stared expectantly at Mortem.

"So," he said uneasily, "there was another way to ensure you could assemble the root, but doing so meant we'd have to leave the Oblivion defenseless while I summoned your father back."

"You what?" she growled.

The power of death backed up a step, lifting his hands. "Look, there was a good chance that your soul link with the immune would be enough. We did not want to leave our realm vulnerable if it was not needed."

"Ye nearly *killed* her," Jagger snarled. "What would've happened to yer realm then, ye moron? Ye should've brought him back yesterday so we could heal Plank with the *purgium*. She would have had time to recover afore assemblin' the root."

Black magic crackled over Mortem's skin. "Careful, mortal."

Jagger stepped up to the power. "Nay, immortal. Ye listen to *me*. She could've just died because ye decided to meddle in things ye don't understand. Ye do that again, and I don't care how powerful-like ye be, I'll come for ye."

Mortem's crackling faded away. "Noted. However, we knew that even unhealed, her link to her father would certainly be enough with her soul link to the immune. Luck would have it that the *amare* was the last part, anyway. The Earth Mother said when the assembler touched the completed root of magic, simultaneously her mortality drained, and the root healed the bond with her sixth father, *giving* her the surplus of mortality needed to form the weapon. So," Mortem announced, "the link with the immune wasn't needed *at all* in the end. Which is no doubt why he's still standing."

From the corner of her eye, she saw that Plank was straightening. "And why is Plank still standin'?"

"Because he's dead. The dead cannot be rendered unconscious."

"So what? Ye can summon people back from the dead?"

"Of a sort," the power of death said. "The dead are all around us. In the Oblivion, they are visible, but here I can revive them if I wish—which I rarely do because it's highly uncomfortable and unbalances the realm. I can encourage a shadow of them to appear or a more physical apparition of them as you currently see."

"And the a'parition actually be them," Ebba said, mouth drying.

Mortem nodded.

"He's here. And ye said the root of magic healed me as it drained me." She inhaled. "Does that mean all o' the cracks in my soul be healed?"

The weight of Plank's eyes were on her, yet that her soul was healed was the least of her current worries.

Plank was back. For now.

What was she meant to say that she hadn't already said? If Ebba dared to believe he was really here, what would that do to her?

"Little nymph."

She closed her eyes.

"Little nymph, I know ye're mad, but let me explain."

The *thwack* of flesh forcefully meeting flesh drew her out in time to witness Plank's head snapping back. Jagger stepped away, dropping his fist to his side. Returning to her, he looped an arm around her waist.

Plank's eyes watered. "Shite, what was that for, ye cur?"

"For breakin' her heart when ye were always harpin' on about how ye wouldn't," Jagger replied coolly.

Plank glared at him. "I made a promise to another long afore I made one to Ebba."

"Then ye shouldn't have made another one." Jagger squeezed her tight.

"I learned a few things. The sit'ation changed."

Ebba's skull was catching up. In that moment, she just felt defeated. Her pride wanted to turn away from Plank because Jagger was right; he'd nearly destroyed her with his actions. The larger part was desperate to talk to him and understand.

She swallowed her pride. "Talk, then. Help me to understand why ye left us." *Left me.*

"Ye've changed, little nymph," he said softly. "And I'm knowin' that be my fault. We've been watchin' ye since I left."

"Who's we?" she muttered, already knowing the answer.

"Me and Felicity. I found her again."

The joy in his voice was like a dagger under her ribs. "Ye're the birds who kept followin' me," Ebba said in a flat voice.

Jagger glanced at her, but she didn't take her eyes off her father.

"Aye," Plank admitted. "I figured when you started tryin' to kill us that ye'd put that together."

On the tiers behind, the Thunderbird started to rise to full height. The Earth Mother reached up a hand and forced him back down, shaking her head.

"I did," Ebba said, dead calm.

Her father blanched. "That was how it all started for me. When Felicity was killed, half o' me went with her. But right when she died, I was formin' a soul link with ye. I was a quarter here and three-quarters not. Eventually, yer fathers, wily buggers, built a ship and named her after my wife. They dragged an oath from me not to leave."

That he'd remain alive as long as *Felicity* remained afloat. She knew that part.

"For all my stories o' magic—which were handed down through her family," he added, glancing at Ebba, "I never much put stock in what came after death. I hated death because it got to keep her company and I did not. When we first met the Thunderbird and he spoke of vessels, doors that I'd sealed shut for a long, long time were opened. Afore then, I'd always known that not even death could truly sep'rate me from her. It was a whimsical knowledge. But after, I saw that she'd never been that far away; that we truly could be together again. She'd probably been waitin' all these years for me just like she'd waited all those many years for me when she was alive."

Ebba remembered his sad ballad—the tune he'd whistled in a daydream for as far back as she could remember.

"Then *Felicity* sank," she prompted him.

"Then *Felicity* sank." Plank sighed heavily. "It was like when she first died, except worse. Because now there was hope. The reasons to leave began to outweigh the reasons to stay."

Anger churned in her gut. "Leavin' us to put together the weapon without ye. Leavin' us to fight Cannon and the pillars. Nearly ensurin' we failed and the entire realm became tainted!"

Plank's eyes watered, and he dropped his head. "Aye, little nymph. These are the things I learned after joinin' Felicity in death. Ye recall she had six sisters?"

"Felicity be an assembler then?" Jagger asked.

Her father dipped his head. "She never knew the bonds with her sisters were so strong—otherworldly—until Mutinous killed one of her sisters. Felicity fell into the same state as ye did, catatonic-like. She should've died but didn't because o' the extra soul link she shared with me—just like the one ye share with Jagger. Except afore her other sisters had time to bring her to me, Cannon caught up with them and murdered her. I didn't know any o' that afore I left ye. Believe me, if I'd known ye'd die for my passin', I'd never have done such a thing."

"Ye knew it'd nearly destroy me," Ebba said bluntly. "And ye knew it'd hurt everyone else. Yer actions were selfish."

Plank looked from her to Jagger. "Ye have yer own soul partner, little nymph. Tell me: How would ye feel if he were suddenly gone? And I went down fightin' to keep the tainted pirates at bay."

"That be a lie," she snarled. "Ye turned yer back on Cannon's stampedin' crew when ye could've kept swinging yer cutlass. Ye placed yerself there in the narrow passage on purpose because ye'd already decided to go!"

Plank swallowed. "There were too many o' them. I wouldn't have survived anyway."

And so he gave up? She was too furious to give any credence to his words. Everything out of his mouth just sounded like an excuse for leaving them in the lurch.

"Ye don't feel the same intense draw to us any longer," Plank said.

Ebba stared at him. "What?"

"When the weapon be assembled, soul links hibernate. For all assemblers. It's a way to ensure they don't keep dyin' over and over. If I'd waited to die now instead o' leavin' ye afore, ye wouldn't have gone through half the pain. Ye would've been able to mourn me as a normal person mourns."

The breath caught in her chest.

"That's my mistake," Plank choked out. "Ye're right, I was selfish and I was weak. I tried to figure everythin' out in the Locker so that ye'd be safe when I left. I told myself that was enough and that I deserved to be with Felicity after so long. But truth is, as soon as I left ye, I learned what I had cost ye. And I'll have to live with that guilt for the rest o' my existence."

Ebba crossed her arms, feeling inconsolably lost. "Why did ye choose her over me?"

"That wasn't the choice I made. I made the choice to stay here past my time to be with ye. Bein' yer father was one o' the greatest joys I was ever privy to. And I ain't talkin' o' the soul link. That be faded now, and the love I feel for ye hasn't abated in the slightest. A soul link is magic, little nymph. That don't mean it doesn't mean nothin', but the soul link is *magic*. What I share with Felicity and what you share with Jagger, that be real and unchangin' through the storms. It be stronger than magic itself. As real as the moon and the stars. More real than sumpin' like life or death."

She dropped her arms, tears pooling in her eyes.

"For near-on twenty years, I loved ye more than death," Plank said, stepping until he was directly before her. "Now I be reunited with my wife, my heart has just grown, and I'll love ye even more from the skies."

She widened her eyes in a bid to stop the tears from falling. Was it just her hopeful heart that wanted to believe him? That he'd lived for her was a hard concept to grasp. The moment that was burned into her memory—Plank glancing back at her in Davy Jones' before turning to face the stampede of tainted—had always seemed to her like he gave up. But if he was meant to follow Felicity into death when she was killed, then every day of Ebba's existence, he'd made the choice to fight on. Each day waking up and knowing he wasn't meant to be here. Each day making the effort. And he *had* made the effort. She almost couldn't fathom it. Until *Felicity* sank, she'd never guessed at his unhappiness.

"Was every day like hell for ye?" she sobbed, the tears finally escaping her. "I should've noticed. I should've done sumpin'."

Plank covered the gap. Jagger's arm fell away as she fell forward into Plank's arms, sobbing.

"Nay, Ebba," he hushed. "There's to be no blamin' yerself. Watchin' ye grow was the greatest honor o' all."

Not blaming herself seemed impossible.

If she could believe in his reason for accepting his fate, then perhaps she could believe in the rest in time. When all was said and done, if Jagger was gone, could she live for someone else for twenty years and love them enough to be happy? When someone had one foot in death's door, their choice to live for others—no matter how long—showed the immeasurable extent of their devotion.

Plank hadn't left because of her. He'd lived for her. And Ebba was lucky enough to have been on the receiving end of that love for over eighteen years.

She stretched her arms around him and gave way to her tears.

"I miss ye so much, Plank," she stuttered between shuddering gasps. "It ain't the same without ye."

He stroked her hair. "But me and Felicity will always be with ye. Never forget that. We ain't gone. We're just in a di'ferent form. One with wings."

Ebba contemplated that, sniffing hard. "What's it like to fly?"

"I'd rather sail. Ye ain't missin' out on much there."

He hesitated. "Mortem, could ye bring Felicity back for a spell? I'd like Ebba to meet her."

When the power of death spoke, his voice was thick with tears. "Of course. She was always a favorite of ours."

"The *only* reason I sorted you into a vessel," the Thunderbird snapped from the tiers. "Believe me, you were set for hell. She asked me to pull a few strings."

Yet another startling example of the Thunderbird's fairness in sorting souls. . . .

Ebba pulled back and wiped her face. When she was done, she stared at the woman now standing beside Plank.

"Ahoy, Felicity," Stubby boomed from behind.

Ebba jumped, looking back to see that everyone else had gathered behind her. How long had they been there?

"Hello, everyone." The woman smiled prettily, her gray eyes crinkling. Her auburn hair was pulled back into a thick braid that hung over her shoulder, the tip reaching her waist. "Long time no see. Thank you for caring for Plank."

Ebba couldn't take her eyes off the woman. It wasn't that she was still struggling not to see Felicity as someone who'd stolen her father. It was that *Felicity* was her home for so long. A part of Ebba had always imagined the ship as her mother. To meet the namesake, no matter her fathers' nefarious reason for naming the cedar ship after Plank's wife, left Ebba in no small amount of awe.

"Ebba-Viva," Felicity said, her smile dropping. "I fear you must hate me. I'm so sorry Plank did what he did *when* he did." She glared at him. "I told him what an idiot he was."

Plank stole a kiss from her, and Felicity's smile returned full-force.

She turned back. "I've felt that pain. I'm so sorry you had to go through that alone."

Ebba studied the wife of her father. Felicity exuded warmth. Her eyes were friendly. She was like a less prickly version of Verity. All genuine love, caring, and quiet manners. Exactly as Ebba had always viewed the ship, if truth be told.

No one spoke, and she felt the tension mounting as they awaited her reply.

Would she ever have a chance to speak with Plank and Felicity again? This might be her only opportunity for closure. Even confused and reeling, she'd be lying if she pretended there wasn't an urge to assuage the guilt Plank clearly felt.

This would help everyone move on.

"Ye had to go through it alone, too," Ebba muttered to Felicity.

"I did."

"Are yer sisters all with ye?"

Felicity nodded, sighing happily. "They are."

"And it be true about the links fading now that the root o' magic be assembled?" Ebba didn't love her fathers any less. But she'd be glad to be rid of the panic that had plagued her for so long. Her fathers abandoning her on Maltu may have ramped that panic up big-time, but everything after wasn't truly their fault, just the root ensuring Ebba would be able to carry out the job when the time came.

"Yes," Felicity said without hesitation. "You'll be much more comfortable in their absence with the root together. Though those protective urgencies, the threat to your life, and the need to be close to them will reappear whenever the weapon is deconstructed."

Caspian called from the back. "How do you know all of this?"

Felicity lifted her chin, eyes searching until they came to rest on the Exosian. "Because when I died and learned what I was, I made a point of learning everything I could. Many immortals have lived for thousands of years. I've spoken at length to most of them, a task that took me all through the Oblivion and took the better part of two decades." She shot a look at the powers and then back at Caspian. "The three of you have already discovered most of what I know, but I'm happy to answer any other questions you have. I didn't learn everything, but I may be able to help."

Feeling eyes on her, Ebba darted a look at Plank.

He arched a brow and glanced subtly at Felicity.

Some faint amusement tangled with the lingering hurt within her. Hurt that Ebba could see would one day fade now that the root was assembled and the last crack in her soul was healed.

She arched a brow back at Plank and nodded, smiling. She approved of Felicity. . . .

Her father beamed.

. . . However, she was still a pirate, and he'd hurt her bad.

She turned to Mortem. "Will Plank and Felicity stick around for a bit?"

The power of death dipped his head. "I cannot drop the defenses again to banish them yet. Perhaps not until we leave to battle."

Good.

She turned to Plank. "I can see why ye never slept with any o' the women throwin' themselves at ye all those years," Ebba mused aloud.

Felicity's brows snapped together, and Plank glanced at her nervously, edging away.

Everyone shied away, powers of Oblivion included.

"Time to head back?" Mortem blurted as Felicity's fists bunched. He blurred away, the other powers hot on his trail.

She'd worried about her fathers getting back up the stairs, but she shouldn't have. They were surprisingly mobile when survival was on the cards.

Ebba observed Felicity cornering Plank against the tiers as Marigold, Verity, and Caspian followed everyone else at a more sedate pace.

"That was mean," Jagger whispered in her ear, leading her after everyone else.

Ebba glanced back at Plank, who shot her a death glare.

An evil smirk spread over her face. "Aye, and it felt right good, too."

TWENTY-TWO

"Is yer kin okay, Marigold?" Ebba asked the matronly woman.

Marigold lowered herself onto one of the large cushions scattered through the ruins. They were back in the large open-ceilinged room alongside the edge of the red water that marked the official border of the Oblivion.

"As well as can be, my dear," Marigold replied quietly.

Usually a dignified, stern presence, Marigold's strain over her missing family members showed in her pallor and slight slouch on the cushions.

Ebba watched her carefully, hoping the eldest of her sons, his wife, and his two children would be found alive. Maybe they could be saved from the taint somehow. None of them could give up hope.

"Would you like anything else to eat, Ebba-Viva?" Felicity asked from the cushion on her direct right.

She was still here. Mortem had said dropping the Oblivion's defenses again to banish the pair was too dangerous. Secretly, Ebba suspected the power of death harbored a serious soft spot for Felicity. She must really like cats or something, Ebba thought. *Everyone* appeared to really like Plank's wife, and Ebba had a strong suspicion she would become one of them.

She perched on a large purple cushion, wedged between Plank and Felicity. Everyone had eaten and enjoyed a brief respite from the assembling of the root. Personally, she felt that dying and coming back to life should have earned her a day's break, but now that the weapon was formed, an energy had filled their crew.

"Nay, I'm stuffed," she said.

On her other side, Plank announced, "Good. Then it's storytime."

Locks groaned loudly. "Are ye serious? That was the only good thing about ye dyin'."

Felicity laughed, the sound like bells.

Smiling at his wife, Plank drew out a leather-bound book Ebba couldn't fail to recognize.

Her scrapbook. She licked her lips. "Where did ye get that?"

"Stubby just gave it to me."

Aye, she bet he did. Interfering old coot. But Ebba couldn't bring herself to be mad.

She stared at the scrapbook. Plank was here—for the time being. Reading the memories without her crew being full and whole hadn't felt right before. She'd been so angry at Plank for leaving, but after their talk, Ebba had a better understanding of the circumstances leading up to his death. She still didn't like that the crew weren't the same as before. But. . . .

She took the scrapbook from him. "Aye, okay. Mayhaps one or two o' them."

Ebba scanned the note on the first page again, relieved when the burning behind her eyes didn't immediately start.

The next page was covered with writing. And the opposite page. She thumbed through the pages. *All* of them were filled with writing. Ebba wasn't sure what she'd expected—just a few lines here and there? But the book was filled. Every page used.

She lifted her head and peered around at her crew on the

surrounding cushions. They smiled back at her, and a traitorous lump rose in her throat.

Tearing her eyes from them, she glanced at Jagger on the cushions to her left. He nodded, and her chest loosened a fraction.

It was time.

Ebba returned to the first memory and slowly read aloud, "*From Peg-leg to Ebba. Toilet trainin' Viva is provin' to be a right nightmare. She has realized grown-ups don't wear diapers, but instead o' goin' to the poop like we've showed her, she has taken to disappearin' into the hold between the barrels to sh—*"

Her face reddened, and she cast a furtive look at Jagger. "I'll save that one."

Caspian and Jagger snickered loudly. Her fathers smiled at one another, clearly seeing nothing mortifying about the story.

How many of these memories were about toilet training?

She cast her eyes over the next one. Safe.

Ebba read aloud, "*From Barrels to Ebba. Today, our seven-year-old daughter started a fight with some children from the Neos village. She managed to bring two o' the older boys to the ground. Thankfully, we arrived just as she submerged the head o' a third one underwater. He didn't quite drown, which is good news considerin' the boy was the son of our trade contact there. Durin' the fight, she lost one o' her baby teeth, and instead of being upset, she decided it looked 'right fierce.' When questioned about why she'd started the fight, Ebba declared, 'I ain't takin' flamin' shite from no soddin' bugger.' In the wake of the incident, my co-parents and I have started a curse jar.*"

Her crew's laughter rang in her ears. Ebba chuckled to herself, grinning at her fathers.

"They likely deserved it," she said.

Peg-leg winked. "Aye, lass. That be why I left a gold coin under yer pillow for the missin' tooth."

Barrels shook his head. "You had your portrait painted that afternoon and were minus one of your front teeth."

She knew that portrait. Each of her fathers had a copy in their shacks back on Zol.

Turning the page, Ebba scanned the next one and threw a smile at Plank.

She spoke, "*From Plank to Little Nymph. Ebba just turned four, and we've told her she's now old enough to climb the shrouds without us watching. Afore she went up today, I told her that the riggin' led her all the way into the sky. Her eyes went as wide as saucers. It was all I could do not to chuckle at her wonderin' face. She's just losin' that pudginess that babies have, but it ain't quite gone yet, and she be so cute it breaks my heart. After I told her about climbin' to the sky, she asked if the stars would be around her, and I said aye. I said that while up there, she could talk to the birds and the sun, even to the moon—they might not reply, but they were listenin'. Ebba left for the crow's nest, and the rest o' us cracked a bottle o' brandy, listenin' as she sung and chatted to the birds and sun for the next two hours. She fell quiet after that, and I climbed up to find her sound asleep, the sweetest smile on her face that I ever did see. My daughter be my reason for livin'. And that day will remain as one o' the best o' my life.*"

No one spoke as she finished.

Ebba stared at the page, tracing the words with her blackened fingernails. Glancing to Plank beside her, she opened her mouth. And shut it. So caught up in actually reading the scrapbook without falling apart, Ebba hadn't stopped to think about what she'd say to her fathers after.

And what did she say to Plank when he'd soon be gone again? Nothing could possibly convey the pained love she felt in this second. The joyful agony. The razor-sharp and heart-warming sting.

She didn't want any hurt to tinge her words because in a matter of hours, her father would be gone. Those words would linger always. They had to be perfect.

Plank's eyes were filled with tears, and that was her undoing. Thick, salty tears spilled over her cheeks as her father pulled her into his arms.

"Ah, little nymph," he said, cheek pressed into her hair.

"Thank ye. I can't say—"

He inhaled deeply. "I know, Ebba-Viva. Ye don't need to speak. This moment be perfect without words."

She relaxed against him, realizing her father was right. Ebba pressed an ear to his chest, determined to enjoy the time with him. Even when she realized his chest was silent—not disturbed by the regular thudding of a living heart—she just clung to Plank tighter, cataloguing his smell, the feel of his arms, and the rise and fall of his chest as he rocked her.

He pressed a kiss atop her head. "Ye'll be all right, little nymph."

Ebba pulled back, wiping her sleeve over her face. She peered up at her father. "And so will ye," she said, voice hoarse. "That gladdens my heart."

Reading the scrapbook had been a good thing. She had her own memories of him, but *more* precious was having some of his too.

The Earth Mother clapped her hands, making both Ebba and Plank jump.

"Yes, very nice, very nice," she said. "But there are things to do. After a, frankly, *thrilling* ceremony—"

"Less o' a cer'mony and more o' a life-and-death thing," Stubby muttered.

"Seriously, did you two find that thrilling?" the Earth Mother continued, turning toward the other powers.

Mortem hummed. "The very last bit where the immune and bearer held her up was the best part. Best one I've ever attended. So dramatic."

"Poetic," the Thunderbird added, tilting his head. "The ultimate catharsis."

"Right," Peg-leg drew out. "So let's focus. We've got the weapon, and that be evenin' the battlefield a scant bit. But we still need a plan to defeat the pillars." He blanched, glancing around. "Where be the weapon?"

Everyone froze.

"I have it here," Caspian called.

They turned to study him. The root of magic was hovering in thin air beside him.

Ebba asked, "Are ye holdin' the root in yer immortal arm?"

He nodded, grinning as the root twirled in the air. Or Caspian twirled the root. With his invisible arm.

"That could take some gettin' used to," Locks said.

Verity didn't seem bothered. "There's no harm with him holdin' it? The root doesn't corrupt immortal flesh, correct? Just mortal? There isn't any risk of him becoming like the pillars if exposed?"

The Earth Mother dipped her head. "The king bearer will not be affected by the root unless he uses his mortal flesh to hold it."

Grubby reached out and jabbed a finger between the root and Caspian's body. He yelped and clutched his finger after. "Shite, there be sumpin' there."

"Fascinating, isn't it?" Caspian asked.

They'd seen a lot of creepy things, but this ranked somewhere between Plank coming back to visit as a shimmering version of himself—with his dead wife—and Grubby being a selkie. Ebba stopped the thoughts in their tracks, sensing that she could continue that game all day.

"You know, it *does* change our attack," the Thunderbird said, sending a jolting pain under Ebba's ribs. "A mortal has never wielded the weapon against the pillars. In history, the powers have always carried it. The pillars won't expect such a move."

Surprise was a good advantage.

"But won't it be better if one of you wield it? You're already powerful," Caspian said, placing the root down by his side.

"Probably," Mortem said. "The root's power is consistent. It isn't amplified by the individual's power, but our knowledge of how to wield the root is something to consider."

The Thunderbird hummed. "And yet the root took the king bearer's arm."

The powers fell mute, exchanging a leaden look.

"None o' that," Peg-leg snapped. "Talk out loud or not at all."

Ebba suspected there was a silent 'ye flamin' sods' at the end of that.

The Earth Mother's eyes flashed. "Everything happens for a reason."

"And . . . you can see those reasons," Barrels said.

"The greater the power of the object I'm scrying, the harder it is to see. Glimpsing any future to do with the root takes nearly all of my strength for several days. All but a wisp of my powers are being used in the Oblivion's defenses, so the last readings I took happened before our defenses went up. That is how I knew that if all went well, you would meet us here."

Stubby leaned forward, glancing around their crew. "Mateys, I like the idea of chuckin' a bit o' unknown at the pillars. We made the mistake of underestimatin' their speed and their allies before. We didn't get a chance to use any o' our ploys. We can't let that happen again. Whatever happens, *we* have to attack. Not just react."

"They'll have their own plans," Plank said. "And they have yer kin, Barrels. They have to know ye'll go after them."

Ebba glanced at Plank. He'd said *ye'll.* Forgetting that he wouldn't be coming was all too easy when they were all sitting around like old times.

"Yes, but we know what they'll go for," Jagger said. "They want the root."

"And they want it intact," Caspian said. "They don't want the weapon in parts, if possible. Can the pillars sense the root is formed?"

The powers nodded.

Mortem answered, "They would have felt it the moment it was restored. All higher castes of immortals would have. That's why we love the assembling ceremony in particular. The immense power is tantalizing."

"And the root can only be taken apart down here. As soon as we leave, they block off the Oblivion," Ebba said.

The Thunderbird turned to look at her. "How did you know that?"

"Makes sense."

"That would have been nice to know on the first failed attempt," Mortem said, tapping his lower lip. "But yes."

Verity straightened. "You said that we need to draw them away from Exosia, away from the strongest center of their power. And that we need an immortal army to battle the tainted."

"Already sorted." Mortem waved his hand in the air. "I sent Marjory to tell everyone."

. . . "Who's Marjory?" Ebba asked in the quiet wake of that tidbit.

"My servant."

"The servant with one eye?" she clarified. "Ye sent a servant to ask everyone to come and fight the pillars?"

The Earth Mother shrugged. "Less of a request, more of an order. And what's wrong with servants? Do you have something against them?"

Ebba frowned. "Nothin' apart from thinkin' they be livin' wrong. Caspian was a slave once."

"Not really, Mistress Pirate," he replied.

"We digress." Barrels cleared his throat. "I have a suggestion. How about we split into three groups to brainstorm? The trinity will form one. And two or three of the crew can partner with a power each."

Stubby was the first to grin. The rest of them followed, Ebba adding hers. The time to divide the powers and interrogate them was nigh, but she was glad the job hadn't fallen to her.

She dragged her cushion out through the opposite archway, which overlooked the apple-red ocean of the Oblivion.

"This kind of feels like a school exercise," Caspian said, laughing lightly as he dropped his own cushion beside hers. The root of magic hovered in the air next to him.

Ebba reached out a finger as Grubby had. She encountered resistance.

"It's real," he told her.

"I know, matey. But my skull and eyes are havin' a war. I swear I should've felt it afore now. It's only there when ye're holdin' the root?"

He nodded. "Certainly. Though there were occasions when I really felt it was still there. I remember trapping it in the door once. I thought I'd gone crazy, but maybe it did appear sometimes. And maybe there's a way I can make it appear without holding the root."

"Worth a shot, ain't it?" she replied, lowering onto her cushion.

Jagger dropped his cushion and plonked down. He waited until Caspian sat to say, "The root be assembled. So everythin' we know be out the scupper. I can't be sure I'm even immune still."

Caspian's eyes narrowed. "The immune's job is to remain level-headed to decide when the root should or shouldn't be assembled. I feel we can safely assume you would retain that immunity whether the root is whole or not."

"The pillars will still want him," Ebba said. "Though not as much as the root."

"Could be a decoy," the Exosian mused.

"Feel free to gamble with my life." Jagger snorted.

The two men grinned at each other.

"How do we draw the pillars out?" Ebba asked after a beat. "If I were them, I wouldn't leave where I was strongest. Especially not after the powers and the trinity had beaten me that way once afore."

Caspian met her gaze. "I have to agree. As much as the powers say otherwise, the battle surely has to take place on Exosia."

Jagger straightened, silver eyes darting back and forth. "They won't unless they deem the risk worth it."

And when would that happen? "Ye mean if the weapon is within their grasp? Or ye?"

"*Or*," Jagger stressed, "a direct hit to them. The taint is everywhere, and the taint is what fuels their power. Maybe we're lookin' at this wrong. When the warriors in my tribe hunted larger game, we exhausted the animal before going in for the kill."

Ebba screwed up her face. "Ye're tellin' us to treat the pillars like a boar?"

"Aye, why not try to weaken them first?"

Okay. "But the whole point is that their taint can't be confined anymore."

"We could take their food source away . . . which seems hard to do seeing as it can spread through living things we can't contain, like the ocean," Caspian said. His amber eyes fixed on Jagger. "Or we take away the people they've tainted."

Uh. "If we knew how to do that, we would've done it already," Ebba said.

Jagger's face was alight with excitement. "But we've never tried. We've always had sumpin' else that demanded our focus. We've used the *purgium* afore." His face clouded. "I just can't believe that everyone who be tainted is lost to us. *A whole realm o' people.* There has to be an answer, one that even the powers don't know of. We've done enough killin' and hurtin'. I ain't signin' up for puttin' down tainted mortals and immortals if we win. And I doubt either o' ye wish to either. So why don't we figure out how to heal people o' the taint now while we can use it to hurt the pillars? Or at least to wave a big red flag in front o' their eyes?"

The last time the pillars were defeated, the tainted were slaughtered. From the powers, she'd gathered that the taint had spread far slower last time. This time, Ebba doubted there were any mortals left unaffected by the pillars' evil.

What else could they do? Go to Exosia with elaborately made plans that would fall apart as soon as the pillars revealed their own strategy? No, they had to draw them out. And if that failed, to weaken them somehow.

"I agree," she said firmly. "We have to try."

"That sounded a lot like 'We're doing it,'" Caspian said, arching a brow at her.

Probably because that was what she'd meant. She pursed her lips.

"So I always thought the root would just do whatever it was supposed to—like when we all touch and glow. But that don't look to be the case. We'll need to figure out what the trident does first."

Caspian stared at it. "I agree—and I always thought the same, too."

"Well, ye read books. Can't ye learn?" she said reasonably.

Jagger snorted.

"In a few days?" Caspian asked. "Let's not form our plan around that. What have we learned about the taint?"

Ebba thought of Jagger holding *veritas*. "Knowing the truth helps."

"Being in the air and the light helps," Jagger added.

"*And* that the black stone we encountered in Davy Jones' Locker could not transmit the pillars' power."

Jagger and Ebba stared at him. The Exosian's lips curled into a triumphant smile. "Davy Jones' had purple water and black stone. Where paths meet has purple water and black stone. I'm willing to bet that the stone stops all magic—not just the taint. That has to be why it's only found in places where the realms touch."

A wisp of hope bloomed in her heart, squeezing it tight. Could there actually be something here? Ebba's mind worked furiously.

"Remember when we all touched, and the remainin' taint left Jagger?" she said. "We should explore that."

"Can that still happen when the weapon ain't in parts?" Jagger asked.

Ebba hummed. "Good notion. We should test that." She reached out a hand to touch them both, avoiding the root of magic bobbing between her and Caspian.

The glow immediately erupted from their bodies. Each of them was washed with bronze, gold, or silver as had always been the case.

But there was a new addition.

Ebba stared directly into the sky at the solid beam of white light that shot out of the trident. The blazing beam wasn't the tiny jet that had led them toward the next part in weeks gone by. *This* beam had a circumference of a grog barrel, and as Caspian moved the trident, the beam moved too.

The pillars didn't like white light.

"Shite," she whispered. "That changes things."

TWENTY-THREE

"All set?" Mortem said cheerfully, squeezing between what Ebba thought must be a centaur and a polka-dot orb that just hung in the sky but seemed a pleasant sort.

She studied the barrels of grog strapped to a row of scaled beasts that Verity had informed her were dragons.

"Aye," Ebba mumbled, darting her eyes from creature to creature. She imagined Plank must be having a field day with all the immortal creatures. He'd always been obsessed with stories of magic.

Every creature capable of flight or hovering had been called to battle. The air was the only untainted medium left. They couldn't risk adding to the pillars' army by letting all of the immortal creatures join the fight. The blue beach was packed with all manner of winged immortal creatures. The masses of their flying army extended back through the tunnel and out into the landing as well.

"I'll have to let your father loose soon," Mortem said, studying her.

Ebba sighed, glancing at Plank again. "I know. I shouldn't say thank ye after ye nearly killed me, but . . . thank ye for givin' me time with him."

"I am death," he reminded her. "The complexities of loss are my traits. So believe me when I say that closure never fails to heal if closure can be had. I'm glad you had it. Few are so lucky."

She nodded, hearing the timeless wisdom behind his words.

Plank and Felicity sidled between a woman with a stretched neck and the legs of a crane, and a monkey with wings and a tongue that kept lashing out whenever a sprite ventured too close.

Felicity took Ebba's hand. "I'm glad to know you at last, Ebba-Viva. Thank you for taking such good care of him. And thank you for being strong enough to let him go."

Not that she was given a choice, but Ebba appreciated the sentiment all the same. She kissed the taller woman on the cheek. "Nice to meet ye, too, Felicity. I wish I'd known ye afore ye died. Ye would've fit on our ship just fine."

Plank pulled her close next. "I have to go."

"Ye were already gone," she spoke into his chest, hugging him tight. "The extra time with ye was just pirate luck."

"Do ye still love me, little nymph?" he asked.

She swallowed the lump in her throat. "Always, Father."

"I love ye, too. And I'll always be with ye. Just stop tryin' to kill me and Felicity. Ye know that if we die as vessels, we truly die."

Ebba chuckled. "Yeah, sorry about that. Don't shite on my deck, and we have a deal. Any chance ye'll consider stayin' in the Oblivion instead o' joinin' the fight?"

"None."

"Thought I'd ask. But please be careful, Plank. If ye really die, I'll be truly mad." More than that. To know that there'd be no chance of ever seeing him again, even as a bird or apparition. . . . Suffice to say, Ebba now felt a whole heap sorrier for Caspian over the fate of Montcroix. Not that her friend would be going to hell unless he angered the Thunderbird in some way.

"Oi, Viva," Jagger shouted. "Want to ride the dragon with me to Maltu?"

She pulled away from Plank to shoot him a look. "Ye can ride that dragon yerself. I'll be goin' on a Daedalion." Call her old-fashioned.

Ebba glanced back and stared into empty space. "Plank?"

The trill of a bird echoed from high above, and she tilted her head back to look at the two dancing birds. Her murderous intentions were gone, so that boded well for the couple. But a sharp pang had taken its place. Seeing Plank made it easier to mourn him, perhaps, but it offered new hardships that weren't there before, too. Knowing Plank was there but being unable to talk to him . . . that would be a fresh torture. Yet Ebba knew without asking that Mortem shouldn't revive Plank and Felicity time and again. They weren't alive any longer. Not in the same way as Ebba and the rest of the crew. Though Plank could still interact with the living, he and Felicity had moved on to the next chapter. There was a reason death existed, and that reason was to balance the living. Ebba had seen hell break open because the balance of light and darkness was upset. She couldn't ask Mortem to let them stay. Not even as a balm to her selfish heart.

Now that Ebba could feel again, she'd grieve as normally as anyone else who'd just spent two days with an apparition of her deceased parent who was now a bird.

Mortem gripped her shoulder and then let go, lifting into the air. He soared high above the gathered creatures, and the other two powers joined him. They flew partway up the funnel of Charybdis and faced their immortal army.

"Some of you have been here before, thousands of years ago," the Thunderbird stated, wings tucked into his sides. Ebba had an inkling that before the next two days were through, he'd be creating a storm of epic proportions.

He continued. "The powers will lead the way with the trinity. The rest of you will follow in our wake. Be prepared for attack on all sides from the moment we exit. We do not expect the pillars to come to us, but this cannot be assumed. Do *not* allow yourself to be trapped and drained. And—" He glanced to where Ebba stood. "—this time, your objective is not to kill the mortals but to corral them by whatever means possible. Incapacitate them if you must, but do not kill them. There is a chance that the trinity has figured out how to save those affected by the pillars' evil—including our immortal brethren who have been captured, drained of power, and tainted."

Gasps rang out in the midst of the immortal army.

"Until we know if this will succeed or fail, you are under orders not to kill anyone. Keep the tainted from attacking the trinity. Attack the pillars alongside us. Triumph is within our grasp."

A dragon roared, and Ebba jolted, her heart sputtering at the fearsome sound.

"A valid point, Graf," Mortem replied when the dragon had finished. "I know many of you were unhappy to be ripped from the mortal realm and confined in the Oblivion. We had friends there. Family. It *is* clear that we cannot repeat our past mistakes of locking ourselves away with the pieces of the root. The trinity is currently working on a different solution."

Bastard.

Ebba tried to look confident as the entire army of immortals looked her way. When the gathered mass of creatures returned their attention to the powers, she shot an alarmed look at Jagger.

He returned it. They hadn't gotten that far yet. And honestly, the powers would need to collaborate with them for that.

"Uh, that's a problem."

She turned to find Caspian behind her.

"Aye," she whispered back. "But one thing at a time."

Ebba turned away as the powers wrapped up and the immortals began to form lines.

They were really leaving to fight the pillars. She felt sick at the thought of coming so far to fail. Surely their chance of losing should be less by now after surviving any number of their enemy and somehow getting here. They should have confidence to spare, but Ebba felt none of that. Because she'd been face-to-face with Pravitus. No matter that they'd have three powers on their side, an army of immortals, and the root of magic, it still wasn't enough.

"Caspian," Jagger shouted. "Want to ride to Maltu on the dragons?"

"I do," Stubby said, pushing past her.

Peg-leg tapped past, Locks in his wake, and Grubby not far behind.

She blinked after them and turned to Caspian whose amber eyes were burning.

"Yes!" he called back, hustling after the others.

"Then come on," Jagger yelled, climbing up.

Ebba peered around her, muttering, "What just happened?"

Verity ambled over, wrapping an arm around her shoulders. "Boys happened, Ebba-Viva. Girls become women, but boys just become bigger boys wrapped in the casing of a man."

She watched Jagger and Caspian, each astride their own barrel-bearing dragon. After everything they'd been through, on the cusp of leaving for a battle that could kill them all, their boyish excitement struck her with odd strength.

Verity rested her head against Ebba's. "Come on, woman. Let's go hitch a ride on a Daedalion and make sure none of our boys kill themselves."

Her gut twisted anew.

Jagger had mentioned the air bubble where fear didn't exist before she assembled the root. Ebba knew that this was one of those moments where fear couldn't be a factor. Certain jobs just had to be done.

Her life had been one air bubble after another.

But this could be the last one, and there was hope in that.

"Let's save our boys," she agreed solemnly.

THE IMMORTAL ARMY circled high over Maltu within the cover of the clouds.

Ebba directed her Daedalion lower, and the rest of the trinity and the crew descended as they waited for the powers to return from scouting. Thus far, they hadn't encountered any sign of the pillars.

Which just served to make her extremely nervous.

What if Sherry and the other brothel girls were down there? And what if they were but couldn't be saved? Ebba and the others were about to throw everything they'd learned at the tainted to try to save them, but what if that wasn't enough?

"I found an isolated group of tainted at the high eastern point," the Earth Mother said, appearing beside her. "I suggest we begin there."

This was it.

"Lead the way," she told the Earth Mother.

Ebba waved to the others and pointed east as her Daedalion followed the power of creation.

How much of her childhood was spent on the island below? She didn't recognize it . . . even as they passed over places she'd spent months at and vividly recalled in her memories. The town and marketplace of Maltu had sat in the middle on the southern coast. The gaol the navy men had marched her fathers to should be below. All of the features of the island were lost to the black soot-like taint.

But as her Daedalion flew farther and farther east, a sneaking suspicion grew within her.

The Earth Mother could not be serious.

If someone had told Ebba that she would end up back at the governor's mansion one day, she would have laughed and then maybe spat in their face.

The mansion had definitely seen better days. Grime covered every trace of white paint. The trees were scoured and burned, and the manicured landscaping was a lost remnant. Apparently, the tainted had thrown a massive violent party here for the last couple of months. Broken brandy bottles littered the space. Scraps of clothing and splintered furniture were strewn over the steps leading into the lobby.

And a very, very naked Governor Da Ville roamed the lawn.

"There were more before," the Earth Mother said, frowning at Da Ville.

Jagger and Caspian hovered either side of Ebba on their dragons. She didn't want to shout and alert the governor to their presence, and the creatures couldn't land until the ground was free of taint—if that was even possible.

Her Daedalion's wings beat fiercely to keep their position.

Did she want Governor Da Ville to be the first person healed of taint? Nay.

Did she prefer to test the theory on him instead of any of her actual friends? Aye.

Ebba signaled to the others, and they nodded.

"Okay, start with the grog," she said.

The Earth Mother flicked her hand and unstoppered the nearest barrel. She circled a finger, and an orb of black liquid floated out. The cork was replaced, and the Earth Mother studied the governor.

She pointed her finger like a gun, and the liquid shot directly at Da Ville, straight into his mouth.

Grog. Something any pirate would drink without thought, but they couldn't waste a drop. Not when it was laced with ground-down magic-resistant rock. Verity and the Earth Mother had spent all day yesterday on the job, ensuring the powdered black stone wouldn't harm those who swallowed it.

Ebba leaned forward as the governor fell to his knees and began convulsing.

"Sumpin' be happenin'," she said excitedly.

Jagger signaled to the Thunderbird, who lowered closer to the ground and twitched his wings. A gust blew over the governor, and Ebba was taken back to a time when she'd breathed her first gulp of fresh air after being confined in the belly of *Malice*. How the air had cleared her skull of dark cobwebs.

"Take me down," she told her Daedalion.

The hawk-woman hovered over the ground. Jagger, being

immune, dropped from his dragon first and strode to her. She dropped into his arms.

"Only because the ground be tainted," she told him.

"Keep tellin' yerself that. Ye love it," Jagger replied.

Caspian leaped from his dragon, the root of magic in his immortal grasp, and Ebba wasted no time slapping a hand on his chest.

Their glow lit up the sky, and Ebba tapped Jagger, who let her down. Though not without a wink.

"Point the root at the damn ground, ye dolt," Jagger said brusquely, staring up at the solid white beam that blasted from the end of the trident.

The beam that none of the powers had seen before. Ebba knew it meant something and that it had to be used. They just didn't know how yet.

"Right," Caspian said hastily, pointing the pronged ends at the patchy grass.

The white beam, roughly the size of a barrel end, shot into the ground before them instead of the sky. Lush grass shot up to their knees. Flowers erupted and unfolded their petals in seconds.

"It's healin' the land," Ebba whispered. "Move the beam around some."

"Fast-like," Jagger said, eyeing a flower that was up to his hips.

Caspian began moving the root back and forth as they approached the governor. He was still convulsing on the spot, hair and bits blowing in the Thunderbird's strong breeze—bits that Ebba would never be able to erase from her mind. And as the edges of their glow encompassed his body, Governor Da Ville began to shriek, arching in rigid agony.

"That's only with our glow touching him, not the actual beam. Good or bad?" Caspian asked, eyes searching the once immaculate garden.

Ebba pushed them both forward. "We need to see his eyes."

Governor Da Ville stopped moving.

Caspian directed the beam away as they leaned over him.

His eyes shifted to them, the barest sliver of color shining around the outsides.

"I think it worked some," Jagger said low. "Bring the glow back to touch him. Just in quick bursts. Who knows what blasting him with the whole beam will do."

The governor's face twisted, and he launched to his feet, throwing himself at their trio.

Caspian yelled and wrenched the root up.

Ebba gasped as the beam of light connected with the governor's chest, going straight through him.

The governor screamed again, body shuddering, eyes wide open. Which was how each of them were able to see the black receding from his eyes until only the watery blue Ebba remembered from so long ago was left.

Caspian aimed the trident at the grass under the governor's feet as he collapsed.

"Oops," he said. "That was a reflex."

Jagger snickered.

Ebba squinted at Da Ville. "He's still breathin'. Just knocked out."

Two birds flittered in front of her face, wings beating erratically.

"What is it?" she asked Plank and Felicity.

Caspian's gaze dropped to the trident. "He's saying more are coming from inside the mansion."

The pillars had felt the loss then. Ebba smiled grimly. Perfect.

Still touching, they turned to face the entranceway of the mansion as a horde of tainted ran out, shoving each other in a bid to reach the trinity.

"What do ye say to seein' if just the blast works without the grog?" Jagger asked them.

Ebba replied, "I hate to waste grog if it ain't needed." She had a feeling that it might still come in handy.

"Sure. Worked for the governor." Caspian was already lifting the trident's steady beam to the closest tainted mortal.

A feral grin graced her face.

The pillars wouldn't even know what had hit them.

EBBA COLLAPSED in an exhausted heap beside Jagger.

"At least the mansion grounds be taint-free," he said, pulling her against him.

They'd cleared the mansion and its grounds of the pillars' darkness so their army could land. The powers had erected defenses around the property. For a while, tainted had raced up the hill from town, and Ebba and the others had blasted the evil out of them.

Then, abruptly, the tainted stopped coming. The pillars had definitely noticed the loss of power. Enough for them to change tactics. Just what their next strategy would be was anyone's guess.

Two Daedalion scouts had tracked the retreating tainted to a gathering on the western tip of the island closest to Exosia. Either the pillars wanted to draw them to the point of Maltu where they'd be strongest, or they were trying to minimize the loss of their power. Maybe both.

The decision to monitor the healed tainted to see if the root's magic had actually worked was unanimous. Though pressing on to heal everyone else was tempting. They'd had a victory today, and rushing into the next challenge headfirst felt rash, especially when the pillars so clearly wanted them to shift away from the mansion.

Caspian leaned against the tree opposite them. He stretched his legs out on the other side of Jagger's. "So we know we can heal people of taint. That's something."

It was a huge something. "I wonder how long they'll take to wake up." Or if they'd wake.

The unconscious and healed Maltu residents were laid out on the lawn and being cared for by the one-eyed servants like the woman from the landing. There was a horde of them, apparently.

"If we have to shoot each person with that thing, it's goin' to take a lifetime," Jagger said. He sounded half asleep. She was in about the same state.

Caspian settled the trident beside him. "We have little idea how to really use the root of magic. I'm certain it does more than shoot a beam of white light. I wish we had that book the trinity kept."

Her fathers traipsed over and plonked to the ground beside them.

She took one look at their faces. "No luck?" They'd been scouring the island with the dragons and Mortem, looking for Barrels' kin and Sherry.

"None, I'm afraid." Barrels peered over to where Marigold sat with her remaining family members.

Peg-leg clapped him on the back. "Not yer fault, m'hearty."

Barrels sighed. "I just hope they're all right."

"We were just discussing the root," Caspian told them. "Wondering if there's a better way to heal everyone faster."

Her eldest father replied, "The powers are frustrating to get answers out of sometimes, but they really will be the best educators on how to use the trident. We have experience with magic and magical creatures but none at all with wielding it."

Caspian's face darkened, and Ebba eyed the change. If her friend turned into a pillar by accident from using the trident, she'd be really put out. Ebba was going to double-check that with the powers of Oblivion again.

"Enough talk o' the bloody root and pillars and evil," Peg-leg announced. "Let's have some normal talk for once."

Locks eyed him. "Did we ever talk normal, matey?"

"Ye didn't, ye strange bugger."

Ebba smiled with the others.

Stubby groaned as he leaned back against a tree. "Lass, I hate to say it, but next time ye get beaten up, I may not kidnap Jagger and start a war with the largest pirate crew in the realm."

He punched Jagger's shoulder.

"Nay hard feelings about takin' ye hostage?" he asked Jagger.

Jagger's response was dry. "Nay hard feelings."

Ebba bit down hard on her trembling lips.

"Do ye remember when Grubby's toe knew the way to the *dynami*?" Locks asked in the silence after.

She laughed loudly with her fathers.

Caspian cracked a grin. "Ebba got mad at me because I questioned the reliability of it as a navigational tool."

Ebba shared an amused glance with him. "I did, didn't I?"

"What about when Cosmo thought we weren't aware he was Prince Caspian?" Barrels whooped.

Their laughter swelled, and Ebba sat up, hugging her knees to her chest as she listened.

"Riding the crocodiles across that pond after hanging in the cages was a weird one for me," she threw in.

Jagger chuckled loudly. "I got free of the parapet and then watched ye all ride them straight across to the other side. Never seen anythin' like it. I thought the whole lot o' ye were bloody bonkers." His chuckle deepened.

"Remember when Locks wouldn't shut up about Verity all the time?" Grubby added. He smiled his toothy smile.

Locks abruptly stopped laughing, which sent the rest of them into howling mirth.

Ebba wiped tears from her eyes.

Peg-leg patted the air, rolling his eyes. "I know ye all want to get it out of yer system, so just do it—"

"—When the *purgium* gave back your leg and took the other," Barrels roared.

Their hoots rang out loud and unabated in the night air through their small oasis in an otherwise tainted realm. A trill rent the air, and she tipped her head back, watching the two birds in the branch above.

The larger white bird lifted his wing in a wave.

"Mateys," Stubby said, his belly still shaking with intermittent chuckles. "Whatever has happened and will happen tomorrow or the next, I'm right glad it was with the lot o' ye. Flamin' pirates though ye may be."

"I wouldn't kill any o' ye anymore," Peg-leg said, peering around the group.

"Aye," the rest of her fathers chorused.

This time, her tears weren't from laughter.

"Viva, why're ye cryin' over that?" Jagger asked.

Her voice choked. "They wouldn't kill each other. It's so beautiful. That be everythin'."

He pulled her back. "Right strange one I've got."

Strange it might be, but her fathers had just said they loved each other—in their own way. After decades of carrying the taint, that admission for someone they didn't share a soul link with was a beautiful and heart-wrenching thing to witness.

"I could hear your laughter from all the way in the mansion," Verity snapped, stomping up to them, her hands behind her back.

Stubby reached across Jagger and shook Ebba's shoulder, pointing at Locks.

Ebba coughed to cover her laugh at the terror on her father's face. He had absolutely no chance against Verity. *No* chance.

The ex-soothsayer smiled suddenly, drawing out a fiddle from behind her back. "Laughter is a great idea, but music is even better. Barrels, do you still play as well as you did while dancing on tabletops in Febribus?"

Barrels drew himself upright. "I daresay my execution has slowed down with the stiffening of my fingers, and I rather think my dancing days are over, but overall, my musicianship and skill has improved with age."

Grubby nodded frantically.

Locks scoffed, "He means aye."

Verity passed the instrument to her eldest father.

"What would everyone like to hear?" Barrels asked.

"'Heart was Free on the Sea'?" Peg-leg chimed in.

Caspian arched a brow. "Nothing that will make me vomit, please."

"What about Locks' song to recall his girlfriends on all the islands?" Grubby asked, beginning to hum the tune. "*Maltu harbor, see the barber, turn right, Delight.*"

As one, they turned to Verity.

Locks squeaked.

"I'd love to hear it," she purred.

Ebba had a feeling Locks might be in big, big, ex-soothsayer trouble. She'd checked her laughter for her father's sake, but no one else was troubling to do so. Peg-leg was even shaking Grubby's hand.

Poor Locks. No doubt he deserved to be tortured. Judging by the healer's wide smile, he would be.

"What about Grubby's selkie song?" she asked when they puttered out.

Barrels set the fiddle under his chin, plucking a few strings, loosening and tightening until he was satisfied. Smiling to himself, he drew the bow across the strings, and his smile widened as he nodded at her to lead the way.

Ebba filled her lungs, singing with gusto:

There once was a lad who swam rather well
And no one thought much of it.
In a race against a shark, he won every time,
Yet no one thought much of it.

He did not rise up for a breath;
He flopped on deck, did not suspect
He was a selkie
A selkie.

There once was a lad who knew just where to go
By dipping his toe in the water.
Prior to this, he neglected to say

He'd been hearing voices.

When young he was hit by the boom;
It's the only way he can't have known
He was a selkie
A selkie.

Her fathers took hold of the song and sang it through a second time. Immortals gathered around—an eclectic mix of horns, sparkles, scales, and wings.

Marigold and her family came and sat with Barrels, and the princesses joined their brother to listen.

This was what Ebba was fighting for. These moments.

And for the chance for everyone else to have the same.

TWENTY-FOUR

The cold woke her.

Ebba rolled onto her back on the grass and blinked up at the sky. Bruised clouds smudged the sooty canvas.

She sat, searching the garden around her, shoulders sagging when everything appeared normal.

"Just the Thunderbird whipping sumpin' up, lass," Stubby called from the other side of Jagger.

They'd fallen asleep where they'd sat singing and talking until the wee hours of morning. Her fathers and friends were sprawled across the lawn, immortals covering the space around them. At least those that slept. Or slept on the ground. Some were hovering in the air, their eyes closed. One, with the head of a dolphin, swam through the air in a circle, its outside eye open. Strange how the creatures' animal tendencies were preserved in the mix and mash of forms the immortals took.

She watched the one-eyed servants milling around the healed tainted. "Some have woken?"

"Aye, lass. And seem right as rain. Mortem checked them and said there ain't a speck o' taint left in them."

Ebba released a pent-up breath. "I'm so glad. What's the Thunderbird stormin' for then?" she asked, standing up to step over Jagger and sit by Stubby.

"Some sphinx scouts reported to Mortem sayin' ships had set sail from the Exosian wharf. Thunderbird started a storm, and they've turned back. Some were comin' from the other islands, too, so he's surroundin' this island with storm. Mortem said that won't keep the pillars from bringin' an army, but it will dent their numbers."

Ebba blinked sleepily. What was a sphinx? "Good news then. Anythin' changed at the western tip?"

"Not last the Earth Mother said, but she's been holed up with Caspian for a scant bit." He stared across the garden at the marble steps of the mansion.

Caspian sat there with the power of creation, trident at his feet.

"He didn't sleep a wink," Stubby said. "Tryin' to learn how to use the thing."

"Knowin' he didn't sleep a wink would mean ye didn't sleep a wink either," she replied, surveying his drawn face.

He shot her a look. "Sumpin' about dyin' just keeps me up at night."

They shared a grin.

The polka-dot orb she'd glimpsed in the Oblivion whizzed over their heads, chittering.

"Ye know," she said with care, "I'm wonderin' if we should give the powers the trident for battle. They understand magic far more than any o' us, smart as Caspian is. Even with that beam o' light, I can't help but wonder."

"Aye, lass. But the powers be limited by thinkin' as immortals do. Just as we be limited to thinkin' by mortal standards. The pillars be immortal, so mayhaps a mortal strategy will work better against them. Caspian be the one to take the root. The realm is his, and his sisters and friends be inside it. Ain't no one'll ever care as much about the realm as someone from the place with sumpin' to lose. And the powers ain't got that."

The Earth Mother and Mortem would probably just drink tea and make a new one.

"Plus," Stubby continued, "I'm inclined-like to agree with the Earth Mother. Caspian lost his arm for a reason. I'd wager there be a mighty good reason a beam shoots out o' the giant fork."

Giant fork. She snickered.

"Ye're goin' to shoot the pillars with it, ain't ye?" he asked.

"Aye, what else would we do? Make a bed o' flowers at their feet?"

"Just checkin'. Just checkin'."

Ebba looked again to where the healed mortals were laid out. Since when had she started calling her fellow humans 'mortals'? In a way, Ebba did feel removed from the rest of humankind now. To wake up being cared for by a one-eyed creature wouldn't bother her in the slightest. Governor Da Ville and the rest they'd saved yesterday would be having heart attacks—if not from the sight of Marjory and her pals, then from the ordeal they'd just been through.

If they could beat the pillars, the realm was in for one hell of an immortal shake-up.

Mortem's head popped into existence in front of her face.

"Wake everyone up," he purred. "My cats have spotted movement."

"Pillage is here?" Ebba said, calming her thundering heart at the power of death's sudden appearance. But they'd left him at the ruins.

"What?" Mortem's eyes flicked to her. "No, don't be ludicrous. My sphinxes."

He disappeared, and she nudged Jagger with her boot. His eyes flew open, and he patted the ground next to him before doing a double-take at her on the other side. His shoulders sagged.

"Mortem has news," she said, standing to wake the others.

She left them to get their bearings and joined Caspian and the Earth Mother on the stairs.

"Learnin' good stuff?" she asked her friend.

His eyes were red-rimmed, and some of his hair stood on end like he'd been struck by lightning.

"Hey." Ebba addressed the Earth Mother. "Caspian def'nitely can't turn into a pillar from using that thing, aye?"

The power of creation tore her gaze from the trident. "Of course not."

"Not even if the magic travels into Caspian's mortal flesh from his immortal flesh?"

"The trident is often used on mortal flesh, assembler. It must be held by immortal flesh. The king bearer is safe."

"Just checkin'," she said, plonking down next to him.

Caspian glanced at her.

"So?" she prompted. "Start talkin', landlubber."

His lips quirked. "I have a slightly better understanding, yes. Whether that will be of any use remains to be seen. The Earth Mother has said I must simply talk to the trident to make my intentions known."

She waited for more. When it didn't come, she asked, "That be it?"

"You recall the awareness that filled each of us when the root was assembled? The trident, or the force *within* the trident, is a sentient thing. It can converse with me through emotion and I with it through thought. If I ask the correct questions, it might answer or deign to show us something. Except asking the right questions takes a better knowledge of magic than I possess."

He stared at the trident, which sat between him and the Earth Mother.

"No one'll care as much about the fate o' this realm as someone from it with sumpin' to lose," she said sagely, borrowing Stubby's words. "A mortal strategy might be all that's needed against an immortal foe."

He studied her, amber eyes flickering. "You think so?"

"I know so. Plus, this ain't just on ye, matey. Ye're holdin' the thing, but Jagger can be the brains, and I'll be the brawn. Ye can just stand there and splash flowers around the place all pretty-like."

Caspian winced. "I knew that'd come back to haunt me."

"I was goin' to wait until after we won but then thought we might all die, and I'd miss the chance."

His quiet laugh faded as Mortem strode through the defensive white barrier.

"A development," the power of death stated when he reached them.

Her sleepy fathers shuffled closer. Jagger came to join her and Caspian on the steps.

"Your mortal kin have been sighted at the western point," Mortem told Barrels. "Or at least mortals fitting the descriptions you gave my scouts. Three orange-haired children and two parents with orange hair. They are corralled off from the other tainted there."

Marigold gasped, covering her mouth with a trembling hand. "Are they alive? Are my babies okay?"

Barrels moved to her side as Mortem answered, "Yes. They're tainted but physically well. And clearly bait."

That was a certainty. "They really want us to take the battle out to the western tip."

"We haven't had a chance to rid the island of taint there," Caspian said.

"And we have the highest ground here," Jagger added after. "Easier to defend."

"Closer to the mainland, Exosia, also," Mortem said, echoing her earlier thought. "Obviously, the realm cannot be risked for a handful of people, but I thought—"

"Ye know what thought did?" Peg-leg growled. "Pissed the bed and blamed the blanket."

". . . I don't follow," the power of death said, his face falling.

"It means a'sumptions be useless. They may be landlubbers, but they be Barrels' family. O' course we'll save them."

Mortem slid a glance to the Earth Mother, who glanced at the trident. Casually, Caspian leaned down, and soon the trident was hovering in his immortal grasp.

"If not for the people, what are we fighting for?" Caspian declared, standing up and scanning the gathering of mortals and immortals.

No one spoke.

He continued, "We will save Barrels' family and any others trapped in the pillars' grasp."

The Earth Mother began to rise. "But—"

"However," Caspian stressed, glancing at her and waiting until she resumed her seat. "That does not mean we must play their game." He scanned Ebba's fathers, eyes coming to rest on Jagger and her.

"Tell me: What would a pirate do?" he asked.

Her fathers talked over top of each other, but Ebba couldn't take her eyes off the Exosian who was listening and dipping his head at intervals in response to her fathers' suggestions.

Either she was a coughed-up fishbone . . . or Caspian had just shut the Earth Mother up with a single look and taken complete control of the situation.

If she wasn't mistaken, her friend had just become a king.

"REMEMBER, GRAF," Ebba told the dragon, "aim yer fire on the fuse. Not the barrel o' gunpowder, or ye'll blow up the . . . the. . . ." She glanced at the long-necked female crane with the massive talons and trailed off.

The crane woman took to the sky, barrel in her grasp, joining the one hundred or so others already up there. They'd leave the barrels of black-stone grog here for now and only take the explosives.

Caspian had asked for the pirate solution. Barrels of gunpowder was the answer. Turned out the Earth Mother was rather good at creating it.

She waved to her fathers and Verity. They'd already said their goodbyes. Marigold and her children had chosen to fight, sending the grandchildren away with the one-eyed servants, the princesses, and the healed tainted until the fight was over. Princess Sierra hadn't been impressed that she couldn't fight, but Caspian hadn't budged.

The Earth Mother soared into the air. She turned in a full circle, hair levitating around her.

"We fight!" she boomed.

The barrier the powers had erected around the mansion dropped away, and the powers flashed to the front of the mobilizing army, heading west.

Most of the immortal army went with them. The sprites remained. A handful of Daedalion. And a dragon.

Ebba, Jagger, and Caspian stood in the middle of the mansion gardens, the trident lashed between the dragon's shoulder blades.

Caspian clambered onto the dragon first.

"Knew I'd get ye on here," Jagger whispered in her ear, hoisting her up from behind.

Ebba didn't dignify that with an answer. This was business.

He hoisted himself up behind her and locked both hands around her waist. She did the same with Caspian.

"Maybe this wasn't in my best int'rest," Jagger grumbled in a low voice.

She clung onto her friend with an iron grip as the dragon bounded and beat its wings in strong, solid strokes. They leaped into the air, gaining height in powerful bursts of speed. They would remain slightly apart from the rest of the army. But not too far.

Bait. That was what the trinity had been reduced to. Something the powers said had never been attempted because of the obvious risk of the ploy going belly-up.

The dragon swooped to the side, and her stomach lurched. She bit back on her yelp.

"There's Barrels' kin," Jagger yelled over the wind.

Ebba squinted ahead and down. As they caught up with the

immortal army and swooped in a wide circle, always hovering slightly apart from the others, she caught sight of the tainted.

And Barrels' orange-haired kin at the very tip of the westernmost limestone cliff.

"Def'nitely a trap," she muttered.

Some people had no finesse. Guess finesse was optional when an immortal was that powerful. But if there was one thing that managing Peg-leg's moods had taught her, it was that sometimes, going in sideways was the best choice. They circled a few more times, slightly apart from the army like a buzzing mosquito.

"The pillars ain't takin' it," Ebba said. Leaning forward, she shouted in Caspian's ear. "Let's make a splash."

He shifted to unlash the trident. The three of them were already touching, so as soon as he made contact, their glow exploded. He wasted no time aiming the beam straight down at the tainted.

She didn't have time to celebrate as the white beam blasted into them, scattering the tainted throng.

The skies darkened in the space of a blink. Not the angry black of a storm but the oily slickness of the pillars.

"They're comin'," Jagger said, his voice edged.

Had the pillars just been waiting to see who had the trident? Her heart galloped in her chest, and Jagger's thumb moved up and down on her stomach. She swallowed her reaction and craned to scan the skies.

"Starboard," she gasped.

To the right, far offshore, three of the pillars were unfurling, their hands outstretched in a replica of what happened at Charybdis. Viscous black poured from their raised palms. The other three were nowhere in sight, but she'd seen this before.

"They be surroundin' us again," she said over the wind. "We can't let them do it. That be how they erect the black sphere around us. Then they squeeze until everyone within be tainted. We gotta get out o' their circle. Thirty degrees to port side," she shouted at the dragon.

The dragon swung its great head to peer at her.

"Fly left," Caspian called.

The immortal immediately banked left.

Behind them, the black pouring from the three pillars' hands was spreading upward like an orb split through the middle.

Jagger squeezed her tight. "There be another pillar on the right."

They were trying to box them in. "Faster," she urged the beast.

The dragon flattened, and the surge in speed nearly sent her flying.

She peered directly downward over Jagger's arm at the distant ground for a second until the immortal straightened.

"Matey be down there," she choked.

The others didn't reply, and Ebba squinted back over her shoulder in time to see a tornado of glittering black-glass splinters rising into the air, aiming directly at the middle pillar.

Mortem?

The oily half-orb suddenly halted, and as Mortem moved closer, slowly the upper and lower edges of the orb curled inward like the jaws of a black monster.

"Mortem," she yelled. "It be a trap."

Lightning struck the sides of the pillars' trap. The Thunderbird screeched from high above and reared in front of the jaws, flapping his great pearly wings.

The pillars' jaws didn't slow.

Mortem had stopped spinning in their midst, and was blurring away, but the jaws slammed shut around him.

Jagger cursed. "Caspian, use the bloody trident."

"Circle around," Caspian told the dragon, awkwardly attempting to aim the trident behind.

Ebba peered back over her shoulder at the black jaws. The power of death was attempting to get out, like a rat trapped in a pillowcase. Bulges appeared in the oily net, but a fourth pillar had joined the others, and no cracks appeared despite the efforts of the Earth Mother and Thunderbird.

Where were the other two pillars?

She spotted the fifth off to their left, black already pouring from his hands. It was the one she'd healed. The half-mortal one. Pravitus.

"Keep yer eyes out for the last one," she told the others, scanning above, left and right. "They be playin' us."

She was probably tempting fate by only looking either side and above like this. If she were them, she'd. . . .

Ebba blanched. "Watch out below—"

A battering ram struck the dragon from underneath. Jagger's arm was ripped from her and hers from Caspian. The glow cut off, but that was the last thought on her mind as she somersaulted up through the air from the sheer force of the sixth pillar's impact.

With the dreadful certainty of a bullet shot into the air, Ebba slowed at the apex of her climb and began to fall. Her fall was gradual at first, picking up faster and faster.

Her breath caught in her throat. She twisted in the air, searching for Jagger and Caspian.

The dragon was free-falling to the tainted sea, a gaping hole in its stomach.

Jagger was falling, too, below and to the left. The lead pillar, Pravitus, was bursting after him, hands outstretched. The sprites were closing on Jagger from the ground in a wave.

Caspian, though. . . . Ebba twisted.

The pillar who'd thrown them from the dragon had him suspended in the air by the neck, the smoking tendrils that cloaked it curling closer to the trident.

No.

A Daedalion screeched, ducking below her, and Ebba thumped onto its back.

"Caspian and the root," she wheezed.

The Daedalion spiraled upward, beating its wings frantically, bringing her level with Caspian. The Exosian gripped the pillar's wrist with his mortal hand, the trident in his immortal grasp.

Two Daedalion dived from high above and scratched their talons down the immortal's back. Smoke uncoiled from his back and struck at them like flies. The hawk-people plummeted to the ground, unconscious or dead.

Black crept into Caspian's eyes. "No," she whispered, pushing up into a crouch. "Take me closer."

The pillar's inching power enclosed on the trident, and Caspian wrenched the trident upward, plunging the pronged ends into its stomach.

The three ends appeared out of the pillar's back.

It was as though all of the barrels packed with gunpowder had exploded at once. The sea itself drew up, erupting high.

In a second, the five black forms of the other pillars arose in a wide circle.

"Ye can't have him," she said angrily, throwing herself from the Daedalion. Ebba launched herself at her friend, circling her hand around his waist to grab the trident.

She wrenched the root free of the pillar's body. Arching back, Ebba pulled as hard as she could on Caspian.

They began to fall together.

He twisted in her arms, glancing at her with amber eyes as they plummeted, the five pillars hard in their wake. Her Daedalion dived for them, talons outstretched.

Smoke whipped out, striking the immortal's wing. With a shrill screech, the Daedalion began to spiral down.

But he'd given them a few seconds they hadn't had.

"What now?" Caspian asked.

Fall faster than the pillars. She hadn't thought through the next part. High above its counterparts, the pillar Caspian stabbed had recovered and was bolting after the other tight-knit group of five.

Lightning collected the two pillars on each end, leaving three chasing after her and Caspian.

Ebba sucked in a breath as the smoke whip flashed. There was no time to dodge it. Pain exploded on her cheek. White fire licked the wound, and she cried out as the entire realm disappeared for a breath.

Black ebbed in. Closing. Her grip loosened.

Falling.

"Ebba."

"Ebba!"

Someone shook her, and Ebba forced her eyes open. A hand connected with her uninjured cheek.

She shoved at Caspian. "I'm awake, ye soddin' weasel. What is it with ye and slappin'?"

He was staring at her face, aghast. Shaking himself, he lifted the root to her face. The cool metal—or whatever the trident was made of—spread a pleasant chill through her, leaving soothed skin in its path.

Wait, were they still falling? She twisted and shrieked at the rapidly approaching ground. "What're ye wastin' time healin' me for?"

"The Earth Mother is coming for us. Where's Jagger?" he called.

Bloody well looking after himself. He wasn't daft.

"We're goin' to die," she announced, studying the limestone cliffs as wind snatched at her borrowed tunic and slops.

The pillars hadn't come alone. Immortals of all shapes and sizes clashed below, her fathers no doubt somewhere in the mess.

"The Earth Mother is coming to get us. Don't worry."

Don't *worry*? Did he even realize they were about to splatter over the ground?

"The sphinxes are attacking our army," Caspian continued. "The pillars must have gotten to them. Or Mortem, I guess. He controls the cats."

"Caspian," she cut in, her eyes wide on the rapidly approaching ground, "ye need to shut yer gob."

He didn't have time to answer.

Strong arms wrapped about her waist in a boa-constrictor grip. The Earth Mother's hair covered Ebba's face, and she shifted to see through the blonde strands.

"We need to get to Jagger," Caspian said.

"The immune is fighting on the ground," the power of creation boomed in an age-old voice, picking up speed.

'Course he was.

The Earth Mother dropped them at the far point where Barrels' kin were.

Or had been.

"The ground is tainted," she said in horror, picking up her feet in a jig as if that could stop the taint from taking her soul.

Caspian gripped her arm. "No, it's not. I blasted this entire section to free Marigold's family. We're safe on the tip here."

"Ebba!"

She whirled and glimpsed Locks expertly tossing a net over a sprinting tainted.

Behind him, Grubby picked up a barrel and threw it bodily into another.

"Where's Jagger?" Caspian hollered.

Jagger was where Jagger was. Which was usually in the crow's nest. Ebba glanced up and was rewarded with a flash of flaxen hair.

She cupped her hands around her mouth. "Oi, Jagger."

He didn't turn, fighting something she couldn't see. He was thrown back, feet slipping on the edge of the cliff above.

Jagger waved his arms, toppling back. But before she could voice her shriek, he'd twisted in the air, taking hold of a swooping sphinx. He grabbed the edges of the creature's wing, holding on as the tainted immortal lost stability and careened for the limestone ground. Jagger abandoned his hold close to the ground and landed in a soft crouch.

Straightening, he jerked at the sight of them. "Viva," he said in relief, gripping both of her arms.

She stared behind at the injured sphinx. "Nice."

"Are ye done?" Caspian asked him drily.

Jagger shrugged. "Aye."

Ebba glanced up, too, and swore. "The pillars be formin' the barrier again."

The six had spread out in a huge circle. Mortem was nowhere to be seen. The sprites were attacking one pillar, the Earth Mother and Thunderbird two each. The other immortals attacked the remaining two, but the air was filled with immortal creatures, both good and bad.

The sky above Maltu was in chaos.

"We need a ride," Caspian rushed to say.

"I'm thinkin' we need a better plan first," Jagger said.

"When ye shoved the trident through the pillar, it hurt him." Ebba's mind worked frantically. The entire realm had shaken when that happened. "But he was fine within seconds. Let's just try to blast them with the beam from here first. We have no idea what will happen."

She and Jagger shared a glance and slapped their hands to Caspian's back in unison.

The trident lit up, white light bursting from them.

"Aim it at one," she called. "It be time to see what the root's beam can do to the pillars."

Caspian obliged, and the beam shot directly at one of the pillars, hitting the immortal squarely. His segment of the forming barrier disappeared.

Her friend didn't need encouragement to move to the next, but the pillars were now alerted. Their allies were weaving to intercept their blast. They'd be healed by the beam, but the pillars would just taint more and more of the people they'd brought.

That wasn't going to work.

"The pillar I just shot is already back in formation with the others," Caspian said.

How was that possible?

"Aim at the barrier instead," Jagger suggested.

Caspian shifted the trajectory of the trident. The root's power shot at the pillars' barrier, and Ebba's mouth hung ajar as the black orb shattered, sending the six pillars flying.

"They be a hive mind," she said. "Anythin' we do to one, the others will feel." Her fathers had said that when she'd healed one of them, the other five had begun to move sluggishly.

She saw the problem with her words as they left her mouth.

"But we just shot the beam at one of them and the others weren't affected." Jagger beat her to it.

The three of them looked at each other, the beam shooting errantly into the black oily sky as the pillars recovered.

"So why were they affected when Ebba healed Pravitus, but not when the beam strikes them?" Caspian said in frustration. "What's the difference? What are we not seeing?"

Unless they were looking at this completely wrong. Everything they knew about the pillars had been told to them. They'd barely experienced anything firsthand. The Earth Mother changing the term 'trinity' to 'three watchers' should show them how easy it was to mislead others.

If Ebba only went on what she, herself, knew from experience, then. . . .

"Not a hive." She lifted her head slowly to stare at them. "They ain't a hive at all. Or they are, but—"

"They have a leader," Jagger said, twigging on.

"Pravitus was their leader. He held the trident the most, so *he* was corrupted by the root of magic first." Caspian's eyes were wide and burning.

Ebba's chest felt tight to the point of implosion. "The other five have *his* mind."

Jagger's breath came fast. "The other five mightn't have been involved at all. Everythin', the taint, their joinin', *everythin'* started with him."

She recalled something from when she was caught in Pravitus's clutches. Ebba thought nothing of the evil whisperings in her head at the time, but. . . . "When he was close to me, tryin' to take my soul, he said, 'Yer will be mine'. He didn't say, 'Yer will be *ours*.'"

The powers told them that the trinity was the first to succumb to the taint. That wasn't true at all. The first to succumb were *the other five pillars*. Their will belonged to one person. The will of every tainted being belonged to just one person. The other pillars were immortal puppets.

"Decoys," she whispered as the anarchy swirled around them.

Stubby hobbled up to them, puffing. "Ahoy. Just checkin' if the three o' ye are goin' to do anythin' useful or just stand there."

They stared at him, mute.

Stubby jerked his thumb to where the white beam was shooting into the ocean, sending water hissing outward.

Caspian jerked and lifted the tip. "Oh."

Ebba snagged Stubby's sleeve. "We need to get word to the powers and all the immortals with explosives."

"A few o' the sprites be actin' as messengers," he said. Holding two fingers to his lips, Stubby whistled shrilly.

A small orb of white light zoomed for their location.

The sprite saluted them, standing to attention.

Jagger leaned in close. "First, ye need to tell a dragon to come and get the trinity. Second, ye need to tell all o' the sprites to spread a message to our side. Tell the powers and every untainted immortal with explosives that when we next shoot the beam o' light, they're to attack the pillar we're pointin' at with everythin' they have."

The sprite nodded rapidly.

"Everythin'," Ebba said sternly. This was all or nothing.

The sprite paled and zipped away.

Stubby contemplated them. "Figured sumpin' out, did ye?"

She dipped her head.

"Smooth sailin', then," he told her, turning away. He freed a dagger and launched it at a tainted who was leaping for Verity, striking the tainted in the chest.

"You aren't meant to be killing anyone," Caspian called after him.

He waved over his head. "Fingers slipped. Gettin' old."

"Old my ass," Caspian muttered.

"Dragon ahoy." Jagger drew them both back to give the creature space to land.

The ground reverberated, and Ebba bit back a groan, peering to the tentacles at the lip of the cliffs. "Kraken ahoy."

"Matey," Caspian said with a sigh.

"Was he that big afore?" Jagger asked, silver eyes rounded.

"Nope," she said. The tainted kraken had apparently been eating everything in his path since they'd left him in the Dynami Sea.

The dragon landed heavily, and they ran for the immortal. Ebba pushed Caspian up ahead of her.

"We can't all touch or the trident will light up," he grunted, pulling himself into position. "Someone has to balance at the back."

She faced Jagger.

"Yer balance be better," he said.

Ebba narrowed her eyes. "Is this about the time I tried to kill ye? Twice?"

"Nay, it be about me havin' seen ye at work in the riggings," Jagger said, hoisting himself up.

She grumbled, using the dragon's hind leg to jump up onto the creature's back. The dragon—likely encouraged by Matey's cantering approach—began its powerful take-off before she'd found her seat.

Ebba slipped sideways and shouted, throwing her body to the right to correct the movement. She clamped the dragon's sides with her thighs, righting herself, and focused on seeking purchase on its scaly skin.

No use. She focused on her legs, trying to sway with the immortal's rocking motion.

"Just like a ship," she whispered shakily.

Jagger was glancing back at her, one arm around Caspian and the other stretched out to her in case she ate dirt.

He quirked his brows, and she nodded, blowing out a breath.

The sprites bolted everywhere through the sky, and Ebba sincerely hoped the pillars couldn't sense the shifting of their force as the immortals with barrels began to climb. The two powers continued throwing their magic at the pillars to no avail. Without Mortem, they were losing.

Where was Pravitus?

Ebba searched each of the pillars, beginning with those the powers were attacking. She turned in a circle and ducked as a sphinx's claws slashed the space where her head had been.

"Shite," she yelped, the hairs on her arms rising. Releasing a slow exhale, she peered at the pillars again.

There he was. Direct south.

She turned back, trying to act casual. "He's behind us. Don't look."

Jagger turned his head to the side and nodded, moving forward to repeat the message to Caspian.

Ebba tracked a sprite to the Earth Mother. Another to the Thunderbird. Those with barrels were subtly positioning themselves above the chaotic battle.

Her heart took off again as great, thick coils of smoke began whipping out from each pillar. They'd abandoned the barrier, probably realizing it painted too easy of a target for the root's beam. The smoke whips struck at immortal after immortal, and Ebba watched their army topple from the sky, her heart in her mouth.

They had to strike now!

She shuffled up behind Jagger, just shy of touching him. The muscles in her legs coiled. Her arms shaking as she waited to make contact.

"Hold on tight. This is it," Caspian bellowed at them and then yelled to the dragon, "Now!"

The dragon circled sharply, and Ebba had no choice but to wrap both arms around Jagger's waist or be thrown off. She buried her face in his shoulder blades, shouting as the world slanted violently and straightened.

She wrenched her eyes open and blinked to adjust her vision.

Just like every time they touched, the glow had erupted from their bodies, coating them in bronze, silver, and gold. A beam shot from the three tips of the trident Caspian held, shooting directly for Pravitus.

The pillar began to whirl away, but the beam caught his shoulder, sending him spinning wildly to the right. Flames shot out from the other dragons, directed at him.

Then the air was alight with the hiss of lit fuses.

The immortals launched their missiles at the pillar from above. Most missed, but some made contact. Reds and oranges streaked the sky, the heat of the blasts scorching her face.

"Go higher," Jagger said. "Above him."

The dragon didn't wait for Caspian's call, climbing through the air again. They banked around the Earth Mother whose face was furious as she formed a crackling ball of lightning between her hands and launched it at the pillar.

Ebba searched for the other five pillars, finding them immobile in the air, hovering. Their attack had ceased.

Out over the black ocean, the Thunderbird screeched, funneling wind at Pravitus. Caspian kept the beam trained on the pillar as best he could as they continued their climb on the dragon.

"I'm going to pin him to the ground," Caspian called back over the chaos.

Ebba would have been disappointed if he didn't plan just that.

The dragon brought them above the pillar, and Caspian adjusted the root's beam. The light burst downward, striking Pravitus and bearing the half-immortal down to the ground.

The oily barrier overhead had disappeared long ago. The immortals were surrounding the immobile pillars, who weren't putting up a resistance.

Pravitus was the captain, all right. And how well he'd fooled everyone for millennia.

The dragon tipped into an almost vertical dive to follow Pravitus to the ground, and Ebba flung her body back in response.

When the immortal stabilized, Ebba straightened, pulled up by her grip around Jagger's waist.

The dragon beat its wings in a steady, slow rhythm, hovering them just above the ground. The pillar lay pinned to the limestone cliffs to her immediate left.

He snarled upward, thrashing against the strength of the beam that was only just making contact on his right thigh. Caspian swung his leg over at the front, training the beam more securely on the pillar's chest.

"Keep contact," he said tersely.

Jagger reached out and grabbed his belt. She did the same with Jagger's belt, knowing that she would fall on her damn face before letting go.

They slid to the ground awkwardly, and the beam wobbled over the pillar's body but maintained contact.

And there he was. Pravitus.

A murderer. *Worse.* A devourer of souls. A master of deceit. Someone corrupted by the very weapon they were using to defeat him. Was he always bad? Had he formed the council thousands of years before with the intention of causing so much destruction? Or was the trident, the root of magic, the real villain in all of this?

As she stared at him, the white beam flaked away his beautiful, cold exterior, exposing the black-eyed, rotting monster beneath. The stench of his corpse made her gag, and she resisted the urge to cover her mouth and nose.

They circled to the pillar's head, led by Caspian.

"Ye were a clever bastard," Ebba told the snarling pillar. "But not as clever as a bunch o' pirates. Do it, Caspian."

Jagger spat on the pillar. "Aye, do it."

And her friend, royal-lubber though he was, lifted the trident high in the air. Without a trace of triumph in the grim set of his mouth, the king plunged the weapon through the pillar's gaping face.

TWENTY-FIVE

Ebba shuffled onto her side, making sure not to break the contact between her bare foot and Caspian's calf.

She reclined on Jagger's lap as he stroked her hair. Somehow, she expected there would be a lot of this in their immediate future.

They'd spent hours ridding everyone on the island of taint, mortal and immortal. After some debate on how best to heal the land, Stubby had recommended taking a page from the Earth Mother's book. As a result, Caspian had shoved the trident in the ground so its beam of white light could pulse down into Maltu Island.

It appeared to be working; flowers bloomed for as far as the eye could see. The trunks of the trees had thickened, their foliage bursting back to life. The sprites were tracking the progress of growth across the island and would report back when the flowers reached the eastern tip.

Unfortunately, incapacitating Pravitus hadn't removed his taint from the realm. But they'd known that from the last time the evil was contained. However, healing the *other* five pillars of taint had caused exponential loss to his power.

The other five pillars showed no sign of waking, laid out on the westernmost tip of Maltu where the Thunderbird could keep track of their state from above. The trident's beam hadn't killed the five—in fact, it appeared as though the root had merely healed the immortals like everyone else. No one knew what toll thousands of years of taint would have on the beings. The five would be watched and observed closely—if they ever regained consciousness.

The Earth Mother was holding Pravitus captive in an orb of her white magic without issue as she kept vigil over the recovering Mortem, who'd been pinned on the ocean floor and drowned several times during the battle. The pillars hadn't fully managed to drain and taint him, and the sliver of black around the immortal's charcoal eyes was now gone.

The sprites came zipping toward them, squeaking.

Caspian smiled and moved his leg away from Ebba's foot. "Done."

"Don't sound so damn happy," Jagger replied grouchily. "We've got a whole realm to do."

Ebba tipped her head back, eyeing him. "Does widdle Jagger need a widdle nap?"

He slid a hand down to cover her mouth, bringing her other hand up to plant a kiss on the back.

"I wonder how they managed it last time," Caspian mused, grimacing at their display.

The Earth Mother glanced at the orb containing the pillar. "Mortals and immortals were able to flee to the Oblivion because the taint didn't spread as quickly. Those who were tainted, we slaughtered in the battle and soon after. There were far fewer than now."

It couldn't be possible that they'd have to kill an entire realm of people. Ebba wouldn't do it. With the pillars contained, maybe every untainted being would have to move to the Oblivion. Her eyes fell on the root. Except when the root was removed from the Exosian realm, it took all magic with it.

She sat bolt-upright. "If we're takin' the root into the Oblivion, then all magic will come with it. The taint is magic."

"Why would we wish to transfer the taint to the Oblivion?" the Earth Mother asked.

Oh. Right.

"No," Caspian said, shifting to face the power of creation. "Ebba is on to something. Magical creatures are resistant to the taint. Only if trapped can they be drained."

The power's eyes swirled, and she snapped, "And what about the immortals contagious with the taint? The root will drag all of them back to the Oblivion with the taint."

"Not if we heal them first, Papatuanuku," Jagger countered, straightening. "There seem to be far fewer immortals than mortals."

The Earth Mother leaned back. "Well, yes. That is correct. We have low fertility rates. And sometimes, instead of babies, we make other things." The power gestured around the realm.

Ebba gasped. "If there ain't as many immortals, we heal them, then take the root into the Oblivion to rip the taint away from mortals."

The power closed her eyes, and high in the sky, the Thunderbird screeched.

"Once Mortem wakes, the powers of Oblivion will gather the tainted immortals for you," the Earth Mother said. "But I warn you. The taint being ripped away so suddenly may not bode well for mortals. It is engrained in their souls."

They fell silent, looking at one another.

"We've all been tainted," Jagger said with a grunt. "It ain't ever easy comin' back from it. No one with it would want to stay as they are—not in their right mind. I would've rather risked death to be rid o' it."

"Aye." She and Caspian added their soft agreement.

"What if we loosened the taint like with Da Ville?" Ebba said, pushing her dreads back. "The black stone grog. Wind. All o' the things we've learned could make the healin' easier."

Caspian nodded. "We could target the areas of islands with the most people."

"And while the immortals are bein' healed, we can keep healin' others with the trident before we take the pillar and the root to the Oblivion," Jagger said.

The power of creation growled. "There will be a black stone prison awaiting him, I assure you. All of us will reinforce it and place it where none shall find him. I'm of a mind to fill Pravitus with the black stones and sew his lips shut," she said, tapping her lip. "Mortem could probably embed shards through his skin."

Ebba winced.

"The trinity would like to be part of the pillar's imprisonment plan," Caspian said.

She wasn't shoving rocks in anyone's mouth.

"The pillar is an immortal," the Earth Mother said.

"Who has caused widespread destruction in my realm," Caspian said. Whether his twitch of the trident was purposeful or not, the movement caught the power's gaze.

She cast a shrewd glance at Caspian. "Of course, king bearer. And during such time, we shall also discuss the future of the root of magic."

He dipped his head regally, and Ebba held back her grin. King Caspian was peeking out a lot these days. Seemed likely he was here to stay.

"The trident sure caused a whole lot o' trouble," Ebba thought aloud.

Caspian looked across at her. "It knows, and it's sorry for it."

"It's speakin' to ye?" Jagger asked. "Like a person? She or he?"

"The root doesn't have a gender that I can discern. And it does not speak but conveys feeling." Caspian studied the trident. "It is the root of magic, nothing more and nothing less. But like a person, it learns."

Ebba tilted her head. "That be why it took yer arm this time and not when the trinity last defeated the pillars?" Clearly the root had figured out the solution to Pravitus's evil far before them. She wondered if the root's beam of light had been a new addition or something undiscovered by past trinities because they only possessed mortal flesh.

Just when she'd stopped feeling like a pawn, there it was again. "Be nice if the root had spoken to ye the entire time."

Jagger nudged her. "Does widdle Viva need a widdle nap?"

She glared at him, unable to stop the curving of her lips.

Her fathers plonked down around them.

"How is everyone?" she immediately asked.

Barrels' eyes were bloodshot. "Bertius was killed."

Ebba blanked. The name sounded vaguely familiar. One of Marigold's sons.

"I'm so sorry, Barrels," she said. "Did the hostages fare okay?"

He wiped his face. "I'm not sure how the children will go after what they were put through, but everyone else is here and well."

Surprisingly few of the immortals appeared to have perished, but then the powers had mentioned immortals were incredibly hard to kill. The dragon who'd first carried them to battle was dead. The majority of those the pillars' smoke whips had connected with were dead. Other than that, the final tally would only become apparent with time. As Barrels had conjectured, the real toll of the pillars' reign wouldn't be physical and would span generations.

There was much to do, but one thing Ebba would make certain of: In centuries and ages to come, all mortals would be educated on the pillars. Records that couldn't be removed from the Exosian realm would be created *somehow*. She was determined. Pravitus wouldn't ever be allowed to gain power again because mortals and immortals alike would be armed with knowledge and truth.

A bird swooped down, and a white speck dropped onto Locks' head. He dabbed at his forehead in shock as Verity burst into peals of mirth.

"Plank just shat on me," he whispered. His face deepened into an ugly purple. "I'm goin' to kill him."

He stood painfully and half-limped, half-ran after her sixth father, who was already out of reach.

Ebba laughed with the others, happy to do so unless Plank decided to give her a turn. She found Felicity in the branches overhead shaking her head. The human gesture was odd on a bird. But dead people inside of birds was pretty odd, too.

The ground vibrated, the shards of limestone on top of the cliff leaping around them.

Ebba peered up at Matey.

"Matey!" Ebba leaped up and hugged the closest tentacle. "Ye be okay."

Ink tears fell from both eyes. "How can you even look at me?"

He collapsed on the cliff, covering his octopus head with two of his tentacles, and wailed, "I'm a failure. An embarrassment." He dropped a tentacle to peer out at her. "I nearly killed the three watchers."

Ebba stood and crossed to the closest tentacle, patting him awkwardly. "It weren't ye, Matey. It were the taint. I'm fair sorry that we had to leave ye in that state. We weren't sure if the *purgium* would kill ye, so we thought it best to wait—"

His beak clicked as he spoke. "I thought you left because you hated me for messing up the plan."

"Nay, Matey," Ebba rested her hand on his cheek. "Never. Ye know ye're a friend o' the crew for life. Ye have no idea how happy I be that ye're okay. Mayhaps don't eat the evil ship next time, though, hmm?"

"I got carried away," he admitted, dropping his other tentacle. "You're looking, like . . . not miserable. You're better now?"

She sighed, glancing over to where Locks still chased Plank. "Long story, but I swear I'll tell ye everythin' once the pillar be locked up." She jerked her thumb at the Earth Mother's orb.

Matey screamed high, rearing back in a slithering mess of tentacles. "*That's* one of the pillars?"

The pillar, but Ebba didn't want to enter into that conversation for the third time in as many hours. "He's contained-like. Don't worry yer head."

"Right, okay. So. . . ." Matey swirled the tip of a tentacle in the dirt covering the cliff. "Are we all still friends then?"

"Of course," she said, patting him again. "We couldn't have defeated the pillars without ye. We wouldn't have known anythin' without yer grandfather's records."

"And I made you a promise," Caspian called from behind her. Gripping the trident, he approached the kraken. "When the realm is free of taint and the people cared for, I will take up my throne."

Caspian might've run from the kingdom once, but she'd be the first to admit that neither of them were the same people they'd been at the governor's mansion. Not by a long shot. Not only was her friend taking up the mantle, he *wanted* the mantle, and that meant the most. He glanced at her, smiling, and Ebba beamed back, her heart filling.

Matey gasped, drawing himself upright, diamond-shaped eyes shining.

"Matey, the Last Kraken." Caspian tapped him with the trident as high up on the creature's tentacles as possible. "The kingdom recognizes your pivotal role in freeing the realm of evil. Rise now as Sir Matey."

Ebba cheered with the others, sniggering at the blank bafflement on the Earth Mother's face.

"So what now, mateys?" Stubby asked as she joined the others again.

"Huh?" Matey asked him. "Did you say my name?"

Stubby closed his eyes. "I'd forgotten how annoyin' that was."

"Back to Zol, I guess," Verity said as Locks re-joined them, covered in bird shite.

"No one say a flamin' word," he spat at them.

Peg-leg's eyes watered, but aside from a few sporadic coughs and wheezes, they managed to obey. There would be time later.

"I'll take Marigold and the others back to Exosia when all is safe,"

Barrels said next. "I'll retrieve Pillage from the landing, of course. Though I'm not sure how I feel knowing Mortem uses him to spy. . . ."

Grubby looked at the water and shrugged. "Guess I'll spend time with my other kin."

Ebba frowned at her fathers. She'd never thought about after they won. Doing so had been pointless when winning seemed almost impossible.

"Sherry ain't here, so I ain't sure," Peg-leg said, staring at his hands.

Jagger turned to him. "Ye fear the worst?"

"Aye, I'm afraid so. Brandy and Margaritta were found. I'll search the island again, but she ain't been brought in."

Ebba's heart twisted for the fiery brothel matron who'd saved her gullet against Pockmark in the alleyway so long ago. "I be right glad for the sake o' Brandy and Margaritta. But I hope Sherry be found," she told her father.

"So do I, lass. Can't help wonderin' if I could have gotten here somehow to save her." He choked and broke off, hanging his head.

They fell silent.

Stubby pursed his lips. "Two of my ships were destroyed. So I'll build a new ship."

"Cedarwood," Ebba said immediately.

"A cedarwood ship," he said wryly.

"Make sure it can fit out o' the hole," Locks put in.

Stubby scowled at him but then lifted a shoulder. "That's all I can think o'. Don't know I'm good for much else than bein' a pirate."

His comment turned her thoughts inward. The others all seemed to know what they wanted to do next. Ebba hadn't a clue other than the same surety she'd always possessed that her life would be spent on the sea.

Jagger took her hand, squeezing. She tilted her head up to meet his silver gaze, and the breath caught in her throat.

Well . . . maybe she had a bit of an idea.

"Jagger and I will be needin' to borrow that ship when ye're done, Stubs," she said. They had a few things to do.

EPILOGUE

Ebba stepped out into the castle gardens, running both hands down the sides of her black corset. She'd threaded moss-green ribbon over the curved tops of the corset that covered her breasts. Beneath the corset was a tunic with sleeves that kept dropping off her shoulders—purposefully, because in recent weeks, she'd discovered the sight of them doing so drove Jagger wild.

And when he was wild, he stopped her heart in her very chest.

She'd exchanged her usual slops for a black skirt that was raised high on one side, and she'd left her beaded dreadlocks down, pinning one side back with a shell hair clip Jagger made for her nineteenth birthday. Rather than adding more beads, she'd kept everything just the same. Rattling hair would be fearsome, but Ebba valued the memento of the beads even more than that. The memories with her fathers. The hardship and trials she'd endured. And that love had returned them to her in Jagger's hands.

Her golden hoop earring was on display, and her new gold-stud nose piercing was everything she'd hoped it would be.

Jagger had suggested that wearing sharpened deer antlers as wings might be dangerous for Caspian's guests, so to complete the outfit, Ebba had just foregone her boots for sandals she'd borrowed from one of Jagger's many sisters and never planned to return. *Finders keepers.*

"King Caspian," she said, striding to join her friend at the parapet overlooking the cobalt ocean.

He turned, opening his arm. She smiled and leaned in, hugging him with one arm even though he kind of had two. The one-armed hug was their thing—no matter how fancy and two-armed he got.

She pulled away. "What're ye doin' out here? Yer party be inside."

Caspian was twenty-one. Which was apparently a big deal on Exosia.

"It's still so easy to remember when the sea was black," he said, shaking his head.

She stared at the sea. The last dregs of sunlight had cast the sky in golds and purples. "I don't think I'll ever forget it," she admitted. A year had passed, and that was yet to happen, anyway.

"How is everyone?" he asked, pushing his simple gold crown back into place.

She turned away from the sea and leaned against the stone wall. "Locks and Verity are happy on Zol, all lovey-dovey and sickenin' to be around. Stubby and Peg-leg made us promise to come back for them soon, or they'd die from the grossness o' it. Grubby goes between Zol and his selkie kin out by Kentro and is happy enough—ye know him."

Caspian smiled.

A year had changed her friend. And she'd always been okay with him changing as long as it was for the better. These changes were. He'd put on much-needed weight and possessed a quiet confidence that was nothing like the brutal, fearsome strength of his father. Certain times called for certain leaders, perhaps, and this time demanded a fair and just king who would always put his people first.

"Did you see Barrels?" he asked her, fiddling with the tassel of his cloak. Reminded her of a curtain, but she kept mute on his royal-lubber fashion choices.

"Aye, he's just inside."

Never really a pirate, Barrels had remained on Exosia and taken up the post of royal quartermaster. With the rest of her fathers mostly in one place, Ebba missed him fiercely. There was a time when the soul bond between them wouldn't have allowed the separation, but each time she visited and saw how happy he was, she knew he'd made the right choice.

And he'd taken Pillage with him, so there was that perk.

"Queen Saliha visited last week," Caspian said after a lengthy pause.

Ebba groaned. "What'd she do?"

"She held a polo tournament in the ballroom. In the air. The ball was a diamond she pilfered from my treasury. And instead of horses, the sprites rode stray cats."

Laughter burst from her lips. "Ye'd think that sleepin' through the final battle would've deflated her ego some."

"Not Sally's."

"Not Sally's," she agreed. Her sprite friend had shown up for a bender four months ago. Somehow Ebba knew it would be an annual event. Apparently, having a month off for every eleven worked was okay when you were queen of the sprites.

Or maybe it was just Sally.

Or maybe it was that Sally liked watching Jagger work with his tunic off.

"How're yer sisters?" she asked him.

He blew out a breath. "Anya's fine. She was recently engaged to a duke whom I believe is a great match for her." Caspian chuckled at her repulsed expression. "My sister is *happy*. It's how things work here. Though I can already see Sierra won't follow that path. In fact, she has been on at me to let her join you on a quest."

Ebba liked the younger princess. Feisty wee thing. "She be welcome—"

Caspian cut her off. "It's too dangerous."

She pressed her lips against a smile. That hadn't stopped him—and Sierra was far more bull-headed than Caspian. The young princess had already attempted to sneak onto their ship twice. When she turned fifteen, Ebba was accidentally going to let her come on a quest.

Frowning at her friend, she asked, "Hey, where be the trident?" She leaned forward and peered around to his other side.

"What. *This* trident?" he asked. With a wave of his hand, the trident appeared.

"Nice trick," a voice called.

An arm looped around her waist. Ebba melded against Jagger's side, splaying a hand over his chest.

"When did ye learn that one?" Jagger asked him.

"A couple of months ago. Despite having immortal and mortal guards, I was never comfortable with the trident in plain sight."

After eons without the root of magic, it was decided not to deconstruct the trident again. The threat of the pillars was too fresh in everyone's minds, and it didn't make sense to Ebba that the very essence of magic should be scattered into pieces. As long as there was a ruler worthy of such power, the trident should be granted. And, boy-oh-boy, had the powers of Oblivion wanted the trident back—the Earth Mother in particular, who'd clearly entertained the notion of ruling the mortal realm again. After taking the root of magic into the Oblivion to remove magic—and the taint—from the realm, the trinity decided the answer to leaving the trident there was a big, decisive no. At least for now, the realm needed a mortal at the helm.

If the root took Caspian's arm so he could hold the trident, why would they ignore such a sign with the battle over? Neither she nor Jagger could hold the blasted thing. Jagger had borne too much burden on behalf of others to ever willingly choose to do so again. And Ebba had never wanted the responsibility in the first place.

No. Out of the three of them, Caspian was the perfect choice.

And she and Jagger would always stop in to keep him in line, lest his head grow too big for his crown and curtain clothes.

"What else have ye found out?" she asked. Each time they visited, he'd discovered more and more—the trident was a constant puzzle for his eager mind.

His eyes burned bright. "As you know, I had discovered that each piece worked with its individual qualities but *more.* The qualities of the *scio* can be expanded to ensure an entire room of mortals can understand an immortal. I used that when the Daedalion visited recently. The *purgium* can heal without demanding sacrifice. I believe it draws from the *dynami,* but that's just a theory. I can affect the mood of a room with the *amare* and *fortudo,* and I can sense truth from lie with the *veritas* when someone is speaking to me. And after having a number of prophetic dreams in the last two weeks—"

"Is that how ye knew we'd be here?" Jagger cut in.

Caspian grinned at him and nodded. "*Veritas* only confirmed truths we already knew before, but as part of the trident, I receive glimpses of the future."

"That would be handy." Ebba's eyes rounded. "Can ye see anythin' ye choose?"

He shook his head. "I haven't had time to explore that too much. But"—his cheeks pinkened—"I did see something last week."

Why was he blushing?

"I'll meet my queen tomorrow," he blurted. "In the rose garden."

Ebba covered her mouth with both hands and pulled her friend into a tight hug. "*Caspian,* I'm so happy for ye. Did the root tell ye anythin' about her?"

He hugged her back. "She's softly spoken and has hair the color of butter. When she dances, the entire world fades away. Her name is Shirina, and I will love her to the end of my days."

Happiness for her friend filled her entire being. "Shirina," she repeated, her smile wobbling. Caspian's rapt, disbelieving expression had her precariously close to tears.

"We'll have three children, all boys. She will love me more than life itself, my perfect match."

Aye, she was going to cry.

Ebba patted his shoulder roughly, clearing her throat. "Ye may be skippin' the tiny steps there, matey, but I guess the root would know." Her heart felt close to the bursting point. On some level, though she'd never regret the undeniable love she possessed for Jagger, Caspian being alone had always rankled and even angered her in a way. For a long time now, he'd deserved so much more than life had given him. And that was about to change. Her kind-hearted, intelligent, *strong* friend would soon find his joy.

Ebba blinked furiously, and her voice trembled as she said, "I'm just so happy for ye that I can't speak straight. I can't wait to meet her. I love her already."

"I just hope I deserve her," he replied, fidgeting. "The sword has already seen our future. I can't screw it up, can I?"

Jagger sniggered, and she swatted him, using the action to wipe at her face.

The pair paused to watch her.

"I ain't cryin'," Ebba told them angrily.

They knew how things worked by now.

Dutifully ignoring her tearful moment, Caspian asked, "Anyway, what about the two of you? Where are you off to next? Dare I ask?"

"We just spent time with my family, but we're ready to spend some time on the ocean now," Jagger said, lips curving.

They'd returned to Neos as soon as her fathers on Zol had finished the new ship. Jagger's family were alive. The tribe had taken refuge down in the caverns. They'd been tainted with everyone else but freed of the darkness when the trident was taken into the Oblivion. A few of the tribe were killed in the violence the taint naturally brought, but considering she and Jagger had expected to find the tribe's remains, discovering most of them alive and well was a time for rejoicing.

Ebba snorted. "What Jagger be tryin' to say is that I'm a strong flavor and his family may need a few sips afore they warm up." Half his siblings and his father had come around by the end. She'd work on the others when she and Jagger next went to Neos.

"Really?" Caspian frowned, darting a glance at the man by her side.

She arched a brow. "Bein' the princess o' the Pleo tribe earned me some points to begin, but I lost them awful quick when they realized I didn't have tribe manners."

The king's eyes flared. "You killed someone?"

"She just roughed up a few o' the warriors who tried to tell her how to dress," Jagger said, kissing her temple. "It be good for the tribe to get a shake up. Ain't good to live in a bubble."

She glanced up at him. "Though in yer mother's defense, I *was* stealin' a few things I couldn't get by honest means. She was dead right on that front."

Caspian's shoulders shook, and he chuckled as he asked, "So not back to Neos for a while?"

"We'll go back a few times a year, most likely," Jagger said. "We both find it hard to be on land too long."

He could say that again.

Ebba shot an amused glance at Caspian. "Did ye know they've made a song about how Jagger—"

"Viva!"

"—defeated Ladon?"

Jagger glared at her.

Caspian burst into a deep, booming laughter. "You're kidding?"

She eyed the fuming pirate, speaking to the king from the corner of her mouth. "I'll sing it for ye later."

The king threw her an amused glance. "And what of your blood parents, Ebba?"

"Aye, they be mostly okay. Did the same thing as Jagger's tribe, really. They went down into the cavern where my crew met the Earth Mother for the first time. Aroha was pretty glad to see me. Cried as much as normal and kept yappin' on about me savin' the world. The chief is still a flamin' sod—nothin' has changed there. They like Jagger a lot more than they like me, too. He's better at respectin' their culture and the elderly and stuff. But it was relievin' to know my blood parents pulled through everythin' okay. Well, as okay as anyone did."

"I'm relieved to hear it," Caspian said. "Relieved that *both* tribes made it through."

"We're goin' to map out the Dynami Sea," Jagger announced loudly, ignoring them. "Stubby and Peg-leg'll come with us. Maybe Grubby. We'll scour it as far as possible in each direction and record the immortals we come across."

"Is that safe?" the king said, still smiling.

"We be pirates," she reminded him, adding, "and Matey always comes along these days. He'll sulk sumpin' fierce when he hears about yer party."

"We shouldn't tell him about it," Jagger blurted.

Ebba agreed. When he missed out on festivities, Sir Matey sulked worse than Peg-leg.

Caspian stepped forward and gripped her shoulder and looked between her and Jagger. "I'm so glad to see you both. I hope you'll stick around for a couple of weeks at least."

"I think the *Plank & Felicity* will be safe enough docked in the navy's wharf," she said, arching a brow at him.

Being friends with the king had its perks. And was great for business—not that they'd ever take advantage of their pirate monopoly on Exosia. Overly. Subtlety in business appearances was an art she'd learned from her fathers, and Jagger always was a crafty bugger.

Caspian sighed happily and released them, ambling back into his castle to join his adoring masses.

Ebba leaned over the parapet, staring at the sea.

Jagger came up behind her, circling her waist and resting his head atop hers. They stood in silence, watching the sun go down—a nightly ritual.

Her eyes drifted toward where their sleek vessel bobbed in the wharf, its blue sails—so they were instantly recognizable to the navy—furled. Instead of a ship cat, they now had two ship birds—Plank and Felicity—who guarded the ship. When she was on deck, Plank's favorite place was her shoulder. Ebba thought a pirate bird was the perfect fearsome replacement for filling her hair with beads, but Jagger wasn't optimistic the whole bird-on-a-pirate's-shoulder thing would catch on.

"Viva?" Jagger hummed.

She relaxed into his warmth, closing her eyes. The connection between them was a near-tangible thing, a buzzing that ranged from comforting to white-hot attraction to infuriating and usually a glorious mixture of all three at once. "Mmm?"

"Will ye marry me?" he said huskily, brushing his nose against her ear.

Ebba smiled, a wild happiness filling her. "Nope."

Laughter choked in his throat. "I'll catch ye in my net one day."

"Aye, Jagger. I know." She nuzzled back into him. It was only the seventh time he'd asked—she was keeping track. "And one day, I'll be happy to be caught." *Or to catch you.* "But there be a whole heap o' things to see afore I make ye my wife."

With Jagger's rich laughter echoing in her ears, Ebba-Viva Fairisles inhaled deeply and gazed upon her beloved ocean.

Her home.

EARTH'S WARRIOR
(Last Battle for Earth: Book One)

Now Available!

FANTASY OF FROST
(The Tainted Accords: Book One)

Now Available!

ACKNOWLEDGMENTS

In late 2016, while researching another series, I came across this quote.

> *"Everybody is a genius. But if you judge a fish by its ability to climb a tree, it will live its whole life believing that it is stupid."*
>
> - Albert Einstein

That night, I met Ebba-Viva Fairisles. A teen who was smart at surviving and being a pirate but not much else. Ebba wasn't confined by society's expectations of gender or acceptable behaviour. In fact, she saw academic smarts as a weakness—or useless at the very least.

Her six fathers and pirate upbringing aside, Ebba's character appealed for so many reasons. First and foremost because the world tends to judge genius by how well children and teens (and adults) perform academically. This is—as Mr. Einstein noted—simply incorrect. Why do we force stars through triangle holes?

We encounter geniuses every day—a hairdresser who competes at cross fit games on the weekends, a builder who can visualise a house on an empty section, a shopping clerk who loses herself to painting each night, a fisherman who speaks four languages—the list is endless. Yet we are taught to think lesser of some vocations, personalities, and ways of life.

If this series has taught me one thing, it's that I must always be on the lookout for that quality or skill that makes a person uniquely, ingeniously *them*. Ebba, Grubby, Caspian, all of the characters in *Pirates of Felicity*, are geniuses. *You* are a genius, exactly as you are—no matter your appearance, sexuality, ethnicity, disability, or wealth.

So maybe I should start by thanking Albert Einstein for his tree-climbing fish wisdom. Smart lad that.

Secondly, I'd like to roll out a barrel o' grog for the characters in *Pirates of Felicity*. Saying goodbye to my characters is by far the worst part of my job. Three years in their company wasn't enough.

Thank you to my husband. I love you more and more each day. Except for Saturdays. I don't want to be woken for a damn walk. This seemed like the best platform to inform you of that.

Big hugs to my family and friends, in particular to my fourteen-year-old sister, Megan. This is the first series of mine that she has read. Her enthusiasm alone made releasing this story worthwhile. Love you, Meggy-Moo! (Lol, I hope your friends read this.)

My beta team, advanced readers, and manuscript team are an absolute joy to work with. Writing is a lonesome job. Don't mistake that for a complaint because I'm a total lone wolf 83% of the time. But sometimes the day starts flat and then I see one of your posts yelling at me for a certain ending or for killing a ship—or passionately informing me that Jagger is the wrong choice. Perks me right up. *Thank you* for setting sail with me on this journey.

There are many authors that make me smile daily. So many that I thought about listing them and it got ridiculous. Honestly, I always thought people with online friends were a little strange. Adult Kelly knows better—or is also strange. The author community brings me so much joy. Thank you, tribe.

A heartfelt thanks to my swashbuckling manuscript team:

Editor One
Melissa Scott

Editor Two
Robin Schroffel

Proofreaders
Patti Geesey and Dawn Yacovetta

Map Illustrator
Laura Diehl

Cover Designer & Illustrator
Amalia Chitulescu

And finally, my readers. I hope you finished this series feeling like you embarked on a pirate quest and won the fight. In magic, in adventure, and in love, we must always believe.

Happy Reading, m'hearties.

Kelly St. Clare
Escape into Fantasy

ABOUT KELLY ST. CLARE

When Kelly is not reading or writing, she is lost in her latest reverie. Books have always been magical and mysterious to her. One day she decided to unravel this mystery and began writing. Her works include *The Tainted Accords, Last Battle for Earth, Pirates of Felicity, Supernatural Battle,* and *The Darkest Drae.* Kelly resides in New Zealand with her ginger-haired husband, a great group of friends, and whatever animals she can add to her horde.

Join her newsletter tribe for sneak peeks, release news, and disjointed musings at kellystclare.com/free-gifts/

ALSO BY KELLY ST. CLARE

The Tainted Accords:

Fantasy of Frost

Fantasy of Flight

Fantasy of Fire

Fantasy of Freedom

The Tainted Accords Novellas:

Sin

Olandon

Rhone

Shard

Last Battle for Earth

Earth's Warrior

Rebel's Crusade

Traitor's Mandate

The Darkest Drae (Trilogy) Co-written with Raye Wagner

Blood Oath

Shadow Wings

Black Crown

Pirates of Felicity:

Immortal Plunder

Stolen Princess

Pillars of Six

Dynami's Wrath

Veritas

Eternal Gambit

Mortal Trinity

Supernatural Battle:

Vampire Towers

Blood Trial

Vampire Debt

Death Game

Werewolf Dens

Shifter Wars

Moon Claimed

Wolf Roulette

www.ingramcontent.com/pod-product-compliance
Lightning Source LLC
Chambersburg PA
CBHW020932310726
48980CB00007B/746/J

9780648334453